ALSO BY ANTHONY GIARDINA

White Guys

Recent History

The Country of Marriage: Stories

A Boy's Pretensions

Men with Debts

NORUMBEGA PARK

NORUMBEGA PARK

Anthony Giardina

FARRAR, STRAUS AND GIROUX

NEW YORK

Farrar, Straus and Giroux
18 West 18th Street, New York 10011

Copyright © 2012 by Anthony Giardina
All rights reserved
Distributed in Canada by D&M Publishers, Inc.
Printed in the United States of America
First edition, 2012

Library of Congress Cataloging-in-Publication Data
Giardina, Anthony.
    Norumbega park : a novel / Anthony Giardina. — 1st ed.
        p.   cm.
    ISBN 978-0-374-27867-0 (alk. paper)
    1. American Dream—Fiction.   2. Self-realization—Fiction.
3. Domestic fiction.   4. Psychological fiction.   I. Title.

PS3557.I135 N67 2012
813'.54—dc23

                                                    2011032253

Designed by Jonathan D. Lippincott

www.fsgbooks.com

1   3   5   7   9   10   8   6   4   2

For Nicola, Henry, and José

It often appeared in European maps of North America, lying south of Acadia somewhere in what is now New England. Norumbega was thought to be a large, rich native city, and by extension the region surrounding it. The name connoted a romantic antiquity that New England appeared to lack.

—from the *Wikipedia* "Norumbega" page

Champlain in a small pinnace explored the coast of "Norumbega," which later became known as New England, as far as the south side of Cape Cod, looking for a better site. He found none.　　　　　—Samuel Eliot Morison, *The Oxford History of the American People*

ONE

MR. WANT

Autumn 1969

1

The Palumbo family, beholden to tradition, drives every year into the country on the last weekend before Thanksgiving to buy the turkey. Beyond Lexington, beyond Bedford and Concord, where the country opens up and darkens, there are still farms where large cages hold white, startled birds. "That one," says Joannie, the little girl, pointing, then runs back to the car, and before she is even inside, she covers her ears against the knowledge her big brother chooses not to protect her from. In the backseat, keeping her company as he's been ordered to, Jack repeats it: "They cut off their heads." Already (he is eight), he has mastered a certain smile that will make him, years later, catnip to women. But not yet; now he is only Jack, her tormentor.

"I wish he'd be nicer," Stella, watching the scene between her children from the cages, says to Richie, and Richie, chuckling mostly for show, touches her neck. He carries with him a keen awareness that people are watching them, that their lives are on display here and they must behave differently, affect a certain refinement. There are rural people here, of course, shopping for turkeys, but also men in pressed khakis, men who belong, mysteriously, to this world of "the country." Something of who he and Stella are as a couple must not be too much on display. He tries to affect the smile of the native, and when he touches Stella, it is with the delicacy that he imagines other men, bankers, might adopt when touching their wives.

The children are waiting in their steamy warmth when they lug the bird back to the car, the look on Joannie's face, Stella can see, remorseful.

"It wasn't yours, Joannie," Stella says. "That one was too small. Because remember we're having Aunt Betty and Uncle Carl and Josie and Phil, and your cousins."

For Richie, even the recital of these coarse-sounding names diminishes all of them in the car (he wants to tell Stella to hush, as if others might be able to hear) after this breath of a richer, subtler world. But Joannie's face comes forward: Let it be so. Let me not have consigned a living creature to death. Jack, beside her, is smirking. He will tell her later that their mother lied.

It is a wonder to Stella, the difference between them, Joannie's birth a modest one, the baby slipping from her without a sound, almost without a will to live, and what seemed a full minute of terror before a cry could be coaxed out of her blue form. After Jack, who broke her, ripped her open, all red limbs and blood-soaked organs, a butcher's carcass they had handed to her and told her was a son. For eight years she has been trying to fold Jack's excess into a being more manageable, a little man in a sailor suit, someone she might more wholeheartedly love.

As soon as the thought appears, she runs from it—not *love* him? Inexcusable. But then it's only one of a great string of unhingements that seem to define her lately. Her sense of life (she thinks sometimes) was formed by a June Allyson movie, or a series of them, seen most likely in the early fifties, when she was a young woman, while Richie was in Korea and they were not yet married. She remembers nothing of the plots of those movies, only a sense of strong, bullheaded husbands, noisy, demanding children, and, hovering over them, June Allyson, pert and smiling, one end of her smile lifted to suggest that some joke lay at the heart of a married woman's existence and if only women learned to get it, everything else would fall into place. Somehow Stella has failed to get that joke, and a more complicated set of feelings has emerged.

About sex, for instance. The way, over time, it has become more of a need: embarrassingly, more for her than for Richie. And about the house they are consciously looking for, the great upward move that has come upon them with the force of a demand.

Richie has been promoted—head of production control at ComVac, the defense plant where he works; he's now making thirty thousand dollars a year, a king's ransom. They have been living, since before the children were born, in a house on Bryant Street in Waltham, nice but too small now that the children are growing. And Richie has become dissatisfied with it—with the house and with their lives within it—for reasons that are mysterious to her.

Her three older sisters are wild with encouragement that she and Richie should join them and their husbands in the developments—heavily clustered with Italian Americans—that have begun pushing into the woods of Waltham and Winchester, Natick and Lexington. But the garishness of her sisters' big new split-level houses puts her off, their air of immodesty. To her they are like houses with too much lipstick on them. Look at me, those houses seem to be saying. Find me alluring.

Richie, too, feels that those houses are inadequate, but there the agreement ends. He wants something else, something almost indescribable. Thirty-nine years old, Richie understands that he has caught a wave, his ascendancy buoyed by a distant war. Seventy percent of the contracts ComVac receives are for war-related materials. He can justify making his money on the blood of boys only because it could so easily have been his blood that was shed, in 1952 or 1953, to feather the nest of a veteran of World War II. Such economy always prevails; it doesn't bother him. But something else gnaws at him. If they are inevitably to rise, he feels an obligation to rise in a certain way. It is not his brothers-in-law's houses so much as their lives that disturb him.

His brother-in-law Frank, for instance. Frank has taken to wearing a peace medallion over his turtlenecks. He runs the AV department in their local school system and loves to goad Richie for his work in the "defense industry." "How many bombs this week, Mr. McNamara?" Richie endures this; the sight of Frank, balding, with a paunch and those ridiculous sideburns he's grown, never appears as a real threat. It is becoming *like* Frank that scares him, accepting a kind of upgraded Italian Americanness that takes the form of split-levels, of sofas and "artistic" lamps. There is another possibility he can sense—though never precisely enough (which is the maddening part)—for himself and Stella, for his children.

It comes to him at odd moments, his own dream of elevation. On shopping trips to Boston—when Stella, like her mother before her, gravitated toward the North End markets where peddlers hawked vegetables and grains from open wooden carts—Richie caught sight of an old Protestant church, or the glass-fronted S. S. Pierce on Tremont

Street, where the Beacon Hill crowd bought tinned specialties, food-stuffs sealed behind colored wrapping. He wanted to be there.

It was an odd dream to have, for someone of his background. His father had been a mason, a Sicilian immigrant, a dark, sullen man who loved to smoke cigars under his grape arbor in Watertown. That Richie had chosen to get an education—even the minor, largely technical night school education he'd managed to piece together—had come as a surprise, and, to his father, not a particularly welcome one. The dream had started then, on Richie's trolley rides into Northeastern in the early fifties, before he was drafted, when he was a young man taking night classes, his nose to the wind of a city that seemed to him thrilling. He'd developed a sense that value resided in the old parts of the city, the venerable buildings, in the feeling of life you caught while watching a man in a long woolen coat and a muffler walking at night, a newspaper under his arm, in autumn. Where was such a man going? To what set of rooms? Some elemental elegance existed, lay in wait, but how did you get to it?

The house on Bryant Street was not it. Returning each evening to the house, with its small, exposed yard, the sounds from every adjoining house intruding—the Lampports' marital spats, Louis Antonellis yelling at his brood of daughters. No. This was too far from the man in the woolen coat, the muffler, the lit windows of the apartment houses near the Museum of Fine Arts, his stop for the Northeastern night classes. It was not enough, and this thought, this goad is with him so often now that even here, with the turkey in the backseat, in the warm, domestic enclosure of the car, thinking of the men he has recently been among at the turkey farm, the long-coated, mufflered man's distant cousins, he finds himself distracted. He has not been paying attention to the road for several miles. Suddenly nothing looks familiar. Did he make a wrong turn or miss a right one? Rather than coming out of the bucolic turkey farm landscape into the world of gas stations and stores—an opening into civilization he would have expected by now—he finds he is going deeper into the wild, deeper into field and stream, thicket, stone wall, wooden bridge. He needs to turn around but doesn't.

There is a new quiet in the car, though he is certain that none of them have yet caught on. Sometimes you can feel trust, as a father, and know how misplaced it is. How people—people you love—can look at you and see facial hair and largeness of feature and believe that along with these comes command. It doesn't. Of course it doesn't. But he cannot admit the mistake, cannot quite say to them, I have gotten us lost.

He is waiting for a road sign, the indication of a route. The dark is coming. The vegetation has grown heavier. Yet it is undeniably lovely out here, the dark trees stripped, the clouded November sky leaking a substance the color of chalk at its edges. Something keeps him going in this direction.

It is Joannie who says, "Are we going home?"

"Of course we are, darling," Stella answers. It would not occur to her to think that Richie doesn't know where he is going.

Jack knows, of course. Jack knows and is watching him. In the rear-view mirror he can just see Jack's face. The boy never dreams, never loses himself. He studies things, doglike, intent, as if at any moment a salvageable scrap might fall from the table. His son, at the age of eight, already his opponent.

It is unclear how long they have driven before they come upon the town. The lights of houses at first. Leaves blow across the wide, darkening main street. A stone library, a white church, not Catholic, a village green in the shape of an icicle, in which stands a monument. It is pure instinct that makes Richie stop.

"Are we lost?" Stella asks, but not with concern.

He peers up at the monument, which stands fifty feet high and has at its summit the figure of a man in a tricornered hat, a Revolutionary War hero. (The name on the base seems to have been rubbed away, but something is written there about "riders.") Beyond it, a partially broken white fence, a house facing the village green, its windows lit. He steps out of the car, and as he does, the strangeness of the town gives way to something else. Is it the combination of light and fallen leaves, late-fall dusk, the order of the town, the benevolent order laid down for two centuries, everything old, the primordial hush, the sense of safety here? Looking at the stone library makes him want to be a reader, he who never picks up a book.

He waits just long enough to feel the cold breeze against him, leaves blown against his feet. In the window of the house near the green, he sees the figure of a woman leaning forward, laying a cloth over a table. She is in a formal-looking dress. Her hair is tied in a knot behind her head. She has prepared dinner. Her family will soon join her, warm faces seated around a table.

"Richie?" he hears from inside the car, and turns to see Stella inclined toward him. Stella insisting they go back. It is Sunday night. Dinner has not been prepared. The children.

In the center of the town is a store, its windows many-paned. Don't they need to pick up something? Milk? He wants badly to know what waits inside the store.

When he gets back into the car, it feels immediately like a surrender, the way a drunk must feel when his children come to the bar to fetch him, their expectations thick and limiting. He moves the car forward, but he can't leave.

"Now I know we're lost," Stella says.

"What's the name of this town?" he whispers.

It is the sign outside the library that tells him. NORUMBEGA. He has heard the name, the old, unaccustomed Indian sound of it set here, in this part of the state, against names like Harvard, Sudbury, Ayer, like a town making a deliberate attempt to hide itself, or to claim its specialness.

It is when he is past the end of the green, past the library and the store and ready to turn, that he spots it. The house has three stories of windows. Some of them are lit. It is not yet so dark that he can't tell the house is painted in some shade of green, the windows trimmed in yellow. Smoke lifts from the chimney. The short front yard ends in a weathered fence, a lamp shining against the encroachment of dusk. It is a feeling that resembles first love, the completion of a thing already started long ago.

As he stops the car to study the house, Stella sighs, picks at something in her lap.

Joannie, in the backseat, leaning forward, thinks, I will know if the turkey I picked is the one they killed if I can *see* it. Let me see it. She says a brief prayer, descending into a place that feels comforting to her, a place of God and angels, immense light, a secret room. When she emerges from it, the turkey no longer matters. Jack waits, deeply aware of his father.

"Wait. I'll just be a minute," Richie says, and gets out.

They all watch him approach the house.

"Your father's going to ask directions," Stella says. She knows, and Jack knows as well, that something else is true. "We must have taken a wrong turn somewhere, but your father will right it."

For a moment Jack feels something he will fight against for years: he remembers a year ago, seeing his mother walking down the street

8

toward their house, holding a paper bag containing groceries. He had been in the front yard playing with friends. Where was Joannie? Who was watching her? He can only remember in the sight of his mother's figure the sudden perception of some lack in her, some integral vulnerability. It is a feeling he has about women, that they must be saved. It is never those words that appear to him, only a feeling. His mother walked like a target, there for anyone to throw something at. She wouldn't know how to duck or dodge.

But he could do nothing, because the man who has walked up to the doorway of this strange house is in charge, at least for now. The door has opened. An old woman stands there, being polite. An intense yellowness of interior space settles over his father, who has become deferential—if he were wearing a hat, he would be holding it now. Jack is embarrassed for his father, for the need in him that only he, Jack, sees. And then the more exquisite embarrassment of watching his father pushing on the door, to keep it open, as the old woman tries to end their encounter. In another moment, Jack believes, his father will kneel before her, grovel.

Stella sees this, too, and tries not to. She turns away, considers the town. It is dark, overgrown, old, and as she thinks this, she knows that Richie has not approached the house to ask directions. Some part of her knows that whatever he is doing is a way of welding her to this place she finds so dark and unattractive. She closes her eyes. There is a hallway that is life. Doors open, and you must enter, you have no choice. They are never the doors you want to open. Smile against that, June Allyson once said.

2

They were an old couple; their names were the Greeleys. The man had patches of white hair and a remote air, as if he had just witnessed your golf swing and was offended that you'd been invited into the club. But he was frail, clearly on the way out. It was always dark when Richie arrived, and he was never fully welcomed. He smelled wood burning in the nearby fireplace, and as winter came on, lacings of frost formed attractively on the windows.

Richie had resisted it at first, this mad idea of his, after the first night of his inspiration, seeing it after the fact, after his embarrassing presentation of himself to Mrs. Greeley at the door, as a bit crazed and certainly unrealistic. But something kept pulling him back, usually after work on his way home. The house never lost its beauty or its irresistible appeal. Then began a series of formal visits.

On each of his increasingly awkward visits he tried to peer farther into the house and was more and more intrigued, the house familiar somehow. He caught sight of the small room off the long kitchen, not big enough for a proper living room, but holding a fireplace and two comfortable chairs, a table between them where lay knitting and a copy of Samuel Eliot Morison's *The Oxford History of the American People*, a book he immediately decided he should procure and read. There were signs that the house was never properly cleaned. Behind the kitchen he sensed more than saw the large porch, its windows broken into tiny panes like the windows of the store in town, where he always stopped on these visits, sometimes simply to wander through the aisles and notice the things that did not appear in his local grocery store: shortbread, English biscuits, jars of mincemeat. The little store might have been an outpost of S. S. Pierce.

He tried to temper the strangeness of his visits to the Greeleys by making himself useful. Was there anything they needed? "No, I drive, you see," Mrs. Greeley said. "And we have a son, he lives in town."

"We're not selling," she said finally, directly.

He was sitting at the table. "We don't want to move, you see," she said. He saw steel in her, and an echo of her husband's instinctive disdain.

"Look," he said, "I'll stop coming if it makes you nervous. But eventually it will happen. Eventually you'll want to sell. All I want is the chance to make the first offer."

She nodded, her face caught in the passing shadow of a need she would not admit to.

"And one other thing," he added. "Since I'm not coming back, and since I expect I'll be making an offer someday, I'd like just once to see the upstairs."

She hesitated, not entirely certain whether to trust him. But his manner was businesslike, and she finally gave in. "Go ahead. You'll find the stairs just past the bathroom over there on your right. But don't touch anything, please." Then she decided not to trust him, and she followed him up, with what he could see was difficulty.

There were three bedrooms on the second floor, two on the third, where the roof sloped. He went into one of the bedrooms, where their son must once have slept. A diploma from Bowdoin hung on the wall. There was a washstand and a mirror, and when Richie flicked on the light, he saw a picture of a boy and a girl dressed for a prom, the boy in a white tux, his hair in a close-cropped postwar 1940s cut, the girl leaning down, her eyes slanted toward him, a big, secret smile on her face, as if she were already starting to undress for him. The photograph captured abandon, blondness, and wild good health. Jack will sleep here, Richie thought. Jack will wake to this: the Bowdoin diploma, the fields that stretch endlessly behind the house.

"Your son?" he asked Mrs. Greeley, who was standing guard behind him. She did not answer.

After visiting the Greeleys, he sometimes walked into the Norumbega library. There were lights on tables, stacks of books, the new bestsellers in their slipcases. A woman in a Dutch Boy haircut sat behind the counter, eyeing him with mistrust. It was as though she wanted to be alone here, silent and prayerful in this cathedral.

One night a woman came in. She was wearing a camel hair coat. It was a spring evening, still light out, though just barely. The woman was a blonde; he had seen her putting out a cigarette at the entrance. "I've left the children in the car," she said to the librarian, imperious, known here. "But I have to have *Bullet Park*. You saved it for me, didn't you?"

"Oh, I did," the librarian answered. She was a different woman now, a benevolent keeper of the town's secrets.

"Good." Then the blonde leaned forward. "Do you know who's driving me crazy?"

"Who?"

"Norbert Oakes. He's driving me crazy."

The librarian shook her head and stamped the book, and then the woman took it and walked quickly out of the library.

At home that night, Stella had wanted to talk about a battle two of her sisters were having, a battle so inconsequential he could not pay attention. The incident of the woman in the camel hair coat was still with him. The way she had trailed cigarette smoke, perfume. And Norbert Oakes, what had he done? Through the window he could see Eddie Lampport depositing his garbage, the man's habitually slopeshouldered walk and the lifting and lowering of the garbage can's lid. Richie had already checked on the children, the first thing he did when he came home. In Jack's room, he'd picked up a toy airplane from the shelf while Jack, still awake, regarded him. "So it's the air force for you, is it, young man?" Richie asked, and felt the light, solid structure of the plane Jack had put together. Jack took it as one of his father's non sequiturs, the things he said because he had to say something. Jack had no intention ever of joining the air force, but he nodded his head, and Richie put the plane down. There were moments between them, as if each were acknowledging a breach that had no real reason for existence. They were both male, both of a certain physical, athletic nature. Yet they had never bonded in a simple, masculine way. Richie wanted something enormous for his son, but if there was a bridge between the small boy on the bed and these expectations, he couldn't locate it, could not find the lever that, as he pressed down on it, would allow him to feel the weight of his son rising. The photograph of the Bowdoin boy, the Greeleys' son, came to him—all that potential, all that hope—but here was his own son, in his blue pajamas, nodding his head as if his father had just said the most nonsensical thing in the world.

In Joannie's room it was different. He still had possession of Joannie's body, though not in the sexual way. He could climb into bed with her, snuggle, kiss her neck, rub her bottom. She was spawn, female, a baked thing still soft enough that pressing your thumb into it could change its shape. He loved her warmth. He noticed that on the wall near her pillow a small drawing of Mary had appeared, torn from a catechism. It was Mary being lifted up to heaven by angels. Joannie's body turned to him. Her eyes opened briefly, imploring him from out of a dream, then closed.

"Why does she have the Blessed Virgin up on the wall of her room?" he asked Stella when he came downstairs.

"Let her go through it," Stella said. They worried sometimes, the excess of it all, Joannie's young religious fixation, her reflexive making of the sign of the cross. Then Stella told him about her sisters' argument. She knew where he had been when he came home late like this, but though he wanted to tell her everything—the library, the woman, *Bullet Park*, the name Norbert Oakes—he knew she would scoff at whatever he presented. She did not like the idea of Norumbega, had never liked it from the beginning.

"Stella," he said when there was a pause. "I want you to trust me."

"I trust you."

Better if she'd said the opposite. Better if some fight could be had.

12

"Stella, I don't want to live where your sisters live."

She nodded. It was pointless to say that a multitude of choices lay between Bryant Street and the wilderness where he wanted to camp them all, that tree-darkened place whose name made her think of Indians.

"I go there, I feel like I understand something. Why should those people have all that? Why shouldn't people like us have it? You remember, when our parents came here, they all huddled together? Little ghettos. Newton Highlands. Watertown. Waltham. Well, we're still huddling in ghettos. It's just the houses have gotten more expensive."

"You don't have to say that."

It was true. None of what he'd said touched the depth of his feelings. He looked around the house and felt something powerful: the way a life could enclose and smother you if you didn't fight hard enough.

"It's just I worry," she said.

"What do you worry?"

"That we'll take too big a bite."

He smiled.

"Of?"

And again, no answer to that, though she could see it clearly: a depth of loneliness waiting for them. You married a man and you married his ambition. No part of that ambition took in with any seriousness her belief that when a woman looked out her kitchen window, she should have access to the kitchen window next door: a woman like her, doing the same thing.

He insisted that she come upstairs—it was always his way of finishing a conversation—and she told him she had the rest of the cleaning up to do. When she finally came up, she took a long time undressing, then in the bathroom. It was punishment, of course; delay, and false at its heart. He wanted sex in order to control her, and she wanted it for chaotic reasons of her own. That night it was as it always was, though he had to work harder at the beginning, fighting her forced resistance. Some trace of their kitchen table argument was in her glands, hardening and pushing him away until she couldn't bear it anymore and softened. She shook her head from side to side, an act of sex that would have been indistinguishable, to anyone looking, from the continuation of a conversation. Her scream when it came was so sharp it surprised even him, and he covered it with his mouth a second or two late.

3

Richie's office at ComVac was at the end of two long rows of desks, with men working on either side of the room. His office was glass-enclosed, his secretary, Dottie Pace, seated just outside.

Usually, though, Dottie was in his office with him. They loved to plot the life of the department together. Dottie had clipped bangs and short hair that hugged her head tight, and Richie liked to remark on her likeness to the singer Keely Smith, joking, when things were going particularly well, "Sing 'That Old Black Magic,' Keely." In response Dottie would always primp and lift one leg like a flapper. It was one of the joys of work to have a secretary and to smoke the occasional cigarette with her and to have her know you in a looser, easier way than your own wife knew you, a relief, really, to deal with a woman this nearly male.

It was sharp-eyed Dottie who noticed the top brass poking their noses into the office one day late in the spring. Sam Keller, the company's general manager, and Lou Cedrone, a VP. All they did was peek inside. They were in suits, and the men in Richie's office—boys, really, with shaky deferments and pregnant wives—were stripped down to white shirts and loosened ties. Dottie looked up from her typewriter. To see these men here was not so unusual, but the look of calculation the two executives wore when they were looking inside the office drew her suspicion. When they were gone, she slipped into Richie's office.

"You notice?" she asked. "Keller and Cedrone?"

"What?" Richie said. His notion of the office was like a safe child's sense of home: it will always be thus.

"Snooping," she said.

At lunch she sat with the secretaries of other departments, listened to the gossip, attentive to the tiniest of movements in the firm. One Christmas she had given each of her young nephews a magnet set in which tiny metal shavings under plastic could be drawn by magnet to alter the features of a man's face. She thought of the movement of the company that way: the smallest changes in one department drew energy in a certain direction, and soon the entire face was affected. All the men, Richie among them, she thought of as innocents who didn't know they required protection. Two days after the appearance of Keller and Cedrone a man named Ray Desmarais appeared in the doorway. He was a large, block-shouldered man who had once been a standout lineman for Brockton High, then pissed away a scholarship to B.C. But even without the degree he had risen to become a department head at ComVac. He retained the huge shoulders and the mean, crushed-looking face, the blunt forehead crowned by bristly curls that jutted out aggressively. When Desmarais came into the office, he started shooting the breeze with Lenny Johnson, whose desk was last in the long row. Richie noticed this and stared down the row until Desmarais looked at him and smiled. Under normal circumstances Ray would have approached Richie in his office then, but that day he didn't. There was something at once bold and secretive in the way he stood there smiling, and that was the day Richie understood that maybe Dottie had been right, something might well be going on.

If it was anything, it was the shootings, Dottie suspected. You couldn't sustain enthusiasm for a war when innocent students on American campuses were being shot and killed. The war, enthusiastically fought or not, might still drag on, but it was the job of Keller and Cedrone to see beyond the next few years—when military contracts could easily dry up—into the far and dazzling future.

That fall Dottie got sick. It was something she didn't fully understand, something to do with her ovaries. She tried to ignore it, but found herself bent over double one day after lunch. She grabbed enough files to see her through the week and brought them home with her. She called Richie a couple of days later. There was an important file she'd forgotten: Could he bring it by?

To get what she needed, he had to open her desk. In the side drawer was a packet of Kleenex, two mismatched buttons, a hairpin, and a box of staples. Otherwise it was empty. Dottie had been so much a fixture of his life—comic, slightly extravagant, small and yet large—that to see these signs of a kind of internal emptiness moved him deeply. His first instinct, looking up at the room full of men who depended on her entirely, was to take up a collection to buy her flowers. But he could imagine her scowling at that.

He brought her the file on his way home from work. She answered the door in a bathrobe. She looked embarrassed, not quite meeting his eyes. Richie had never been to her place before, and when she invited him in (reluctantly, it seemed), it felt at first like an invasion. Her apartment was still, neat as a pin, as empty of her inner life as that forlorn drawer in her desk.

"Sit down. I'll make some coffee," she said. "But I want to talk to you. I've been thinking." She spoke as she went about efficiently making the coffee. Under the thin bathrobe she wore blue pajamas. On her feet were a pair of slippers that may once—it was hard to tell—have sported bunny ears. "What they're seeing is the end of the war. That's clear enough."

"It's gotten quiet, Dottie. I don't think we need to worry."

"Shut up," she said. She could do that. He had never taken offense. "I spoke to Jane O'Neill in shipping. Sylvania got a contract we wanted. Raytheon got the SAM-D missile. So here's my little worry. They're looking ahead, and they're seeing less and less to go around. So here's what you have to do. You have to request a meeting. You have to have an idea. There's no reason our group works only on missiles. Production is production. We could be working on something else."

He smiled. The worry was real, but he didn't think he could let her know he shared it. "You're too smart, Dottie. You think too much." After he'd said it, he winked at her.

"Don't. Don't do that to me," she said with utter seriousness.

"Okay. Tell me what else we should be working on."

"I'm seeing an empty desk where I'm used to seeing you. Or somebody else sitting there."

"Okay. But you're supposed to be recovering. This is getting you all worked up."

"Don't give me that. It's something stupid with my insides. It'll pass. But if you don't come up with a project for us that takes us into peacetime, *that* scares me."

"Okay, I'll do that."

He had no intention of doing anything. The myth of "peacetime" had no valence for him. He also didn't like it that there was no longer any joke between them, no possibility of asking her to sing "That Old Black Magic" and having one of the boys in the office look up and say, Jesus, are you two *married*, or something?

"So you heard me," she said. "I think this is very very important. If I weren't sick, I'd ask for the meeting myself."

At work in the next few weeks he was warier than he might otherwise have been of the presence of outsiders hovering at the door. Finding none, and finding, on the evening news and in the papers, no sign that the current administration was serious about winding down the war, he felt at least momentarily safe.

•

He had started taking the Norumbega paper that summer. He was no longer welcome at the Greeleys', and he didn't want to miss news of them, Mr. Greeley's death, especially. He was just in time. It occurred early in the fall. They were Episcopals. There was no wake, but he attended the church ceremony in Concord that had been announced in the paper. It was a brief affair. The minister made mention of a wire company "Tom" had owned and managed, where he had been "stalwart" and "fair." Richie could see the widow in the front row, and beside her, her son, the former Bowdoin boy. The son had hair the color of fine-grained sandpaper, deep-red skin, and his father's nearly detached-looking jaw. The son kept looking around, as if counting the sparse congregation. He looked both restless and confined, an overgrown ruffian was Richie's impression. Richie took a seat far back in the church. Beside the son sat three teenage girls, all of them with straight blond hair and wearing fine gold chains.

There was some delay after the service, when the hearse did not immediately leave the curbside. Ronnie Greeley (the son's name, Richie had learned from the paper) stood beside the long black car smoking a cigarette. Richie stood in the church doorway, uncertain whether to follow the family to the gravesite. Ronnie kept looking up at him, and he could tell that Mrs. Greeley, mostly hidden within the car, was explaining who he was. Finally Ronnie approached him, hitching the belt riding under his serious gut.

"Why don't we step inside here," Ronnie said.

"Fine, sure," Richie answered, and tensed.

Up close in the vestibule, Richie tried to superimpose the younger face, the tuxedoed boy in the picture, on this wasted face before him.

"I understand you're the man who's been harassing my mother."

He hovered uncomfortably close to Richie now. Was that whiskey he was smelling?

"Not harassing."

"Huh?"

"I said, not harassing."

"Well, call it what you will. *Stalking*, would that be a better word?"

"I love the house."

"Is that right? That's why you're here, at my dad's funeral? Because you love the house?"

Richie folded his hands and considered the adolescent way this man had said "my dad."

"I asked you a question, sir."

"To show respect. That's why I came. I stopped by and visited them, to let them know I was interested. When they told me not to come anymore, I stopped coming. But I got to know your father and I respected him."

"Is that right?"

One of the blond girls had entered the vestibule.

"Daddy, Grandma wants you," she said. "We're ready to go."

"Okay, here's what I want," the son said, ignoring his daughter. "I want you to leave her alone now." He moved change in his pockets.

Richie felt he was witnessing a performance, though he didn't know of what.

"Are you going to just stand there?" Ronnie shouted to his daughter, waiting behind him.

"We're ready to go."

When enough time had gone by, Richie asked, "Is she going to be all right?"

Ronnie, having moved toward the door, turned on him a surly, revolted look, as if he'd fully expected Richie to be gone by now. But there was still in this man's face a doubleness: in the act of dismissing Richie, he was trying to look hard enough at him to determine something.

"I could stop by, see how she's doing," Richie said.

"I'd have to have your legs broken then, wouldn't I?"

On the drive home, having decided not to push things by following the family to the grave, Richie had to wonder how it was he had so quickly gotten past the fear, why it had been so easy to face up to this man. What he couldn't shake then or afterward was that he had seen weakness in this closed world. The man in the long coat and muffler had whiskey on his breath, staggered a little, looked for excuses not to return to the soft, beautifully lit rooms. Terrible to think of what he was learning. At the same time—he couldn't deny it—a door had opened.

He did visit Mrs. Greeley that fall and felt no risk of having his legs broken. She seemed not unpleased to see him, though confused and made frail by loss. She spoke as if she had just put a great many things in order, though she had no idea where to locate all those orderly piles she'd made.

"My husband was president of a wire company. Sterling Wire," she said. (They were drinking coffee.) In another class, his own class, a woman would have ended a sentence like that with a questioning upward tilt in her voice. But here language was fortified by assumption: of course Richie would know Sterling Wire, and where the offices were located, though he didn't. He let her talk. She told him the history of the place, just to hear her own voice, he assumed. She seemed to recognize the moment when she felt she had said too much, and she began to wish he would go.

"Are there things—" he asked. It was late fall. A year had passed since he'd first laid eyes on this place. Sometimes Stella suggested that they look at other houses elsewhere, but he ignored her. "Gutters? Have you looked at your gutters? I could clean them out or get them replaced if they need it. I could do that. Winter," he said, "requires a lot of work."

She looked as if she hadn't considered that. He had a hint of his power, lay back on it.

"Your son, he's taking care of things, is he?"

"Oh," she said. "He comes by."

"But does he *look*?"

"I don't know what you mean."

Where was the car? he kept wanting to ask. She had once assured him that she drove. But if that were so, where was the car?

"A house like this is a precious thing. It's old, though. Things go wrong. Wood rots. There are tree branches that need to come down. You're used to—forgive me—you're used to living with an old man."

He stared down between them, at the table.

"I want to stay here," she said, and then it was as if she were ready to get mad at him. He'd overstepped, suggested her husband's incompetence, and his name, after all, was Richard Palumbo. That was on her face, too, that breach.

On his way out, she followed just behind him and tripped. He put his hand out quickly and caught her, but she was rattled. He wondered if it was serious, if she was losing her sense of balance, and he thought afterward that she was probably thinking the same thing.

He waited a week, then called Ronnie. "I'm worried about your mother."

"Oh, fuck."

19

"She nearly tripped. You know about their hips. The bones get soft there. This happened with my own mother."

It was not a lie; before her death, she had been in a wheelchair.

"Listen, you don't think I know about my mother's health? You presume I don't know this?"

Richie held back, then chose to go on.

"Do you check in on her? You don't want her to fall, because she might never walk again."

He wondered at his own presumption and was not surprised when Ronnie answered unintelligibly, a garbled *yawp* of offense.

Still, it was a business move; that was all it was, planting a very gentle threat into a hostile negotiation, to be dismissed out of hand by the opponent, who would of course be haunted by it later.

"That's all," he said. "Keep an eye on your mother."

Having planted a possible lie, he began to suffer from what he might have called a moral confusion. Things weren't absolutely clear. Was he forcing Mrs. Greeley out, planting doubt where it didn't need to be? Christmas came and went. In January he went to the house with an ice-breaking instrument and broke up the ice on the front walk, then laid down sand. Mrs. Greeley did not come to the door, but he thought he caught her looking out at him. It would help if she opened the door to him. He would feel better if he could ascertain that she was truly weakening. A curtain moved suspiciously, but that was as much of her as he saw.

There were skaters on the Norumbega pond when he drove past, girls with long blond hair and long, colorful mufflers. They all resembled Ronnie Greeley's girls. Black-haired boys had set up a section for ice hockey, and they chased the puck hard, their hats flying off. The girls watched, then didn't watch, then watched again. The arrangements of bodies seemed precise, not accidental, gorgeous in their fixedness. It was like a dance, the behavior of a secret society on display. He imagined Jack in the scene, and it became surprisingly easy: an older Jack, a teenager, a golden boy, flying across the ice with the bare, high trees in the background, privy to all the secrets these children hoarded. It was the sort of moment when any doubts he still harbored disappeared.

Then the boom fell in the spring of 1971.

A meeting was requested at ComVac in the office of Lou Cedrone. Keller was not there, being away on business.

"Look, be forceful," Dottie said to him in his office, when she could no longer stand the fact that they weren't talking about it.

"For all you know, this could be a promotion," he said.

"I tried to warn you. You wouldn't listen. Word is Desmarais is taking over here."

"Where'd you hear that?"

"Scuttlebutt."

Lou Cedrone's office had model sailboats on the credenza. Cedrone had a ketch he sailed on a lake in Lynnfield, and there were pictures of him on the boat with his family. He had a wide, oblong face shaped like the sort of plate Stella's sisters served hors d'oeuvres on. He didn't shave well, and there was something mismatched in his clothing. Cedrone's authority derived from a mysterious source.

In the room also was Desmarais, his eyes lowered, trying to look grave.

"Richie, we're shifting," Cedrone began. "There's no other way to put it. I'm being blunt. You know when a boat gets hit by a wave, things shift, then they settle?"

Richie had no idea why Cedrone thought a nautical metaphor appropriate.

"Looking ahead, there's a presidential campaign next year. Nixon's going to want to bring this thing to a close."

"What thing?"

Cedrone looked at him as if he were being sly, or else dumb.

"You know what I'm talking about."

"War is constant," Richie said, more eloquent than he'd expected to be. "First this one, then another—"

Cedrone said nothing.

Desmarais interrupted. "Lou's talking about a new direction for the company, Richie."

When Richie looked at him, it was as though everything that was raw and uncultivated about Ray Desmarais was on display: as though he hadn't brushed his hair, as though his teeth were sharp and flecked with yellow stains.

"World War Two ended," Richie said. "Remember? We were all just kids. We thought, well, that's that. We missed it. What was it, four years later? Korea?"

"We know. You went over there," Cedrone said.

21

Richie didn't answer right away. They were missing his point. "This is not about me. You go through periods of peace. They never last. The contracts will come in, believe me."

Desmarais was tapping his foot, impatient.

"Tell him," Desmarais said, and looked at Cedrone.

"This is about *shifting*," Cedrone repeated, and shrugged. "No crisis here. No disaster. A few layoffs. You'll have to do it. We've prepared a list. Ray's department and your department are merging. Think of what an animal does when it senses danger. Hunkers down. Shrinks. And the defensive parts—the quills, whatever—they go out. That's us. That's ComVac. Right now. We want a smaller, leaner, tougher production control. Ray in charge. You'll have eight guys, and you'll report to Ray."

"Eight?" Richie said. He had twenty now.

He thought of them and started counting. His boys. A sound came out of him that he couldn't control. He was immediately embarrassed by it. He saw these two reacting to it, their eyes meeting.

"What's coming is computers," Desmarais said.

"Sure," Richie said. "And war."

"You've got to get rid of that attitude," Cedrone said. "Nothing changes so much for you. Eight guys. We've got contracts for that missile you're working on. New things will come in, things related to defense, but not enough to keep twenty guys on. Under Ray, you'll learn something new."

Under Ray.

"How long has this been in the works?"

Again, Cedrone's and Desmarais's eyes met, and Desmarais worked at the nap of the rug with his foot.

"This comes from on high, Richie. We're the unfortunate messengers."

"What about Dottie?"

For a moment they didn't seem to know what he was talking about.

"His secretary," Ray Desmarais said. What was worst about it was that it was said with a note of kindness.

"Look," Desmarais said. "I've got my own secretary, Rich. I like her. Connie Furlo. I can't take your secretary."

"She's gotta stay."

"We'll find a place for her. Is that okay? Will that work?" Cedrone opened his hands, as if he were being beneficent.

"We don't need two secretaries," Desmarais said, but not meanly—a problem of logic.

"Somewhere in the firm," Cedrone said.

"That's a promise," Richie said.

There was silence. He had a sense of something now—the change had been presented to him as a fait accompli, but had it really been that? "From on high," they'd said. How much higher up did things go? A smugness had come over the features of Cedrone and Desmarais, the closer's look. He had been expected to put up more of a fight.

"I pick the eight I keep."

He could almost hear in the sound of their breathing their immense relief.

Outside Cedrone's office, Desmarais wanted to shake hands, but Richie couldn't lose the feeling that he'd given in too easily; there'd been a fight to be had and he hadn't gone in full bore. He wondered how much this had to do with his obsession to get to Norumbega. In *those* negotiations he'd been fearless, brilliant. Did a man have only one fight in him? He thought of Jack on the ice. Something had closed down in him, like in those old movies where they wanted you to look at only one thing so they blacked out everything on the screen but a hole of light.

He went back to the office. Dottie's eyes were like two headlamps you see creeping up toward you through the dark at the end of a long road at night. As he approached them, he looked away. She came into his office.

"Bad," he said, still not looking at her.

She sat. He couldn't tell her the whole story. Ray Desmarais's secretary, Connie Furlo, was brash and blond, like Ginger Rogers.

"Explain the whole thing to me," she said.

4

"Eighty-five thousand," Ronnie Greeley barked into the phone. "That's the price. Take it or leave it."

"That's outrageous." Fifty thousand was the most he thought he could reasonably be asked.

"Take it or leave it."

"What do you need with that kind of money?"

"That's the question?" Ronnie Greeley laughed. "That's the question you're going to ask me?"

"No one could pay that kind of money."

"Oh yes they could. In fact, I shouldn't tell you this, but the city would like that lot for the police station."

"What?" His heart fell suddenly. "And raze the house?"

"Sure. It's centrally located. Up to me, that's what we would do," Ronnie said. "I'm no sentimentalist, but my mother is. She seems to think we have a deal with you. Yes or no?"

"I need a day."

He looked at the numbers every which way. He considered what they'd have to do without. Then he told Stella.

"No" was the small, plaintive word that came out of her. They were in bed, the lights out. She pulled a sheet over her face to keep him from seeing her crying.

"No," she said again.

"Stella."

"It's like the worst thing. There are all these things that can happen to you, and you think—that thing, that awful thing, what is there, a ten percent chance? And then it happens."

He tried to pull the sheet down so he could see her face, but she yanked at it.

"No," she said again.

They scuffled over the sheet, and he won, holding it down, but even in the dark he could see how drawn her face was.

"Why do you hate it?" he asked.

She had stopped speaking. It was that awful silence that had been like a third partner in the marriage.

"We won't know anyone there," she said finally.

"We'll meet people."

"Never. We'll never meet them. Why should they talk to us?"

It had not occurred to him. In the silence of their bed, he grew afraid. Some elementary support had been taken away. Sometimes he said to himself, I am not the head of production control at ComVac anymore, and it was a sentence so terrifying in all its implications he had to close his eyes against it and press down internally, as though a lump inside him wanted to grow. It was not failure, exactly, but it was not ascent, and he had come to believe in ascent as a male obligation.

"You don't understand," he said.

"What don't I understand?"

To help make the decision, he drove to Norumbega, bringing Stella with him. The June sun was filtered through high clouds, so that there were shadows and then moments of intense light. The town seemed to him dreamlike and within his grasp. The words "You are no longer head of production control at ComVac" lost their primitive power because here ComVac faded, moved from its central place in the universe. But he also felt nostalgic for the sense of himself rising, himself and the war, the vise-grip of safety. There was no more net, no security under him, only these houses in their light and his wish that they might speak to Stella as they spoke to him.

Near the town pond was a place for cars to be parked. It was illegal for non–town residents to park there. The sign read NORUMBEGA PARK, and below it was a list of restrictions: no fires, no use by anyone but town residents. A section of the pond was visible from the road, but a more secluded section could be approached only by a path. "You have to see this," he said, and led Stella halfway down the path. He stopped when he saw that there were teenagers on the beach and a teenage boy was out on a floating dock in the middle of the pond. The blond girls wore the skimpiest bathing suits, pink and green strings that stretched across their backs, their soft, very white buttocks barely covered in low-cresting bottoms. They were immensely pale, these children. They flicked their long hair behind them and went into the water, and Richie and Stella watched them as they surfaced, treading water, their voices low and private and unhurried, secretive, as if clipped into shorthand. He would have preferred to show Stella this scene unpeopled. The presence of the kids made him feel slightly old, dowdy.

The boy on the dock helped the girls up and then stood there with them. He put his hand on the back of one of the girls, then lowered it until it reached the bottom of her suit and then snapped it. She slapped his hand away. He did it again. This time she looked at the boy and in a single, unhurried gesture removed the bottom of her suit, then the top. She stood there, her young breasts bobbing slightly, pasty, uplifting in the early summer light. The boy was convulsed with laughter. The others made a great deal of noise. The girl executed a perfect dive. Then the boy took his own bathing suit off and the girls in the water laughed, shouting and pointing. The boy made a proud display of himself, turning around so that he was fully visible to Richie and Stella, his equipment shockingly purple against his white skin.

25

Richie placed his own hand against Stella's back, and they moved away awkwardly. They were quiet as they settled in the car, Richie hugely embarrassed and feeling intensely the failure of his plan to impress her. But when he turned to her, he was surprised to find that Stella was smiling.

In the bank in Concord where they passed papers, where the figures he was signing a promise to pay rose again in their true, monstrous height, he had to work to block out the image of that naked girl, the self-displaying boy, and Stella's mysterious amusement. Beside him, Stella had dressed formally and seemed a different, reassuringly sober woman. She had brought one of her sisters, Betty; they held pocket-books. Her older sister acted protectively, as if Richie might try to slip something past Stella.

He was entering the unimaginable part of his life. That was how he thought of it. He could see his brothers-in-law retreating, humbled, old. And Betty, too, with her money and her big carpetbagger's purse. If he would have no ascent at work, there would be this other.

They moved in in late summer, just before school started. Before that happened, he visited Mrs. Greeley. He had a tape measure with him, that was his excuse, to measure the rooms, but there was really something he had to find out.

She looked grim, closed in on herself, when she let him in. She had no words for him. He held up the tape measure.

"Oh, go ahead. You might as well," she said.

He pretended to measure rooms. Occasionally he checked on her. She was sitting in the kitchen, like a dog hiding in order to nurse a wound.

Finally he came to her.

"Mrs. Greeley."

"I never tripped," she said.

"I saw you," he said, trying to be gentle.

"My balance is just fine, thank you. I'll live with Ronnie. They don't want me there, of course. It'll only be a matter of time before they figure out a way to send me somewhere else. But Ronnie will get the outrageous price you paid for this place. Which you never should have paid, by the way. If you had come by, I'd have told you not to pay it."

He had no answer.

"He saw how much you wanted it. You know what he calls you? Mr. Want. That's his name for you."

He thought of going.

"I was concerned for you being alone here."

"Is that what you tell yourself? I'm fine. I can walk. Look."

She got up and walked a straight line.

"Why did you let him sell it?"

She didn't answer. In her eyes was a plea, as if it could all still be undone.

"Tell him I'm all right," she said.

He tried to leave.

"Tell him," she repeated, uncomfortably loud.

When they moved in, he realized their furniture was all wrong. It was not a thing you thought about until you saw it, but there was nothing left in the bank, so they would have to live with it. Once, they had expected their lives to fit a certain pattern, and their furniture reflected that. Looking at it in this new context, Richie had a depressing sense of how much of him had already been given over to his brothers-in-law's world. The furniture they'd brought was full of the angles of an imagined future that, he realized now, had already dipped into the past. The expectations inherent in their couches, their brightly colored low-slung chairs, had been that the Kennedy years would go on forever, the early sixties' cha-cha rhythms prevail; "Moon River" and the theme from *Mondo Cane* would continue to be the defining songs.

The fit was not perfect, but it would change in time; they would become the people they were in his vision. Stella would dress differently, in fur coats that nearly touched the ground, and he would read and smoke a pipe. One day his own children would come home from school and Joannie would ascend to her room with hardly a word for him. She would call him "father"; the phone would be ringing off the hook, the village swains lining up.

Jack, too, would become unapproachable in his perfection. Football. Ice hockey. Baseball in the summers.

At Christmas, bands of carolers would come to the house. Jack! Joannie! Snowballs would be lobbed playfully against the windows. Come out! Come join us! Jack would regretfully put on a muffler. Damn,

I've got chemistry finals to study for, he would say. Joannie would re-
fuse to go out until a boy came to the door and begged.

On the night they moved in, Jack sat in the room he'd been given,
not his first choice (he'd wanted one of the rooms on the third floor).
His father insisted that he sleep in this room, with a picture of a boy
and a girl left hanging on the wall. Jack had wanted to take it down and
his father had looked embarrassed. "Leave it up just a little while,"
Richie had said. The room felt overlarge, old, haunted even. He could
hear his parents downstairs, his mother's unhappiness humming like
the faint drone of a mower in a neighboring field. After supper he'd
returned to the room and waited for it to be dark. He looked out his
new window on the long green-and-yellow field behind the house, a
scene that meant nothing to him. He knew there was something in his
father he needed to endure, but he had always known that. It was late
August. He stood at the window.

He would be going to a new school. Vacantly, like a thought about
a future so distant you know you really don't have to think about it, he
imagined hitting someone. That would be his way of making himself
known. He could almost see the face of the boy he would hit.

Once darkness fell, his parents seemed to have forgotten all about
him and Joannie. They were downstairs, no longer arguing, but in a silence he knew enough not to trust. In the dark, he took off his clothes
and stood at the window. Naked, he went to the middle of the large
room and stretched his arms out to both sides, as if to measure this
new space he was being asked to operate in. It was a much larger room
than any he'd ever lived in, and for a moment he felt that, felt the newness and possibilities of the space. Then he went into Joannie's room.

She was taping her pictures to the wall. She had the life of Mary
down now, each one cut from a separate catechism so that the nuns
who taught CCD were perplexed: Why did each catechism have one
picture missing? He sat on her bed.

"Listen," he said. "This is what you've got to know."

She didn't look at him.

"Joannie, it's important. This is why you have a brother. Girls who
don't have brothers never learn this stuff."

She turned to him, so that he could see the fear in her, though this
had happened before, and she knew enough, he believed, not to fear
him.

"It's all right." He went closer to her. "Look." He was holding his

28

penis. "You see this goes back? You see this skin, it goes back." Underneath the retracted foreskin, the head of his penis was red. Joannie looked at it, but she had started to cry.

"Oh, stop it. Come on, stop it. You want me to put my clothes on? I'll put my clothes on if it bothers you this much. But then you'll never learn this stuff. You'll go through your whole life and it'll be Mary, Mary, Mary. You want me to put my clothes on?"

She nodded yes. He looked around her room. It, too, was different, and everything felt different.

After Jack left, Joannie hoped he would take his time coming back. The picture she was in the process of taping up was Mary's visit to her cousin Elizabeth, pregnant with John the Baptist. "And it came to pass, that, when Elizabeth heard the salutation of Mary, the babe leaped in her womb" was written underneath. She pressed the picture into the tape behind it so it held. (Her parents had told her not to tack things up here, it could ruin the walls.) Mary's face was beautiful and young as she entered the room, greeting her cousin. Joannie had colored in Mary's robe—blue—and she had rouged Mary's cheek.

What Joannie remembered then was an event that had happened a year before, when she was seven. They had all been driving in the car that December, near Christmas. It was nighttime. The lights of the stores were bright, and her mother had insisted that they stop. Her mother ran into a shop, then emerged holding a package. Once she was back in the car, Stella looked at Richie, and Joannie had seen. Just a little girl, she hadn't wanted to see, but there it was, the determining truth of her young life. Terrible to remember. Nonetheless, a certainty.

What she had begun to understand after that moment—that revelation—was that if she were to avoid the thing she'd seen in her mother's face, she must love Jesus not simply as another presence at the bountiful table, but as the table itself. She must defend herself. This was her life now.

In the meantime, there was much to endure. In her notebook she wrote the words "Jack is the devil" and waited for him to come back.

TWO

LAC BLEU

Spring 1979

1

They were studying *Hamlet* in senior English. On the cover of the book, Laurence Olivier stood in tights, holding a sword that was not a sword at all, but a long and pointed rapier. Spring of senior year. Jack inhabited a body that was not suited for *Hamlet*, or for any kind of deep thought, though he knew he was intelligent. In fact he had great respect for his own intelligence, enormous respect, but it was something he hoped he wouldn't need for a while. When Mrs. Bowman talked about Hamlet's procrastination, that was something Jack understood, because a whole area of life—thought, ambition, discipline—felt like something you could put off for a long time if you were alert to what was speaking to you now.

What was speaking to him was a voice saying, Lean forward and blow on the neck of Sandra Champlain, the girl in front of you. Lean forward and avenge me, my son. Sandra Champlain wore her light brown hair in a long braid she had just rearranged so that it rested against her left shoulder blade. There was a gathering of fine hairs on her neck, and he couldn't help but imagine that Sandra Champlain must be hairy all over, that the pattern of down flowed, in rivulets and tributaries, to the place where it fell into that fine, familiar dank pool. He could see it without closing his eyes. And the ooze there. He could see and even smell the ooze at her center. That was his knowledge, how the biology and the topography of Sandra Champlain worked, so that when he leaned forward, as he did now, and breathed against her neck, he could feel, before she flicked her hand at the spot on which he'd breathed,

33

that some impulse must be running through every fine hair, the way wind sweeps across beach grass, until it reached that place, and a corresponding impulse would have started down there, in Lake Champlain.

Mrs. Bowman failed to notice, so he did it again. Before he did, he considered Mrs. Bowman and wondered why it was not the same imagining the network of hairs that led to that place in her. As he imaginatively took off the beige sweater and the matching beige shirt she wore, he could see all the currents in her stopping someplace, someplace twisted and dried out. The place where *Hamlet* lived was a kind of gully. In order to get to *Hamlet*, the flow had to stop.

This time Sandra Champlain turned around. Annoyance coupled with embarrassment made her face red. She was one of the girls who wanted to have nothing to do with Jack Palumbo, the rich and accomplished girls not yet in touch with themselves. They were all in a tizzy about their SATs. For a couple of weeks during the winter, that was all the girls had talked about: "scores" and "1400s" and "Brandeis" and "Wellesley" and "Bryn Mawr." They were trying hard to get to the gully, to the dried-out place. O Hamlet, what a falling-off was there. Jack had not bothered to take the SATs.

Girls like Sandra Champlain even had the balls to wonder what he was doing in the advanced classes at Norumbega Regional High. "They put me here," Jack answered once, sullenly, not to Sandra Champlain, but to another girl when they were assigned to work together on a project and she had grown annoyed with him. He had "tested" well. His parents had made a big fuss about it. Our Jack's a genius. Except he was no genius, just smart enough, he knew very well, to belong here.

And in this room he could count at least one girl he'd been able to distract from the SATs. Two, if you counted certain incidents that had taken place in the den of a girl named Heather Plympton. But "incidents" didn't count, so he settled into the memory of the other girl, Barbara Ingersoll, who was now holding her pencil between her teeth, two rows to the left of him, leaning forward, hanging on to Mrs. Bowman's every word. He settled so deeply into those particular memories that he was soon hard, embarrassingly so.

The bell rang.

He watched Sandra Champlain join the SAT brigade on their way past Mrs. Bowman's desk, watched her look back at him and say something to a friend that, he was sure, had the words *"breathing* on me" nestled somewhere in it. She would never awake, he thought. She would live a Rinehart penmanship kind of life; she would die in a good house, never having wavered outside the lines. They were all gone then, but he was still sitting there because he couldn't very well get up.

Mrs. Bowman leaned back in her chair.

"Well, Jack, did you stay to discuss *Hamlet?*" she asked.

She knew very well why he had stayed. She had high school vision. He felt diminished by the way she was staring, making him feel he was only one of hundreds of boys who had popped unfortunate boners at the end of class over the many years of her career.

"No, ma'am," he answered.

"Well, I'll be here another five minutes," she said. "And then another class comes in. I guess you know that."

"I do."

The look in her eyes went deeper than boredom with his particular problem. It was like she was letting down her guard for a moment, unafraid of showing him just how sick she was of telling class after class, over the years, about a prince who couldn't make up his mind. Boys like Jack, Mrs. Bowman knew very well, had no problem making up their minds. It was as if right now, in his intimate presence, she was considering a radical proposition: revise all of literature so it conformed with the way things actually were. They shared that moment. Like both of them were pushing open the heavily annotated gates of Elsinore and stepping outside.

On the cusp of their agreement, he stood up. He still had it. He knew she noticed. He did not go close to her desk. Nothing was particularly provocative in what he was doing. He might even have been carrying himself with a certain shame. But on his way past her, he saw her cheeks color, and her hand went out and did something to the air, something small, but still, something he knew it didn't strictly need to do. The world was constantly new. Every erection was something that had never existed in the world before. In moving past her as he did, Jack thought he might only be reminding Mrs. Bowman of that very basic fact.

The halls were silent when he came out. He had to wait by the lockers a few minutes until he was at half-mast. A girl was coming down the hallway, and when she saw him, her eyes lowered and she walked close to the opposite row of lockers, the way a girl on a dark street, seeing a potential assailant on the other side, might strive to make herself invisible. Like she had to be afraid, this girl. Like Jack Palumbo would ever rape anybody. Or even touch them if they didn't want to be touched. Though sometimes they didn't know that about themselves, and that was how he had left his mark here, by knowing it for them.

It would be his only mark. After freshman year he had stopped playing sports. He knew he wasn't good enough to be outstanding, though he was good enough to play. When he quit, it had driven his father crazy because his father saw it as a way they might enter this town that they had never really entered, this town that had always, in ways subtle and not so subtle, denied them full admittance. A headline in the local paper saying JACK PALUMBO SCORES AGAIN might have done it, according to his father. They were all seated in an old-fashioned sleigh and Jack was the horse drawing it and his father wanted to crack the whip. Go score, Jack. Win some games. From his position as the horse, Jack could turn around and see them all on the sleigh, his father with his anxious face and his desire for social movement, and his sister and his mother under blankets, just trying to keep warm. Seeing them all this way, he knew he didn't have to move. Let the snow fall on them until they all grew tired and moved inside. Someone—his father sometimes, but mostly himself—would then unshackle him from the harness and he'd be free to roam.

He had arrived at his math class, but something held him back. Mr. Winslow, young but already starting to gray, was moving back and forth in front of the class, holding a stubby piece of chalk. It was the moment of the day when the male teachers' shirts all started coming out of their pants, and something in that detail made Jack not want to go forward, as if doing so, sitting in class, opening his book, was to enter a world hopelessly limited and confining. Still, if he just stood outside the door like this, Mr. Winslow would see him and the game would be up, so he shifted his body so that he could see inside without being seen. Now his vision was of his fellow students, his fellow math scholars, seniors, boys and girls, some of whom came from the moneyed places in this town, the big houses and the fathers who drove Bentleys into Boston and came home late at night, that whole world his father had secreted them into.

They were not all moneyed, of course. The high school was located in this rich town only because once upon a time it had been decided that Norumbega had enough land and was central enough so that busing kids in from Abingdon or Wansett was feasible. So there was this oddity of poor kids, farmers' sons and daughters, and factory workers' sons and daughters sitting alongside girls like Heather Plympton, whose father had once been the president of a college. Money had gone into Norumbega Regional. While the other towns paid what they could, the tax burden on people who lived in Norumbega was enormous—his father complained about this all the time—so girls like Heather Plympton, rather than being shipped out to private schools, were thought to do well by staying put. Further, they all pretended not to notice that when they went home at the end of the school day, a chasm didn't open between girls like Heather Plympton and girls like Ellen Foley, whose attention Jack had managed to attract. Ellen Foley's father was a janitor and an alcoholic, but immense discipline had won Ellen a full scholarship to Wheaton. Given this girl's dedication to a goal beyond the moment, it had surprised Jack at first when she agreed to sleep with him, and her ardor had almost scared him. Scared *him*.

Now she was looking at him, her expression just a bit confused. Why wasn't he in math class with her? Her expression changed, and it was that change that made him back away finally. Out of sight of everyone now, he leaned against the wall. He would not go in. Her demand was always a little too much for him. Not the sexual demand (though that, too, always took something out of him). The other demand. He stared out the window at the end of the hall, looking out at the athletic fields at the side of the high school and beyond them the woods. He could imagine the feeling of busting out at the end of the day, that first deep immersion in the smells of this perfect spring. He thought sometimes his life would be perfect if it weren't for the fear started up in him by that small, unassuming-looking girl who had stared so hard at him, with her unanswerable demand.

At five o'clock Jack had to go to the pizza parlor to pick up the car.

The pizza parlor had been a store in the center of town when they first moved in. His father had been responsible for the conversion. NORUMBEGA PIZZA, the hand-painted sign now read, underneath it the word SUBS. His father insisted even now, deep into spring, that the store's tiny windows retain the frosting, the mock snow they had put up to outline the windows back in November. Jack might say something—it

37

looked stupid, unseasonal—but his father had a strong feeling for this little structure and would answer with something like, Oh, people, when they stop, they should feel like they're stepping into another world, Jack. That was supposed to be his father's great business acumen, which had landed him as the night manager of this place. Five nights a week his father was there after his regular shift at ComVac, and he was there Saturdays, too, inhabiting this little world that was so important to him, this "other world" where the snow didn't melt until June.

Christina Thayer was working behind the counter. It was always a little bit of a shock to see her there and then to see the way she looked at him, as though something unpleasant had once happened between them. It wasn't a surly or hateful look, and it wasn't as though she were scared of him. It was a wariness. At the high school, where she was a senior like him, she managed to keep a distance from just about everyone, which made you forget sometimes how beautiful she was—blond hair, dark eyebrows, but something else, something placid and unfindable, and what he suspected was a deceptive air of repose. Why had she needed to come here to work? She was a wealthy girl, or at least a girl Jack had always assumed was wealthy.

"Back here, Jack," his father said. Jack could see him through the opening, sprinkling cornmeal on the long table where he rolled out the pizza dough. He was wearing the embarrassing chef's hat. Jack went inside.

"You come for the car?"

Jack nodded.

"Mow the lawn?"

"Not that it needed it."

He had looked up while mowing shirtless and seen Joannie watching him from her window. Then she'd ducked out of sight. She did that sometimes; she watched him. He thought of it as the profane side of his little sister peeking out from behind the veil of assumed holiness. It made him smile now.

"Good to get a good start."

His father always wanted something at these little meetings. He wouldn't just hand over the keys. He wanted some nebulous connection, a checking in on Jack's life. Jack's life had been closed to him for years, but his father believed that the sullen boy who presented himself for inspection was the true Jack.

"I've been having a conversation with Christina," his father said.

38

Jack heard the tone, braced himself. "She tells me her mother just sent a down payment to UMass for her."

Jack turned and saw Christina in profile. Without knowing why, he felt a stab of pity for her.

"Jack, maybe this is all my fault, but I don't think so. When were you supposed to apply to college?"

"I don't know. Christmas, I think."

"*Christmas?*"

"Yes."

"And we never talked about this?"

"No. We never did."

"I asked you about dates. You said you were on top of it. You even mentioned some schools, as I recall. I expected you'd be telling me something soon."

His father had been laying out the bolt of long, spongy dough. Now he stopped.

"You didn't apply anywhere, did you?"

Jack didn't answer. He could read the genuine pain under his father's air of confusion.

"You frustrate me, Jack."

"I know that."

"What?"

"I said I know that. Can I have the keys?"

"Where are you going tonight?"

Richie knew, in a limited way, that his son was a ladies' man. He imagined his son's exploits in the same relatively innocent terms with which he'd once considered the exploits of his old army buddies, the ones brave enough to visit whorehouses in Seattle before they'd all been dispatched to Korea. That was as far as his understanding, or his imagination, went, and he didn't want to push either. He simply hoped his son's exploits would not embarrass him.

"Listen, if you're not giving me the keys, I can walk to where I'm going. It doesn't make that much difference."

Walk to Wansett. Seven miles away. Not likely.

Jack's father made him wait while he rolled out two sheets of dough. All this time he wore the silly baker's hat he was so unashamed of. Looking at his father in this getup, Jack had to wonder: Was it the job of families to find the one member who would have no trouble separating from them and then to try, in increments, to break his heart?

After what felt like a long while, Richie handed the keys to Jack. "We have to talk," his father said.

"You need any help?"

"Too early. You want to come back in an hour, we can use you."

He would or he wouldn't. He would have to see.

"Bring your mother a loaf of bread."

Jack grabbed one out of the bin near where Christina was sitting, waiting for the first customer. She watched him as though what he was doing was a kind of theft.

Ellen Foley's tiny house was at the end of a cul-de-sac. Inside, her parents would be huddled away in their bedroom, watching TV. He didn't know when or where Ellen's father did his drinking. In fact, he wouldn't have known her father was an alcoholic if Ellen hadn't told him one night, as if the information should make him feel sorry for her. The secrets of families were amazing. Here you came to this quiet little house where everything seemed so calm, and the girl you came to see told you of rages, of things broken, of the grip a small man in working clothes could hold over women. When did Mr. Foley's rages happen?

Here's what Jack knew of Ellen's mother. One night he had taken Ellen home from a date and found as he was dropping her off that he had to take an enormous crap. He asked Ellen if he could use their bathroom, he didn't think he could wait. There was only one bathroom in the Foley house. It was near the parents' bedroom. Jack was used to space and privacy for his bodily functions. When he released himself either sexually or digestively, he gave himself room, so he didn't think to temper himself at all when he used the Foley bathroom. When he came out, Ellen's mother was in the hall, holding a cleaning brush and a bucket. She didn't look at him or greet him. She just waited for him to move past her so that she could go to work.

"You're late, Jack," Ellen said when he arrived at her house.

He had felt guilty enough about his father's disappointment over his lack of college plans that he'd put in an hour behind the counter, working beside Christina at Norumbega Pizza. If there was a way of making subs delicately, Christina knew how to do it. He had wanted to say to her, Put more on. More meatballs. More sausages. For Chris-sake, smother the fuckers.

40

He held up his hand and put it under Ellen's nose to explain his lateness.

"Ugh. You're going to smell of pizza sauce now."

They sat on the front steps and were quiet. He listened for what was going on in the house, the TV and the drinking and the beginning of her father's rage. He was listening now, all the time, for the insides of things. That was his task. Others would go to college, but his own education would consist in figuring everything out.

"What do you want to do?" she asked.

"This is nice." He leaned back.

"We could go inside. We could sit in my room and listen to records."

"Why don't you show me your college application again?"

She slapped his knee in reproval.

"Maybe we can improve it. Or how about the graduation poem? You working on that one?"

"You're an evil boy."

"But you are, aren't you?"

"Yes."

She leaned forward, put her hands over her knees, and rested her small chin there.

"What's your metaphor?" he asked.

That was the rule. Mrs. Bowman had announced it. To compete for the prize of graduation poet, you first had to submit, and have approved, an acceptable metaphor.

"Oh shut up."

"No. Tell me. I'm interested in acceptable metaphors."

"I'd like to see you up there. I mean, it would stun everyone. Jack Palumbo, reading a poem."

"Well, maybe I will."

She looked at him, shook her head, then turned away.

There was a party they'd casually agreed to show up at. Jack drank a little at the party, not a lot. He drank with boys, and Ellen was at the other end of the party, which took place in someone's basement. She was with the smart girls, the ones who were loose enough to go to a party and drink. Heather Plympton was one of those girls, and every once in a while she looked at Jack with an expression that had in it both the memory of the incidents that happened in her den, incidents that stopped short of intercourse, and a rising above those incidents, like they hadn't mattered. There was always a risk, if you'd been with as many people as Jack had been with (which, if the truth were known, was not as many as he'd been credited with), of a kind of social embarrassment, but one of the wonders of this spring was the way all the seniors had agreed to treat the past like an island they were getting ready to leave, an island they'd been marooned on for four years, and now, in leaving, they were released from responsibility for who they'd been during that time.

By the lake, afterward, in the Norumbega Park lot, there were other cars. They knew them by sight. Some of the kids inside them had already finished and were swimming in the lake. Jack and Ellen had never done that, because they had started in February, when it was too cold; after they'd finished in the car, Jack had liked to slide across the ice and get Ellen to follow him, a big, long running start and then a long slide. Now that it was warm enough to swim, Ellen had moved, emotionally speaking, well beyond the desire to engage in anything communal. When they heard, as they did now, the sound of a small group swimming, she recoiled from the coarse language coming from the lake.

"Sluts," she said. "Jack, I don't want to be a part of this anymore."

"Where do you want to go, then?"

"How about a house? How about a *bed*?"

He didn't say anything. He didn't have to. The night would proceed.

"What time do your parents go to bed?" she asked.

It was a funny question, but he looked at the car's clock.

"They're in bed now, probably."

"And your sister?"

"My sister goes to sleep with the angels. And wakes with the birds."

"We've never done it in your bed."

He was leaning against the driver's side door, and now he smiled.

"Ellen."

"What?"

"We sleep close together at my house. All three bedrooms are on the second floor."

"I know that. So?"

"So, Jesus, don't you think they'll hear us?"

"We can be quiet."

She placed a hand on his knee, and he turned away. There was this terrible thing about helplessness. How her doing that could startle him and cut his thinking off, so that something stupid might happen. And he didn't want that.

"I'm sick of the lake, and I'm sick of the slutty girls out there. Sometimes I don't want to be anywhere near them."

Jack swallowed. Her hand was traveling up his thigh.

Then suddenly she took it away. Though he didn't want her to keep leading him into helplessness, he hated when she removed it.

"Promise me something."

"Oh, shit."

"Jack. Promise me. When you're married, when you have kids, when you're like a *man*, will you call me up?"

"And say what?"

"I just want to know what happens to you."

"And *you*? Don't you think you'll be married and have kids?"

Ellen grew quiet and went into that space of hers that he thought of as a great emptiness. If there was an image that came to him at such moments—these ones he dreaded—it was of Ellen Foley in a desert, or anyway in a deserted place, in rags. Wind was blowing against her face.

"Sometimes I think I'm going to be very unhappy."

"Why do you think that?"

"And you, you're going to be fine."

He didn't challenge that. He believed the same thing, most of the time.

He reached toward her and held her chin. Kissed her. "Ellen, don't go away." Already her eyes were dead. "You want me to take you home?"

"No. Please. No. I want you to hold me."

The car was a '76 Oldsmobile Cutlass. It was just possible to slide over and hold her. He did that, aroused but at the same time respectful of the fact that this was the place—this psychological Hades of hers—where they never made love.

"Did you drink too much?"

She shook her head.

He went on holding her. He thought he could fall asleep. His right leg was asleep. By any rational standard he knew he should have ended things with Ellen by now, ended them as soon as he'd discovered this darkness of hers, which he wanted to have nothing to do with and which too often consumed his evenings. But things weren't rational. They just weren't.

When some time had gone by, he said, "Are you feeling better? Soon? Anytime soon?"

She shook her head.

"Will it make you feel better if I take you to my house?"

"I don't know."

"Do you want to try it?"

It was risky, but he would do anything for her, even stupid things, when she was in the grip of one of her depressions. He drove to his house and parked in the driveway. All the lights were off except one in the kitchen and one they left on over the back porch entrance. It was close to midnight.

He led her in, and they stood in the kitchen. He could tell right away that she felt better, or at least she was trying to fool him.

"It always smells good in here," she said.

It was true. His mother's domain. Sometimes, when he came home late at night, he found his mother here. She'd become a night wanderer. Her sleep was erratic. If he'd caught sight of her in the kitchen tonight, he'd have called this whole thing off.

"I wish I lived here," she said. "In a house like this."

"Listen, we can't go up to my bedroom."

"Why not?"

"Ellen, it's too risky."

She came close to him, led him in the dark into the little room off the kitchen, where they sat on the small sofa, from which he had to remove *The Oxford History of the American People*, the book his father had been trying to finish for as long as he could remember. She reached for him, and that was that. With Ellen he couldn't even describe what their sex had evolved into as "sex." There had to be another name for it. It was like the body and the clutchings and the juices were put to some purpose other than pleasure. He didn't know her when he fucked her, and though there was an undeniable excitement to it and a depth he had never found with other girls, he didn't entirely like it. He preferred seeing conventional things in a girl during the act: fear, and maybe a tiny bit of struggle, a grappling with all the things that kept them on the far side of enjoyment, then their final triumph over those things. But with Ellen you went into a dungeon where it seemed a lot of other people lived. Her father with his secrets, her mother with her cleaning brush and her pail, that small house on the cul-de-sac. His penis was put to some use he could never understand.

Then, too, it was exhausting. It went on. He always wanted to sleep right afterward, so much did he feel he'd been put through the wringer.

44

He lay his head against her smallish, warm breasts. She stroked the hair that fell against his neck. He pretended for a moment that she was someone else. Like he would look up and this other girl would smile and make some joke and he could believe that life was a sailboat and all you had to do was keep the sails open and receive the wind as you skidded across a lake where tiny ripples surfaced. Clichéd as it probably was, that would be his poem, if he ever got around to writing it. If Mrs. Bowman would ever accept his metaphor. He smiled at that thought and, lulled by Ellen, her hand on his hair, drifted into sleep. He knew he was naked and that some vague danger lay in this fact, but he told himself there was time. Whatever that danger was—it was slipping from him—it could be righted. There was time.

It was the heat, the waking in the night feeling that you were burning. How suddenly it came, and unexplained. First she thought of it as a presentiment of death, until she mentioned it to her sister, and Betty had said, "Oh, ya, them, they call them the hot flashes." Betty had put the stress on the last word. It was a kind of explanation, though not quite enough. "You know, and then afterwards you dry up." It would have been good, Stella had always thought, to have an older sister of some delicacy, someone who might explain things fully, but that had never been Betty's way. Early explanations of sex had come out in the same coarse manner. "They push it up ya," Betty had reported on her early married life and then shaken her hand to indicate pain, so that when Richie had come back from Korea, some part of Stella—inadmissable, a ghost self—had wished he had died there, so that she could have avoided the pain.

Now there was this other side of it all, waking her, so she had to strip herself naked, even in winter, and lie on top of the covers, waiting for it to pass. Was all of life this passiveness, this being done to, the body simply a clearinghouse for pain? She waited. But lately, even after the heat had left her, she couldn't get back to sleep. Lying beside Richie, listening to him sleep, his open mouth.

Tonight she got up and went into the bathroom, not the one connected to their bedroom (she didn't want to wake Richie), but the one in the hall, the one the children used. She wet a washcloth, ran it over her breasts, belly, not looking at herself, or trying not to. On her way back to the bedroom she passed Jack's room, the door open. He was not home yet. It must have been past one. Panic, and then she looked out the hallway window and saw the car there, so she knew he was somewhere within, downstairs.

She tightened her robe. Sometimes, on these late nights when he came home and found her alone, wandering, they talked. It was the new thing in her life, to talk to a son. As he was growing up, they'd passed each other as if there were no need for deep acknowledgment. She'd wanted to hasten his growing up so that he could be out of the house and she could be alone with Joannie. She had never liked the male part of Jack, the sealed, malodorous inner room of a boy, a place as unattractive as any on earth, things growing erratically and wild, hair, ears, the sudden mustache, the love of noise, the profound hiddenness. She prayed he'd be all right but had no idea how to make him so.

But then out of that, and just recently, he had changed, as if he had newly learned how to be gentle. Coming home late at night, he approached her as she sat with her tea, the single overhead light on. She did not even try to imagine where he had just been. "You okay, Mom?" His face open and receptive, though she could not tell him, could not begin to express the burning, the revolt of her own body, the helplessness she felt. If the tea was not already made, he sometimes lit the burner under the kettle. It was possible to believe he would be someone's good husband someday, that he had come out from under the yoke of Richie and the shackles of boyhood, emerging into something generous.

Now she looked forward to seeing him, and descended the stairs, where she saw that the kitchen light was on. She might have missed them, the two bodies on the small couch, so much did she anticipate finding Jack in the kitchen. She was not looking for him there, and her first sight made her body turn all the way in the other direction, so that she nearly headed again up the stairs.

"I'm sorry" were the first words out of her mouth, as if they'd been awake.

It was only the realization that they were not, that they each slept profoundly, and beautifully, that made her turn. The girl's small breasts, thick with aureole, like a pregnant woman's, squashed softly against Jack's head. Her head leaning forward, the short hair and child's face, her body pushed back against the couch by his larger one, which lay sprawled and open. She moved forward cautiously to get a better look at Jack, then found she couldn't turn away, though she knew she should.

He was a thing she had made, but she had not seen him naked since he was small. The light on them was like the dim light in museums. She stared as long as she thought she could. Then she turned finally and headed up the stairs.

The image had been implanted. She could not quite blink it away. Nor did she want to. Jack had changed since they'd come here, to this house; the evidence on display was only the crudest evidence, but in that crudity she felt she had taken a peek inside him. Sometimes she felt grateful to Richie for bringing them all here, though she never said it, and she could never speak to him of this thing that linked her and Jack, though here, now, in the dark, she was beginning to understand it.

The heat in her body had left her as she lay beside Richie, replaced by something else. Something had happened to her, too, in coming here. She, too, had changed. Moonlight came in through the window. She concentrated on it a long time, thinking of Jack's body and smiling slightly before closing her eyes.

2

Sometime back in the mid-seventies, four or five years after they'd moved in, Richie had noticed that the shelves in his beloved store in the center of town weren't being restocked.

He'd been attentive. Shopping in the little store had been, for a long time, his chief form of civic life. At the beginning he had attended meetings of the board of selectmen. Few others had been in attendance, so few that the selectmen, seated on the stage of the town hall, stared out at Richie in a way that made him uncomfortable. It was not that they were hostile; instead, he felt as though his desire to belong were too much on display: Who else but a man nakedly desiring of a place here would sit through the long, tongue-tied plea for overtime pay made by the man whose job it was to plow the streets of Norumbega during snowstorms? Looking down at Richie after the resolution of this particular issue, the selectmen might have been saying, You see what it is, this vaunted belonging? It is all the parceling out of pennies, the endless adjustment of rights and deeds. After several months Richie stopped attending.

The store was something else. He always lingered longer than he strictly needed to, pretending that the purchase of necessities required long deliberation. He wanted to see who else lived here, to peer at the town's interior life. Women came in and made their purchases quickly, talking in a kind of shorthand to the girl behind the counter, a parochial world communicated in their brief exchanges, the names Bill or George spoken of like local deities.

There were two stores in the one: the aisles of sundries—Comstock squash filling, Del Monte tomatoes, packaged breads—were succeeded by the counter on which the two great cheese wheels, white and orange, lay. There on the counter, as well, were the wrapped packages of cookies baked by a local woman, the tightly wrapped zucchini and carrot loaves, breads from a hippie bakery in Cambridge, organic mints, and small chocolates from Holland. These you were expected to pick up at the last moment. Popping one in his mouth on his way out the door and receiving the first caress of Norumbega spring air was, for Richie, a benediction: impossible not to be inflated with a sense of the goodness of your life, the immense privilege, the stunning beauty of the everyday when the everyday has been sufficiently sculpted. It was this relation of commerce to well-being that had entranced him, and it was this—the disappearance of these dear items on the counter—that he had first marked. And been distressed by. Only afterward did he notice the growing scantness of packaged goods.

From time to time he had been aware of a man behind the counter. Rarely alone there, the man joked or chatted with the countergirl, clearly supervisory. Occasionally the man disappeared into an office at the rear of the store, from which Richie could hear the sound of an old-fashioned adding machine. Also sighs, exhalations, and the odd phone conversation, sounding at once relaxed and mysteriously charged.

One night the man was alone at the counter. The wheels of cheese lay uncovered, and Richie had to stifle the impulse to tell this man to cover them. The man greeted him with a slight twinkle in the eye.

"Late shopping?"

The storekeeper's voice was patrician, soaked in a brine of social irony Richie was unfamiliar with. His hair was black, graying, worn slightly long in the back. He was older than Richie. Put him in his mid to late fifties, but physically youthful. He wore a tweed sport coat, open shirt. He was nowhere else but behind the counter, ready to receive your money; simultaneously, he gave the effect of disdaining commerce.

"This is your store?" Richie asked.

"It is."

The man looked curiously at Richie, and from a slight distance. A smile appeared to be crawling toward his lips, as though he were looking for an *excuse* to smile.

"I can't help but notice . . ."

"The stock is thinning?"

Richie nodded, unsure how far he was being invited in.

"You notice correctly. We're going to close."

"No."

Richie had no time to shape the word, to pull back on the pure expression of his longing.

"I certainly didn't mean to offend you."

The man was looking at Richie now, invitingly, teasing him toward familiarity.

"It's all right," the man said, stepping back without moving. There was something in his manner now, a way of looking at Richie like a generous teacher recognizing untapped talent in an otherwise lackluster student. "Stores close all the time, you know."

"But not this one."

"Oh? Are we special?"

The man took his money and bagged his purchases.

Richie went to the door—no response occurring to him that wouldn't make him sound foolish—but turned at the last minute to find the man regarding him with continued, unwarranted interest.

"Something else coming in here?" he asked.

"Not that I know of." The man opened his arms. "A great emptiness, I think."

"Nobody's buying it, then?"

"Are you interested?" The man raised his eyebrows, the appearance of a commercial instinct reassuring to Richie.

"No, no. It's a shame, that's all."

"Indeed," the man answered.

"How long before you—before you close?"

"Hmm? Oh, that's not been decided."

The man was already past this conversation. Stupid to linger. Richie stuck out his hand.

"Richie Palumbo."

"Yes, you've got that house," the man said. He took Richie's hand a second late.

"The Greeley place," Richie said, surprised at being known, and with an accompanying pride.

"Drove the price of things up here, didn't you?"

"Beg your pardon?"

"That price you paid. All our assessments went up."

He understood now. The stares of the selectmen had not been as empty as he'd assumed. And the brush-offs, the failure of others to greet him in the five years they'd been here not all inherent snobbishness.

"I—"

"Oh, don't apologize. You wanted that house, and you were willing to pay whatever it took."

"That's about right."

"Bunch of parasites in this town. Most of them inherited their money, and their houses. Someone with a little spirit comes in—"

His smile showed teeth now. And something in his eyes, taking Richie in all over again.

"You live in town?" Richie asked.

Immediately he noticed a mild retreat reflected in the man's eyes.

"I do. Yes."

He should have known, was the inference. That he didn't said all that needed to be said about his outsiderhood.

"Well, your butter will melt," the man said, eyeing Richie's bag, another joke he was expected to get. Then the man's hand was out again.

"Norbert Oakes," he said.

That night in bed, Richie remembered. The woman in the library, when he'd first started haunting the town, the long coat, the cigarette, the librarian's catlike smile. "Norbert Oakes is driving me crazy." It excited him. He had made an inroad; it was like at last following a trail of crumbs that led into the inner, hidden life of Norumbega.

When was this—'75, '76? That middle time. Inflation, and the last helicopter taking off from Saigon. The time of shame and curiosity, when the future life of the nation took the shape of a question mark. Gerald Ford was like the man behind the curtain in *The Wizard of Oz*. Great forms and puffs of smoke appeared on the screen, but the man at the center had a halting manner and cleared his throat. It was the first time in Richie's life when he felt no one in charge, the enterprise itself up for grabs.

At work, it was the age of Desmarais. As Richie had predicted, things had not changed so much at ComVac. The number of contracts received from the Pentagon had held steady; the development of computers could not maintain a hold on engineers whose imaginations had been trained and sharpened by a close concentration on torque and velocity, the sexual shape and thrust of missiles.

The truth was that Ray Desmarais had outfoxed him, staged a kind of coup by means of those harsh eyebrows, that indefatigable linebacker's face. Desmarais now oversaw all the defense work and was unexpectedly hands-off. Richie had his eight men.

Dottie had been moved to another department. Their encounters were in the cafeteria, occasionally in the halls. She kept something behind her eyes, like a covered plate she was bringing to someone else's house. He still felt it should be his, whatever she was carrying. The workday contained a sequence of tiny heartbreaks like this.

In the summer Desmarais's son came and was given a desk. The boy was a junior at Rensselaer, then a senior, finally hired permanently. His face was a replica of his father's, squashed and blunt and feral, on top of a stocky body. Bluto, Jr., Richie called him under his breath. Bringing the boy in was Desmarais's way of assuring his dominance. Richie thought of bringing Jack to ComVac in the summers, but something in his son's profound relaxation—what Richie believed was a terminal lack of drive—made it seem unlikely. From his adolescence on, Jack had taken to the golf links, become a caddy, and had no intention of working indoors. Occasionally, driving past the country club, Richie caught sight of Jack's form, right hip thrust out casually, the regulation country club hat on his head. Some slow world had become alluring to Jack, the world of golfers: his son had come closer to the town's social nucleus than Richie himself ever managed to come. If there had been a belief held that at a certain point Jack would turn to his father and say, Teach me something, that belief was receding, though Richie had not lost it entirely.

So what had happened to them all since coming here? Had it all been dispersal, each of them seeking a private quadrant in which to function? Joannie, even now, in what should have been the bloom of her early teenage years, remained hidden—physically behind long bangs that covered her forehead, but more deeply behind the door of her room. She remained permanently, Richie thought sometimes, a little girl, fearful, abnormally attached to her mother. Their time alone together consisted of their Sunday morning drive to Mass (Richie and Joannie were the only two in the family who went) and the forty-five minutes of the ceremony itself, when he listened to her reedy voice rising on the hymns. It was like witnessing a shocking inner part of her. Often he wanted to ask her if she wanted to stop for coffee or a snack afterward. Though she was respectful toward him, always kind, an anticipated awkwardness held him back. What would they talk about sitting in some coffee shop?

The grand surprise of those early years—the one happy surprise—had been the way Stella took to the house. She had a pride about it—her kitchen, and the garden at the back. Her sisters came, and they sat on wrought iron chairs under an arbor she had had him build. The sisters held cups of tea and didn't know what to say, because Stella had so clearly gone away from them. They made broad efforts to return her to a common language. She nodded, as if she would allow them to talk about whatever they wanted, but felt no need to contribute. She'd become a reader. Books from the Norumbega library—*The War Between the Tates, The Easter Parade*—were to be found on chairs, on her bedside table. It was a Stella he didn't quite know.

In bed, she had grown more forthright. This was the other surprise, though in truth it was less a surprise than an escalation. He excused Stella her growing sexual enthusiasms. In fact, they frightened him a little, and it was perhaps as a result of an unconscious, undefined pulling away from her that he found himself alone much of the time. Then there was the problem of the mortgage. For a time—a suggestion made by one of the brothers-in-law, one he could not be seen to have taken at the time—he had been looking for a business, something secondary, to be attended to at night. "You ought to get yourself into something," his brother-in-law Carl had said. "This place will eat up everything you've got." They all knew what he had paid for the house, knew the mortgage, knew his income. In the old days, Stella had kept nothing private.

So the store intrigued him, though he could not figure out at first whether his interest lay more in trying to solve his financial difficulties than in preventing Norbert Oakes from slipping into the magic wood, never to be known.

When he next saw him, he asked, boldly enough, "No takers?"

Norbert Oakes looked at him, the effort to remember arresting his face for seconds.

"Ah. No. No. I doubt there will be."

Richie was annoyed that there were others nearby in the store. He lowered his voice.

"Maybe we can talk."

"Talk?"

"Alone."

The man's eyes did not light up as they would have if he were reacting, excitedly, to being saved at the last moment by a potential buyer. You could not tap so easily into Norbert Oakes's inner space.

"To talk about a sale, you mean? How delightful."

The word disconcerted Richie. He was afraid Norbert Oakes was about to point him out to the other shoppers for some eccentricity he wanted Richie to demonstrate.

"I'm not sure—a sale," Richie murmured.

Oakes drew him out silently.

"I had an idea."

One evening, by arrangement, they met in the back, in the office. Oakes kept a calendar there—a picture of a Mexican woman carrying a pot, one hip thrust provocatively toward the viewer. Otherwise, there was only a maze of papers on the desk, bills, and one of those old-fashioned checkbooks, large and formal as a wedding album.

Oakes leaned back and folded his hands. "I'm all ears."

"Well. My idea," Richie began. "First of all, let's establish, you're closing the store because business is bad."

Oakes looked at him an uncomfortably long moment, smiling. Talking to this man was like undergoing a tutorial in human mystery.

"Let's say that," Oakes said.

"It's not true?"

"Like most things, it's partly true." Oakes licked his lips. It was as if he couldn't wait for the next thing Richie would say.

"So business is not so bad, but you want to move on."

If there had been something in Richie's tone that was just a bit condescending—the seasoned man of business speaking to the amateur—Oakes butted against it. His eyes grew hard.

"Why don't you just tell me the idea?"

"There's no place to eat for miles around."

Oakes waited. Then he said, "So, a restaurant?"

"No," Richie said. "A restaurant isn't something I could do. It's important I keep my job. I'm thinking of something I could manage at night. Something that would require a partnership."

Then, emptiness in the eyes of Norbert Oakes.

"Go on," he said finally.

"You would have to hold the note. You own this place, right? The building?"

Oakes nodded.

"I'm tapped out at the bank. I couldn't go to the bank and ask for a loan with the mortgage I hold on my house."

"Oh, I think they'd be delighted to loan you money. No one else is asking them these days. Things are going for a song."

"I think you would have to hold the note," Richie said again.

Oakes looked back at him, for the first time with what Richie felt was respect.

"Tell me what you're thinking of putting in here."

"There are two things people will always patronize. Pizza parlors and Chinese restaurants."

"Yes," Oakes said, and leaned slightly backward.

"Well. I'm not Chinese."

The idea seemed to rise before Norbert Oakes like something fanciful, an idea so far out of left field he was delighted by it. "Good God," he said. His foot, one leg folded over the other, began to tap. "A pizza parlor. In Norumbega. Good God."

The smile was full, though not exactly a smile of simple agreement. For a moment Richie saw a complex mechanism behind the smile, the very switchboard of Norumbega, wires crossed and uncrossed. It flashed for a second, a secret he was about to be let in on.

"Tell me, Mr. Palumbo," Oakes said. "Do you fish?"

Norbert Oakes's canoe was one of those chained to a post and upended on the shore of Lake Norumbega. The chain was rusty, and Oakes, fitting the key in, said, "It's only a pretense, of course, that this thing is secured. I know very well the kids break in. They take it out." He grimaced as he fitted the key in and turned it. "So long as they return it, I don't mind."

He had brought along two rods, oars, and a basket. It was late afternoon and Richie had left work early. Oakes had also brought a pair of what he called "waders."

"Why don't you take the front?" he said, and the two of them rowed to the place on the other side of the lake to which Oakes directed them, then got out.

"Now this is called portage," Oakes said, smiling, in the grip of a kind of competence never fully on display in the store. "You learn this in camp. We all went to camp, you know. Camp Chippewa and Camp Runnymede and such. Camp was very important."

Richie lifted the back of the canoe and listened to Oakes from behind. There was something sly he couldn't quite read in the words. Was Oakes making fun of his ignorance, or was he making fun of his own privileged past? Oakes had insisted that he put on the waders before the portage for a reason: they were sinking a couple of inches into muck.

Eighty feet later they faced another, much larger lake. Richie had not seen it before and did not try to stifle his exclamation.

"Yes," Oakes said. "You don't see it from the road."

The water must have been freezing; its color was such a deep blue as to dip into realms of black. Dark trees at a distance—immensely tall, their color the green of the illustrations in old children's books. A large bird swooped over the trees. This is the forest primeval, Richie found himself thinking. The heart of the world.

"Of course it's a rotten time to fish. I don't like your schedule at all," Oakes said, steadying the boat. "Get in."

They rowed to the center. Dazzled, Richie asked about worms.

"Worms?" Oakes smiled. "We don't use worms. We went to camp, Richard. We learned to tie flies." He put on a pair of glasses, opened the basket. In a plastic case were an assortment of colors, small, feathery things the size of women's earrings. Oakes opened one and lifted it. "We won't catch anything, of course. We won't fool a single fish at this hour of the day. But we can at least learn the rudiments."

He showed Richie the wrist movement involved in casting. Richie watched the line loop and drift in the air as if it would never land. Something gorgeous in that, an elegance that seemed to have nothing to do with catching fish. Oakes explained the technique, and they drifted, casting; Richie stopped doing it awkwardly after half an hour.

The sun had dropped behind the stand of high trees before Oakes said, "So. Pizza."

The word felt, at that moment, like a profanation. Richie had been thinking of Ray Desmarais. He had been thinking how permanently barred Ray Desmarais was from this secret lake, unseen from the road, jewel-like, and, with the fading of the light, sinking deeper into blue. It embarrassed him, the world he came from, the watercoolers and the men who needed a shave by three in the afternoon, pen holders lining the pockets of their shirts, and the lighting at ComVac, installed on the cheap during World War II and never updated.

"Yes," Richie said. He was hesitant to go on, but Oakes's look demanded it.

"The way I see it, the largest cost would be in conversion. Putting in an oven. This is where we'd have to borrow. The inside will have to be gutted. But after that—well, let's say we open at three. Get someone to come in, get us started. It's fairly simple. I could manage it at night."

He spoke slowly, still with the sense of awe that the lake drew out of him. His image was of himself looking in, checking on things, taking calls from the house. But not really working. Working in a pizza parlor would mark him ineradicably as the Italian interloper. He saw himself and Oakes outside the store, two men of business, their hands behind their backs. Proprietors.

"And where do I come in?" Oakes was tying a new fly. He looked at the water the way a man might study his own lawn.

"I assumed we'd be partners."

Oakes grimaced again, though he didn't mean to offend.

"I'm not sure I'm quite the type to put on a baker's hat and . . ."

"Oh, neither of us would do any baking."

Oakes smirked. "So who makes all these pizzas?"

"We'll hire someone."

Oakes cast, then looked at Richie cagily. "Yes, of course. Now, here's the fact, Richard. The bank will loan us money because, short of this idea, there's no idea. The store sits empty. So we gut and we build and we . . . hire someone, and we hope against hope that the good citizens of Norumbega and the surrounding boroughs have a taste for pizza." He smiled at that. "Personally, I find the idea delightful, but I cannot speak for my townsmen. We may fail, in which case we owe a lot of money."

"We won't fail."

Oakes was reeling in.

"Oh?"

"No. No, we won't fail."

Oakes gazed at him a long time, as if he were trying to gauge the provenance of a work of art. "This is the attitude that built the great wharves of Boston."

Richie tried another cast.

"That conquered the heathen Indians. 'We won't fail.' I stand in awe. You think we can actually make money?"

"I do."

It was a minor shock, but one he was still absorbing, that a man like Norbert Oakes might be hungry for money. That he, Richie, could give this to him did not seem such a great gift. The pizza parlor was an idea that seemed to him insubstantial and utterly real at the same time. Elbow grease and vats of sauce. Subcontractors and wreckage. All of it could be made to happen. You visited a bank, you wrote checks. He felt unafraid of that. Work. Unafraid. It was what Oakes could give him that seemed the true prize.

"Yes. I wanted you to see this," Oakes said, gentle now, nearly private in his tone as he studied Richie staring out over the water of the lake. "I've christened it—it's a bit pretentious, actually—Lac Bleu."

As it turned out, there was no problem with the bank. Their risk was an equal one. A man named Guy Procaccini answered an ad they placed in the papers. Richie observed him baking pizzas. A grizzled man who smoked cigarettes between batches and sometimes forgot to check the pies in the oven, resulting in several burnt ones.

Guy Procaccini took a taxi to Norumbega. (He'd lost his license.) He complained that it was eating up his wages. Once, Richie noticed cigarette ashes in a pie he was boxing up for a customer, and stopped him in time. Procaccini's rage flared.

"We can't have that. We're trying to build up a reputation," Richie said.

Procaccini's eyes continued to burn. "So we cover it over with sauce. They'll never know. A little ash. They'll never know."

It was the beginning of Richie's understanding that the business would not succeed unless he addressed it hands-on. His respect for his customers—his need for their approval—was too great, the interchange fraught. It was not long before Procaccini was fired and Richie, on his

way home from ComVac, donned an apron and a baker's hat that resembled the cap he'd worn in Korea. It meant opening later, but Richie
knew how to bake pizzas. Though he hadn't done it regularly in years,
it had once been his Sunday night specialty. Stella helped him with
the sauce until he was able to master it on his own. His management
skills—his careful way of laying out a job beforehand—served him well.

"Oh, this was not how it was to be," Norbert Oakes said. They
fished early now, Saturday mornings at first light. They met in the parking lot, where Oakes sipped from a thermos, his eyes lighting up at the
sight of Richie like a man regarding a woman he had not thought to
win so easily.

"We were to be two men of business, country squires, counting our
money while the solid light fell," Oakes said, the line between his teeth,
breaking it off.

"We'd have gone bankrupt if we'd kept Procaccini," Richie said. He
caught trout now. They fished from the shore of the inner lake, the flies
dropped just so. The water in the morning the silver of a weighted cloud.

The sly tutorial—"portage," "this is how you tie a fly," "we all went
to camp"—had given way to something else. They were partners. At
the end of every week they read the ledgers and rolled coin together
like brothers. They bonded over numbers. Profits were slow in coming,
but Richie could sense their arrival.

One night, baking pizzas, Richie saw Oakes's form outside the
window, watching him. He went out to him.

"I worry about you," Oakes said.

"What do you worry about?"

"Too much work, Richard. All day at that business of yours, now
this."

"You could help," he said. "Take the counter. We wouldn't have to
pay the girl."

"That's what I came to talk to you about, actually," Oakes said, and
cleared his throat.

Their conversation was being conducted by the rear door. Oakes's
car, a fir-green Jaguar, lay shining in the same light that fell upon their
Dumpster.

"My daughter," Oakes said.

Again he cleared his throat, an uncomfortable obstruction there.

"What about your daughter?" Richie asked. Oakes's private life had
been a mystery, Richie's respectful questions largely unanswered.

"I have a sixteen-year-old girl. I'm thinking we could hire her. That is . . ."

What was this sudden shyness, this asking Richie's permission? When Oakes entered the confines of the baking area, he always sniffed luxuriously—a brief rapture running across his features—but treated the utensils as if he were too awkward and butterfingered to pick them up.

"She's sixteen, as I say."

"Is she a good worker?"

Oakes laughed, but it was indistinguishable from a cough. "Where would she have learned that, do you suppose?"

"You ran a store."

"Egregiously, yes. And with plenty of help. I'm not like you, Richard. I'm not a very good hands-on man."

"You've never talked about your family."

Occasionally, at moments like this, there was a return to their first conversations, where Richie had a sense of confronting a house where certain windows seemed to be wide open, others boarded up.

"I have a daughter. I think it would be *good* for her, is what I'm saying, to come and learn here. Learn something, at any rate."

"Well, yes," Richie said.

"Good. Well, perhaps I'll have her drop by."

Was there a moment of silent pleading before Oakes turned away? Then the Jaguar ticked and he pretended it needed to be attended to. Within it, his face changed from what it had been a moment ago. The brief moment of vulnerability fell away. He became again the country squire, the scourge of Norumbega, to be feared by women in long coats.

Oakes's daughter, Christina, arrived, at the tail end of her braces period. Her skin recorded the passage of a mild and recent attack of acne. It was healing nicely, a few red spots jutted from the top of her cheeks, that was all. Richie noticed the caked makeup she had put on inexpertly. Her smile was a brief eclipse of her lower lip by the braced teeth, followed by self-consciousness. In all this imperfection was an announcement—the clear heralding—of wonders to come. She would be a beauty.

When Stella was pregnant with Jack, they'd gone to see the movie

Exodus. At some point in the movie the character of Karen had appeared, a small blond girl demanding, effortlessly, something from the audience. (They knew beforehand, in the way you knew in those days, that Karen would die violently, the future of the nascent State of Israel embodied in her delicate frame.) Beside him, at Karen's entrance, Stella had gasped. It had been a mildly troublesome introduction to the notion that women could be drawn to the beauty of other women. But to call it "beauty" was to miss half of what it was. Certain girls carried on them a quality that tucked beauty into the folds of a larger garment. They were some ideal of what a girl could be, calling us, effortlessly, to be better in their presence, to be aware of everything in us that is awkward, hairy, and inappropriately hungry.

All of this—the advent of the young woman she would one day become—Richie saw as he taught Christina how to use the cash register. But at the beginning, she was sixteen. Did she know his son, Jack, at the high school? he asked, to make conversation. "I think so." She nodded, too quickly, just to be friendly and agreeable, Jack having made, clearly, no impression whatsoever on her. Richie was neither happy nor disappointed about this.

He would have liked to ask, as they became more used to each other, about her home life. Did she live with Oakes? Did she have a mother? (Why did she use the last name Thayer?) But you did not crack the vessel of such a girl by pressing too hard. Her shift ended at eight—Richie was alone for the last hour or so of occasional orders—and when it was still light enough, she bicycled home.

"How's that daughter of mine doing?" Oakes asked one night as they were rolling coins from the soft-drink machine into papers suitable for deposit.

In the wake of Procaccini, profits had come. Still not large, but promising to be larger. The addition of "subs"—Richie's idea—had made a difference.

"Good," Richie answered. "She's a wonderful girl."

"I'm glad to hear that." Oakes's eyes sparkled; he might have been waiting for more. Richie rarely saw them together, and their interchanges told him very little. Oakes always seemed deferential in her presence, staring at her without seeming to be staring. As for the girl, her eyes seldom rose to meet her father's.

"Teach her something, Richard."

What exactly did he want her to be taught?

Other girls came and went, and a few boys. On weekend nights they always required two behind the counter. Christina's braces fell away; her skin cleared. She wore her hair tied in a knot in the back. She rode off on her bike in a direction past the library. Some nights Richie wanted to follow her—just to see, he told himself, where she lived.

"You don't live together?" he asked Oakes one Friday night.

Oakes looked up at him over his glasses, impenetrable.

"We don't, no."

"She lives with her mother?"

Oakes made a neat closure of the coin wrapper in his hand and set it aside.

Richie did not at first recognize the feeling that had begun to come over him after a year or so, as he drove or—more frequently, after Jack got his license—walked home. On Friday nights he often carried more than a thousand dollars in bills and coin the half mile to his house, but he never thought to fear being robbed. He saw not a soul, only the windows of houses, lit against the dark. He had become the man in the muffler, the man in the long coat; some hungry and heat-seeking traveler might have watched him and been filled with envy, except for the baker's pants, which made him look like what he was, a tradesman. Still, there were compensations: money enough to secure his place here and, in season, fishing with Oakes. He had the lake. If it was not the whole thing, it was at least something. Coming home, he always heard Stella call down to him from upstairs, where she lay in bed with a gardening book or one of the thick novels she read. They had taken their places here.

On those nights, when Jack was nearly always out, living his secret life, Joannie stayed mostly in her room. She sometimes came down to greet him. If she was in a particularly good mood, they'd watch television. Though the shows were often silly, they were a way for the two of them to spend time together. Richie wanted to ask why she never seemed to go out. Her hair hung in what he thought of as a clumped, unattractive manner, but he could see that underneath, she had Stella's earthy young beauty, and at times he had to fight the urge to pull her hair back to reveal her face. He noted the intent manner with which she studied the television shows they watched—*The Rockford Files, Dallas*—and hoped that what he saw there, particularly as she was exposed to the scenes of flirtation and seduction, was interest. Joannie had begun receiving literature from religious organizations;

photographs of nuns and black children in Africa sometimes graced the envelopes.

The really troubling thing, though, was that Joannie's presence could not distract him from his most difficult thoughts, not like in the old days when he'd come home and climb into bed with her. Sitting with Joannie in front of the TV, he could not help but think of Christina. There had been a moment one recent afternoon when he stood behind Christina as she was hoisting something. The fabric of her T-shirt lifted over the fabric of her jeans, and a slip of skin—two inches, three—had appeared. He retained the exact color of that skin—soft brown in summer, with a single pimple resting on the left side of her lower back—and the shape of her buttocks in her jeans. He could not stop thinking of it—in bed, even sometimes at work. Joannie's presence could not draw him away from it.

In November, before the start of the Christmas season, he and Christina laced the windows with wisps of snow from aerosol containers. Then they stepped outside to gauge the effect. A look of childish happiness settled over her features. He wanted to put his arm around her. Like a daughter. He wanted badly to get away with that as an excuse, wanted to believe that was all it was. But if that were the case, why did he feel he needed to lash his arms to his sides?

Nothing in these stored-up images amounted in his mind to anything so crude and dismissible as a sexual fantasy. He would not defile himself or her that way, by imagining them in an act of penetration. In his imagination she was not penetrable, at least not by him. She floated in an ether located above the region of the limbs. She was like the town itself, he thought sometimes, everything gorgeous and elusive about it in human form. And so, following this logic, what he convinced himself he wanted was not her body, but her acceptance, even her love.

One night, cleaning up, he asked Christina a question about Jack. He was not sure what answer he was looking for or how she might offer him reassurance, but his unhappiness over Jack's lack of college plans forced it out of him.

"I'm disappointed in my son," Richie said, then cleared his throat.

"Why?"

"He's not like you."

They had worked together for two years. Many of their conversations were in shorthand. If she had not become like Dottie—how could she?—there was still a hope that in speaking, he would be understood.

So the sense of her hiding something—the air had seemed to bristle immediately at his question—was troubling.

"What do you mean?"

"Going to college. He never even applied."

She looked relieved.

"What were *you* talking about?" he asked. "Something bothered you."

"No. Nothing."

He gave her a moment. What had been there, inside her hesitation, when he suggested that Jack was not "like her"?

"Is there something about my son I should know?"

"No. I mean, he's a popular boy."

Richie attempted to study her. You couldn't go too far. But she was holding something back. She knew something.

"He's popular with girls," she said.

He nodded, as if there were some deeper meaning there. He felt her judgment of Jack. Jack had gone for the cheap, the obvious in life. Was that what she was telling him? Was that the town's embarrassing judgment of his son?

It ended their conversation. When they were done with the cleanup, he went outside to watch her as she mounted her bike to ride home. It was something he liked to do, but tonight, as she turned back to him, pushing off on her bike, he felt too revealed, as though he wore his longing on his face. As she glanced back at him, was that pity he saw?

Unmistakable, though, something else in that look: a revelation in her beautiful face of some longing of her own. Not for him, certainly. But for *something*. She carried her mystery away. She rode under the high trees that formed twin columns along the majestic main street, and he watched her until she disappeared.

3

The appointment had been made for four in the afternoon. Stella needed to pick Joannie up from school and then drive what she had been told was approximately an hour and a half out to the priory in Lancaster.

Joannie had explained—assured Stella more than once—that this was simply an exploration. "Just a visit," Joannie said. With her CCD teacher and a group of other girls Joannie had already visited the priory in the spring and come home glowing. She'd recently told Stella that she wanted to go again, to visit with the nuns. "Just to ask questions," the girl had said.

Because she could not yet drive, Stella would have to take her. Joannie had made the call—the appointment—herself. She'd been nervous to do it. Stella had watched her, her young girl's hands shaking on the receiver and her voice pitched too high.

Driving was still a challenge for Stella. Out of necessity, she had taken it up after moving to Norumbega. On Bryant Street, everything essential had been within walking distance or an easy bus ride away. She'd been unusual for not having her license, but it was one of those fears of hers she had decided it was not really necessary to overcome. Until Richie moved them to the country. Here it was just too much of a bother to take a taxi to every doctor's appointment and to wait for Richie on the weekends to do serious shopping. So there had been a succession of Sundays when he taught her, and the simple shifting of positions—her behind the wheel, him in the passenger seat—felt like a threat to some agreement they had lived by.

Joannie was quiet on the ride, her hands folded in her lap. Stella tried asking a couple of questions, but when Joannie answered in single syllables, she stopped. She remained in the right-hand lane the whole way. Anyone could pass her. That was fine. Let them.

The priory was at the end of a long road in the woods. The nuns were housed in an enormous stone cottage attached to the church by a covered walkway. No sooner had they parked than a nun appeared at the door. This woman did not smile in greeting, but stood with her hands clasped low against the folds of her habit.

"You must be Joan," the nun said when they were close. Still without a smile, though not unkindly. Her face was austere but beautiful, without makeup.

Joannie bowed her head and wore a beatific smile. Stella could have sworn she was holding herself back from running into the nun's arms and shouting, Take me! But that was only her—Stella's—fear.

They were ushered into a room. All the furniture was old, donations from other people's houses. On the walls were religious paintings that might have been scavenged from a dump, marked by water stains. There were crucifixes and a small library, organized by theme and labeled: PRAYER LIFE. SAINTS. VOCATIONS.

"We have some very fresh banana bread," the nun said. Here was

64

the first smile. In another life she might have been the prettiest woman in the neighborhood, with handsome children and an enviable air of competence. "Sister Catherine baked it this morning. And tea, of course. I'll bring you some. What do you take?"

It was quiet. Stella sensed movement from other rooms. Joannie seemed fixated on a sequence of internal thoughts, which Stella wanted to prod her out of. But then there followed the keen sense of how young Joannie was. She seemed a child here, far too young to be considering some other life. Surely the nuns would take note of that and discourage her. Stella was remembering a Halloween two years before, when Joannie had dressed as one of the girls from *Little House on the Prairie* and gone out with a group of girlfriends. After the amount of worrying that she and Richie had done about Joannie's isolation, it had been thrilling to watch her run down the front walk to meet her friends. It was one of the rare occasions when she seemed to have spirit and to want to be a normal, functioning member of the world.

The nun—Sister Anselm—returned with slices of banana bread on a plate and two cups of tea.

"I'll be speaking to Joan alone for a while, if that's all right. Then we'll talk together. We'll be just upstairs."

I've been praying, she might be saying, and you have interrupted me.

Then they both left. Stella stared through the window glass at birds in the yard, wondering what they must be talking about upstairs, how far Joannie's "exploration" had in fact gone, feeling left out entirely of something huge.

She picked up a book—*The Interior Castle*—and touched the cover but did not open it. She felt that the first lines she read would contain an accusation, something that would apply to her personally, so she left it unopened.

She listened for some signs from above, from the room where Joannie and Sister Anselm had gone. She half expected to see Joannie emerge in a habit, to hear Joannie say, I won't be coming home. She touched her heart, which had begun thudding at the thought. The beautiful nun would smile with a kind but superior wisdom. You having failed, we can take over now. The difficult thing was the unexpected pleasure she could sense at the edges of that thought: Now I can be alone with Jack.

There was no way to shoo away the guilt accompanying such a

thought. Where had it come from, out of what fissure in the brain? It had been the same with her pleasure over her first orgasms, a year or so after her marriage, when Richie learned to slow down. They had been thrilling, but the horses of guilt had reared up immediately. You weren't supposed to have such pleasure. In the 1950s there was no permission. She looked at her married sisters and imagined that it did not happen for them, and this was the very beginning of her distance from them.

But then had come something deeper, something to separate her even from herself. She had come to depend on those orgasms, sometimes even outlasting Richie, wanting more from him even when he was finished. The wanton in herself seemed a separate person, not to be admitted to, a second being she could not fully accept as a part of herself.

Coming to Norumbega had offered her a surprising distraction from all this. Very soon after moving into the house—sooner than she had any right to expect—she had come to love it. The way the light came through certain windows. The distances she stared out at from the back. At last to have enormous space for a garden. As she got more and more into it, she thought of the garden, of her whole backyard, as a spiritual retreat. She had not known on Bryant Street that it was possible to situate oneself in a corner of one's yard at a certain hour of the day— six o'clock on a May afternoon, say—and watch the sun fall over the trees and notice shadows. Each tree its particular shadow. Lilac and mountain ash and Dutch maple. Early leaves made a kind of lattice. It seemed a gift, to sit under an enormous sky in a quiet that felt vast.

She had become a reader, too. A new, more dignified Stella had begun to emerge. She had come to believe for a time that this new devotion of hers would replace the absorbing need for sex that had become such a private, personal embarrassment, that light and neat rows of vegetables and the tops of trees—and trips to the library—would become the ordering principle that had thus far eluded her. That this new life took her away from people—from her sisters, even from Richie— she had come to accept. There were nights, after sex, when it seemed that Richie wanted to say something to her, but though she sensed this, she never asked. Didn't want to know, not really. Terrifying, really, to *discuss* need and desire. Better to keep it at a distance.

At times now, during the night, suffering through the hot flashes, she saw them as a suitable punishment, almost welcomed them that way. Suffering to offset pleasure. If anyone were to say, You have wanted too much to be alone, she would answer, And look how I pay for it. Look. There was at least that balance. But then had come the night when she came upon Jack and the girl naked on the settee, and she'd understood the limits—even the self-willedness —of her spiritual retreat. How much Jack's body held a vivid display of her own—well, what was the word—*wantonness*. Or was it simple physical munificence? Acceptance of the physical gifts we are given. With that thought came another: You do not have to punish yourself for this.

The next morning, the morning after she'd come upon Jack and the girl, she could not meet her son's eyes. Some old part of her wanted to chide him, scold him for letting himself be found that way. Jack made his own breakfast, which was to say he poured milk over cereal, took three gulps, and left. She was always in a robe on Saturday mornings; he was due at the country club. Joannie came down earlier than usual, expecting Stella to cook for her. That morning, she asked Joannie to wait. Then she went to the front window and watched Jack. His long legs. The stride in which the upper part of his body leaned slightly forward, as if into an invisible wind. All anger had gone out of her. For the first time in his life, she wanted to ask him things. How to do this, really. How to inhabit proudly the sensual realm. At the moment of his leaving—he would soon be gone—she wanted to know Jack. Even to take instruction from him.

And suddenly she had no tolerance for Joannie's slow breakfast. She wanted Joannie to go upstairs, to sleep later. She felt now that they had been like two fussy old women all their lives, huddling together in a shelter. She had broken a little from Joannie that morning. Terrible to think that—they had been so close, though was it really closeness or sheer, dogged protectiveness? The moment Joannie had gone up to dress, Stella stepped out into the garden, holding her robe closed against the chilly May morning, asking the garden to save her.

And of course it hadn't. She was waiting for Jack when he came home, flushed from his day outside, sweat around the brim of his cap. "What?" he asked her, and because in his world, Jack's world, he could only believe her confusion to be nothing, a minor flaw in his mother's painfully simple being, he smiled widely and patted her on the head. She listened to him taking his shower. She soaked his hat and laid it out to dry.

You have lived wrong.

Those were the words that came to Stella that afternoon in the priory. But wrong *how*? How *exactly*? Don't stop there, her mind seemed to be saying. There is something that exists after guilt. Something important. Listen to it.

"Mrs. Palumbo?" Sister Anselm called.

Stella was being called back. A stairway lay to her left. She stood.

"You can come up now."

The room at the top of the stairway was not a room, but a landing. Two old chairs, needing to be reupholstered, the faded green of a supermarket cabbage. Joannie had not touched her banana bread or her tea.

Sister Anselm looked as though she were trying to work her way toward a greater friendliness, but reserve held her like an unignorable cold.

"We've been talking. I'd like you to know what we've been talking about."

Stella wanted to smile at that moment, as though it mattered to her, what she was about to be told. She wanted to pretend to be a concerned mother.

"I want you to understand, as I've told Joan, we could never accept a young woman at sixteen. Joan is at a formative stage. She feels she has a vocation, but it needs to be tested."

Stella finally managed a smile. She understood not a thing that was being said to her. Vaguely, she thought, Had Joannie asked to be accepted? Was she that bold?

"I've advised prayer."

Then the nun leaned forward.

"Do you pray, Mrs. Palumbo?"

"Yes," she answered very quickly. "Oh, yes."

Sister Anselm seemed to take in the lie. The tiniest movement in the pink lids of her eyes.

The nun hesitated. "Young girls like Joan. I can remember this very well. One tends to be alone a great deal. One hears what appears to be God when it may in fact be something else."

Joannie seemed to hear this in a way that made her blush. Her head lowered, as if in reaction to a slight blow.

"We need to expose that internal listening to some kind of light. I was going to suggest that Joan work."

"Work?"

"Yes. In the world somewhere. Volunteer. A hospital. A school. Some-where she could be tested."

Stella turned to her daughter.

"And date. I know that sounds perhaps unexpected. But yes, Joan should date. Normal high school activities."

Joannie blushed further. Stella wanted to smile. Yes, good advice.

"We're a contemplative order. Do you understand what that means, Mrs. Palumbo?"

Stella turned back to her, shook her head.

"We're not in the world. We pray. That sounds like a dreary life, I'm sure. It's not."

Sister Anselm was drawing a line separating them. It was as though she existed on the other side of a river, at a great distance from them, and Stella was being asked to see Joannie's spiritual life as a thing a good deal less than what was required. Stella wanted to tell this nun that since childhood Joannie had tacked religious pictures on the walls of her room. She did not need to *date*. She was happiest in church. It was that simple, really. She wanted to defend her daughter against the rejection this nun seemed to be holding over her. Stella did not wish her daughter to be a nun, but if Joannie chose, she had every right. It was sheer motherly competitiveness she was feeling.

"She's always been a religious girl," Stella said.

The nun smiled: I will allow you to have said that, it means nothing.

Joannie turned away, looked out the window.

Stella touched her hand and felt an incomprehensible impulse to-ward knocking things over in this room.

"Shall we pray?" the nun asked.

They knelt, the floor hard against Stella's knees. She was expected to close her eyes, but couldn't. Instead, she watched Sister Anselm's eyes close. The nun's face instantly softened. She might have been twenty-five at that moment, except for the lines around her eyes. Stella wanted to witness her rapture, but it felt like an intrusion, so she turned to Joannie. Joannie looked at her—was that a simple goodbye Stella read in her eyes, or was the girl acknowledging failure? Joannie closed her eyes, tightened her face as though she were holding urine inside her, God a full bladder that must not be allowed to leak out. And here was the difference. The nun relaxed in prayer, as if to let something in, while Joannie tightened, to keep something out. She needed to help

69

Joannie, had no idea how. What about *Little House on the Prairie?* Stella wanted to say. What about the way you ran down the walk with those phantom creatures, your friends? Wasn't that fun, that night? Don't. Don't abandon the other part of life. But Joannie continued to clamp her eyes shut, blocking out the world and all that Stella was coming to see were its perfectly acceptable pleasures.

4

The senior class had decorated the big dining room of the country club, a room Jack had been instrumental in securing, earning himself a nod of thanks from the prom committee. A great papier-mâché volcano sat in the center of the room, spouting smoke created when Ronnie Harlow, voted Class Dork and reveling in the honor, poured water over dry ice secreted inside. The theme of the prom was "Evening in Pompeii." Irony reigned that spring at Norumbega Regional High.

The girls were dancing with each other. Looking at them through his own mild drunkenness—their clear, pinkish skin, the way they'd pushed themselves into their mostly sleeveless gowns, their breasts squared and tucked away so that the line of cleavage became a hard, dark maternal crevasse—Jack noted that they all seemed forcibly grown up tonight, apprentice matrons, ready and eager to become their mothers. It made him feel disappointed, as though the interim life—the life where you were not still in high school and not quite yet in anything resembling adulthood, the life he thought of with an ecstatic appetite (especially since he had recently decided he would live this interim life in New York)—were something his female classmates were all too ready to leap over.

"You know what I want to see them do right now?" the boy next to him, Buddy Piper, asked. Buddy Piper had curly hair and great height, and a confidence that overrode the adolescent acne he had never quite managed to lose. "I want to see them—do you know what Nivea is?"

"Sure," Jack said.

"I want to see them take off each other's fucking gowns and rub Nivea all over each other." Buddy Piper's face scrunched up and approached Jack's in a way that seemed overly intimate. "Wouldn't that be good? Instead of this bullshit? Some porn thing? Some major nipple thing?" Buddy Piper made a motion with his little finger to indicate an erect nipple. "You ever see one of those movies? Girl sex movies?"

"No."

"Where girls do it to each other?"

"I think I get that when you say girl sex, Buddy."

Buddy shoved a flask against Jack's ribs. "Here. Have some," he said.

The game they were playing, without great skill, was to hide the flask from the eyes of the faculty chaperone, Mr. Shelton.

Jack refused Buddy's offer. He was drunk enough. He didn't like the way he was feeling distant tonight, separate from Buddy Piper and his Nivea fantasies. Separate from everybody.

"I do not want any," Jack said. "I do not want any, Mr. Piper."

"The fuck." Buddy looked at him with a slightly twisted grin and took a swig from the flask just as Mr. Shelton turned to look at him. Buddy was expected to hide it then, but he didn't. He closed the cap more slowly than he needed to, and Jack was disappointed to note the indifference of Mr. Shelton, a man he respected.

Jack got up. On the excuse of having to take a piss, he left the row of boys with whom he sat.

He had the keys in his pocket to the room where the members stored their golf clubs. Opening the room, he smelled that leathery, oiled, and cut-grass smell he had come to associate with the exclusively male world of Saturday mornings, when he hoisted Ron Sargeant's or Tommy Paul's bag of clubs over his shoulder and waited for the man's coffee to kick in, at which point he, Jack, would be acknowledged with a smirk or a smile or a dumb question about his sex life. It was a casting off, that moment, that he had loved. The world of Saturdays was like going off on a boat, except the water was grass, exquisitely sculpted, spongy, and pliant. He chose Tommy Paul's bag and removed the driver and then found a basket of balls and stepped out, not even to the driving range, but to a spot just off the club deck, and started whacking balls out into the dank night. Repeated actions like these led to an unconsciousness, where you were hip or wrist or ankle, that was all you were, and each combination of bone and sinew became a malleable liquid in which you felt you were swimming. He was nearly in that state when he realized someone was on the deck behind him.

Loosen was the first word he heard. It was a male voice, and when he turned, he saw Mr. Shelton there.

"Loosen what?"

"Pretty much everything."

The man had his hands in his pockets. He wore a tuxedo, like everyone else at the prom, but his looked more worn-in, more like it fitted his body.

"I feel pretty loose."

"You might *feel* loose, but look . . ."

Mr. Shelton stepped off the deck, took the club from Jack, placed the ball on the grass, and in a lovely motion sent the ball arcing into the unseen green.

"That was very cool," Jack said.

Mr. Shelton nodded and stepped back.

"Now you."

Jack hit the ball, not particularly well, made self-conscious by being watched.

"Oh, hopeless."

"I was having more fun before you started watching me."

"Yes. Well. Your friends are all so drunk I'm going to have to take their car keys away. I notice you're not. Can you drive them all home?"

"Sure. I'll take care of them."

There was silence then. Still with his hands in his pockets, Shelton kicked at the grass lightly, just skimming the top, as if he were kicking away dew. Jack remembered reading *The Great Gatsby* earlier in the year in Mrs. Bowman's class, and now for a moment what he thought he was seeing was what that man Gatsby would have looked like if instead of becoming a bootlegger he'd become a high school teacher.

"Whose clubs are they, by the way?"

"Tommy Paul's," Jack said.

"Is this something I need to report?"

"No. I caddy."

"I know you do, Jack. I know your life."

"How's that?"

Again, Mr. Shelton smiled. Jack had a sense now of messages being sent, with great subtlety, by this man. He knew enough to know they were not sexual messages—Mr. Shelton didn't want to blow him—but the man was looking for some shift in the level at which they related, a shift made possible only by the imminence of graduation.

"You'll go—where, next year?" Mr. Shelton asked.

At first Jack didn't understand.

"You mean college?"

"I do mean college."

Jack looked off into the dark where they'd sent their balls, distressed by this turn in the conversation.

"You know I'm not going."

"Of course. It's a great worry. Any concrete plans?"

"Sure. Yes."

"And do you care to share them?"

"I'm thinking New York."

Mr. Shelton nodded. He asked silently for the golf club back, but this time he placed it like a shovel against the grass, as if to see how much force he could apply without making a hole.

"What are we thinking, a room at the YMCA? A—what?"

Jack didn't answer. He didn't like the question, the tone that insinuated a lack of imagination.

"Look, it's not too late, you know. I could contact some people at Brandeis." Shelton was smiling. A briskness had come into his face.

"No. I don't want you to do that."

Mr. Shelton hesitated. "I could, you know. I could call someone up."

They looked at each other. Was Mr. Shelton showing off for him? Showing off his worldly prowess, his ability to affect change by picking up a phone?

"Otherwise you're going to—what, buck the tide? Do something bold and 'interesting'?" Mr. Shelton smiled.

Jack felt his only power now lay in holding back, in not allowing this man to get to him. All of them, they wanted to make you just like them.

"My friend, come here."

Jack hesitated, suspicious.

"Oh, please. Here to the window."

Mr. Shelton preceded him. They both looked inside. From this distance, even more than Jack had noticed before, the girls seemed to have aged considerably and the boys looked dunderheaded, dullards, too large for the smallness of their brains. He understood viscerally why the word *dick* had become such an appropriate put-down.

"I ask you to look at them," Mr. Shelton said, stepping back.

"I'm looking."

But now he could smell Mr. Shelton's aftershave and was disappointed in the man for wearing it. He didn't like the way his mind was traveling, imagining Mr. Shelton preparing for this evening. Why would a man, an apparently heterosexual man, volunteer to chaperone the senior prom? He wanted this to end now.

"What do you see?"

This was a game. Jack didn't answer.

"Or"—Shelton laughed gently—"maybe the appropriate question is, Do you want to be their equal, or do you want to serve them all your life?"

As much as he might have been prepared for the question, Jack was still taken by surprise.

"Let's do the roll call, shall we? Hickox. Plympton. Thayer. Hartnett. Shall I go on? Wilmot. Harris. And excuse me, what is your name?"

Jack still didn't answer. On "Thayer," by some force of serendipity, he had landed on Christina. She was sitting in a backless copper-colored gown, her blond hair pulled up in a French twist. She looked friend-less and isolated, and also, in a way Jack could not have put together rationally, equipped for life in a way these others were not. Though he had often encountered her in his father's store, they had managed to ignore each other, and her presence in the high school—distanced, muted—had been easy enough to ignore. But tonight it all seemed different. It was as though her high school loneliness and her great, un-charted beauty had given her a head start and put them tonight, oddly enough, in the same place, at a distance from their supposed compa-triots. He felt drawn to her in a way that made him question his own level of drunkenness. Christina Thayer had come to this prom with a boy nobody knew, someone from another school, a boy tall and aristo-cratically ugly and, if Jack had to hazard a guess based on his move-ments, gay.

"Do you think your particular talents alone will earn you a place in the meritocracy—"

"Oh, please," Jack interrupted, annoyed.

"You know what that word means?"

"Don't insult me, okay? I know what a meritocracy is."

They just looked at each other. Jack held back. He did not want to fight with this man. Mr. Shelton—whatever older-man desires he'd brought out here tonight vis-à-vis Jack—seemed an obstacle, that's all. Jack had seen something in that glimpse of Christina Thayer that sug-gested to him a whole new shape to this evening.

74

"Listen," Jack said, "I appreciate this, I really do. I appreciate that you care so much about me, you're willing to call Brandeis, and . . . you know."

The slight disappointment in Mr. Shelton's face was troubling to Jack. This man had taken a risk coming out here, talking to him this way. But what Jack wanted to tell him was that it would have been better if he'd stuck to golf lessons. This was something adult males, Jack's father included (Jack's father *especially*), seemed not to understand. Their physical behavior was the entirety of their power, and thus of their teaching; their every move was seen, fully taken in, and analyzed by boys. It was when they tried to put their "wisdom" into words that power leaked out of them.

He turned away from Mr. Shelton's face to see Christina Thayer rise and, her date taking her hand, move to the dance floor. The song that had begun playing was the Troggs' "Love Is All Around," a decent enough tune, and at the first bars the girls who were still dancing with each other turned away to look for their beaux, as if some mating signal existed in certain songs. He watched the way Christina moved, separate from the others, dancing only because it was expected. Her back was exposed in the gown, as perfect a thing as Jack had ever seen, no excess of skin, but an exquisite tapering against invisible bones, and then her ass, which he didn't strictly want to look at now.

"Jack? Are you out here?"

Ellen Foley was standing in the doorway. Ellen looked good tonight. Her gown was blue, she hadn't tried to do anything fancy with her hair, and she was wearing her glasses. She was cool enough not to be taken in by what all the other girls were taken in by. All things being equal, he knew he should have been happy with her. Or happy enough. A summer of fucking, and then they would part. Their relationship would not survive distance, would not survive the gap between Wheaton and New York. He knew that. But no, you didn't think about comfort when a new, huge challenge appeared before you.

"This *song*, Jack." She bent forward from the waist, half laughing, as if mocking the romantic longing she genuinely felt. "Come on. *Please.*"

He hesitated a moment.

"You'll excuse me," he said to Mr. Shelton. "Looks like I've got to dance with her."

"Of course you do."

When Jack was halfway to the door, he turned back. "Yeah, maybe a room at the Y. I don't know. I could fuck up so easily."

He offered Mr. Shelton that small allowance of dignity. Then he went inside.

He danced with Ellen, but his eyes were on Christina almost the whole time. He tried to get her to look at him, but she was doing that thing of hers, so familiar to him from the high school corridors, where she seemed to be looking out at you, or over you, from behind an invisible screen. Something in this excited him, though. Ellen was close against him, trying to read him.

"It's all right, you know. We could go now."

"No," he said.

"*No?* Is Jack Palumbo saying *no* to me?"

He smiled. "I'm having a good time."

She knew he was lying. She was not exactly hurt. It was, instead, as though she knew that something was going on and she was determining, in her own way, whether the greater advantage might be gained by pursuing it or by letting it go.

When the song was over, she adjusted her glasses.

"Okay, so we'll stay and we'll have a good time."

She waited a moment, forcing a little too much ironic fission into those last words, then went back to her group of girlfriends. On her way, she turned around, having thought better of her decision to let Jack's mood go unexplored. In thirty seconds of looking at each other in silence, they had a conversation. Ellen knew how to read the renunciation of her that was in Jack's face now, in his shoulders and even in his hands as they sank into his pockets. She watched all this for a minute, took it in, felt a large impulse to smother what was happening to him, then decided against participating in her own humiliation. Jack went and sat in a corner of the room, his heart beating very fast.

He was on the other side of the volcano now, so that he wouldn't have to see what Ellen was doing. He didn't want to tell anyone his plan. He wanted to be very quiet about this new thing that had been developing in his mind. If he sat here long enough, Christina Thayer would turn to him. He knew that, and that was about all he knew. She would see his face, she would blush. It was as if he had the power in this moment to see the future.

But it didn't happen. Christina never looked at him. People were starting to leave the prom. At a certain point Ellen came looking for him. The scene they were about to have felt redundant, and he waved her away.

"You cruel boy," she said. She sat beside him a few moments. It felt heartless, but he was measuring his own heartlessness against something more powerful.

"Who'll I get a ride home from?"

"One of your friends. One of your friends will drive you."

"Jack. People told me you were cruel like this, but I didn't believe them. Stupid me. This is an aberration, right? This is one of those Jack Palumbo moods."

"Just don't cry, all right?"

"Oh, don't worry. I won't. I'm going to believe this is one of your moods."

What moods? he wondered.

She sat there a moment, the heaviness coming over her.

"You fuck. You utter shit."

He watched her leave, but not the whole way. You couldn't watch a girl's back. You couldn't do it. There were those places in their bodies where all the vulnerabilities lay. The back and the neck. Lives had been wasted, he was sure, because a man looked too long at a girl's receding neck after trying to break up with her.

When Ellen was gone and he was tired of waiting for the moment he'd been so certain would happen, he went and sat at the table with Christina and the strange boy. Others had left. There were empty places.

"We should go," Christina said to her date after Jack had sat there a moment.

The strange boy had been looking at Jack. A crooked smile came over the boy's face. "Who's this?" he said.

Jack didn't answer. Deep coral spots had appeared at the center of Christina's cheeks.

The boy looked from one to the other of them. "I don't get this," he said. "Something going on here? Explain this to me, please."

"His name's Jack Palumbo," Christina said.

"Okay," the boy said, waiting for more.

Christina looked at Jack then, for the first time. She had more composure than he'd expected.

The strange boy laughed at the uncertainty and mystery of what was going on.

77

"This is Barney Hunt," Christina said, and then seemed to retreat from her willingness to take Jack in, returning to her more characteristic shyness and embarrassment.

Barney, still laughing a little, still weirdly smiling, put out his hand.

"I don't want to shake his hand," Jack said.

Barney's smile took a while to drop. No, he was not gay. Something surly and spoiling for a fight was in Barney Hunt's eyes. Watch out for these aristocratic guys, Jack thought. You can never judge their capacities.

"I just want to ask a question," Jack said.

"What's that?" Barney Hunt asked.

"Not of you. I don't want to ask you a question. I want to ask Christina something."

She looked at him for three or four seconds. On the plate before her were the remains of dessert—some kind of lemon cake she'd eaten only a few bites of—and the nosegay Barney Hunt had probably bought her. One flower—a small yellow rose—had been dipped accidentally in lemon frosting.

"I want to know why you settled for UMass," Jack said.

Barney Hunt's look was quizzical. Christina looked at Jack with an arrested look of surprise.

"I mean, you could have aimed higher. I want to know why you didn't aim higher."

"This is the big question of the night?" Barney Hunt asked.

"Yes," Jack said.

"Maybe she doesn't want to answer you."

"Look," Jack said, staring him in the face. "I don't know who you are. I don't know where you came from. I don't particularly care, all right? I'd like to ask Christina a question, which comes out of . . ."

He stopped, a little embarrassed for himself because the next words weren't coming. He knew, in an unformed way, what they were, but they weren't coming. He felt the lack in himself for the first time, as if he should have been more eloquent. Meanwhile, Christina's skin was deepening in color. He would have liked to come up with the words to comment on that, too, but they were not to be found. He felt he understood the situation at this table so completely—the way she was compelled by him without being able to admit it—it was a kind of brilliance, but you had to attach words to brilliance, otherwise what was it?

"Do you want to answer him?" Barney Hunt asked.

"No."

She had spoken very low. It was almost unhearable.

"Huh?"

"I said no."

"Okay, you heard her. You have a date, buddy?"

"Buddy?"

Jack wanted to punch him. But no, to achieve what he needed to achieve, there could be no punching.

"I sent her home," Jack said.

Now Barney Hunt didn't know what to make of Jack, what to do with him, what to say next. He shifted in his seat.

"Why don't you go get the car, Barney," Christina said.

Barney Hunt looked at Christina. "And leave you with this guy?"

"It's all right. I think I can handle it."

It made Jack like her more, this little moment, and then what came after it, her looking at him, unafraid.

Barney Hunt settled back in his seat. Clearly, he didn't care for being dismissed. He reached into his pocket and fished out a set of keys and then dangled them before himself, as if there were something very cool in doing this, in showing Jack that however he was being dismissed, Barney Hunt lived in the realm of cool.

"What, you want to meet me at the entrance?"

"Yes," Christina said.

Barney Hunt looked once more at Jack, to let him know he was just slightly disappointed this wasn't going to end in blows.

When Barney left, Jack assumed his seat, moving it a little closer toward Christina, but not perilously close. He touched the edge of her plate.

"Who is he?"

"My cousin."

"Ah."

She looked down a little, not at Jack. But she wasn't nervous anymore. It was amazing to him that this closeness didn't seem to scare her. Right now, inexplicably, that glass filter between her and the world had disappeared. It made him very, very curious.

"You know what I love?" he asked.

Her head tilted toward him microscopically.

"I love the way you ate, like, three bites of this cake."

She waited. And then when she spoke, her voice was very soft, almost like she were feigning a lack of interest.

"Why do you love that?"

"Because it's like—you. It's like this incredibly gentle thing. Like your stomach is so small, or something, that's all it can take. Or— *something.* I want to know."

He moved a fraction of an inch closer and watched her rear back just that much.

For which she seemed to silently apologize, as though she'd determined to be brave and at that moment had failed.

"It's okay," Jack said.

"What do you mean, though?"

He thought she was afraid of what she'd just said, the implicit tiny invitation she was tendering.

"I mean, there are these things that people do and you just want to know why they do them. You want to go into that place that's like their—*motor.* Their—the *locus,* all right? The locus."

Surprised, she looked up, looked at him.

"Nobody thinks I'm smart, Christina. People think I'm just a dick. For four years I've been walking around this high school, and it's been like—there's Jack Palumbo, the dick. And you know what? I have remembered *everything.* Every book we've read, I remember everything about. And I know words."

He laughed. He was being so wildly open with her, not entirely sure where it was even coming from.

"*Locus.* That place in you that ate those three bites of cake—I want to know that place. I want to go there."

He stopped. It seemed he was going too far. He saw the part of her that was beginning to resist, wondering if he was playing with her.

"Christina, you came here with your *cousin.*"

"I wanted to have . . ."

She hesitated, looked around the room briefly.

"I wanted to have an experience like everybody else. I wanted to know what this was like."

She seemed embarrassed by having spoken so many words. "I've got to meet him now," she said, and started to stand.

He reached for her hand, to stop her. What he got was the nosegay, which she had lifted. He held the nosegay, feeling foolish at first, and then, when it was close to his mouth, he reached out with his tongue and lifted the lemon frosting off the yellow rose. Afterward he felt even more foolish, as if he'd put on display some part of himself he didn't want her to see. It was a bad move, too bold, but it had its effect. Her skin deepened into a color he thought had never been named. Her body had just invented it. He was hugely excited by that.

"I've got to meet him," she said again.

"I'll go with you."

They walked through the room, which was now full of empty seats.

At the entrance there were others, lounging. Cigarettes. There were gazes at them, this odd couple. Boys with red-veined eyes. Girls whose skin was slick with sweat.

"—cko," someone called. His nickname, more intimate even than Jacko, its longer form.

"Where will he pick you up?" Jack asked.

"Here, I think."

They stepped off the front landing, into the dark.

There was a highly charged silence, and Jack told himself, Don't touch her. The very movement of the world right now depends on you not touching her. The last song was playing inside, the chords slow and uncommitted to, as if the song would break up before it was even finished. From Christina, Jack felt he was about to receive something. An energy he thought he could read was inside her.

"Here he comes," Christina said.

Jack could see the headlights.

"Okay," he said.

It was important that she see him, Jack, fading. It was important that she see him as about to be lost to her. Thinking this, Jack thought to himself, This is my genius, this is my fucking genius. To know exactly how to make her want me.

She did not turn to him as she got into the car. Barney Hunt was playing music loud, as if that might cut him off from Jack. She stepped inside. She looked at the glove compartment and then held up her nosegay and looked at the rose he had licked and not at him, and then she drove off with Barney Hunt.

Graduation was held every year on the football field. A makeshift stage for the seniors and rows of seats set up for parents and special guests. The stands themselves, facing one side of the field, were left for spectators, and they were nearly full.

Several of the boys had worn nothing under their graduation robes, or nothing much. Stella, in the fourth row, noticed that. Jack marching in with the others; she saw his legs, the fine black hairs.

A girl was reading the winning graduation poem, something about a cat's-eye marble, the glimmering thing inside the marble a metaphor for that trapped thing that was about to come out of all the seniors. Stella thought she recognized the girl, but her concentration was on Jack, the way he seemed poised up there onstage, at the exact midpoint between impatience and readiness. One recent night he had made her tea and told her his plan. New York. He had seemed eager, wonderfully young, and though everything about his plan—its unformedness, its vague hope—frightened her, she had pretended to be thrilled.

The scholarly and civic awards were being announced by the principal. The Norumbega Garden Club Award, the Wansett Memorial Fireman's Award, the Alison L. Pepper Award for Scholarship in the Sciences. The list was seemingly endless, but would Jack win one? It had not occurred to Stella to wonder, much less to expect, but now she found she wanted it. She wanted, one more time, to see him rise out of his seat and tramp across the stage, to see his bare legs and the pair of old sneakers he wore, to watch his body lope over to the podium, a bit slouched, as if there were an inherent excess to his being he had to make a false apology for.

Stella clutched Joannie's hand. Joannie seemed to be shrinking into her seat, cowed by all this life, this high school celebration, and Stella wanted to remind her of what the nun had encouraged her to do: embrace this.

Three-quarters of the way through the awards announcements, Richie began to lose the last shreds of his own hope. Not that he'd had much to begin with. Seeing that his son had worn nothing under the graduation robe had been a blow to him, but then he noticed that most of the other boys had followed suit. Perhaps some of them wore shorts, but the display was the same. The main difference was that these other boys, with their big shoulders and their large, confident heads, were being called, one after another, to the podium to receive awards. Tonight they all looked like thugs, red-faced savages with combed hair, but they were also creatures of acknowledged achievement, and as Richie took this in, as he watched each of them cross the stage to shake the principal's hand, the thing that had been eating him since the night Jack told him he would not be going to college rose up in him like bile. Ashton Philbrick had won the Sargeant Family Scholarship, given to the senior best embodying the scholar-athlete. John Lerner received the Selectmen's Prize, given to a civic-minded senior. Richie knew enough town scuttlebutt (working in the pizza place made him privy to just about everything) to know that Philbrick was headed to Princeton, Lerner to Tufts. Neither boy wore pants, but as each of them crossed the stage, their nakedness seemed to exist in concert with the opposite of nakedness: the parts of them that were determined and ambitious and restrained, disciplined boys, clothed boys. Once, Richie had believed that just by coming here—just by offering Jack Ronnie Greeley's room and the lake to swim in and the frozen lake to skate and play hockey on—would turn Jack into someone like Ashton Philbrick. But up there on the stage, wearing that big, stupid smile, Jack was telling him how wrong he'd been.

Something else had been necessary. He had never quite figured out what it was. He had tried to read Samuel Eliot Morison's *The Oxford History* for some clue to the American entitlement. He always got lost in the stories. The Civil War. Oliver Wendell Holmes's great tribute to war: "War, when you are at it, is horrible and dull. It is only when time has passed that you see that its message was divine." His own war had not been like that, not divine, more something he had muddled through, a small man's survival. Yet others took gold from the experience and passed it on to their sons. Ah, God, he thought, the weight of everything misunderstood, mismanaged, misapprehended in those words. He would never come close, he would never understand.

Christina Thayer's name was being announced. She had won the Heidi Langworthy Memorial Scholarship, named after a girl who had drowned in the lake twenty years ago. Richie sat up, surprised, though he shouldn't have been, that Christina had a life outside the store, that she was—or must be—a kind of scholar. She crossed the stage to polite applause, the reserved girl he had come to love, and though love was still in him, and pride for her, it was mixed with anger because Oakes, not Richie, would get whatever credit was to be bestowed. Oakes was sitting far down the row behind Richie—he'd noticed him at the beginning of the ceremony; noticed, too, that he'd come in rumpled clothes, as if this evening meant next to nothing to him. But now Oakes was the one who got to burst with pride. Oakes, who had been nothing but an absentee father, driving that Jaguar, not even giving his daughter his name. That was how unfair the dispensation was. But then Richie turned to look at Oakes and saw something that surprised him— Oakes's face leaning forward in a gesture of supplication, the man half standing. Richie turned away from him, embarrassed by the nakedness of that look, just in time to see a look pass between Jack and Christina.

Richie's thoughts stopped there. He wanted to run the film backward. They had shared a look, his son and this girl. Had he made it up? He had almost convinced himself it was something he invented, until he noted the new seriousness and appreciation in Jack's face, and the way Christina seemed to be absorbing it, blushing and looking down at the floor of the stage as she passed before Jack. Had anyone else seen it? Richie looked to Stella, then at Oakes, who'd settled back, his pose now so casual Richie had to wonder if he'd made up the previous pose.

Christina was back in her seat now. Jack was still looking at her, but she was not returning his stare. The final awards were being announced. The last name was not Jack Palumbo's.

It was fully dark by the time the seniors lined up by rows to receive their diplomas. The red light on top of the power station on the hill above the high school blinked. The lights had come on over the field, and to see the seniors lined up, the boys especially, brought out in Richie a strong burst of nostalgia, enough to overwhelm his previous emotions. They resembled a row of army recruits waiting to go in for physicals, the look men take on when they must become passive, must have something done to them rather than do a thing themselves. A stored-up energy resided in the boys' arms and legs, something touching to him. If he could forget the brief incident between Jack and Christina, if he could move beyond that—and he was trying hard to—there might exist in the scene before him the very thing he loved most about Norumbega, the reason he'd forced his family to come here in the first place: the elegance and the cadence of this town, the way its very being was like an imposed rhythm, a barely heard drumbeat. Not all the students were rich. But even the poor ones, the bused-in boys and girls, seemed to hear that beat.

Hearing it himself, he was able to hold on to one last hope for Jack.

He'd noticed an unevenness in the applause the graduating students received as they went up to receive their diplomas. The athletes, whether Lerner or McCarthy, Gilpin or Feidenkevitz, received whistles, were greeted by the blowing of horns, hard and guttural cheers, primarily of other males. The beautiful and popular girls—whether they were truly liked or not—received loud and sustained applause. But there were others, too many others, who received only perfunctory applause.

He wondered what kind of applause would greet Jack. Perhaps the evening would contain a surprise after all. Perhaps some respect for his son lingered here, among the teachers, among the parents and the students themselves that would amount to an elevation of his hopes. He himself had not been much acknowledged tonight. Even the best of his customers, while smiling at him, had not come forward to shake his hand. "We won't know anyone there"—hadn't those been Stella's words of warning at the beginning? And they didn't, still. He'd once convinced himself that a large part of what had kept them at odds with the greater citizenry was Jack's refusal to play the games these others had played. If Jack had only wanted to apply to college, to play baseball or run track or do any of the things that brought people together on the sidelines. But it was Norumbega Pizza that had really cemented their place. He had to admit it now. That great defining act of his, so necessary to their staying here and so isolating. But Jack had a life separate from theirs—his caddying, his existence as what Christina had termed a "popular boy"—and Richie hoped that separate life would manifest itself, because as he saw Jack rise, ten or twelve bodies from the front of the line (they were up to the M's), he became afraid that silence would greet Jack's name, or tepid applause that if it could speak, would say, Who? Whose name was just called? I don't recognize that name. Oh, yes. Oh, yes, the son of the pizza man.

David Nurse was being called to receive his diploma. Then Nancy O'Brien. Dan Oberlander. And behind them Jack, drawing closer. Richie noticed that a stillness had come over Jack, an embodied calm. His face looked dark, and at that moment, Richie had to admit, extraordinarily handsome.

"Alyssa Jane Packer."

The closer Jack got to the front of the line, the more Richie found himself clinging to a wild hope that Jack's name would elicit not just a huge burst of applause, but a *thunderous* burst. That he himself would have to turn around and acknowledge it, the father of the most popular boy here. That it would undo everything.

"Alan Philip Padula." Jack was next, and the applause Alan Padula received sounded to Richie like applause that held something in reserve, as though the seniors and their parents knew instinctively to hold back because the *next* senior was the boy to call out of them the unrestrained.

And then it happened.

In his revved-up state, Richie did not at first hear the sound that followed the announcement of Jack's name. But he saw very clearly the flare that had gone up above the stage. It had burst, sending pink ripples over the heads of the seniors, causing some of them to put their hands over their heads to protect themselves. It brought back to him, if only briefly, Korea, and an instinct—one he'd found laudable in himself, in that war, at the onset of a loud noise—to protect the person next to him, in this case Stella, and beside her, Joannie. He had begun to throw his body on theirs when he stopped himself, as if grabbing hold of the word *firecracker* in mid-motion, and of the reality behind the word. Stella had hardly noticed, fixed as she was on Jack, an exclamation coming out of her mouth, one that Richie read, strangely, as delighted surprise.

He heard the other sound finally, the sound other than the sound of the firecracker, though it was not easily distinguishable, taking the form of a chant he couldn't make out. It seemed to go "-*cko, -cko, -cko*," and underneath it, on the speaker system, a song: "*Skyrockets in flight / Afternoon delight.*" Another firework was tried, and failed, at which point the principal, rather than shake Jack's hand, raised his own hands angrily, went to the back of the stage, and seemed to chide someone there. The song went off abruptly, followed by loud laughter, and Jack, at the front of the stage, at the point where he should have been shaking the principal's hand, instead waiting, looking as though he were trying very hard to keep himself from being convulsed with laughter.

"Do you see what happened?" Stella was saying, very excited and laughing herself. "They're shooting off firecrackers in honor of him. In honor of *Jack*."

She looked at Richie and was a little shocked, taken up short, to see how bereft he looked, and she thought he didn't yet understand.

"In honor of *Jack*," she repeated, but he still didn't get it, and it was not something, she realized, they could share. Though there was no time to think about it—she wanted to see what happened next—a hard but unsurprising truth had just landed between them. All those years of sex, Richie, and we can't laugh about this?

She looked down at Joannie and noted that Joannie looked troubled, confused by what had just happened. She held her daughter's hand tightly, as if to infuse her with her own enthusiasm.

The principal was calling for calm. Jack was still there at the podium, and the principal put his hand on Jack's shoulder and said, "Now, I know it's not John Palumbo's fault, but we're not going to go shooting off fireworks until the appointed time. Please. Discipline, people. This is only a night of celebration so long as nobody gets hurt."

Hushed, chastened, the senior class fell into a silence in which could still be seen the traces of large smiles.

Stella was wrong. Richie had seen what the joke was, but to him it was a joke *on* Jack, and a humiliation. And his worst fear did come true: after the principal shook Jack's hand belatedly and handed the boy his diploma, Richie's son—still smiling, but as if in a world of his own—crossed the stage in nearly complete silence.

One night in late June, Christina asked if she could leave work a few minutes early. She had her mother's car, a tan-colored Volvo, parked behind the store. Richie said yes, and as soon as she left, he put up the BACK IN 15 MINUTES sign and followed her.

It was before eight o'clock, still light. He followed at a distance, and it was not far. He knew she would not be suspicious of a car traveling at this distance behind her; her look as she left had been too determined, too forward-looking. She pulled into the parking lot by the lake. Richie parked on the road, masked by firs, and watched.

She walked farther in, along the path, past the sign for Norumbega Park, with the posting of the rules, and he stayed far enough back to be unseen. Jack was waiting by Oakes's canoe. He unfastened it easily and smiled after he'd done that, though there was no false pride in the boy. Richie could tell that even from a distance. Something gentle and masterful in his movements. A certainty, a delicacy and care in the way he stood apart from Christina, allowing her immense room. As if the boy wanted to say, At any moment you can change your mind.

Christina's posture was harder to read. Not tentative, but not certain

87

either, she looked like a well-trained girl forcing her way up the ladder onto the high diving board under her mother's encouraging but slightly worried gaze. She held her hair behind her head in one hand. Jack, Richie could tell, aching to touch her but holding himself back. A restraint almost classical in the boy's body. He held the boat for her. She took off her sneakers and stepped in.

Richie watched them for as long as he could. The girl was at the front of the boat, Jack behind her, rowing, so that the well-defined muscles of his back pressed against the fabric of his shirt. No one else was on the lake. The heat of the day had lowered so that the trees on the far side were shrouded and vague. Jack and Christina were becoming dark figures now.

He might have intuited something years before, the day he brought Stella to the lake and they witnessed the naked children on the float—the anti-order that had in fact existed here, an anti-order that mocked him. Instead, he had willfully turned away from what was true in those teenagers' actions, believing that the world was balanced on the sight of a woman seen through a window at dusk, a woman laying her table in a house as old as American history.

The fulcrum of the world was located somewhere other than the place he'd tried to put it. Jack had understood this better than he had. The prizes were not to be asked for, not earned, not sidled up to. *Seized*. Richie himself was a fool, had always been one. Jack and Christina had disappeared by now, the two beautiful young people. They were on the inner lake, Lac Bleu. Oakes had taught Richie to fish with flies, and he had felt, in that instruction, a godly hand leading him into the desired territory. But Jack was laying hold of the lake as if he'd always known no one needed to bestow it. It was there for the taking. Not by means of a respectful education, but savagely.

Jack had still not touched her. Had never touched her. This had been the one unbreakable rule. His reputation had always preceded him and filled a certain kind of girl with disgust. For years he'd seen that disgust in Christina, but it hadn't mattered, she'd been nowhere in his range. But as with other girls, a certain moment arrived. He read it the way a dog smells things miles off. They saw shadows lengthening, these girls; they saw, in harsh light, the dimensions of their rooms. The neat piles of college applications and the books stacked up on the shelves of their desks. *Ethan Frome. The Return of the Native.* College, the promised thing, discipline and reward, all that they'd counted on gave way like unhardened cement under the impress of a wished-for step that still frightened them. Life could not be all discipline. There had to be a kind of wildness, too. That was the moment when he walked by and saw the look, the hooded eyes, the signs of how they didn't want to feel what they were feeling, and certainly didn't want Jack Palumbo to know it. He always tipped his hat, mentally, to this secret they didn't know they'd just shared. It was an essential part of the compact, his saying, I know it. I am the disgusting creature you have never wanted to be near, but I have just seen what I've seen, and if you are ready, at any point, I am here.

And then, in the next stage of the negotiation, he had to let them know how much physical discipline he had. How he would never pounce on them or even touch them until the moment came when they had to be touched, and then it was, as often as not, they who took his hand and led it to where they wanted it to go. He had to allow them the embarrassment of this, and the pride they often felt, an awareness he liked to stoke in them that it was they who were seducing him. *He's not so bad.* He could almost hear the words in their heads. *He's not what they say.* Or maybe they thought it was they who were changing him, disciplining him. Let them think that. Let them have the illusion.

That was how it had gone with Christina. First the recognition at the prom, then the slow demonstration of safety, the long convincing of her that nothing at all would happen until she was ready to make it happen. Until the night she told him about her father's canoe, and he had to pretend he didn't know, that the easiness of the lock wasn't a high school legend, that the soft spot on the other side of the water, on the grass by the hidden lake, wasn't a place he'd taken other girls. She'd said, "I can ask your father some night if I can get off early, while it's still light," and he'd nodded, that was all.

Facing the water of that inner lake now, Christina was tentative with the buttons of her shirt. She lifted her fingers and smelled them, blushed. Jack knew what she was smelling, his father's sauce, heavy with oil and herbs. She dipped her hand into the water and went on removing her shirt, then her jeans. She stepped out of them until all that was left was the black bathing suit that fitted her like a hand touching every curve and swell of that soft, magnificently tapered body. He knew she was a little embarrassed by her own perfection. He imagined

89

her running past mirrors, dodging her own pride. He also knew that lately she'd have been looking at herself more closely, in anticipation of this moment, studying her own bush as if she'd never quite looked at it before, turned on by herself.

But now the moment was here, intruded on by many other things. The coldness of the water, for one. She stood, mid-calf deep, and shivered, crossing her arms around herself.

"It's freezing on this side," she said.

He had the feeling that every word, everything he might say would be wrong and come out sounding as awkward as what she'd just said.

"Have you been here?" she asked.

He took his time before nodding.

He saw what that did to her face, the total lack of newness this represented to him against what was entirely new to her. It affected him. Something he hadn't expected landed on him.

"Aren't you coming in?" she asked.

It was a moment he'd anticipated, but what crept up on him unannounced was a kind of dread he was startled by and didn't recognize.

He stopped a moment, trying to align himself. He had to tell her, in one way or another, that he hadn't brought a bathing suit. He had anticipated this, even planned it: with false apology taking off his pants, ushering in the next development. Now it seemed crude, this tired tool of seduction, something to be ashamed of. Not for *her*. He couldn't countenance that girl in the water being seduced that way, then abandoned. It was too cruel.

So he shook his head. He watched her disappointment, which registered as confusion. Then he crossed his arms and looked away.

He heard her go into the water. When he turned back, she was swimming, the disciplined crawl of a girl who'd been taught to swim by experts, in camps. When she'd gone far enough out, she turned back to him, her hair wet, her face in shadow. Even at this distance he could see that she was looking at him to ask why it wasn't going as anticipated. It would have been all right, she seemed to be saying, if he'd dropped his pants and had nothing on underneath. That moment would have been part of the next step that had existed at the edge of her fantasy.

She treaded water a long time. What she couldn't begin to understand was what was happening to Jack. He did not want to take her. To take her would be to ruin everything. The feeling was entirely new to him. He was at a distance from his own history, wanting to discard it. He understood nothing at all. Again he shook his head.

He wanted to kneel down before the image of Christina, vulnerable and perfect in the water. The urge was so strong he had to step back mentally from it, to try to impose some reason on himself. Nothing clear would come, except for the dimly apprehended fact that if he were ever to take her, it would not be here, and not like this. In order for that important thing to happen, he would have to become someone else, someone entirely new.

THREE

THE PLACE
THAT OTHER PEOPLE
CALL THE WORLD

Late Summer 1987

1

The only walk allowed her in the day was between the midday meal and the three o'clock Office of None. Joan—now Sister Gertrude—could take the walk only at the pleasure of the mother prioress, who made it clear that she was restricted to the main road leading into the monastery grounds and the parts of the woods belonging to the monastery.

Even with the permission, there were still two sins she could not avoid every day that she took the walk. The first was the thought she had when she passed the monks' abandoned gardens: the monks—the brothers—were lazy. Why, having formed and raised these beds, had the men who sat across from her during the seven prayer services of the day allowed the work to lapse? Peas should be seen hanging from the vines in spring, to be replaced by lettuce, onions, chard, and later zucchini and tomatoes, until finally, by this point in late summer, the green outlines of squash should be visible. She traced the succession of vegetables from memory, from her mother's garden—more vivid to her here than it had ever been at home. As she confronted the overgrowth, she could not help but imagine the brothers as they stood outside the monks' enclosure, musing, clueless, over the stalled engine of a car. She had no clear idea of what fraternity boys were like, but she had the same idea most girls had from the movies. She imagined the monks in their cells, taping up pictures of girls to the walls and opening beers, those men in stiff black robes expelling farts and joking with one another in that frat boy way she'd learned from movies seen on TV long ago—*Where the Boys Are*, or the one that Sister Julian had mistakenly brought back from the video store last year after Christmas, the very first year the priory had a VCR. *Animal House.*

Where did such thoughts come from? It felt to her like the kind of meanness and smallness that came from being too much alone with herself, part of the problem she'd encountered, and had to deal with, since coming here. Individually, she loved each of the monks and accepted each man's idiosyncrasies, just as she'd had to do (and not without effort) with her fellow sisters. They were farm boys from Manitoba and parochial-school boys from Buffalo and Schenectady, boys who must have been good-looking in their youth but now had a rubbed-raw look, as if their skin had been shaved too long and too harshly with a dull razor. For one of them she had even developed, to her great astonishment, what she had finally allowed herself to call a crush. Brother Joseph, from Manitoba, had seemed to her, at the beginning, youthful, sweet, endearingly awkward. When, after both nurturing and fighting the crush and assuming that it signified the fatal flaw in her vocation, she finally summoned the nerve to confess it to Sister Anselm, the mother prioress had not appeared shocked. "We do develop these things," the nun said, before adding more cautiously, "Some of us." There had been disappointment mixed with Joan's relief, her great crisis reduced to a commonplace. Wasn't it—the care of her immortal soul—supposed to be more important than that?

It had been more than five years since the assault of those feelings. Joseph's hair and beard had by now started to go gray; he walked with an odd, lilting motion that was indistinguishable from a stoop. They laughed together about many things. Attending their relationship was a sense of how ruin and decay will come to all things if you simply allow them. She was six months to the end now, six months to her final vows, full commitment to this life. And though she could almost laugh now at what she had felt then, the towering self-importance of desire, she was still not free from finding fault with herself for the simplest things.

But then there was also the second and larger sin.

At the place where the firs opened, there was a spot where she could stand, unseen by anyone on the road. It was all right to look, that much was permissible. But if someone should appear, she was only to answer questions, not to converse, never to initiate. And she was certainly not to do what she habitually did: draw an invisible line separating the monastery grounds from the land belonging to others, to step over it and breathe the air, as if to show herself, daringly, that it was still possible to leave.

In fact, there was not much to see from this spot. Next to the monastery grounds was an alpaca farm with a strong wooden farmhouse. A cage in the back sometimes held a dog. The house's trim—the shutters and the line of piping that ran just under the roof—was pale blue. She had marked the progress of the painting when, during the summer just past, two men—an older and then a younger, a boy, really—had been completing the job. Occasionally she saw the house's mistress, a tall, thin, attractive woman with long blond hair who favored jeans and fashionable boots that reached all the way up her calves.

That was one view. Then, directly before her, was the road, and on the other side of the road a white one-story building with a sign: LANCASTER CURLING CLUB. In the two years she'd been taking this walk, not every day, but as often as she could, she had wondered what this might be. A curling club. She had looked the word up in the priory dictionary, but it had not helped: a game played on the ice with something called a curling stone. Still, as little as this represented in the physical sense, it represented something enormous to her.

There was, she had not been surprised to find, an unquestionable beauty to the life of the monastery, if you could give yourself to it. A rhythmic beauty that arrived in surprising places. When, at the end of the midday service, the list of the dead was read aloud—those monks and nuns of the Benedictine order who had died on this day—she nearly always wept. To think they had done nothing else but *this*, all day, every day of a life. *Give over*, was the voice that spoke inside her then. Be one with them. You were to do this until every desire died. That was it. Your life marked not by event, but by the tolling of hours, the transcendent moments of prayer, the building of the interior castle (Saint Teresa of Avila's words, not Joan's), that tentative, ever-enlarging place where all impulses might go, as to a plain of battle. To God. To be taken by God. This life simply a rehearsal for the one to come. All that, lovely beyond measure.

But then there was the other side, represented by the Rule. Nothing was hers anymore. No decision as to what to read, how to bow, at what hour to pray—even, at the beginning and to a degree still, *what* to pray. Was she to pray not as *Joan*, but as something less tangible, less real as an individual? "You're going to have to give yourself to all this. To *me*,

97

actually." Those were the words her formation director, Sister Julian, had used at the beginning. Julian was a woman with a full, round face and perpetually startled-looking red skin—an indecipherable-looking woman. They'd been in Julian's room—an unusual thing, nuns generally stayed out of one another's cells, but work had been going on elsewhere—surrounded by photographs of Julian's brothers and sisters, a big Irish family, children with heavy jaws, captured in the Polaroid glare of the early 1970s. Being closed into that room with this forbidding woman had been like sitting at a cafeteria table in high school with the least popular girl, who said to you, It will just be us now. The two of us. We will not even get to watch the pretty girls flirt with boys, or the handsome, hulky boys strut in with their baseball caps and ignore us. We will not get to watch, even from a distance, the prom or the talent show or the senior play, all those things that bring color to the faces of others. It is just us, this room, and these impossible rules. Joan, after the strict self-discipline of her teenage years, had not expected to rebel against these things *here*. But she had.

Over time, she had learned that Sister Julian was not so bad. She had a lusty, low laugh she did not try to hold back when on video nights they watched Indiana Jones or *Beverly Hills Cop* and the broad sexual jokes were made. It was she who insisted that they watch just a few more minutes of *Animal House*, until the astonished sisters who remained realized they'd seen the whole thing through. It was she, finally, who taught Joan something of the hugeness of the allowable within the limits of the fixed.

But for all the obedience learned, there were still limits Joan had never been able to accept. That a walk should be confined. That to stare deeply at the world with desire was not allowed. What was one to do with desire—not for a person, but for the simplest things? The wish to know, for instance, what went on in a curling club, to cross this road, to enter the forbidden space out of an impulse no deeper than curiosity. At home, when everything was available to her, she had treated the world with fear. Only here, now, in this maddening reversal, did it all begin to seem alluring.

She was standing in her place, staring at the sign for the curling club, when the sound reached her. A swishing of branches against the ground. She turned, alerted, even a little frightened, expecting to find an animal, perhaps even the dog next door, loose. Instead she saw a boy gathering branches.

She knew instantly that he had seen her, knew she was there, yet he didn't look up. His glance, when he finally offered it, was shaded, as if he wanted to presume nothing. It was for her to say the first word.

But the Rule came back to her. Do not begin a conversation. Maintain custody of the eyes. *Do not look at him.* Which she couldn't help doing. He was a solemn boy, perhaps seventeen. Dark, curly hair and a small goatee. Hispanic, perhaps. Dark-skinned, at least. He held an armful of fallen fir branches, gathered more. He was beautiful in a way that made Brother Joseph's looks seem a little dull.

"What are the branches for?"

There. She had spoken. He looked at her a moment before pointing with his chin toward the farmhouse. Was he surprised by her question?

"She wants them," he said.

Joan thought of the farm woman, her regal bearing, the length of her legs in tight jeans. She knew where she'd seen this boy before. He'd painted the house during the summer. She recalled seeing him, the shock of black hair, high up on the scaffolding. The woman must have kept him on.

It was as much of an exchange as she believed they were going to have, yet when he looked at her, something fell against the plain of his features, a shadow, a hand drawing each of them—eyes, nose, chin—slightly down. The boy showed evidence of a kind of remorse that drew her to him. How odd that it should be him and not her showing guilt. Her instinct was to relieve him of it.

"I'm not supposed to be here," she said.

"What's that, Sister?"

"I'm off our grounds. This is not . . . I'm sure I'm off our land."

"I know that, Sister."

He looked at her again, no doubt thinking her odd. Such a pure young face. She had to turn away from it. How stupid, that after going through all the years of high school—handsome boys all over the place—it should only be now, in this state of enforced denial, that male beauty should begin to appeal to her.

But that was all she was to get. He started walking toward the house, dragging those branches he couldn't hold in his hand.

She arrived back in her room at 2:30. She wore no watch, but her inner clock was a good one. As long as she lingered in the woods, it was never past 2:40 when she returned. She immediately took up the

Lectio she had put aside that morning, the Bible portion she had been studying and meditating on for the past month. There was a slight urgency to what she was doing. The boy was still with her, the sight of him, the effect he'd had on her. The portion she was meditating on now was the tiny section of Chapter 1 in Luke, where the Virgin is visited by the angel.

"The angel came to Mary and said, 'Hail thou that art highly favored, the Lord is with thee: blessed art thou among women.'"

She read from the King James, her earliest Bible. There were newer approved translations, but she preferred the high language of the King James.

"And when she saw him, she was troubled at his saying, and cast in her mind what manner of salutation this should be."

Such moments in Luke were a comfort to her, the humanizing moments, when the great religious figures seemed so vulnerable and touching, so lost. Jesus in the Garden, the night before his trial, asking if it's still possible, at this late moment, to let the cup pass from his lips. That delicious, heartbreaking wish, on Jesus's part, for just a little more life, please. And here, in Mary's story as told by Luke, not the girl with the smooth white face of the Italian paintings, that face bathed in perfect acceptance, but the small, dark Semitic girl interrupted at her sewing, suspicious, gazing at the angel and asking, *Who are you?*

And then, after the announcement of the pregnancy, which Luke had the kindness at least to put in the future—"Thou shalt conceive in thy womb," the angel said—the simple question coming from the girl, "How shall this be, seeing that I know not a man?"

Joan looked up from her reading. Through the window of her cell, a patch of woods. She thought again of the boy in the woods. How shall it be? she wondered, repeating the last. When nothing unusual happened in your life, you fixated on any change. She re-created his face, then forced herself to shift her concentration to the Virgin, to absorb all things into the Virgin, the way that the young girl, on hearing the news from the angel, must have stopped in her tracks, her hands going to her abdomen, as if she felt she no longer owned her own body. A small cry would certainly have come out of her.

Was it unforgivable self-magnification to think of herself in Mary's place—incapable of owning her own body's impulses and attractions—or was it what we were *supposed* to do, the whole myth of religion there to give us coordinates in order to pull our earthly lives into some larger magnitude? She chose to go into it, to feel as Mary must have felt. Doing so had the power, for a moment, to make her gasp, to pour every troubled feeling into the Virgin's accepting body.

Joan's favorite moment of meditation was the late, unspoken moment in Luke's Gospel that existed just before Mary's words of acceptance. The quiet ranging of the Virgin's mind that must have happened. To Joan, the Italian painters all dishonored the Virgin by depicting her in a pose of perfect—and instant—acceptance. In Joan's mind, Mary took a walk. She closed her eyes and imagined it: Mary's walk, without moving from her spot, around Nazareth, the alleys and the views of open fields, women at their work, the hot, panting animals. All this the young girl must have assumed as a birthright, *dailiness*, to one day wash clothes with the other women, to gossip at the fountain, things she loved now only at the moment of losing them. How long a moment could she take? In her head a clock said, You must be back in your cell by 2:40 at the latest. Do not look too long, the angel is waiting. Mary might well have seen, on that walk, a boy she was drawn to. Might have had to close her eyes against him, against desire, against beauty. Something else had chosen her.

The bell rang calling Joan to the Office of None.

Rising, she touched the letter Jack had recently sent her. It lay unopened on the corner of her desk. She made a mental note: It will contain some news of trouble. Pray for him.

2

Jack's first weeks in New York had been more difficult than he'd anticipated. He'd saved five thousand dollars from caddying, but there was still the problem of finding a place to live. A room at the YMCA was out of the question (Mr. Shelton's mocking description of the life Jack was going off to live still hovered over him), so he checked into a room in a hotel near Times Square and watched his money start to dribble away. He'd expected New York to be a place where you could walk down any street and find fat landladies hanging out of first-floor windows, with APT. TO LET signs everywhere. But no, the city had a hard closedness to it; it seemed run by people called apartment brokers, whose files and Rolodexes contained the key to a metropolis that, early on, began to seem mythical to him, near impossible to enter.

101

It took him almost a month before he realized that you could go to a college, or to the coffeehouses near a college, and occasionally see a flyer where someone was advertising for a roommate. He found space in an apartment on Amsterdam Avenue and 111th Street, above a Hungarian restaurant called the Green Tree, with four other men, three of them Columbia students at various stages of academic engagement and one, the actual procurer of the apartment and holder of the lease, a young lawyer. Jack was invited to pay one hundred and twenty-five dollars a month for the tiniest of the rooms, space for a mattress only, a single window staring out on brick. "You just got out of *high school*?" the lawyer, Mark Fink, asked. And then he repeated the question to be sure Jack had heard correctly. Jack revealed the depths of his savings account, and Mark Fink allowed him to stay on a provisional basis, until someone with more of an aura of cityness, of means and the continuing capacity to pay, could be found.

It was interesting, though. For the first month he watched the lawyer bring in a succession of girlfriends. If they were anything like a proper sample, there was a tremendous hairiness to the girls of New York. Mark Fink's girlfriends sported great diaphanous orbs of frizz. Their tight jeans sculpted small, knotty asses, and though Fink favored large breasts, it was often the case that these girls' hair was the widest part of them. They were graduate students in women's studies and paralegals and occasionally a poet. In the morning, while they scoured the cupboards for granola or prepared tea, the pinched intensity of their faces as they readied themselves for a class or for work made Jack think of even the most ambitious girls he'd known in high school as almost bovine in their passivity.

On the rare occasions when these girls were there on Saturday mornings, being in less of a hurry, they appeared in the kitchen in T-shirts and panties. It was meant not to matter, the pinpoint nipples and the cleft of panty wedged between the small buttocks. This was 1979 in New York. Whatever was going on in Norumbega, here a gulf had been crossed, on the other side of which lay a world in which a twenty-two-year-old girl could appear nearly naked in an apartment full of young men and think that the problem, if there was one, was all on *their* side. Mark Fink, when he bothered to introduce Jack at all, introduced him as "our mascot" or as "young Holden Caulfield."

On Friday nights Mark Fink liked to hold informal tutorials in the large, open living room, which faced out on Amsterdam. The subjects were women, movies, and the greatness of certain late-sixties rock groups the assembled acolytes might have missed. (Real estate law, which Mark Fink practiced by day, was never touched upon.) Pot, provided by the lawyer, was an aid to conversation. There were often fewer than four in attendance, but Jack was always among them.

One Friday night Fink treated three of them to a showing of *Apocalypse Now* at the Ziegfeld. Stoned beyond measure, the lawyer could be heard to sigh rapturously during much of the film and had to be hushed by a couple sitting in the row in front of them. Afterward, on the number 4 bus, he couldn't be contained. "Based on what I've just seen? *Men?* You listening? We're on the verge of the Elizabethan age of cinema. I am, like, blown away on three different levels. Coppola is the new Shakespeare. No, no, no—*better.* Shakespeare would never have been brilliant enough to use a song by the Doors."

There were plenty of seats on the bus, but Mark Fink insisted on standing, charged up and lecturing, his hair, a shock of which always seemed to be jutting out from his forehead, making a kind of waving accompaniment to his words. The others on the bus, the ones who were not of their party, stared straight ahead, read newspapers, or looked at Mark Fink as if he were an annoying oddity. Jack was struck, not for the first time, by the enormous indifference of the city, the human blocks of concrete against which pockets of genius flared. That was how he'd come to think of Mark Fink, as a kind of genius of enthusiasm. He'd expected the city to be like that, all clamor and desire, like Mark Fink writ large. But what he was struck by—and what he was coming, oddly and increasingly, to appreciate—was the great dullness that buttressed the place: the unattractive women on buses who wore cheap coats and came from work where they were secretaries, nurses, salespeople; the Puerto Rican men with slicked, oily hair on their way to be doormen; the preponderance of cheap restaurants full of people whose existence was marginal, and therefore at odds with his earlier sense of the city as mythic and unapproachable. It seemed, once you'd passed the physical, you were allowed to warm the bench here as long as you wanted.

Back at the apartment, Mark Fink could not be brought down from his high. He played "The End" over and over, pacing around the living room, his face in a pose of recovered ecstasy. One by one the acolytes drifted off until it was only the lawyer and Jack sitting on opposite sides of the big room, both of them on the floor, their backs leaning against the wall. Mark Fink squinted at him. "Are you still here?" he asked.

"I've been here all night," Jack said.

"No. I mean *here*. You're still in the city? Amazing. Mr. High School Boy. I had you gone a month ago."

Jack said nothing.

"So what do you do with yourself?"

Jack didn't feel compelled to answer. What he did was walk around. His days were spent taking things in. It was thrilling. He knew the great horizontal city from having walked from Washington Heights down to the tip of the island. There were questions no one could quite answer for him. What was the building that jutted out into the bay near the slips for the Staten Island Ferry, the building that looked like an old German rathskeller? What was Queens, and how did you get to it? The Friday night tutorials were a big part of his week. So were the moments when the skinny, small, ambitious large-haired girls came into the kitchen barely dressed while he was gulping his morning coffee. His answer to Mark Fink would have embarrassed him: I'm looking at things.

Mark Fink came close to him. He pushed his wire-rimmed glasses up over his small nose and stared hard at Jack.

"Do you have a job yet, Caulfield?"

Jack loved it when Fink called him by that name.

"No."

"Well, you've got to get a job. You want to stay?"

"Yes."

"Well, that's it, then."

Jack was deeply embarrassed to admit, in front of this man, that he had not yet mastered that aspect of things.

"Okay, listen," the lawyer said, leaning so close that the recently smoked pot was traceable on his breath. "There's a newspaper called *The Village Voice*. We'll get you a copy tomorrow. There are things called want ads. They exist so that this city can suck up little boys like you and get them to do the things nobody else wants to do. Which I assume you're willing to do?"

"Sure. Yes."

"Otherwise that bankbook of yours is going to dwindle and you'll have to go back to that planet you're from. And I don't know fuck-all about you, but I suspect you don't want to go back there very much."

Jack didn't answer, but smiled, feeling something new and not a little exciting: what Mark Fink was doing, he believed, was showing concern for him. Pay attention to this man, and he could be guided, for the first time in his life, by someone whose instincts he fully trusted.

A week or so later he found, as Mark Fink had promised him he would, a want ad in *The Village Voice* for a telemarketing company in midtown on the East Side.

He was put into the phone room, seated in a little booth in a row of other little booths, all of them filled by telemarketers with scripts in front of them. In the script he was handed was a procedure for selling *TV Guide* to those whose subscription was about to lapse, at a savings he was meant to present as astronomical. The cards he was given, containing names and numbers, listed area codes in Ohio, Iowa, North Dakota. He felt the wide range of the country opening before him as each call was picked up, then an ensuing depression. The women who answered seemed mired in long, bleak afternoons. Their husbands were dying in other rooms. The crops were failing. There was probably a good reason they were allowing their subscriptions to lapse.

After three hours and four sales he had done nothing to encourage—a dead man could have made those sales, so eager were the recipients to talk—he went into the office, where the room supervisor, a tall British woman named Rosie, had been listening in on his calls.

"I don't think this is for me," he said.

"No, I can see that. Lack of enthusiasm. But a good voice. Older than you are, that voice." She was not quite looking at him, her attention lingering elsewhere. What had she started out wanting, he wondered, that she had ended up here?

"Listen," she said. It was her word. It was like a card she placed in your hand. "Something's just come up. I don't know if it's for you. But maybe it is. Shall we try it?"

It was apparently impossible to be fired from this job, no matter how lackluster your sales skills. Jack was dragged into the coolly lit inner sanctum of the offices. "I think it's him," Rosie said, and a man, dark, Middle Eastern, in tinted sunglasses, looked him over. It was like being recruited for the CIA, except that what he was handed was a new script. He was to make calls on behalf of the American Management Group, pretending to be a young, sharp, slick sales guy who can never be reached. "Listen, I'm hardly ever in the office, so let me call you back" was written into the script. He was to refill orders for components of an experimental training program the AMG had sold to selected companies in the South.

He had no idea why he'd been chosen for this, but almost immediately after he started making the calls, he found something appealing in the work. Rather than ushering him into bleak and insufficiently stocked kitchens in the Midwest, these calls took him into offices in Atlanta and Memphis, where secretaries and receptionists named Johnnie and Linda Lee brought to even the briefest of interchanges a beautiful slowness, even a hint of deep languor. His sexual thoughts he'd determined, and was trying very hard, to confine to Christina. That was his New York vow, the thing that made him feel good and strong about himself, about the new Jack Palumbo. Still, he found he *wanted* to make these calls. The whole point was to get past Johnnie and Linda Lee to the guy he was intended to reach, but he was content to stop with the girls, to linger. "You're telling me there's really a place in Atlanta called Peachtree Plaza?" he asked one particular Johnnie, thrilled at the sound of her slow responding giggle. The man he was intended to get through to was not available, but Johnnie told him that if he called back precisely at two, she'd put him through.

"You flirt with them," Rosie said when he went into her office for an assessment. "That's cheating, of course, but it's good."

"I haven't gotten through to a single guy yet."

"No, but you will," Rosie said. "You've got the secretaries now, and that's the key thing. And that"—she touched his hand—"was my hunch about you."

In another place, in a different situation, that touch would have meant a distinct thing; here, he knew instinctively, it meant something else. Rosie had no interest in him sexually but had picked up on a quality in him, a latent seductiveness he had apparently not been able to let go of even in this city where he was devoted to repressing his old self. What Rosie was telling him was that the thing that had made him what he was in high school—the very thing he was trying hard to distance himself from here—was a thing he could learn to successfully market. The touch of her fingers on his was the touch of the city's cynicism: We both know what you can do. We both know how utterly meaningless it is. But if you can use it, do so.

He did get through to the men he was meant to get through to—

just as the various Johnnies had promised—and though his initial dealings with them were unpracticed and awkward, he managed to fill about half his orders. And then one day he started to do more than that. During a conversation with a middle manager in Atlanta, he set about scheduling a date for their follow-up conversation and suggested a particular week.

"Oh, no," the man said. "Oh, no." He chuckled. "That's my week. I'll be over at St. Andrews in Scotland."

It took Jack a moment, but he caught on. "That's the golf course, right?"

"It is indeed."

Feeling inspired, Jack started talking golf. Hesitantly at first, then with greater confidence, he sculpted out greens, talked drivers. He kept expecting the man on the other end to cut him off. It never happened. The man responded by singing the praises of the Scottish links, and they went back and forth until fifteen minutes had gone by. The conversation had been dreamy and seemed to have nothing to do with business. It left Jack feeling pleasured and guilty, but when he went into Rosie's office afterward, she was beaming, having listened in.

"Oh, God, you're a genius," she said.

"I talked for fifteen minutes," he said, as if in confession.

"Are you kidding? You talked *golf.* The man's yours for life."

It led to his success at the telemarketing firm; the guys he called began to look forward to his calls. Each day, he crossed the park, rode up in the elevator, and indulged in long, dreamy conversations, flirting with the Johnnies, talking golf with the suits, making up games he'd played over the weekend, naming his scores. None of them knew he was just a kid sitting in a booth on Lexington Avenue. He invented a Jack Palumbo they believed in.

Only after a while did it become difficult—that the city should be like this, a place where you pretended to be someone, and if people believed you were that person, they paid you. As the fall went on, he began to grow more isolated, more resistant to the place toward which he was being pulled. He identified less with the slick and predatory young men he saw on the streets—young men on the way up—than with the denizens of buses and out-of-the-way coffee shops, men who worked, fathers of too many children, something a little sapped in all of them. These were the men he wanted to identify with. He began gravitating to such places just to restore some sense of reality. But then, reality itself had changed for him the night on the lake with Christina. That, anyway, was the way he thought about it.

His every intention and, he guessed, hers, had been that that night was to be a night of sexual completion, that there, in the lake, or on the sandy banks of the lake, they should have finished what they had started the night of the prom. Later, when he tried to attach words to the feeling—more like a blinding whack—that had come over him as he'd watched her in the water, the words he came up with failed him. Was it because he'd seen a vision of her *worth* out there? He liked that word—he wanted to believe it—but it wasn't exact enough, it didn't encompass how much he'd simultaneously wanted her, at the same time understanding that the absolute worst thing he could do with that want would be to fuck her. To do that would be to diminish her, and to lose her. He didn't want to lose her. That was all he knew.

In the end, Christina had come out of the water disappointed. He'd left his clothes on because to have taken them off and *not* made love to her would have felt ridiculous. To her curious, slightly hurt look, he'd not known what to offer but an embarrassed, inarticulate honesty. They'd rowed silently back across the lake, and when they were at her car and he asked if he could see her again, she found it difficult to meet his eyes.

"Why?" she asked, which he supposed said a great deal, but not enough.

Nonetheless, she agreed, wary and defended as before, but willing to let him take her hand. They'd gone to movies, conventional dates that made him feel like a visitor from another planet. So this is what the timid do. Sit next to a girl, afraid to touch her. He'd joined their ranks. Christina sat there in all her ripeness, a nearly palpable glow emanating from her, wanting the touch. It was not her response he feared, but his own too-easy mastery. He wanted to distance himself from it. He wanted a kind of apprenticeship in need, as if only this would make him worthy.

He took her one night to the country club; they walked the links together as darkness fell. He taught her how to set up a tee, how to drive, how to putt. She listened, the good student, alert to what was not being said. She no longer expected him to take her in his arms, but she stayed with him on these nights because the power as to how this would go had passed into his hands. She was like a girl who believed she was going to be taught something. Was this how courtship worked? She was that innocent.

In the gathering dark, he thought this would be the perfect setting for it—this place, the greens, the light of midsummer. But just to look at her was to understand how wrong it would be. To think of her under him—to consider himself using what power he had—had come to seem like a defilement. And he knew too well the feeling that always came afterward—the mild disgust you couldn't help feeling for the girl, for what she had allowed you to do. He could not imagine feeling that for Christina. He was eighteen, and he wanted something else.

The most difficult night was the one when he went to her house and asked to see her room. It was a risk, but he wanted to see it. His father was always after him to give him details of Christina's house. What was it like? his father wanted to know. What was her mother like? All Jack had told his father were the most basic things: the old furniture, the thinness of the Oriental rugs. Less easy to communicate was the sense he got, in entering the house, of stopped life, hushed life, a virginal intactness, as if the air of a domicile could express a sense of waiting. "I just want to see it," he'd said to Christina. That night, her mother was not at home.

They climbed two sets of stairs. This was what he'd always wanted for himself, the private room on the third floor. Christina's bed was heavy mahogany, the tops of the bedposts carved into pineapples. He touched them. Christina's head was bowed. She was expectant that he had asked to see it so that the thing might at last happen. The heavy August foliage intruded from outside the window, Christina's room a kind of aerie.

His erection pressed against his pants. Ellen Foley would have taken advantage. Christina waited. The word *why* did not need to be spoken, so present was it in the room. In erotic difficulty, he considered it. Why not? Except that there was the reason, the fist inside his belly holding him back. He was certain something would go wrong; he would hurt her too much or fail in some other way, and that would form an excuse for it to end.

Sometimes he believed he could see the future. The way his letters to her from New York to UMass would go unanswered. He saw that and held to the belief that sex could come only after love had been unalterably planted. It would even be all right if there were others before him (though he hated the thought), drunken boys she would meet at college. They could all be easily defeated if there was love. The thought was new to him, entrancing.

He touched her neck, kissed her, and said, "This is good," then led her downstairs, taking the steps two at a time, before anything could happen in her room.

When they were in the yard, she had the courage to say, "You're playing with me."

"No, I'm not."

The next words stopped within her mouth.

"I'm not. I swear."

He did not quite have the words to tell her any more than that. They were both stupidly inarticulate on the broad, sweeping lawn behind her house. Let it end. He could wait. Somewhere in him was the sense that he wasn't finished with life, wasn't finished with girls, with wildness, with cruelty, with that whole side of things. She had to be separate from all that. The words that might have expressed this were not yet his.

Yet in New York he found he was wrong. He wanted no one else. He had written her three letters. Descriptions of his life, mostly. He left things out. The Johnnies. The way the Johnnies were his form of sex now. The blow jobs a woman in the office gave in the stairwell, mostly to the black boys. (Jack turned away whenever she looked at him; having that happen would kill New York for him entirely.) He wanted to paint another world for her, purer, greener, and more like the lake. He was carving out that world in the middle of New York, living chastely inside it, holding it up for her to see in the hope that she would come to him. Having proved himself to himself, he was ready for her.

She did not answer his letters, and it became too easy after a while to see her standing at the edge of a college dance, looking at the other girls dancing, trying to figure out how to be more like them, how to dance so your tits bounced, so you could gain the attention of the Colins and the Brendans and the Courts, crude Irish boys from Lynn and Salem who held foamy containers of beer poured from a keg and watched the girls and waited, their faces turning meaty and red. She wanted only normal life, this poor girl. He saw all that; he saw her life, her tepid desires formed in that house in which nothing ever happened. He wrote her a fourth letter. "Come to me. Now. I was wrong," it said. She didn't answer that one either.

One Friday afternoon near Thanksgiving, Mark Fink came home from work and found Jack alone in the apartment.

"Oh, shit. I came home early so that I could do something private."

Jack expected to see a girl's head pop in after Fink's, and he looked beyond the lawyer, waiting.

"Not *that* kind of private. You think I'd think twice about that?"

Fink didn't stop, but went down to his room.

"Don't come in!" the lawyer shouted. "Don't follow me."

In a few minutes Jack crept down the hallway to the bathroom, allowing the lawyer his privacy. But on his way back he peeked into Fink's room.

The lawyer had loosened his tie. His shirttail was half out of his pants. He was at his desk, where he had cleared a space and was pouring out a quantity of white powder.

"What's that?" Jack asked.

"Shit. Is there no privacy to be had on the wide earth?"

"You could have closed your door."

The lawyer didn't look Jack's way. He was dividing the white powder into smaller piles with the aid of an antique letter opener. He was doing this in a finicky way, as if he wanted to accomplish it according to the rule book.

"Just tell me what you're doing and I'll leave you alone."

"Serves me right for renting to a high school kid."

"Is that cocaine?"

"Get out of here. All right? Go read a book."

"No shit. I've never seen it."

Jack came closer. It was exciting to be close to the substance, which he had only read and heard about.

"I am not giving you any, do you understand? It costs too much, and you're like, twelve."

"I'm not asking for any. I just want to look." Jack held out a finger. He was asking to touch it.

"No."

"You give us pot."

"That is *so* different. This is another league." Fink looked at him, a measure of confused embarrassment on his face. "You want to know why I brought this here? Okay? Truth? You want to know why? You *insist* on knowing why?"

"No. I . . ."

"Because when I am not babysitting you guys, I occasionally go to parties. Where it's becoming the drug of choice." The lawyer scratched his ear. "And I don't *understand* the fucking stuff. In fact, it terrifies me. I'm tired of refusing it and looking like a jerk and making excuses for myself. Why am I afraid of this shit? Hmm? What is the fear?"

After that, he continued to look quizzically at the substance. "A hundred bucks. Do you believe it?"

"It takes me practically two weeks to earn that."

Fink started to look around, suddenly determined. "What do they use, a straw?" Then, as if he were forcing himself forward, "No, no, no. Of course not. A dollar bill."

He proceeded to roll one up, then made a smaller division of the powder than he'd originally laid out. He closed one nostril with a finger, held back, as if determining this was the way he'd seen it done, then lowered the other over the rolled bill and snorted a bit of the powder. It was awkward at first. It took him a couple of tries before he seemed to take in any at all. Then he succeeded.

"All right. Shit. Shit. Shit."

The lawyer stood still, sucking in air through his nose, studying his desk, as if waiting for something.

"If anything happens, you know how to call an ambulance, right?"

Jack laughed, delighted that the lawyer was revealing so much of himself.

"Actually, is this it? Is this the way you're supposed to feel?" Fink placed a finger against one nostril and laughed, looking again curiously at the substance. Then he snorted a couple more times, gazed at the pile of white powder as if it were a present he'd opened whose contents had been surprisingly pleasing.

"But maybe you should stop me from having any more."

"All right."

"Life seems extraordinarily good right now. I've done this, right?"

Because of his good mood, Mark Fink treated Jack to a strudel from the Hungarian Pastry Shop on the street below. He watched Jack eat with great, appreciative curiosity, but he didn't want to stay confined, and he suggested that they walk to the park.

Riverside Park in mid-November was all russet, brown leaves clinging to the branches of a few trees, occasional shrouded figures walking.

"Look at fucking New Jersey," Fink said.

He had settled into a bench, slouched back, put one hand over his nose.

"I've just had my first hit of cocaine. Jesus. It feels like there's something *behind* my nose." He blew his nose a couple of times until he seemed back to normal, or close enough. "So what now? A series of parties where I'm not afraid. Where I join the *throng*. We're tipping into the eighties, Caulfield."

He looked over at Jack.

"What happens in the eighties? What happens to the newly coked-up Lawyer Fink? Hmm? Any ideas? Does he survive it *intact?*"

Fink opened his arms as if to embrace the Palisades facing them in the far distance, and at the end of the gesture, his fingers went from being spread to being tilted, so that instead of embracing the far shore, he was pointing at it.

"No matter what happens, that's where I see myself. Over there. Take a train. Take some little choo-choo. Go past all the dead towns of the Erie Lackawanna and keep *going*." He put a finger to his nose again. "Don't stop where you think you should stop. Keep going until you come to some hamlet with a stationmaster. The roofs of houses covered with snow. The little woman inside. The babies. The fire. The cooked *fowl*. The briefcase on the chair." He paused for a second. "That's my future life. Forget the Doors. Forget *Apocalypse Now*. Forget *this*. This *brilliance*." He breathed in and leaned forward so that his elbows were resting on his knees. "The world of brilliance has been eclipsed. The world of brilliance is ours for a *second*. Like love. We go *there*. We go into *that*."

Fink leaned farther forward, touched the ground before him, thinking about what he'd just said.

"Unless . . ."

"Unless what?"

"What do you do, Jack? I've never quite been able to figure it out."

It was almost too bald: the lawyer turning the tables, making Jack the vulnerable one.

"Do you think about it? About what I do?"

"*Think* about it? I don't spend time on it, no. But I notice you never bring a young lady home. You go to this bozo job of yours, but what is your social life?"

It was not in Jack to answer, *This*.

Instead he said, "There's a girl back in Norumbega, where I come from." Then cautious, a little frightened: "She's not exactly there. She's at UMass."

"You're shitting me, right?"

"What?"

"There's a girl back home. And you—what?—you pine for her?"

"Not exactly."

"Then what, *exactly*? You are here, young man. You're living like a monk. And it's passing you by. New Jersey will wait, Jack. New Jersey will always be there. *This* won't."

The lawyer was wearing a big, delighted, but not uninsightful grin as he stared at his bench partner.

"God, you really are young, aren't you? And I'm tempted."

"Tempted to what?"

"To share a little of this with you. This white powder."

Jack smiled, only slightly hesitant.

"Mostly what I'm tempted to do, though, is whack you on the back of the head. Or *push* you. Hell, man. Hell. *Hell.* You don't get to be twelve forever."

"Right. But . . ."

"But what?"

"I've been pretty happy." Jack delivered the words in the tone of the confessional, overly sincere. Still, he meant them.

"Oh, God, listen, this conversation cries out for a cigarette. And I haven't got any." The lawyer stood up, looked around a little frantically for someone to bum a cigarette from. He appeared, to Jack's eye, derelict, untrustworthy, and with a fuck-it-ness to him that was his best quality. Fink ran down to the walkway; he'd spotted a man. There was a brief conversation—the lawyer, from Jack's distance, looked electric and clownish. The man reached into his pocket. Mark Fink gestured to Jack, holding up two cigarettes in triumph, then handed the man some money, which was refused. With the stranger's help, Fink lit them both, then ran up the hill, attempting to keep the cigarettes alive.

"Here here here," Fink said, handing one to Jack.

"I don't really smoke."

"Oh, come on, come on. Smoke." The lawyer sucked on the cigarette with rapturous pleasure. "So you've been happy. You walk around."

"Yes." Jack took in a drag. It felt old to him, this ritual of cigarettes, like high school.

"Pining for this girl."

"Not *pine*. Listen, don't make fun of me, all right?"

"Why don't you go see her?"

114

"No." Jack shook his head. "No. It's got to be here. I go there, it would be like—bad."

The lawyer continued looking at him, like he was trying to keep himself from laughing, and Jack was aware of how intense, how almost fetishistic his behavior must appear.

"I didn't ask for this," Jack said.

"For what?"

Jack leaned forward. He was deeply embarrassed now. Any simple word—and *love* was the simple, inadequate, and probably meaningless word that was on his tongue—would, he knew, sound indefensible. He couldn't possibly tell Mark Fink about the night on the lake, the way the feelings of that night had become a directive for him, how they were still capable of filling him with a strange kind of joy. Besides, those feelings wouldn't count for anything here in this city, with its cruder emotions, its expectation of appetite. He shouldn't have said anything to Mark Fink. Having let out even this much, he felt the weakness of his own position. Christina hadn't answered a single one of his letters. So what was his life? There was that sense that had been with him at the end of the summer, of not being finished with things. But he had pushed it away. In the process, had he leapt too far ahead of Christina? Again, he saw her at UMass, her life, and felt a new and sudden stab of dread.

"For what, my friend?"

Jack looked at Fink, couldn't remember the last thing he'd said. He shook his head, and Fink laughed.

"All right," Fink was saying. "I'm going to go up and do some more. A little more. That's all." The lawyer yawned, touched his nose again. "You can do what you want. Or you can—come. You can come up if you like."

Mark Fink got up. He pointed again to New Jersey, then lifted the collar of his coat. Before he turned away, he smiled in his sly way.

"You know what I feel like? I feel like you're Pinocchio. You're on your way to school. All good intentions. And I'm the fox. Remember? What's the song he sings? '*Hey Diddly Dee, the actor's life for me.*'"

"Actually," Jack said, "it's *Hi-Diddle-Dee-Dee.*"

Fink laughed. "Right. You're eighteen. Forget it."

He started walking up through the park, his hands in the pockets of his coat. Jack thought he looked classic, a man on the cover of a novel, one he'd want to read—a good, serious, complicated novel about a young man in the world dealing with temptation and desire. Why was he so separate from that story? He resented, in that moment, everything in himself that kept him from his crudest desires. He resented his own purity, if that was what it was. A doubt had been planted, that his life had become too much *will*.

And then what came over Jack, on the park bench, was loneliness. How lonely this was. He was going home in a week for Thanksgiving. He didn't want to. Would Christina be there? Would something have happened to her at UMass that she couldn't tell him about in a letter? He grew frightened, suddenly, at his closeness to that moment of finding out.

Fink was nearly at the top of the park. He turned around once to look back at Jack. Then he turned away.

Jack shouted for him to wait.

3

What she had loved best from the very beginning was the prayer at the end of the day, at the close of Compline, the verse sung in the nearly pure dark—"The Lord grant us a quiet night and a perfect end"—the collective wish uttered while the single candle burned in its red sheath; the length and weight of those moments of deep silence until it was time to leave the church and, though it was still quite early, go to bed.

When Joan came here for visits while she was still in high school, she had always come with her mother. They made it a girls-only expedition. ("No men allowed!" she could remember her mother saying to her father; she could remember, too, the not-quite-rightness in her mother's tone.) Her mother always had to prod her at the end of Compline prayers, when the darkness and silence descended, reminding her it was time to leave. There were usually by then only a small number of religious left in the church, a single nun or a single young monk (she had not known then that one of them was required to stay and close up after the last visitor), and her thought was always, No, who would want to go to their bed, to the realm of personal dreams, when there was *this* available?

To be held here within this thick, inhabited quiet was not (as she'd sometimes feared at the beginning) merely an escape from being a plain girl scorned by the boys in high school, and from having failed as a volunteer hospital worker, as she'd done after Mother Anselm had suggested "work." (The "dating" part of the nun's advice she had never taken.) Nor was it just an escape from bearing witness to her parents' marriage as a source of pain. She'd needed to have all that confirmed—that it was more than running from failure—and the feelings she encountered at Compline did that for her. "We have only to make ourselves available," Sister Anselm had said once. "God does the rest." It was true.

There was only one other in the darkened church with her now, and she had not been aware of his presence until he rose and made movements she knew instinctively were meant to let her know he was there, ready to close up. She waited, watching him. Which of the monks was he? He came to sit in the row before her. The small head, the beard. Brother Joseph.

"Sister," he whispered. "It's my night to lock up."

"I know."

"I don't mean to rush you."

The beautiful hesitation of this gentlest of men. He leaned forward and pushed his glasses up the bridge of his nose. He was, of course, utterly sincere. He would wait all night if necessary. He harbored no desire, she was certain, for anything in the world that would prevent his serving the Lord, and if waiting on a nun's prayer constituted such service, dawn would break before he would stir.

"Do you ever think about the world, Joseph?"

She was surprised by her own question—not its existence, but its utterance. The religious had been cautioned not to speak after the close of Compline.

"How do you mean the world, Sister?" His voice was slightly high.

"Things we used to be able to do naturally. Without thinking."

After a silence he said, "I miss basketball. Sometimes. No one here plays, really. And it's not a part of our day."

"My brother would play with you. If he were here."

"Your brother," he repeated, staring ahead. "The one in so much trouble."

"I don't know that he calls it trouble."

She had told Joseph, on one occasion where they shoveled snow together, about the letters Jack wrote to her, ones where he reported nearly every detail of his life. The letters had started when Jack was in

117

New York. The nuns and monks were not to share personal information without permission; nonetheless, she had done it, told him all about Jack's life.

"I could close up, Joseph."

"No, Sister. I wouldn't sleep."

"You take your duty so seriously. All right. I'll finish. I love it here now."

"I do, too."

"The first time I came here, when Father Alfred sprinkled me with water, I wept. I didn't know until then what it was to be so impersonally loved."

Joseph accepted her words in silence. They had come out sounding overdeliberate but undeniably true. The gift of becoming the impersonal object of God's love. The gift of not mattering. The abbot had ended Compline by shaking holy water over all of them, in the dark, the guests last of all. She had felt, at that moment of her life, under the small shower of water, a welcome dissolution. *I am not Joan*, with all the failure that implies. The abbot's water lands on someone and it does not matter who that someone is. *I am not Joan*. I am this body, this consciousness, this accident of God's bounty. At such moments, even now, she felt it easiest to *go out*—to her mother, her father, to Jack, to anyone and everyone within the span of her memory. It was godliness. At the moment of the Mass where time was given for personal wishes, she always found she could ask for nothing for herself.

"I should have learned to play basketball," she said. "My brother could have taught me."

Brother Joseph shook a little, an indication that he was quietly laughing. "Yes, we could have set up a hoop. Played twenty-one."

"Is that what you played in Manitoba?"

"Sister."

"Yes, Joseph."

"I would sit here all night if you wanted, but I'm afraid I'll be missed."

"Of course you will."

She hesitated a moment, then stood. He did, too. Shy and slightly embarrassed that he had to end this.

"It's all right," she said.

He waited for her to go. She blessed herself and stepped out. The cloister walk leading from the church to the priory had long windows, and she stopped to watch the winter night through them. There was enough moon so that the shadows of tree branches stretched across the thin coating of snow. Again, she hesitated. It was beautiful. The moment had something of grace in it. She found she needed that. In her room, before sleep, she would have to ponder the second thing, the truly important thing that had happened to her that day.

She had seen the boy again. Over the past few months she had in fact seen him often, standing in front of the house at the moment when she arrived at her spot. It was as though he had nothing to do in mid-afternoon. A green truck was always parked in the driveway. His, she supposed. A Hispanic boy in Lancaster, had she known the town better, would have aroused her suspicions more than his simple presence did.

Today, though, he was watching her when she arrived, and then he did what he had never done. He moved toward her, studying her carefully over the distance of several yards, as though he were approaching an animal, not certain when the wild thing would bolt.

"Sister," he said.

She nodded her head but did not meet his eyes. She wondered what it was he wanted, why he had approached.

"Angel," he said.

She had no idea what he meant. She looked up. Was he calling her an angel?

"Angel," he repeated, and then she thought she understood.

"That's your name?"

"Yes."

She laughed, relieved, delighted. It did not occur to her to be afraid of him.

"Angel," she repeated. She still did not tell him her own name. She'd grown unused to the social niceties.

"Do you work for her?" she asked, pointing toward the farmhouse.

"Sometimes." He seemed so strange, so frightened of her in his way. Wary, though it had been him who'd come forward.

"I don't see any of the others," he said after a moment. "They keep to themselves, I guess."

"The others?"

"The other nuns. What are you, the wild one?"

119

It took a moment to see the joke he was making.

"Yes. I suppose I am."

He did not smile, though she'd acknowledged the joke.

"It's okay, then? You're okay to talk?"

"I'm not supposed to, no."

He nodded. He had no idea what she meant, she could see that.

"We're not a silent order. But we're not supposed to have—conversations. We do invite people in, though, to our services."

Everything she was saying seemed to push him deeper into the realm of confusion. So she let that sit for a long moment.

The woman had chosen that moment to come out of the farmhouse, and as if on the alert, Angel turned around to regard her. Joan was not sure how visible they were, but when Angel turned back, she caught on his face the same look of darkness—possibly conflicted shame—that she noticed when she'd first encountered him gathering branches.

"We invite people in. We pray seven times a day."

"Not me, Sister."

"Why not?"

For the first time he smiled. "I guess you could say I'm a sinner."

In spite of the smile, she could see how thoroughly divided his allegiance was now. He had to go to the woman. His break was over, she would have some task for him to do. It was in response to his earlier look of shame that Joan determined she would bring the horarium with her next time, the printed hours of the services, and hand it to him. Perhaps the sadness she detected could be alleviated by prayer. It was a nun's job to take on misery, to convert. That was what she told herself. That was the excuse.

In her room that night she prayed over their meeting, attempting to forgive herself for her boldness. In her prayers, she asked the Blessed Mother to take on the task.

She did not see him again for two weeks, though she took the walk every day she was able. After their last talk she had begun to think of him as her challenge. That was the excuse. She did not examine this, or the desire to gaze upon his face, whose beauty kept returning to her. These were inexcusable things, so she didn't think about them.

A letter from Jack had arrived. He asked her if he could bring the girl to Joan's Solemn Profession in three weeks. It would be difficult, the girl's presence would make it difficult—why must Jack come at all?—but she would have to write, to answer. Of course. Bring her.

Every day on her walk she carried the horarium.

On the last afternoon of her walks—she had vowed to herself she would stop them in honor of the upcoming day of her Solemn Profession—she saw the boy again. It was intensely cold, so that colors stood out, with a wind that had laid bare whole swaths of the winter lawn. He did not look her way as he came out of the house, and she thought of calling. But she couldn't. It hurt her some to think that he did not look for her. He headed for his truck. Her heart was beating quickly.

He revved up the truck and backed down the driveway. She waved, unseen. Then she ran to the road, through the screen of trees, holding up the skirt of her habit and praying that she wouldn't trip. At the edge of the road she understood that only if he turned to his left at the end of the driveway would he pass her. This would be the last walk, therefore, her last chance. She could not begin to think why this was so important.

The truck did turn left. He accelerated and did not seem to see her. He turned toward her only at the exact point where he passed her, and his look was strange, like a man coming out of a scene of tension. There was something more adult in his look than she was used to seeing there: older, rougher, where she'd seen before a kind of innocence. The truck stopped two hundred feet down the road, so far that she believed he'd considered not stopping. She closed the horarium inside her fist.

Then the door opened and he got out. He walked toward her wearing an expression of mild impatience. His hands were in his pockets. She had never gone this far. Directly across the street, she could see the white, uncrisp wood of the curling club, a closeness to the outside world that thrilled her. He stopped at a distance from her.

"I brought you this," she said, offering the crumpled paper in her hand.

She opened it first, attempted to smooth it out, but felt the pointlessness of the offering, as if she were using it only to make an excuse for herself.

"What is it?" he asked.

"The horarium," she said. "Remember? The hours. Of our services. You said you might come."

"I never said that."

She handed it over, and he took it, glancing briefly at the slip of paper before putting it in his upper pocket.

"That's all," she said. "You're invited."

She turned away then, adding, "I know you want to come," the brazenness of it bringing color to her face.

"Sister," he called.

She turned but did not look at him at first. Then did. The crudeness, the manliness, the loss of the sweet boy she'd perceived him to be was there in the stance. He was older—twenty-two, twenty-three? Hips and legs. A strength there. *Born to fuck.* Where had such a sordid phrase come from? From some movie Julian had rented? From the world of high school? She was shocked by herself, but accepted it.

"What would I do?" he asked.

His face had changed. She couldn't tell if he was joking with her. If that was a smile, a smirk, or if the question was genuine. She chose to believe.

"You could sit in the back. Listen."

He had no immediate reaction. There was nothing to stop her.

"That's the first word in our Rule. *Listen.* That's the first thing we're asked to do."

She felt a certain strength saying that, Gertrude the teacher. You see, she wanted to say to him, as if he were God's emissary, I am devoted.

"That's all, huh?"

As he crossed his arms and adjusted his expression, she saw, too, how the openness fought with this other side of him, which he had tried to hide from her but which was there in his stance.

"That's all," she said.

And it was. She would go now. It was completed, her task. If God had been pushing her into the woods, asking her to take what seemed a series of foolish, even dangerous unconfessed steps, the fullness of his plan, of his odd means, burst like a small floating object inside her. God asked me to disobey in order that this might happen, an invitation tendered to this troubled soul.

She turned away again. In her first step onto the embankment she slipped and needed to catch herself with her hand. When she turned, she saw that he was still waiting.

"You okay?"

"Fine."

She dusted off her hand. A scratch had appeared, a trace of red. She had scraped against a sharp rock. She tried to cover it, to keep it from him. He was standing in the road, watching her. The embankment was before her, but she did not take the step.

"If you walk a little farther, Sister, it's easier to get back into the woods."

She looked in the direction he'd suggested, toward the alpaca farm. Suddenly it seemed enormous, to go that distance. She had felt this before: God suddenly throwing up a roadblock, God damming the road she was expected to go down.

It seemed he was picking up on this feeling in her when he said, "Sister, I'm not in a hurry."

She turned, finding it impossible to look at him. What did he mean? She hesitated, looked across the road, seeking some kind of escape and finding instead an urge toward bravery.

"There's something I've often wondered, Angel."

"What's that, Sister?"

She closed her eyes, attempting to stop herself, then pushed forward.

"What is—curling? Exactly?"

He looked at her a moment, his eyes narrowed, intensely curious. She pointed to the sign.

"Curling? That?" he asked.

"Yes."

"It's a game you play on the ice. Sort of like hockey. Or bowling, more like. Old-fashioned, like this whole town."

His look changed to one of challenge laced with playfulness.

"You want me to show you, Sister?"

There is no safety, she thought, the thought coming from outside her. So go forward.

"I'd like that," she said.

After a moment he turned and looked again both ways and crossed the road. She was expected to follow. The thrill of it, gray asphalt with twin strips of white down the middle. She'd driven it, of course, but this was different, this degree of exposure, like being in a boat on the sea. She imagined a carful of nuns passing her now, the look she would offer them: one of rapture. She was tasting freedom, that was all. Before the long descent into fulfilling God's wish for her, a walk around Nazareth.

Behind him, she climbed the short, slick hill to the curling club.

"Careful, Sister. It's slippery."

On the other side of the wooden building was a large porch, and on it was a series of heavy-looking black weights shaped like flattened apples with bent cores. The building looked deserted, abandoned long ago. Attached to it was another, longer building made of cinder blocks, ventilated the way hockey rinks were.

An ice pond was at the bottom of the hill. Beyond the pond, a long field, yellow now with dried stalks, brushed with old snow. At the end of the view, hills.

Angel was looking at her, as if trying to figure her out. She saw herself as if from outside. The nun's habit. The rough-looking working-man beside her. Anyone watching would perhaps fear for her. She felt perfectly safe.

"What'd you want to know this for, Sister?"

She shook her head, turned away from him.

"What are you looking at, Sister?"

"The ice."

He seemed then to know her, to know at least what she wanted, a desire she could not have fully articulated even for herself. The relief—the evidence of her apparent normalcy—lightened his features.

"Go ahead," he said.

This was what it must be like to be with a man, she thought. Their perfect ease with giving you physical permission to do things.

"Go ahead, Sister."

She looked at him, grateful that the manliness and the crudity were gone, something more simple and accepting of her in their place.

"Do you think?"

He nodded, and she went down the hill. At the edge, she tested the ice. At home she'd always noticed the pond, frozen in winter, but had never gone out on it. Another of the things that had always been self-forbidden. How was it that she was freer here than in the days of her supposed freedom?

"It's okay. Not deep. If you fall in, I'll pull you out."

Lifting her habit, she stepped onto the ice and attempted to slide. Were she to go in, go under, be saved by him, she could imagine the humiliation of explaining it all to the mother prioress. She went ahead anyway.

Sliding was difficult with the shoes. Suddenly he was behind her.

Watching her at first, watching the difficulty she was having. He stepped forward and took her hand. There was something in this that moved her. The softness of his hand, the darkness of his skin against her white skin. Something went through her, something she would never forget.

"Come on. If I help you." He took a running start beside her. She loved that. The physical boyishness in him. His willingness to meet the world. He was holding her hand and pulling her, and she let out a scream.

"It's okay, Sister."

He let her go. She slid some. The wind caught up the sides of her veil. She wanted more. As if he knew it, he was beside her. He took her hand again. She slid some more. She loved the looseness of it, the way it released something young in her. When she turned to look at him, he looked ruddy, approving of her, thrilled by what she'd allowed herself to do. In that moment she said, Enough. All right. That is fine. Enough. Her heart's beating was making itself known. She felt a deep gratitude. He went on smiling.

"I have to go now," she said.

"Oh, come on, Sister. You're just getting into it."

"No. I have to go."

She was smiling back at him, but she could see his disappointment in her, as if in her physical limitations he saw her closed and frightened parts.

On her way back, she walked more carefully on the ice at first, but then allowed herself what slide she could achieve on her own. She knew he was watching her. She could not lose the smile on her face.

She was halfway up the hill to the curling club before she turned back. He was still waiting on the ice. Would he tell anyone about this? Would this be a part of his life he could ever speak about?

"This is it, you know," she called. "The last time I can come out like this."

He tilted his head slightly, like a dog that doesn't understand what's just been said to him but senses its importance.

She said nothing more at first. Then she said, "February twelfth. I become a nun. There's a ceremony." She hesitated. "You could come."

She crossed the road by herself. Once again on the monastery grounds, she touched her quickly beating heart. Oh, that was wonderful, she said to herself. When she came close to the priory, she sensed its silence and desertion and knew without consulting any clock that

125

she had stayed out longer than usual and she was late for the Office of None. She would enter when it was already in progress. There was a protocol for that. Bow first in penance to Jesus, then to the monks to her right, finally to the nuns on her left. Then assume a place lower than usual in the front row and take up the psalms. Pray for forgiveness. But it did not seem so difficult. She knew that what she had just indulged herself in might not be allowed by the nuns, but it would certainly be allowed by God. At that moment, and as if for the first time, she understood fully the difference.

4

On Saturdays Jack liked to sleep late. When he woke, Elspeth was at the dressing table that was too small for her. She was naked, and her long hair floated down her back until she lifted it, pinned it with the thick barrette she'd been holding between her teeth. In the mirror she saw that his eyes had opened.

"Ah. His Lordship awakes."

It was one of their little jokes, the excess of sleep Jack seemed to require. Another joke was the way he kicked the sheets off himself so that he lay there as naked as she was, so that she couldn't avoid looking at him in the mirror.

They were competitive with each other. It was one of the ways he knew they made whatever they had work (they'd been living together a year), as though they were on a court with a ball and they both knew the ball itself was unimportant, but possession of it hugely so.

He touched his belly to draw her attention there. Jack wasn't fat, but he had developed a belly. Beer and laziness. He was selfishly proud of it, in part because he knew she wasn't happy about it.

She glanced at her watch, which lay on the dressing table. "The train is at eleven twenty-five."

"What time is it?"

"It's almost ten, Jack. You slept."

She was ten years older than him. Thirty-one. Someone had said that was a woman's peak age: everything has come to a place of elegance, like the body holding its breath before entering a big, crowded room. He thought she was too thin, though, that she could use some of his weight. Sometimes when they were making love he had this weird

126

moment of transference, like he was putting some of his weight inside her and it might stay there, it might stick. The implications of this troubled him.

"Are you going to shave?" she asked.

"Do I have to?"

"Yes, you have to."

They were going to visit her parents in Montclair, New Jersey. In the year they'd been living together they'd previously visited twice, and each time had been difficult.

"And I have to come?"

She didn't answer, but in the mirror he could see that her eyes had changed. It was amazing to him what that now-familiar look implied.

By any of the standards of the world, Elspeth was a beauty. She had a longish face with good bone structure, deep-set hazel eyes, and a headful of luxurious chestnut hair, which she tended the way an older woman might tend her own china, with the sense that it was never to be used roughly. Her body was tall, thin, her legs long, and when he grabbed them, she always tightened the muscles so that he could feel how little excess flesh was there. She was an editor in a commercial editing firm—a "shop," as she and her coworkers liked to call it. (It was where they'd met; Jack was the receptionist, or, as his female bosses liked to describe his job, the "eye candy.") Yet with all these trappings of beauty and worldliness, there were still the eyes, the moment when her eyes told Jack that a beautiful woman could have all these blessings yet still feel a want of power.

Elspeth's father was a neurosurgeon. The house in Montclair was enormous, set on the rise of a wide lawn bordered and made private by hedges, with a tennis court and a swimming pool. The doctor had slick silver hair that he combed close to his head so that it curled just behind his ears, and he reminded Jack of an actor he couldn't name, someone's father on a TV sitcom, an actor who was always turning up in the tabloids for DUI convictions. To Jack, on the two visits they'd made previously—a late-summer visit just a few months after they'd moved in together and then a longer visit at Christmas—the doctor had offered a hard eye, some cutting remarks, and little else. There was drinking in the Montclair home, but nothing excessive. The mother had the vague blond air of a woman who has decided to stick with a man through a series of ongoing infidelities, and she put a lot of effort into never quite meeting her husband's eyes. There was a sister and brother, both of them, like Elspeth, somewhere on the verging-on-life-defining curve between twenty-seven and thirty-five. The scene there was bland, with flashes of mild competition and occasional instances of rage. But these visits did something to Elspeth that he did not understand and that she never wished to talk about.

"Nobody likes going home" was Elspeth's only explanation.

True enough. He had last been home at Thanksgiving. It was his family's first holiday without Joan—she had entered the convent that fall—and he and his parents sat around not quite knowing what to say to one another. Mostly they'd wanted to know when and if Jack ever intended to start college. His visit had been dull, but that was the worst he could say about it. It had not made him weird about sex, the way going home did to Elspeth.

At Christmas in Montclair, on their last visit there, after a day that seemed to him only routine—shopping, a dinner of leftovers, an evening of TV—Elspeth had asked him to fuck her in the ass. It was not the first time, not a complete surprise. Ass fucking had recently become a minor trend within her circle. In his three years in New York, Jack had grown used to the way things were taken up, then quickly discarded. He thought of the rage for ass fucking among Elspeth's female friends in much the same manner that he thought of them all deciding, a year or so before, that they'd had to read Jacobo Timerman and spend long nights discussing torture in South America.

Except not quite, not exactly, at least not this time. Her asking him to fuck her up the ass after Christmas had, he knew, not been trendy, but desperate; it had everything to do with the day they'd just gone through. Afterward, when he went over that day in his mind, nothing in it offered a clue as to why Elspeth wanted him to hurt her, in her childhood room.

The obvious assumption was that her father had abused her. Jack was not shy about bringing it up; he had his own guilt on the subject, things he had done with Joan as a kid, but they always stopped short of what he'd have called the unforgivable. "Oh, please, that's so cause-and-effect," Elspeth had said. "My father never touched me." Jack chose to believe her. She would not have hidden this from him, not if he'd pressed. "Can't I just like it?"

On the train home after Christmas, that conversation had happened. Her eyes had lit up with what he thought of as forced mischief, a presentation of herself as wild and unpredictable. He had distrusted this and remained uncertain of what might happen the next time they had to visit Montclair. Now he lay in bed as long as he could, until she said, "All right. Come on. Really. It's time."

Whenever they took the train out to New Jersey, he remembered Mark Fink's little speech in Riverside Park, the day that turned out to be the first time Jack had ever tried cocaine. Mark Fink had been wistful and slightly damning about the little towns of New Jersey, but there was still a melancholy that came over Jack as he passed through these towns now. He had made it to this place, and Mark Fink, he was pretty sure, had not.

For more than a year after the day in Riverside Park with Mark Fink, Jack's life had come to be ruled by the white powder. The velocity with which this happened had shocked him afterward. Like all his life he'd been waiting to pledge allegiance to cocaine, though it made no sense. He'd been good, he'd been careful. He'd been chaste and pure in the city. That had been his New York life before the day in the park.

Afterward, he could still grimace at the recovered embarrassment of certain moments of that year. The bathroom of the marketing research firm where he worked became a favorite place to use. It had made him free and easy with the Johnnies in Atlanta; he'd made assignations with them, told them he was heading south. Could they suggest a place where they might meet? In her listening booth, Rosie heard him, called him on the carpet, eventually fired him. Before that—an early low point—he had given in to the woman, Martha, and the blow jobs in the stairwell.

It was as if, on the other side of the chivalric city he'd been trying to both create and live in like a knight devoted to Christina Thayer, there existed a sordidness beyond belief, and to go from one to the other required only a subtle adjustment of the mind. Or maybe a willingness to indulge one's weakness. Jack thought, too, that this was inherent in him, in spite of who he'd been trying to become, and he excused it as the last of his wildness, the things he had to fully expunge from his body before he could possess Christina. For a long time, he held on to that excuse.

He attended parties with Fink, parties with young lawyers and traders, with blond girls in brief black dresses. The cocaine came out.

He was introduced by Fink as a first-year Columbia Law student, which became a form of permission to fuck these girls in bathrooms in apartments on the Upper West Side. He and Fink would laugh about it on the way home, and late at night he would write to Christina, indulging in the kind of doubleness he'd convinced himself it was possible to maintain. Writing those letters was like walking into Central Park at dawn on a spring morning after one of those parties, onto one of the great lawns, covered at that hour by a layer of mist that stretched before you, the buildings pink and gold in the distance. It was that feeling of an elemental purity coexisting with the night he'd just had, a party with two Southern girls from Bear Stearns, one named Paula and the other named Georgia something, sitting on the side of a bathtub with their dainty fingers up their noses, telling him they weren't wearing underwear. "Want to see?" And then having them both on the edge of the tub, from where he could see rust in the drain and a bar of hairy soap the apartment owner had not bothered to clean. "Tell me about your classes," he would write to Christina. "Tell me about the intellectual life."

In his walks he searched for restaurants where he might take her when she finally came to him. Clean wood-paneled rooms with a handwritten menu in the window. His mind split. You could do the white powder, fuck the girls, go into the stairwell with Martha, none of it mattered. It was part of his apprenticeship in love. Though there came to be an increasing desperation to this belief, he went on convincing himself that the two worlds did not have to conflict.

But finally they did. When Christina wouldn't come to him, he grew impatient and went to her. Took a bus. Coke up his nose in the Springfield station, where he waited for the connecting bus to Amherst. It was late spring. He'd made the mistake of arriving during finals week. He found her in her room, cramming with a girl named Marie, who, when they were introduced, smiled at him knowingly. Some joke lay in his existence, a story Christina may have told her.

"You never answered my letters," he said to Christina when they were alone. He lay on her bed, exhausted by the trip. He slept while she studied, and he waited. Her hair was different, as if she were trying to make herself a clone of Olivia Newton-John, the year's reigning goddess. He watched her in the light of her desk lamp, noting the changes in her, and he knew that she wished he would go. But eventually, he believed, she would stop studying, would lie on the bed with him, they would sleep together, it was time. Late at night a boy came to her door. Christina answered with embarrassment, making excuses for Jack's presence. Jack could see the boy in the shadows, handsome, a normal college boy in a rugby shirt, red-haired, some Irish high school athlete starting to grow his hair long, thinking it made him wild. The dormitory corridor had an air of great secretiveness, coded and hushed like an army barracks after dark. It was a child's world, Jack thought, strangely proud of himself for having survived his year in New York, for knowing what to do at the lawyers' parties, what to drink and what to say. He was a figure of great sophistication sitting on Christina's bed, though none of them seemed to know it. After Christina had dismissed the boy, she said, "Jack, you have to go."

"Why? Is that your boyfriend?"

She didn't answer.

"My psych final is in the morning."

He'd reached for her then. He remembered the visit to her childhood room and how much she'd wanted him.

"Do you sleep with him, Christina?"

She bit her lip, turned away from him, toward her desk.

Finally, though, she'd given in. The long-delayed event he'd held back from happened, but only because he practically begged and wouldn't stop kissing her and promised to leave after they made love. But though he felt that he was forcing it, and that from the beginning there was something wrong in it, he was surprised at her response. The shrouded angel of Norumbega Regional High came, if only briefly, alive. Perhaps the Irish scrum half of the corridor had primed her over these last months. It was awful to think of. She seemed not to love him for it, but to become embarrassed. Even pleasure could not make things right or make him feel anything but the missed timing, the utter folly of this event. They did not know how to talk to each other afterward. On her bed, he had taken out the cocaine he brought, and asked her to share. She refused. When he thought about it on the bus back to New York, he understood it was the worst thing he could have done, but it had also been deliberate, as if to give her a convenient excuse to reject him. Maybe he had needed to end it that way, to let her know—and to admit to himself—that he had fallen too far for this to be, anymore, a possibility.

There were further descents. One night on Rockaway Beach, to which Mark Fink had enticed him when the weather turned warm,

131

the lawyer stepped into the waves fully dressed and declared that he was leaving the law. One by one he'd taken off nearly every article of clothing, until Jack had to witness his amazingly skinny body stripped down to his underwear, the waves hitting him one after another, Mark Fink's ribs standing out. It could have been Jack's continuing heart-brokenness over what had happened with Christina; still, this felt like the saddest moment of the year. The depleted way the lawyer looked, this man who had once seemed so powerful to Jack, so in control, charged up and lecturing. Those early days of his discipleship to Mark Fink had been Jack's best vision of New York—crisp autumn days and letters to Christina, and the walks, the endless walks at the beginning, and coming back to the apartment to find Fink and a frizzy-haired girl hovering over Fink's stereo, listening to something wispy and scratchy-sounding with a reverence that lightened their faces and made them, Fink and the girl, look at each other with something that Jack could only believe was love.

To see that same man, that young magician, half naked in the surf at Rockaway, cocaine-charged, surrendering, seemed to Jack a declaration that the world was just waiting to make you lessen and decay. Even in New York something was waiting to open and anatomize your smallness.

Jack had perceived that—the depths of his own fall—and had still not gotten over it a year later when he answered the ad for a receptionist at Short Cuts, the editing firm where Elspeth had looked at his application, then at him, letting him know instantly two things: he was hired, and he was about to enter a relationship that, whatever its great advantages, was not going to give him what he knew, even then, that he needed.

Elspeth's brother, a graduate student studying hematology at NYU, was visiting for the weekend, as was her older sister, a woman who had already gone through several career changes and was now running a day-care center on the Upper West Side of Manhattan. The siblings had decided on a tennis game in the afternoon. The court still held patches of rain from the night before and needed repairs. Jack didn't want to play, feeling lazy and like he didn't want to work for a spot inside the sibling hierarchy. Ned, the brother, said he'd take on both girls.

Jack watched them from the sidelines. They laughed a lot, but never in a way that fooled him into believing they were comfortable with one another. When the ball landed in one of the puddles, Adele, the older sister, picked it up and shook it so that water landed on Ned's face, and Ned had an uproarious response, like this act was an allusion to the years of ribbing he'd had to take as the youngest and the only boy in the family. Jack felt the willed part of it. This was what made him sleepy in Montclair: the enormous effort they all put into looking and acting normal—or what they'd decided was normal.

Midway through this boring game of tennis, the doctor came home. He drove a BMW the color of the yellow band on a honeybee. He carried on him an aura of sweat and of silver chest hairs sprouting through the opening of his shirt, though he was natty, had clearly showered after work, and wore a tie. He sat next to Jack and took out a pack of Parliaments and lit one.

"Hi, Daddy," Adele called from the court, the first to see him. She made a mock pout when she saw the cigarette, and the doctor groaned and half chuckled under his breath.

"They're afraid these'll kill me," the doctor said to Jack while he pulled in a long, apparently satisfying drag. "At the same time, they can't wait for me to die."

The doctor looked sidelong at Jack after he'd spoken, to gauge the reaction. Jack didn't give him one. This was becoming familiar, even after only two visits. There was a kind of pleasure in not returning the doctor's killer serves.

For a while, then, they watched the game in silence together, the doctor's children's passes at glee, at free-spiritedness, growing increasingly depressing. Adele tried the hardest to grab her father's attention, throwing comments his way. Elspeth's face darkened as the game went on, as though each of her sister's attempts at levity took a toll, and Jack started to cheer inwardly: Go ahead, tell the old man to fuck off. But he saw that Elspeth could not go that far within her family circle. Abruptly the doctor got up. He ground his cigarette into the soil at his feet and entered the court, startling Adele as she was preparing to return a serve. The ball fell into a corner. The doctor used his feet to test the places where puddles had formed. They were all silent, waiting on him. He seemed a little unsure on his feet as he started off.

"Keep playing," Elspeth said after the doctor had gone. A physical lassitude had come over the siblings. Adele turned and looked at Jack, and he felt something he'd felt coming from her before: It was his fault,

133

Adele might have been saying, Jack's fault. There was nothing wrong with this family, it was just the presence of an outsider, maybe this particular outsider, that brought out the flaw in the glass. Remove the outsider, hold the glass to the light in a different way, there was no flaw.

"Keep playing," Elspeth said again, this time a command.

At dinner, the doctor uncorked a bottle he'd apparently been saving for a special occasion. Jack studied the label; the words were in French.

"Do you know wine?" Dr. Wooten asked, aware of Jack's perusal, turning to him.

"No."

That was as much attention as Jack suspected he was going to get. The doctor stood at the head of the table. There was late spring light coming through the not-yet-bloomed rhododendrons outside the window. The chandelier over the long table was on. Opposite the doctor, Mrs. Wooten folded her hands, as though waiting out something she knew was going to be unpleasant.

"Here's something I've noticed," Dr. Wooten said. "In restaurants in New York. The finer restaurants." He put a very slight topspin on the word *finer* and released the cork. "And even here, in the finer restaurants in Montclair. Which are all, by the way, run by mafiosi."

"My father's exaggerating," Ned said apologetically to Jack.

"I am not. Mafiosi thugs. The veal has blood on it. The chicken. The—what's that thing they make with oxtail?"

"Osso buco," Adele said, and shimmied up to the table like Daddy was about to tell a good story. Her job was informing people that their three-year-olds weren't slick enough to make it into the high-end daycare center she ran. That, anyway, was how Elspeth had described it.

"Osso buco. Of course. Blood. All over it. You know what I'm talking about. You know blood, don't you, Ned?"

Ned lowered his eyelids slightly.

"Well, anyway, here's what they do. They place the cork beside you, and they wait. The sommelier waits. You know what a sommelier is, Jack?"

Jack hesitated a moment, though he knew the answer. He hated this game.

"The wine guy."

"I taught him that, Daddy," Elspeth said. But she was blushing, annoyed at herself for having taken the bait.

"All right. Good. You're supposed to *know* to sniff the cork. And sniffing the cork, what the *fuck* are you supposed to smell?"

After the doctor had spoken, there was a quiet, no one answering, the sound of Mrs. Wooten's jewelry shifting on her wrist.

"The quality of the wine, Daddy. The bouquet," Adele said.

The doctor looked at her a moment.

"In your next career, maybe you can be a sommelier."

They began to eat, in the hope—Jack could feel it coming from all of them—that the doctor had finished what he had to say. Ned tried to introduce a new topic, a visit the writer Jonathan Schell had recently made to NYU to discuss his new book, *The Fate of the Earth.* For a while, there was animation at the table, a display of great interest, a willed belief that they were a cutting-edge family, attentive, hip, on the cusp of exciting things. But at the first break in this new conversation Dr. Wooten came back.

"So it blows up," the doctor added after a moment. "The world, it blows up. What's this man's name? Schell? There's a Johnny Burke song. You know it?" He was smiling, scratching his chin, an old, rough-hewn paterfamilias for a moment. "*'And sometimes I think,'*" the doctor sang in an uncertain baritone, "*'I wouldn't mind at all.'*"

"Don't say that, Daddy," Adele said.

The doctor smiled, pleased with himself. His fingers went up, shaking exaggeratedly (the others all seemed to notice it), pointing in Jack's direction for several seconds before he spoke.

"Tell me, remind me, what this one does."

After a brief silence Elspeth put down her fork. She continued chewing the chicken in her mouth. She regarded her father with some concern and spoke cautiously. "Jack's taking a poetry course at Hunter College."

"Poetry?" The doctor's concentration felt closely and deliberately *placed*, as if it required an effort.

Elspeth swallowed, took a sip of water. "At Hunter College."

"That's a city university, isn't it?"

Jack was meant to answer. Elspeth turned halfway toward him in expectation. At such moments he always wanted to levitate, float above and away from the house. Nothing good could come of this.

"It's a city university, yes," Jack said. "I pay seventy-two dollars for

135

the course. I go at night." He wasn't facing the doctor. He sat directly across the table from Ned, who looked weirdly encouraging.

"I go once a week," Jack finished, then added, as if to slip a knife into the doctor's neck, "for the good of my soul."

Dr. Wooten smiled at that.

"For the good of your soul. I like that story. Seventy-two dollars. Poetry. Where? City College?"

"Hunter College, Daddy." Adele had spoken.

The doctor continued to smile, then got up abruptly. Adele flinched, like she expected to be hit. The doctor left the room. They could hear him in the next room, the library. No one at the table spoke while they listened to him shuffle around in there, though Mrs. Wooten sighed and touched her necklace and Adele wore a strange smile.

"What'd I say?" Jack asked, a small joke to relieve the anxiety, to which none of them responded.

"Do we have no fucking . . . poetry in here?" The doctor was shouting from the other room. "No fucking . . . Is all we care about Richard *Nixon*? I see more Nixon books in here than you can shake a stick at. How many times can you read Kissinger's *war* memoirs?"

"Daddy, I have some poetry in my room," Adele called. When there was no response, she said, "From college. Some Emily Dickinson. Do you want me to get it?"

The doctor stood in the doorway. "What? What did you say?"

"I said I have some Emily Dickinson. I could get it."

He appeared saddened by her words, not certain what she was telling him, his concentration clearly elsewhere.

"You asked about poetry, Daddy. I said I have some."

"Sit down, Philip," the mother said. She so rarely spoke that Jack was always startled by her hard little voice.

Dr. Wooten took his place at the table. He appeared to be working out some problem in his head. Then, after a few moments of this, he picked up the cork and fingered it, turned it over in his hand like a pitcher palms a ball so as to become deeply intimate with its ridges. Then he flung it at the opposite wall. It startled everyone, but no one spoke.

In bed, in the dark, Jack waited. Elspeth was brushing her hair, standing by the window. No lights were on. Elspeth's brushing seemed to Jack automatic, soothing, like a child sucking a plastic nipple.

"This was a good house to grow up in," Elspeth said.

He thought he might turn on a light now. He'd brought a volume of poetry from his class, an anthology. He was deep into Randall Jarrell, "The Woman at the Washington Zoo." He might read, and wait and see what she did, or what she asked him to do.

"We each had separate little houses in the back. Ned's was in a tree. Mine and Adele's were at opposite ends of the yard. We pretended we were a village. We invented identities. I was Mrs. Willow. That was my name."

Jack yawned inadvertently and was glad she didn't seem to notice. He was being subjected to the suburban idyll now. With every girl he'd ever known who'd had a troubled family, it was the same: once, there had been a golden moment. Before the disaster, Daddy had been raking leaves, Mommy inside baking gingerbread. A scent composed half of rotting apples and half of woodsmoke had been carried on the wind, while the children, the little girls, ran through the yard. They all wanted you to know they were victims of a broken promise, that it hovered, always.

"Who was Adele?" He yawned again.

She put the brush down, sat on the bed. "You don't care."

"Not true."

She stood up, hovered over him. It was almost like she was wanting to start a fight, except not quite.

"What are you doing?" he asked.

She just looked at him, and since it was dark, he couldn't tell exactly what her look was, except that he had a sense of her withholding something important.

"Come on. Come here. Put your boxers on."

He was startled by the command. It was not what he'd been expecting. She put on her own robe, so he obeyed.

"Just my boxers? Where are we going?"

There were only two floors in the Wooten house, but the floors were tremendously long, like the connecting hallways in museums. At the end of one such hallway Elspeth placed both hands gently against a door and listened. Assuring herself that whoever was inside was asleep— it was her parents' bedroom, he assumed—she opened the door adjacent to the bedroom, slipped inside, and asked Jack in. Jack guessed he was being invited into the parents' bathroom for a quick fuck, and he would have the meaning of that to figure out in the morning. But as soon as they were inside, he believed something different.

137

The room had an exclusively masculine feeling and scent—the odors of an aging male masked by an expensive fragrance. He looked at Elspeth's face reflected in the starkly lit mirror, a face drawn and devoid of makeup, her eyes with the slightly startled look they took on when unadorned. Next to her, he saw his belly pushing against the waistband of his boxers and thought he should probably start watching his weight, things were getting a little out of hand.

Elspeth opened the sliding glass doors of her father's medicine cabinet. Inside was a long array of medications. Jack recognized none of them. He was meant to, though, and it was clearly meant to help his understanding when Elspeth pulled out certain of them and held them before him. Tofranil. Sinemet. Elavil. A second after looking at the names, he couldn't have remembered them. Part of the problem of being with an older woman was that you kept having to hold up signs that said, I have not had your life experience. Don't expect me to know more than I know. Up until Elspeth he had always considered himself brilliant about female psychology.

"So?" he said.

She looked at him, not to tell him he was stupid, but to indicate that he had disappointed her. She did not like to have to spell things out. She put the drugs back into the cabinet, as if thinking better of the whole project.

"What? Just tell me," Jack said, and she shook her head.

They heard him then. Jack could see the goose bumps rise on Elspeth's shoulders, the way she went rigid. The bedroom door opened and then the bathroom door. The doctor did not look startled to see them. He wore a deep blue bathrobe that to Jack's eyes looked extraordinarily soft. His hair was barely mussed, like he hadn't been sleeping, but reading.

"I thought I heard."

He peered at them intently, and Jack had the feeling he was going to go right ahead and do what he'd come in here to do, oblivious to them—in any case, deliberately.

"Your young man needs to lose some weight, Elspeth," the doctor said.

"I keep telling him that."

She wanted to leave now. She wanted to leave the room without a scene. Neither of them—Elspeth nor her father—moved, but there are instances of frozenness that contain movement, and Jack had the sense that the doctor, though he'd stepped away from it, was blocking the door.

"When your mother and I were young—were lovers—we used to do this. In her parents' house. There's nothing original about what you're doing."

Elspeth smiled, a pass at relief she would see how long the situation would allow her to maintain.

"A standing-up shag in the bathroom. Generations have done this. I couldn't do it now. The back would give out."

"You caught us, Daddy."

"Yes. I caught you."

He looked at her in such a way that she stopped smiling. Then he glanced at Jack, and at the medicine cabinet.

"But I have to say we had the wisdom to choose a bathroom closer to our own bedroom."

Now he was smiling. "We had that wisdom, you see."

"We're going, Daddy. We didn't come here for that."

In the silence afterward, Jack watched the doctor visibly choosing from among alternatives.

"I came in here for some business, you see." He moved close to Jack, who was standing nearest the toilet.

"Of course," Elspeth said. "We're going."

Before they could leave, the doctor glanced quickly into Jack's eyes, then reached forward and opened the waistband of Jack's boxers and peered inside. His look was at first clinical, then amused. Jack wanted to slap his hand away but had the weird feeling it would be impolite.

In any case, it was only a moment before he released the waistband. It had happened so quickly that Jack hardly had time to feel shock. But then the doctor did something else, staring more carefully into Jack's eyes, searching, and then seeming to find something more interesting to him than Jack's genitals. "Poetry," the man said with an inflection Jack couldn't read.

"We're going," Elspeth said, and went out the door.

Jack followed. When they reached her bedroom, Elspeth went into the connecting bathroom and told him not to come in.

He waited, sat on the bed, got up. Was she crying in there? And if so, for what? It had been a deeply strange scene, but then, here in this house, what wasn't? Should he go in now and see what she was doing?

His instincts around Elspeth were never certain, frequently wrong. The great difficulty for him in this relationship was not solely in their age difference; it was something else, the fact that their relationship was basically devoid of love. Because of this lack, he was denied the sort of freedom of expression that love allowed, where you could make a mistake, even a large mistake, and be forgiven for it. The basis of all of this was almost cold: she'd saved him from the place into which he'd been led by Mark Fink and cocaine. He knew that and was at least partly grateful. But it bothered him that there were places he could not act out of. He was to be humbled by her; that was the understanding.

He was nearly asleep, having given up waiting for her, when she finally came into the bedroom.

She slipped in beside him, sidled up to him.

"Hold me," she said.

He did, and he knew by the way she lay against him that this was to be it for tonight.

"You don't believe me," she whispered.

"What?"

"That it was a good house to grow up in."

"I believe you."

He listened to her breathing—girlish, small, clinging—until she was asleep. In the middle of the night he was awakened by something outside the door, a movement, a body hovering there, walking back and forth inside a very small space. He was certain it was the doctor.

He was certain, too, of something else, that in some way even more intimate than the man opening his shorts and studying the contents, the doctor had witnessed something in Jack's eyes, taken it in, registered it—the unspoken parts of Jack, the parts that had been killed off or silenced by cocaine but were starting to come back. Jack was left with the strange feeling that the doctor knew him, knew something he had been trying to hide—or deny—for a long time.

The doctor worked his shovel around a wheelbarrow of wet red clay. It was midsummer, and they were repairing the tennis court, a job Dr. Wooten insisted on performing himself. The doctor was in a gray T-shirt. Across the material stretching over his chest the marks of sweat appeared in the shape of a downward-pointing archipelago.

Jack was shirtless, assisting. It had been arranged. Dr. Wooten had asked for him especially. "Bring that boyfriend of yours out," he'd said to Elspeth. "I need his brawn." She'd made a sport of quoting her father. "You're still 'that boyfriend,'" as if this suited her, the fact that Jack still didn't have a name. But Jack, by now, knew differently.

"There's this contradiction, you see," the doctor was saying, working the shovel around the clay mixture not because it needed more mixing, but because he seemed to require the physical activity. "You bring them up, your children, to a certain expectation of life. That they will not have to do certain things. Not have to get their hands dirty. Then you see them as adults. Smart. For the most part successful. And all you want is for them to get their hands dirty." The doctor paused. "Like—this," he said. "Like—*us*."

Jack noted, not for the first time, the conspiratorial way the doctor used the word *us*. "Why's that?" he asked.

"Why?"

The doctor had a way of looking at him, as if he himself were surprised that they were becoming intimates. But also with a repetition of that weird peering-in to Jack that had begun on the night in the doctor's bathroom.

"Well, because, at the end of your life you go back. You *return*, as it were, to the earliest values. Your own father's values. Inevitable. They're what seem bedrock. Everything else—"

The doctor made a gesture in the air to dismiss his surroundings, the tennis court, the adjacent pool, the ocher-colored patio awning, the great house beyond. "Wait. Wait a moment." Looking suddenly excited, he went inside and came out in a few minutes with a small volume, from which he read aloud.

"'The cloud-capp'd towers, the gorgeous palaces.'" The doctor looked up at Jack, sent him a playful look, then went on reading with pleasure. "'The solemn temples, the great globe itself / Yea, all which it inherit, shall dissolve / And, like this insubstantial pageant faded, / Leave not a rack behind.'" He clapped the book shut. "What's that? Tell me, poetry student."

"I don't know."

Dr. Wooten studied him awhile to be sure Jack wasn't teasing him.

"It's *The Tempest*. Shakespeare's *Tempest*. You don't know it? *Come on*. They don't teach that in poetry classes? I made a great search of that god-awful library of ours, that shrine to the Book of the Month Club. Tell me, did all of us really think we'd go on reading *Fail-Safe* and *Seven*

Days in May into our dotage? I found *one* volume of Shakespeare. I read it. You did that to me."

Jack, at such moments, did not know how to respond. The doctor was playing with him, he knew that much, maybe believing something about Jack because he wanted to or needed to, or else challenging him to live up to the doctor's own exalted notion of "poetry." Still, Jack could never be sure whether he was being generous to what he perceived as Jack's nature, or just insanely competitive.

The poetry class had ended, and he missed it. He'd loved the image of himself on the subway, riding up to Hunter at night, a reminder to him of the old, lost life of discipline. Then, afterward, the feel of the big, dull stone university disgorging students into the courtyard on Sixty-eighth Street, the subway life, New York dusk. But that had been it. Sometimes he wished this pursuit had yielded more.

"I'm not much of a poetry student," Jack said. "It was just something I did."

"No? Well, the things we do, we do them for a reason, don't we?" The doctor looked hard at him. "You could simply be fucking Elspeth, couldn't you? Instead, you're searching."

Jack had learned to shrug off such shocks and to keep the doctor's insults to Elspeth hidden from her. Still, something lay behind them. Their visits, his and Elspeth's, had increased of late, for reasons Elspeth chose not to talk about. It was the progression of the disease, Jack knew that much. He'd guessed Parkinson's, from the evidence of the turned-down pages in Elspeth's medical books, and she had confirmed it, though not much more. "I don't want my mother to be alone with him," Elspeth had said. There was a sense of approaching danger. And just as the doctor had grown more gruffly friendly with Jack, Elspeth had beaten, within her and Jack's relationship, a subtle retreat. "Tell me what you're so scared of," he said to her often, just to get her to name it. But she wouldn't.

The doctor spread a shovelful of clay over an indentation in the court.

"Here. Rake that, will you? And then, tamp it down. Walk on it. Carefully. My shoes are too good for this."

Jack did as he was told, felt the doctor watching him.

"That's it. Even. You see, you go back to an older world. Your ancestors used to tramp grapes underfoot. To make wine."

The doctor was smiling, as if he didn't mean to say it with a straight face.

"Actually—" Jack started to say.

The doctor was ignoring him, watching Jack's feet. "Mine? Well, who knows? Starvation and desperation. Ireland. Wales. Depression. Drink. *Scotland.* Who knows? It gets lost. My father was the foreman of a cracker factory. Can you imagine it?" The implication Jack heard was, Like you, I come from nothing. At such moments it felt like the doctor had chosen him not for himself, but for what was generic about him.

When the smoothing-out was done, they used a roller to complete the job. This was where Jack's "brawn" was required. The doctor leaned down to inspect. "There's a little dusting we need to add. In a minute. No hurry. Then we'll have to bounce a ball. To see how it goes. Take your shoes off now."

Jack did, and the doctor accepted them, working out the small pebbles embedded in the grading of the sneaker sole.

"I'll tell you what was best, though," the doctor said as he was doing this. "What's best is the beginning. Don't let anyone tell you there are rewards that only come later. It's the beginning. It's the ripeness of it. It's the—well, it's the fucking. As much as anything. The young fucking. Irreplaceable. Don't let anyone tell you different."

He handed Jack his shoes. They moved on to the next indentation and repeated the process, but this time the doctor didn't say anything. The motions seemed to be becoming difficult for him.

After they'd worked a couple of hours in the hot sun—the older man able to do less and less—the doctor went inside and brought out two tall beers. They tapped bottles, and the doctor said, "To poetry."

Jack took a couple of sips and said, "What do you mean, the end of your life?"

"Hmm?"

He knew the doctor had heard him and understood the question, though the man pretended to be distracted.

"You said before, 'at the end of your life.' And you're not, I mean, *old.*"

The doctor smiled. "Come here."

They walked to the edge of the tennis court. Outside the fenced-in area was a row of hedges and then the enormous lawn. It was as though the doctor had taken Jack here just to stare at something they both knew well, the vastness of the yard.

"Elspeth told me it was great to grow up here," Jack said. His speech felt awkward, but called for.

"Did she?"

The doctor's response cut him off.

"Don't start the testimonials yet, please. Don't tell me what a great father I was. I was a *provider.* A damned good one, but still, that's all." He took a few unsteady steps onto the lawn.

"And mean, very mean. Critical as all get out. My children resented me for that. And still do. They *want* something. But you don't do what I did, the discipline, my God—the *self*-criticism—and then turn it off when you come home. Don't even try and do that when you have children of your own. Though I suspect they won't be with my daughter." The doctor smiled. Like so many of his jokes, he kept this one to himself. "Which is too bad, really. I've tried to put in a good word for you."

His words were strange enough, but before Jack could say anything, the doctor's left hand had started to shake, like he was grasping something and then letting it go, in quick succession. Dr. Wooten looked down at his hand and watched it, as clinically as he'd once studied Jack's penis. There was no sadness or deep concern, just a careful watching. When the spasm, or whatever it was, was over, the doctor looked at his watch.

"What would you say that was, thirty seconds?"

"Okay. About."

"Thirty seconds." He put his hands in his pockets. "You get it, and then you lose it. Let that be the wisdom I impart." He looked at Jack. "Poetry student."

When he lay with Elspeth now, he wanted to tell her. He wanted his time with her father—the things the doctor said to him—to inform their intimacy, to deepen it, to give him something in her eyes, a measure of respect that he couldn't seem to get on his own. But he was aware that his chosenness—if that was what it was—implied a rejection of the doctor's own children. Elspeth had picked up on it early.

"It's like him. Be harsh to us. Hard on us, all our lives. Then when things go bad, choose someone else to open up to. What's so special about you?"

"Nothing," Jack said, feeling that was true.

"He sees you as the struggling kid he once was. 'Working class.' He doesn't know that he's landing his affections on the most ambitionless boy in America."

They were in bed, and he didn't want to argue.

"Has he offered to put you through medical school?"

"No."

"Well, that's coming."

"It's actually the poetry. He wants to talk about poetry."

"Oh God." She forced a harsh laugh. It was an ugly thing to hear. What made it worse was that it was she who had encouraged him to take the course. It had embarrassed her a little, at the beginning, that he was only what he was, the receptionist, the man Friday, the ex-druggie, and when they went out to bars to drink with her friends, their supposition was that she had taken him on only for the sex. She ought to have been brave and tough-minded enough to have admitted that, but there was a part of her that found it a little shameful or not quite socially acceptable. When he started reading her poetry books, she encouraged him. It was something to say. "Jack's taking a course."

When he came home from his nights at Hunter, she was sometimes expectant, like something would have happened to him, a latent ambition fired up.

Now, with his ascension in the doctor's eyes, even their usually reliable sex began to suffer. The competition that had been so present in their everyday activities found its way in. There were nights when she grasped his penis, forced it erect, and then stared at it, as if she wanted to hate it or do something cruel to it. Why should he be the one to own this instrument? Certain women wanted it for themselves, as if they believed they were entitled to put it in their pockets, carry it away, like take-out food. She was angry at it for being separate from her, belonging to him, an object of desire attached to a person she was no longer sure she wanted to invest with the power of being desired.

"I could do something for you," the doctor said that fall, as inevitably as Elspeth had predicted.

He and Jack were in the library, a room with a fireplace. The doctor had asked Jack to start a couple of logs going. It was like a scene in a nineteenth-century novel. There should have been brandy on serving trays. Elspeth and her mother were huddled together somewhere else in the house. Though the family still treated Jack like a kind of retainer—he was not to know certain things, he was not to be present at family meetings concerning the doctor's health—he had learned that the doctor had stopped working. One of the reasons there was no brandy on trays was that Dr. Wooten could no longer be trusted to hold a glass without spilling it.

"What would you like to do for me?" Jack asked.

"I could put you through school."

Jack smiled in a careful way.

The doctor looked at him, wanting to be let in on the joke. "What is it?" he asked.

"Everybody wants me to go to school," Jack said.

"Well, it's what one does, isn't it?"

"I suppose."

"But you could never afford it. I understand that."

Jack made a decision to keep silent. The room quiet, the fire crackling, the dog asleep. Outside, the darkness that descends on a fall afternoon of promised rain. He felt like he was betraying his own father. Every opportunity had been there, and the man's desire had been almost ungovernably thick. But what occurred to Jack now, in this room, was what had always been true: if he was going to bend his will to that of another man, it had to be a man good enough. There had been Mark Fink (a mistake), and now this.

"I know you're on a quest. I understand that. I admire it—"

"Listen"—Jack interrupted him—"I don't know what you're talking about when you talk about this quest."

The doctor's eyes narrowed; things had turned unaccountably serious.

"I mean, when you talk about me and poetry."

"Don't bullshit me, young man." Then, in reaction to Jack's look, a tempering smile. "You're too good for this. You know that."

"Too good for what?"

"For this life you're leading. You're a *receptionist*, for God's sake. I'm inclined to think you're even too good for my daughter, for Elspeth, for that matter. You're capable of something else. You've *been* something else, haven't you?"

It was unsettling to have the doctor know that.

"How old are you?"

"Twenty-one."

"Twenty-one. Young Jack. I expect you know everything I'm telling you. Deep down, as they say. I suspect that nothing I'm telling you is a surprise. That you are 'running in place,' as they say. Or maybe running away. Avoiding the thing that's waiting for you, at any rate."

That was the extent of it. Suddenly the man looked cold.

Jack was left hanging in midair. "Do you want me to put another log on?" he asked.

"Please."

Jack felt the doctor watching him as he went about the small chore, appreciating his efficiency in the physical world, his size. When he sat back down, the doctor was smiling again, a relief.

"What does your father do? That is, presuming he's still alive."

"He is. He runs a pizza restaurant."

"Oh God, I love it."

It was odd how, even as Jack tried to bring this man down from his overly high estimation of him, he found himself giving in to small things. He knew that by leaving out half of his father's life, leaving out Norumbega itself, he could please this man. Also, he liked the thought of himself as fallen angel.

"What's waiting for me? I think I'd like to know that. What you see."

"What's inside you." The doctor paused. "See what's inside you, young Jack. You will always fight something, won't you? An impulse."

Under the doctor's gaze Jack felt something stir in himself. It actually became painful when he sensed the man's appreciative gaze withdrawing.

"Are you okay?" Jack asked.

Dr. Wooten's face had become a mask, unapproachable. Jack sensed it was time to leave him, but didn't want to.

"He calls you primitive," Elspeth said to him later. They were at the table in the little kitchen in the apartment in Chelsea.

"'Your primitive friend,'" she quoted. "You know he's going to kill himself."

"No, he isn't," Jack said.

She smiled in recognition of the unforced shock behind Jack's words.

"Take a look at his medicine cabinet the next time we're there. Seconal. Nembutal. In quantity. I tell my mother about them, and she throws them out. But that doesn't mean anything. He just hides them, I'm sure."

"Doesn't she check his bathroom herself?"

"She's not paying enough attention. Maybe she's tired of waiting. It's how a doctor does it, I guess. Pills."

Jack thought that if he were someone else, a more mature person, he would know exactly what to do now, how to soothe her. But the terms she had created for this relationship kept him immobile in his chair. She was to be in charge. He had begun to hate it. Elspeth would never have a child, he thought sometimes, because of the difficulty she would have in ceding half ownership to the child's father.

"When he dies, I want you to move out," Elspeth said.

"Come on. He's not going to die."

"I'm going to want to be alone for a while. I know that."

She was still not looking at him. The morning light coming in through the kitchen window was the only strong light the apartment received. Her profile in it told him she was already exalting herself in grief. She was reciting words like lines from a play.

"There's something you don't know," Jack said.

"And what's that?"

He waited, unsure of how much of the doctor's hand he wanted to forcibly tip.

"At night sometimes, when we're there, I hear him pacing around."

"And?"

"Outside our room. When he thinks we're asleep."

"Yes. And?"

"That's not what a guy does when he's going to kill himself. He doesn't, like—*hover*."

She stared at him like what he'd said was stupid. "No, Jack? What does a man do when he's going to kill himself? Tell me, from out of your vast experience."

Her look was so harsh he started to lift his hand. He did not get it very far up, but she stared at his hand, and it was almost like she was pleased to see that—it confirmed something for her. She got up and moved into another room.

148

"It's breaking his heart," Jack said when he followed her. "The things he can't do anymore."

"Oh Jesus. You're being sentimental. His heart isn't broken at all. He sees the end of his proficiency, that's all, his *mastery*, and he can't imagine living for any other reason."

"Look, maybe I see things you don't see."

"Clearly. Because you're the one he shows things to."

"Are you jealous of that? Is that what this is about?"

"No."

The room was half in darkness. A beige couch with pillows and throws on it. A framed Mondrian print on the wall. Old bottles with dried stalks. Beach glass and art books. A girl's apartment, Jack thought, seeing it for the first time without him in it.

"I think that says a great deal," she said.

"What does?"

"That you were ready to hit me."

"I wasn't. I didn't."

She would hold it. He knew that. It was data she would store forever.

"I've never hit a girl in my life."

"I've spoken to John," she said. "I've asked him if you can stay with them. I didn't just want to throw you out."

John was the proprietor of the store on the ground floor of their building. He sold artifacts, old theater programs, records from the forties and fifties, vintage sixties lunch boxes in mint condition. He lived with his lover in a building a few blocks away. When Jack and Elspeth stopped in at the store, John always flirted with Jack.

"Jesus. I don't want to live with those guys."

"Why not? They'll take good care of you." She paused to look at him. "You won't go back, will you?"

He knew what she was talking about.

"You're booting me out," he answered instead. "I might. I might go back. Who the fuck knows?"

He was saying this just for show. She seemed to know it.

"I think you should examine your rage," she said.

"Oh Jesus."

"I think so. I do."

•

149

On their last trip to Montclair, things were markedly different. It was early January. Elspeth suggested to him that he didn't have to come. This was a far cry from the hurt and wounded look she'd given him when he'd suggested, in the spring nearly a year before, that she go alone. He had once been her defense. Now the notion of his being asked to fuck her up the ass was as foreign as her suddenly tendering an offer of marriage would be.

The doctor was starting to stoop now. His eyes retained a mild amusement when he saw Jack; they took on a fighting look when he regarded the others. But the doctor asked for time alone with Elspeth, in his study.

That night, she rode Jack hard. A surprise, since it had been a couple of weeks since there'd been any sexual contact at all. It was painful, he could tell that she was hardly wet, so her working against him felt as if it was opening and stretching sores on his foreskin. When he came, he howled in actual pain. She cradled his head, touching the hair on his neck with what he read, or hoped, was affection. She was on top of him. He felt that the whole operation had been to do something that hurt him, after which she could afford kindness.

A half hour later he woke to find that she was no longer with him. He felt the damp, warm place where she'd lain, and he turned on a light. She'd taken her pillow. He went to the door and opened it to find the doctor standing there, as if he'd been listening.

"Well," the doctor said, confronting Jack, unembarrassed.

The doctor's stoop looked painful. He glanced beyond Jack, into the room.

"No—Elspeth? Is she in the bathroom?"

"I don't know where she is."

The doctor, regarding him, looked as if he were having trouble controlling his mouth.

"All right, then," he said, and started to move away.

Jack put on his boxers and followed the doctor down the hall, an echo of the journey he'd once taken with Elspeth.

"Why are you following me?"

"I'm worried about you."

The doctor glanced at him, annoyed, then touched the walls for balance.

"*Worried?*" He motioned Jack away, but Jack continued to follow him all the way into the familiar bathroom where he had first encountered the doctor's medical stash.

"Go away. I'm serious now."

"I'm not leaving you."

"You're going to follow me in here, are you? All right. Look," the doctor said, but when he tried to bend down, he couldn't. He opened the door to the cabinet beneath the sink and gestured for Jack to get down.

"Just below the pipe you'll find a loose board."

Jack lifted the board and felt below it. There were two pill bottles. He took them out and stood before the doctor, holding them in his hand.

The doctor was smiling. "You see," he said.

"I guess I should throw these away."

"You guess?" The smile grew crafty, though the doctor could no longer manage the subtlety of facial gesture that had once been his hallmark.

"Why do you want to kill yourself? Why do you want to do that to your family?"

"You can ask that?"

He touched Jack's naked shoulder, but again, it seemed a balancing action.

"Let me have them." The doctor took the bottles, opened them with an effort, laid the pills out on the sink. "We're getting quickly to the point where it will no longer be *possible* for me to do this. Pour me a glass of water, will you?"

"I can't."

"Oh, don't be silly. Of course you can."

The doctor smiled, as if he knew Jack, or sensed a usable weakness.

"Or else go away. Go back to bed. Pretend this never happened."

"You have to tell me why you're doing this."

"Remember," the doctor said. He tapped Jack hard on the chest, smiled, or attempted to. "The fucking. The fucking is all."

"I don't believe that."

"No? Then wait." He laughed. "Just wait."

He reached for one of the pills, dropped one, reached for another. "Fuck." Angry at himself.

"Look, you take these, we can call the hospital, pump your stomach."

"You won't."

"Why not?"

"Because you understand. *Jack*." The words were slurred. The doctor's eyes, red-rimmed, scoured Jack, and the next words were laced with rage. "You understand . . . how *fallen* a human being can be. Don't you?" He tapped Jack on the forehead, smiled as though he'd scored a point.

The doctor then took a pill, poured himself water, swallowed it. Some of the water seeped from his mouth.

"There's a measuredness to this. Not all at once. You throw up then. The whole operation . . . fails."

"Tell me what I'm supposed to understand? I *don't* understand. You keep telling me I'm something that you're making up. You're playing with me."

The doctor ignored him, took another pill. Jack closed his hand over the remaining ones. The doctor looked at Jack's hand and smiled.

He tried to pry Jack's fingers off the pills. Jack could win this. There was no doubt in his mind. But then the doctor's smell hit him, the huge fatigue contained in that smell.

"Am I? Playing with you? Tell me, young man, you've never been in a place you've found unacceptable. Tell me that. Hmm? Because I won't believe it. You have a kind of age in your eyes. Your eyes are older than the rest of you. They tell a story." The doctor waited. "There are two things you can do when you find yourself at your lowest. Correct? You can accept weakness, accept your miserably fallen state. The Christian attitude, yes? We are all of us—less than God. Ah!" The doctor clutched his chest in mock prostration. "But the other—the, to me, more attractive prospect, is to say *fuck* no. I will not accept fallenness. I will not accept it."

The doctor became extremely quiet, focused on Jack's eyes. "Tell me you've never felt that way."

"I have. Okay."

Jack was remembering the night in Rockaway with Mark Fink, the long subway ride home, elevated over Queens, a fight they'd had, so trivial, so junkie-like, the grand eclipsing borough had seemed like a great slough he could drown in. He'd never felt so low as he had that night, not even in the stairwell at the telemarketing firm, the woman Martha going down on him. The self-disgust that followed that willingness to be nothing but the craven physical self. He remembered wanting to jump from the train.

The doctor, sensing the drift of Jack's thoughts, nodded. "We search then, don't we, for a way out. We find some outlet. Poetry. Death. *Something*. Or am I wrong about you? Are you a boy who simply likes to sleep with women who don't respect him?"

He paused a moment, let it sink in.

"Now, please. You'll let me take these, and then you'll hold me, here on the floor. If my wife knocks on the bathroom door, you'll say it's you in here. She won't believe you, but she won't bang down the door and risk being wrong." He opened and closed his mouth. "She won't risk being wrong." He had to hold himself against the sink. "And it will relieve them all. Now, don't be silly. You know what I have. You know my disease. Nothing good's coming. Help an old man. We both know. The great poets have said it."

"You know I'm not that. I don't know shit about poetry."

"Oh, Jack," the doctor said, looking at him, touching his cheek affectionately. "Of course you do. Stop pretending now." Gently then, extraordinarily tired, the doctor lifted Jack's fingers off the pills. He was able to do so only because Jack's hand had gone soft. He took another, with water. "How many is that?"

"Three."

"Three," the doctor repeated.

He took three more, drinking water in measured quantities, at intervals.

"I can't do this," Jack said. He considered going for the door. There would be the doctor's falling, someone finding him, the pumping operation, the hospital vigil, then what he sensed—or knew—would be a repetition. And if he left now, he knew he would not be invited back. All the trust he'd earned would be lost. The doctor, as if knowing this about him, looked at him between sips. He was getting a kind of pleasure out of this, or if not pleasure, he was taking in a victory Jack was helping him achieve.

" 'This rough magic I here abjure.' "

Jack wanted to know what he meant, but could not ask.

When the time came for the doctor to fall, Jack grasped him and they lay on the floor, the doctor's heavy body atop his. For a while there was only the furiousness of thought: a way to seek an explanation for the others. Perhaps he would be able to say, I found him. But then the man's slackening breathing asserted a reality that made the future seem vague. Hold a dying man in your arms, and there is not an appreciable future. It felt uncomfortably like the aftermath of sex: the poses, the attention to the other's movements. It occurred to him that this could land him in jail, but by then he suspected it was too late, the doctor's breathing had slowed to almost nothing, and Jack felt helpless. There was a faint smell of vomit. He touched the back of the doctor's neck, remembering how Elspeth had touched his earlier that night, and reasoned that he might do well to think like a woman now, to think in the language of comfort.

Finally, he couldn't go through with it. Late in the night he wedged himself out from under the doctor's body and betrayed him by waking Elspeth's mother. An ambulance was called. The doctor survived, but succeeded in his quest, on his own, a couple of months later. Jack only heard about this. He'd been exiled by then, living with John and John's lover, Michael, in their loft on Twenty-eighth Street. "Elspeth's father did it, finally, I guess," John had said, coming home one night from the shop. Out of work now (impossible to work with Elspeth when they'd stopped living together), Jack spent the days returned to his old habits, wandering, reading. These were the days when he started writing letters to Joan, landing on her as the receptacle he needed. Not even considering: *Joan*. Only that he had a sister, she was there, she'd always been there to receive him. He provided details he thought later he should have kept out. But he could think of no one but himself. He did not consider Joan at all, could not imagine the reality of his letters being opened, and read, in a houseful of nuns.

He managed to find out where the doctor's service would be, took a train and then a cab to the church in Montclair. Sat in the back, hoping that Elspeth would notice him. In black, she looked classic, severe, beautiful. She gave the eulogy, praising her father for making possible a "magnificent" life. That was the word she used. It was as if she were escaping into a vision. The beautiful childhood mythologized. Unspoken was all that her father had withheld, giving it instead to Jack. It felt like a huge failure to him now, the night he held the doctor and had not been able to stay. Shameful, the knocking on his wife's door, Mrs. Wooten appearing in a nightdress, hair flattened, skin old and creased, annoyed with him, as if it might have been better to allow the doctor to do it. A pact had been made, and he'd broken it. He'd been alone

154

afterward, as the ambulance drove off, Elspeth and her mother gone with it.

He received a note from Elspeth, through John, in the months after Dr. Wooten's death:

> That night, the night he tried to do it, the night you were with him, he told me I should leave you. He said I could only ruin you. He said you had the potential for ruin and the potential for grace. I swear, that was what he said. I fucked you that one last time because I didn't want to believe anything special about you, Jack. You were a boy I'd picked up and hired. Why should you be special? I was the one who wanted to be special in his eyes.
>
> In the end, this is better. You're better off with John and Michael. Let them take care of you. Let them love you. Then take your next step, whatever the hell that is. My father seemed to believe in you. I don't, Jack. Not in the same way.

Ruin and grace. To see it written that way sent him into the deepest depression of his life, as if he'd been given partial but hugely important information about himself he couldn't begin to know what to do with. Like the night on the lake, he was left with a feeling of understanding nothing. He missed the doctor and the level of attention the man had given him.

Afterward he walked around the city remembering the doctor's words, trying to keep alive, as long as he could, the elusive sense of importance the doctor had gifted him with. As long as he could maintain the notion of a battle going on inside him, it was as if his soul mattered. Yet too often, as time went by, he felt that the drift of his life was in the other direction, a direction he was newly determined to fight. The ruin part he always understood. It was the second word, the word *grace*, that came to haunt him.

5

The bishop was to arrive later in the morning. The simple fact served to quicken the life of the priory. They had not seen him since the last

155

Solemn Profession—Sister Monica's, six years before. A short man, white receding hair, a funny movement about the lips, as if he were perpetually remembering something he must mention to his secretary.

The secretary, Father Burgoyne, was to come, too. No one knew him—his was a fairly recent appointment to the Chancery—but he was accompanying the bishop in order to certify that everything at Joan's Solemn Profession was as it should be. His name was often heard being spoken during the morning preparations: Would this or that be all right with Father Burgoyne? This annoyed Joan, that someone who had so little to do with any of them—a dioscesan functionary—should set all their nerves aquiver.

But it *was* nerves, that's all. Like a wedding morning. Joan had never attended a wedding (a cousin, long ago, but that hadn't counted, really), though she could imagine. The pinning of dresses and the worry about hair and the how-will-we-look. And all of it, all the highly keyed anxiety because there would be a moment of penetration later in a hotel room, a moment Joan imagined would be lonely, and disappointing after the high frenzy of the day.

There would be no penetration of her tonight after the ceremony, after the gathering in which she would see them all—her parents, two sets of aunts and uncles, Jack, the girl. They would all be invited into the priory, on any other day a violation in itself. She had received permission to take them into her cell. But she would be left alone, finally. A moment she anticipated more than any of the day's rituals. Her life as an ordinary nun would simply begin. No further anxiety, no sense of a faux pas she might at any moment commit that, if discovered, might lead to exile.

But after all the months and years, she finally had presence of mind enough to understand that she had always overdramatized: none of her sins, none of her transgressions—not even her day on the ice with Angel—would have had that effect. They didn't go far enough. On discovery, they would only have been presented to her by the mother prioress along with the question: Do you want to go on, Joan? The struggle, all along, had been for her to judge.

Dressed, the long gown trailing behind her, Joan went to the window. It would be good to have an actual mirror now. There was none in the room. She touched her hair. Years ago, a nun was expected to have it cut down to the scalp. No more. The feel of her thick hair sent a small charge through her, like a connection to someone she had once been, a girl in a room with no idea what might happen to her. A girl waiting for her brother to come in and show her the next thing about his changing body that had become so urgent to display. What had surrounded her then? Dolls, books, the emptiness of a large house, the wish for more of them, more brothers and sisters, more sounds. To be absorbed. The quest of her life, she thought sometimes. To be absorbed into an organization of the world that did not discount her but did not insist on her at its center. An organization of the world that said, Take your place here. Exactly here.

It might have been enough for her to take her place in a family, if it had been a different family. It pained her now to admit this, though she sensed, in spite of how far she had come, that it was still true. She thought of them all now, over in the guesthouse, assigned to rooms that were no more than revamped cells like this one, only given a little more color. Would Jack and the girl be allowed to stay in a room together? Would her mother's eagerness to see her cause her to knock things over, a clumsiness she would have to control that would be noted by Brother Philip, the most elegant of the monks, their host at the guesthouse? Joan touched the window.

Had it not been winter, it might have been possible for her to see them taking a walk behind the priory. She saw them once a year. Aside from Jack's letters, contact had been minimal. The words of those letters came to her now. Jack's agony in the time after the doctor's death. She could hear a rustling in the hallway, her fellow sisters, her bridesmaids. Sister Monica had already come in twice this morning. "Listen," Monica had said, and read from the first reading, Paul's Letter to the Phillipians, which would be hers to read at the ceremony. "*Dung* is in the reading. Can I say *dung* in front of the bishop?"

"It's in the Bible, Monica."

"Yes. But so is *circumcision*. I couldn't say *circumcision* in front of the bishop."

It was half a joke. Monica was mocking herself. Also, intensely nervous. She needed only Joan's mild reassurance. But in Monica's absence, alone, staring out the window into the day, Joan had to think—with equanimity, not panic—that it was a lie. She did not count all things outside of this life as dung. She remembered Jack's letters and the names. Elspeth. Dr. Wooten. Mark Fink. The succession of women after Elspeth. And the single man the man who had died of AIDS. She would like to see Jack walking by right now. She would tap the window, wave. Today she would have more of him than the letters allowed. There would be touch between them at last. She and Jack, they would touch. And Angel, too, if he accepted her invitation.

Father Burgoyne was a dark redhead, his hair slicked tight against his scalp, high, shining forehead, lips barely there. ("He looks like a serial killer, don't you think?" Julian would say to her later, poker-faced, at the reception.) And right away, seeing him after they'd filed in, nuns first on one side, male clergy following on the other, she wished he wasn't there. A girl does not want to see strangers at her wedding, not this close up, not looking so critically at her, not on the altar.

Still, her family was there, too. She could feel their presence in the church, though she wouldn't look directly at them. Some of the nuns did that as a matter of course, stared straight out at the congregation. They were at fault, but how could you help it, really? Occasionally men came on retreat, one or another particularly handsome; it caused a stirring among certain of the nuns. The presence of women retreatants, too, was known to do it. Given what she knew now, Joan's early belief that her crush on Brother Joseph marked her as a pariah seemed naive. There was sex here, sex in the air anyway, but its power was really no more than the smell of rice pudding prepared by Sister Catherine once a fortnight. They looked forward to it, and then it was absorbed.

Father Alfred read the opening prayer. Monica got through her reading, not tripping on the word *dung*, but stressing it rather too much, Joan thought.

The second reading had been given to Clare. Colossians 3:12–17. *"Put on therefore, as the elect of God, holy and beloved, bowels of mercies . . ."* It struck Joan as odd that the New Testament's earliest language should have been deemed appropriate for her today. Light came in quite suddenly, a break in what had been a gray sky. It caused another kind of stirring. Joan looked at the nuns on either side of her, their rings. The Gospel was Luke, the story of Martha and Mary, Martha's complaint to Jesus that she should be the one to do all the serving while her sister Mary gets to soothe the Lord.

Father Alfred, the abbot, overweight, Scottish, rough-voiced, delivered the homily.

"Will Sister Gertrude be a Martha or a Mary?" he began by asking.

This was a minor shock for Joan, to hear her name pronounced,

158

and so quickly. Her centrality to all of this caused her to blush, though that was silly: of *course* she was central.

"Martha, of course, is the busy one, the practical one," the abbot went on. "She gets the food ready for Jesus's visit. We all know Marthas. They do not relax."

He paused. Was it a joke he intended? The Scottish stress on the *a* in *relax* resonated.

"While Mary, what does she do? She sits at Jesus's feet. She listens. She is seemingly doing nothing. Or let's put it this way: she does nothing *but* relax.

"People say *we* do nothing but relax. We contemplatives. Others act. Others work. We do not. So it would be easy for us to take Jesus's answer to Martha's complaint—'Martha, Martha, thou art troubled about many things'—as an excuse for our soft lives. We could call it 'the better part,' as Jesus does. Mary has chosen 'the good part.' To sit. To relax. To simply listen."

Joan began to wish it was over, so that she could look at her family. But to glance away from full attention to Father Alfred would be considered a fault.

"We must not take it for granted, any of us, that ours is 'the better part.' A contemplative dies when he or she begins to feel the choice is finished, and the choice to listen, to pray, is 'better' than to put those impulses into action. Am I disagreeing with Jesus? Someone needs to prepare the food. Someone needs to sweep the floor. Others of us need to sit at the feet of our Lord and simply listen. Which are we called to do? Which is Sister Gertrude called to do? Every day she will have to ask that question. Has God chosen her, or has she chosen God? Chosen laziness? Chosen ease?" A silence. It went on too long. He was clever that way, to make them pay attention by giving no sense of a continuing thread. Still, the question he'd asked pierced her. What *had* she chosen? It was terrible to feel that the answers weren't available to her, even today. Was she to go on asking about the rightness of this choice all the way to death? "We are here for a simple reason today: to celebrate the fact that after six years of preparation, Gertrude is choosing to take Mary's part. But tomorrow morning, after we've eaten the cake and said our goodbyes, she will have to get up, won't she? She will have to ask herself, Do I want to take Mary's part again? Not because it is the 'better' part, but because it is *her* part."

Father Alfred pulled at the back of his robe, as if to release it from where it had been trapped between his buttocks, unapologetic, as always, about his body. Joan had a moment of embarrassment—would her family see what a coarse life this was?

"At the end of our lives, we might be able to say which is the better part. That is Jesus's perspective. The end-of-life judgment. But we are not gifted with that. We have only our everyday perceptions, informed by faith, to go by. We have to choose, without the comfort of absolute certainty, to be lazy. To be relaxed. To do seemingly nothing. Is this what we are called to do? That is the question that is never quite answered by any of us. We rest in God's words, and we find challenge in God's words."

Joan knew he was finished before anyone else did. His face took on a practiced pose of distance and scrutiny, as though surprised by something he'd just said. Everyone was standing for the invocation. Something was troubling Joan about his last words, though she had no time to seize on what it was. Things were moving too quickly now.

"Sister Gertrude Palumbo, the Lord calls you to follow him."

It was her moment to stand, to face the abbot. "Lord, you have called me, here I am," Joan found herself saying, perhaps a bit too low.

The mother prioress stood, moved out of the choir, came before Joan. Her cheeks were bright, as if she were suppressing a smile. It came as a relief after Father Alfred's implied suggestion of her unworthiness, and Joan smiled back, but Anselm checked her. Joan thought, This is the mother I have always wanted. To be a young girl crossing the street with such a mother would have been to know safety and certainty beyond dreams. She knows the world; she understands it. The brief checking had been to say, Of course we both want to smile. This is joyous. But the time has not yet come.

"Dear Sister," Anselm said. "In baptism you have already died to sin and have been set aside for God's service. Are you now resolved to unite yourself more closely to God by the bond of monastic profession?"

What was the look in Anselm's eyes? As though she didn't know her, as though she were a stranger.

"I am," Joan remembered to say. But her eyes, she felt, were still begging for something. The old recognition. Anselm! Look! It is me, Joan.

Then the bishop stood. His voice was curiously remote; they all had to lean forward to hear it.

"Let us now ask God our Father to pour out His blessings upon the whole Church and upon our sister here, whom He has called to follow in the footsteps of Christ. May the blessed Virgin Mary and all the saints intercede for us."

It was Joan's moment to prostrate herself. She lay on the cold tiles, her face against them, so that she picked up the smell of disinfectant. Someone had gone to the trouble of cleaning this floor, anticipating this moment of intimacy, cheek on tile. (Which of her fellow sisters, she wondered, had been called upon to be a Martha?) I could stay here forever, Joan thought. How much better to turn away from the others, to close her eyes. She heard the saints' names being recited in Latin: *"Joannes Baptista, Joannes, Maria Magdelena, Maria, et Martha."* It ought to have been a comfort. She felt, instead, her distance from them. She was too much with her family now, too much with them watching, feeling their thoughts: This is Joan, after all, they would be thinking, not one of the saints. This is Joan, who used to hide in her room after school, who used to peek out the window at Jack mowing the lawn with his shirt off. Joan, whose terror of the world drove her here—not God's call, but fear. They would not be aware, none of her letters would quite have indicated that she had grown, or rather that something had grown within her.

What was it Father Alfred had suggested? Every day to make the decision all over again. She would not think of that. She would think only of what it might be like to be alone tonight in her cell, away from the names of the saints, the implied comparisons that must leave her wanting. Alone in her cell, she would be free to become what she was— simply a woman conducting her life in a way that made sense. Was that not enough? *"Athanasius. Basilius. Cyrille."* Perhaps Julian would come in, they would speak, laugh, make fun of the bishop and the terrible Father Burgoyne. Then she would be invited back to recreation. The movies and the shared stories she'd been denied during the last five days of solitude. She thought of the Virgin traipsing across the hills to visit her cousin directly after the appearance of the angel with his terrible announcement. The Virgin's search for company, for simple confession: I have come across the hills because I don't want to have this baby, Mary might have found a way of saying. Though I know I must. (Would we have loved her any less for having and overcoming doubts?)

Then, when all the names had been recited, came the *"Libera nos, Domine.*" Deliver us, O Lord. "*Ab omni peccato. A morte perpetua. Per incarnationem tuam.*"

The bishop spoke again; then she was to rise. The moment had come. Her Solemn Profession. All that had come before, prologue. She felt this, felt its importance as she had not expected to, anticipating an anticlimax within the ceremony. Everyone else was sitting.

"Are you resolved to prefer nothing to the love of Christ, to commit yourself to him with a free and joyful heart, and to promise stability in this monastery?"

She reckoned there was no great sin in a moment's hesitation after the bishop's question. In a wedding, wasn't there a moment when the congregation was asked if anyone might show cause why the ceremony should not go on? A voice might rise now from the assembled. One of the nuns, perhaps. She's really not . . . Joan heard the dryness in the imagined nun's voice. Not what? Not ready? A tiny smile came to her lips. At which point she imagined Angel bursting in in his work clothes, that look on his face, the ruddiness our Lord noted in David, the youngest of Jesse's sons, the chosen one. She wants to live a little bit, Angel would say. Joan's smile grew slightly wider. This was surprisingly easy. What she felt was the presence of forgiveness.

"I am," she said.

"Are you resolved to commit yourself to the unremitting search for God in the monastic life, according to the Rule of our Holy Father Benedict?"

"I am."

"Are you resolved to live under obedience, following Christ, who came in obedience to his father's will?"

No, I will continue to find ways to disobey, and hide the fact. I will continue to walk into the woods. Perhaps Angel will continue to meet me. Occasionally I will masturbate.

The voices in her head were not difficult to push away. She knew they were real. But like the words *born to fuck* that had risen at her sight of Angel on the road, they seemed to come from another place, real and yet, at this moment, remote.

The great surprise was to find herself facing her fellow nuns, the monks, Father Alfred, the bishop, Father Burgoyne, and to appreciate that they were all, most likely, more or less like her. The whole range of sin seemed no more than a mongrel dog mucking about in the corners of the church, obedient though always on the lookout for a stray scrap of meat. What Father Alfred said had only begun to make sense. To every day agree to try to do it again.

The mother prioress seemed to be looking at her that way. *You see what I have been trying to tell you, Joan.* She saw them all in their ordinariness: the cup of water and eyeglasses on the bishop's night table, the soiled socks Father Burgoyne might drop in the evening, with distaste, into the rectory hamper. The solitariness of each body pulling up its night covers. *We agree to one thing or another, one view of the world or another, every day. And some of us are seduced by a set of beautiful questions that go by the name of religion.*

Joan read her profession chart aloud, took it to the altar, and signed it. It was then that she allowed herself to scour the room, to seek out her family.

But she did not really get a good look at them until later, during the party. It had all been a blur until then. Angel, of course, had not come. The cake was orange, with bits of fruit inside, its frosting a pale orange as well. There were bottles of seltzer and ginger ale tinged pink. Small sandwiches. Everyone's voices, the nuns' especially, a little higher than usual.

The bishop and Father Burgoyne left early, taking a large chunk of cake with them to eat in the car. ("A little *too* large," Julian commented.) Everything had gone according to the protocol, and there was relief.

Only then could she really look.

Her parents were both fifty-seven. They were aging as she supposed parents must, though there was still something touching, not to say disturbing, in the evidence of it. Gray hair was to be expected, though her father's was still mostly black. Hardest to take were the signs— existing in an aura they carried—of the two of them receding. The vitality she remembered—a battle the two of them seemed always to be waging—had retreated.

Her father, she knew, had always been disappointed in her choice. The smile he wore at the party did not fool her. He had not expected his life with his little girl to end in a room full of giddy nuns, with an orange cake and sandwiches consisting of a single slice of ham. He refrained from hugging her too hard. He wore the look he had worn for a good many years now, a look sculpted in an almost physical way by a failure not of material success, but of some other kind he had anticipated and been denied. In Norumbega, she remembered, he could not look at a tree, a pond, or an open space without envisioning something of his own he believed ought to be part of the scene, something that involved him or his children. He chatted and joked with the two aunts who had come, Betty and Josie. But Joan had the sense that he gave his deepest attention to the girl, Jack's girlfriend.

He turned to Joan at one point. "A beautiful day," he said.

The formality behind it. She thought how difficult it must be for a certain kind of man to grow old, to endure the mild, de-energizing bloat, to exist within a body larger and more tired than he was used to. He kissed her. She remembered the nights of TV, the mornings they'd driven to church together. She could not avoid the sense that in their time together they had missed an opportunity with each other, assuming that a moment would come.

It was her mother who kept trying to supply the missing ingredient of pride. "Oh, we're so thrilled. Your father is thrilled." Afterward she took Joan's hand and squeezed it. The squeeze was meant to function as the stress in a sentence or the exclamation point after it, the bit of grammatical legerdemain meant to give a false declaration more credence. In her mother's face, at the same time, was a calling back to some intimacy, a facet of the past Joan would somehow have to tell her mother she had moved decisively past.

Her mother's face was framed now in a sharply cut hairdo that was more deeply tinged with gray than her father's was. Her hair was thinning, Joan could not help but notice. There was, too, a more pronounced twist to the nose, a more dramatic angle to the jaw. Her skin looked thin as well, with patches of red near the bones. Whatever did she do with her days now? "I thought, when I brought her to you," her mother said in conversation with Anselm, "that you'd never take her." Anselm smiled, though she seemed to miss altogether the warmth asked for and the conspiratorial joke implied.

A few moments later her mother seemed lost. The nuns and monks engaged in their mild, sexless flirtations with one another. Jack was talking to Brother Philip, the two of them looking as if they might be comparing assessments of ballplayers, though Joan could see the way Brother Philip's gaze ranged all over Jack's face. She remembered her mother, who looked suddenly tired.

Joan touched her hand. "Are you all right?"

"Of course. Overwhelmed. A little. It *is* like a wedding, isn't it?"

164

"I told you that." Joan was trying to guess what the woman required now. She had not expected to feel quite this distance. "Would you like to see my room? I have permission to show you."

"Oh. Of course."

She took her mother's hand and led her down the hallway to her simple cell. The bed. The prie-dieu. The desk. The crucifixion on one wall and the Coptic Virgin on the other.

"Oh, my," her mother said. "Such starkness."

It was not a word Joan expected her mother to use.

"But very quiet, I imagine."

"Very."

Stella sat on the bed. "Sit with me."

"Are you all right?"

"I'm fine. What do you do with the quiet?" her mother asked.

"Pray. Sit. Read. There are lots of activities."

What do you do with *your* quiet? was not a question she could ask her mother.

"And you're happy?"

Joan did not feel she had to answer, though she smiled.

Stella's own smile had grown rigid, as though she'd come to the end of her questions and did not know what else to do with her face. What neither of them could quite say was that neither of them was who she'd once been. Stella's long-ago wish to have Joan out of the house, out from underfoot—the result of her late and difficult enrapturement with Jack—had given way, after both her children had left, to inexpressible loss. They had been companions without ever giving each other the name. They had not had to say, We understand each other, because the understandings had gone deep. Stella could not accept at first why visits were so limited, but once she had, she'd been able to move into the quiet, firmly boundaried life she shared with Richie. Gardening and light. Books. There was the new information she'd recently received and now carried with her, the new physical struggle to contend with, which she had kept secret from her children. Still, she had her quiet pleasures. The garden at six o'clock. It could not be called a tragedy, her life. But in this room she felt how much she'd had to close her eyes and mind against the limits of being without a daughter. She was certain the next time she saw a mother and daughter together—in a store, on the street—she would find it unbearable. Sometimes she caught herself, as she drank coffee in one of the little malls that had grown so prominent in the towns close to Boston, thinking, How can I bear such loneliness? But she could. It was a fact.

All of this was clear enough—at least in its outlines—to Joan as she sat beside her mother. Yet she also understood, as she took her mother's hand, how essential it had been for her to go away, to come precisely here, to have endured the solitude she endured. She'd never have left her room otherwise. She never would have been able to bear her mother's sadness, or grown beyond the vision that had afflicted her nearly twenty years before, the little-girl vision that had determined everything.

"That's Jack. Do you hear him?" Stella asked, her hand stiffening, excitement or nervousness or both.

Jack had been guided to Joan's cell by Sister Clare, who disappeared after checking with Joan. He appeared in the doorway, his black hair long in the back, curly, his face thicker, fleshier. Something always challenging in that look of his.

"So this is it? The pad?" he asked.

"Yes," Joan answered. "This is the pad." She smiled to let him know that no joke was beyond her.

It did not seem to bother him, the degree of exposure that his letters had created, the way, looking at him, she was able to know so many of his secrets. He walked slowly to the window, looked outside.

"Nice view."

Stella and Joan both gazed at him. Jack at twenty-six, his clothes not very good ones, still without a college education or even the semblance of a career. He had moved to Boston, but that was really all Joan knew. He worked in a restaurant. He had gone to Boston because the girl was there. She understood that. And that he wanted to be perceived as consumed by love, driven by love as other men were by ambition. They both looked at him, however, as though still expecting him to deliver up some old, promising part of himself.

"Christina looks lovely," Joan said.

"Yeah." His smile was wide, transforming his face, briefly, into something younger.

Stella scratched her knee.

"We're about to be engaged," Jack said.

Stella said, "We'll have two weddings." She took Joan's hand, but there was something off not only in what she said but in how she said it.

166

"First she's got to say yes," Jack said.

"Oh, she'll say yes," Stella said.

Jack turned away, slightly embarrassed.

Before they each quite knew it, Stella left the room, saying, "You two will want to talk," and they were alone.

"Does she seem all right?" Jack asked.

"I don't know. I haven't seen her in so long."

"Different? Does she seem different?"

"This can't be easy," Joan said. Then added, "This day."

"Yeah. But sometimes I think something's going on with her that she's not telling us about."

Joan was still thinking about what her mother had said to Jack about his proposal, not the words, but the tone of it. Stella might have been wishing her way into a good outcome that did not seem as evident to Joan. Christina had seemed aloof today, not deeply connected to Jack.

"You'll be the one to make her a grandmother," Joan said, kindly.

Jack nodded, as if the prospect before him—engagement, marriage, fatherhood—were briefly overwhelming, and she felt for him. It would not go well. Where had the certainty of such a thought come from? He sat on Joan's desk chair, facing her, leaning forward, elbows on his knees, hands clasped. But he said nothing.

It had always been an amazement to her, what they were capable of not saying. Had those long-ago days never happened, those days when he'd insisted she know everything about the corporeal world? About his body?

"You okay?" he asked.

"Yes."

"You good?"

"Yes. Very good."

"You're a nun."

She smiled. It was a sweet thing to say. Then he did something surprising. He knelt before her. She was afraid—then not afraid—that he might be about to cry. But he was smiling, though not happily, as he lay his head in her lap. Resting there. As if that had always been what her body was for, his place of rest.

"This okay?" he asked.

She didn't answer, because she didn't know the answer. But he hadn't waited for it anyway.

He laid his head deeper in her lap. Oh, Jack, leave her now, she thought. It was another of those thoughts she could not control. But she need not speak it. Instead, she touched the hair on the back of his neck and smoothed it. When she made up her mind not to fight it, she allowed the surge of love for him to rise out of her.

Libera nos, Domine.

FOUR

THE HEART'S DESIRE TO BREAK

Fall 1997

1

Their ritual had been solidified by that point in the fall. On Monday mornings Richie would leave Stella at the entrance to Kingman-Deaconess, then park the car in the underground garage. She would wait for him in the lobby; then the two of them would navigate the system of hallways. At the beginning she had considered it a cruelty that on their way to the bank of elevators leading to the adult oncology floor, they had to pass the children's unit—the bald heads of waiting children, the brightly painted rooms full of toys and slides. Later she came to see the wisdom of the hospital's placement structure. What sixty-six-year-old woman on the way to her chemo treatment could feel sorry for herself after witnessing seven- and eight-year-olds sitting with their parents, the little hats on their scraped-raw heads?

The wait was never long. The nurses were mostly young, occasionally pregnant, always upbeat. The chair she was seated in for her treatment was comfortable, and there was TV for Richie to watch while he sat with her. She followed, from week to week, the marital plans of one nurse, the progress of another's toddler. The needle did not hurt going in. The worst she suffered was extreme tiredness. Such progress had been made, even in the nine years between her first onset and this, her second. While the drugs coursed through her, large windows let in a view of Boston, the heavily medicalized district where everyone, it seemed, was either sick or a healer.

Of course there was no hope for her. It was a given, at least in her mind. Nine years before, when the cancer had first announced itself and she'd endured the mastectomy, she had clung to every hopeful word. She'd been on the cusp of sixty then, a promising age for breast cancer. Her lymph nodes had not been affected. The biopsies had been botched, there was more cancer in her breast than they'd first surmised, but once the breast was gone, everyone—the surgeon, the oncologist, the plastic surgeon (she'd chosen a replacement, though she wondered afterward why)—had told her there was no reason to anticipate anything but a normal resumption of activity and, eventually, full healing.

And those had turned out not to be empty words. She had wanted to live. She had lived. There was the surprising vanity of the reconstructed breast, the wigs she had chosen to wear instead of the head scarves. Some part of her had wanted to hide her illness in front of her healthy sisters. She had known there'd be grandchildren, that intense thing to live for, and eventually there had been three, Jack and Christina's three. Richie had surprised her with a depth of support that manifested itself in his new quiet. He was a disappointed man, she knew that, but the fierceness with which he wanted not to lose her might have been enough, by itself, to keep her going.

When, nine years after that first cancer, she grew exhausted during a simple walk to the pizza parlor, when very basic things began to tire her out, she had gone in again for tests and been informed of the spread. Those were her sister Lucy's words—"the spread"—and she preferred them to the official word, *metastasized*. This time she found little use for the precise etymology of cancer—or words like *margins*, *in situ*. This time, at sixty-six, it was clear to her from the very beginning that she would die, and all the positive language in the world could not convince her otherwise. She had seen it in their eyes—those of the oncologist and his young Middle Eastern female assistant—a blankness, like a sheet covering their actual thoughts, evidence they could not suppress through the leverage of hopeful speech.

It was not that she was being a stoic. Far from it. She wept copiously when alone. It was terrifying, death, but she could not believe in any other outcome. There were certainties to life, instinct told you everything. Just as she had once known for certain that her first pregnancy would result in a boy. So she thought she'd better prepare.

In deference to this body knowledge, she elected this time to keep her wigs in the closet and to opt for a head scarf. Her sisters scoffed. Her sisters were luxurious women, full-breasted, grown stout and rich.

"We'll *buy* you the wigs," Betty said. "Those head scarves, they make you look like a Gypsy." The hospital had the wisdom to provide a store for head coverings right next to the infusion suite. She bought three in various shades, and stepping out while wearing one, stepping into the world surrounding Kingman-Deaconess, stopping at a Starbuck's with Richie for a fortifying post-chemo tea, the public gesture made her feel like a woman she'd never actually become in life: a realist, a starer of truth in the face, a woman of maturity and insight. No longer June Allyson, she thought, but Vanessa Redgrave. Sitting with Richie, blowing on her tea, she asked him, "Do you mind? Would you prefer a wig?"

The look he returned her was the one thing she could not bear.

He was, like her, sixty-six, recently retired, and it was, for him, perhaps the worst time this could have happened. There were no distractions. The pizza parlor, yes, but he'd hired a young man to run it five years before and there was only so much checking in he could do. He met a man from work sometimes—Ray Desmarais, another recent retiree. They pretended to play golf, a game Richie had never mastered or much liked. That was his outlet, the one friend who, she knew, was not really a friend.

What had become difficult for her was her need for solitude, and Richie's face, his waiting to be needed. He wanted to do for her, but all she wanted was to be left alone to sit in the garden on a warm autumn afternoon and read *Daniel Deronda*. Read Turgenev, *First Love*. Books she had come to love and to hide from everyone because they were not the books she was supposed to love. Her daughter-in-law, Christina, on her birthdays and at Christmas, gave her sophisticated contemporary romances in which tragedy was overcome and healing ensued. It was, Stella supposed, Christina's work that made her think these books were useful. Christina the therapist. Stella found them useless, especially now. She wanted the full story, the failure of healing, some fictional reenactment of the way life let things rip, obeyed no laws, demanded a full unfolding. She wanted books that did not feel safe.

Her deepest thought—it came to her in the garden, her refuge—was that even within her limits, she had not turned out to be the woman anyone following her life would have expected her to become. Mousy to begin with, less glamorous than her sisters, less hungry for romance, a woman who had never thought about sex. Who would ever have believed that she would become the woman who reached for Richie's penis some nights with such savagery, who'd grown to revere her son's body after turning away from it all the years when it had been hers to selfishly have? (Her deepest regret now—that she had once *had* him and had only wished for him to grow up.) Why did everything—every deep awareness—come too late to make a difference in a life? She would die at sixty-six or, if she was lucky, sixty-seven, of cancer that had metastasized and seemed to have gone nearly everywhere. At a certain point in the oncologist's office, during the listing of "the spread," she had stopped listening, had gazed instead into the large, deep eyes of Rhitu (the name on the young physician's assistant's nametag) and thought to herself, You are lovely. Tell me, what is your life? That was good, she supposed, that impulse.

In part because of this unwillingness to focus entirely on herself, there was one aspect of these ritualized days that might have gone by the wayside—everyone tried to talk her out of it—but that she insisted upon. On their way home from Kingman-Deaconess, she and Richie continued to stop at the day-care center in Watertown, where they would fetch Zoe—Jack and Christina's youngest—just as they'd always done. Zoe was two, far too young to be spending an entire day in day care, even a center as upscale as the one Christina had chosen. That *Boston* magazine had called it one of the five best in suburban Boston was supposed to be some kind of justification. With the two older children, Christina had taken large chunks of time off from work, then continued part-time for their first two years. But with Zoe she'd returned to work after two months and never looked back. Stella knew what that meant.

They had always taken Zoe for two hours in the afternoon, and cancer was no excuse to stop. Heartbreaking to find the children in rows at the tables, having their post-nap afternoon snack, their spines so abnormally straight you wanted to seize them all, lift them up, and hold them. Zoe had Jack's black hair, a tiny widow's peak, dark, embedded eyes. She would look up at Stella and Richie without surprise or particular relief and continue to sip from her cup, rocking slightly in recognition. They were all quiet on the ride to Norumbega, Route 2 opening into the country, the farm stands that reminded Stella of the trips they used to take in search of Thanksgiving turkeys.

Zoe was easy—quiet, mildly curious, willingly entertained. Richie held her in his lap and read her books while Stella went upstairs and lay down, attempting to rest from the sourceless fatigue that she sus-

174

pected was a result of parts of her body ceasing communication, like invaded territories losing their radio power. From their bed she could hear Richie downstairs. She wished he chose better books. He went to the big bookstores in the malls and came home with charmless, colorful ones. He seemed not to know the difference between a book like *The Runaway Bunny* and one like *Mr. Pumblechoke's Trip to the Moon*, which he was reading to Zoe now, and which sounded dreadful. Stella felt the urge to get up and tell him to find a better one, but she fought it. She needed rest. And Zoe was fine.

But the more difficult thing—the thing she considered as she faced the brilliant afternoon light of her window—was that the child was not fine. This gorgeous child had been abandoned by her mother. Anyone could see that, though Christina was the most competent of mothers—healthy, carefully prepared food, planned activities, the best day care. Who could fault her? What anyone with true insight could see was that Christina had gone away, had abandoned not only Zoe but Jack and the two older children. Went through her days alert and highly organized and deeply absent. You could feel the hollows in their house. You could, you could feel them, like the cold spots in lakes.

Don't think about it, she told herself. But what else was she to think about? Sleep would not come. Her exhaustion was too thick, too consuming. She listened to the sounds from below until they disappeared; then she decided she'd rested enough.

Richie had taken Zoe out to the backyard, was pushing her on the swings he'd put in when Jack and Christina's first daughter was born. It was a little cold for this, so Stella took Zoe inside and they played together for the last fifteen minutes, until Zoe was bundled back into her coat, strapped into the car seat in Richie's Volvo, and driven away.

This was the world Stella was being ushered out of. Her son's marriage heading downward, her daughter persisting in the religious life, three grandchildren, a husband who would descend into loneliness and abjection. None of it good (except, of course, the grandchildren), and if there was something she could do within this time she had left, something to magically make it all better—well, perhaps the suggestion would come. What she had now was this hour. It took Richie that long to get to Watertown and back—longer if there was traffic, even longer if he stopped and visited with Christina, which he liked to do. (That cold girl, with such power over men.) But now, this hour, she wrapped up tight. An Adirondack chair, stripped by time and weather of its old paint, had been placed under the grape arbor. The grape fronds were withered; a few unpicked grapes hung blackly. There were only wild aster and goldenrod and the long, stalky yellow flowers, weeds really, that endured into fall. The pleasures of a ruined garden. If Stella had ever written a book, she thought that should have been the title. The late birds came and perched, busy with fright. Such beauty here.

Daniel Deronda was about to meet the mother who had abandoned him. In an early scene in the novel, while Daniel is rowing on the Thames, George Eliot described Daniel with such erotic appreciation that Stella, reading it, had felt an accompanying thrill. Imagine giving away a boy like that! Imagine it!

Yet she had done the same thing, given Jack away early. All these years had been a long effort to meet him again. But had she? She and Jack, had they really met?

It was supposed to be enough—she had anticipated it would be enough, sufficient, a dark bliss—to have this solitude, combined with this light, to help her reach her end state. Already she had asked Richie to spread her ashes in this garden. "Stop," he had said. He wouldn't hear her. She would meld with what she loved. That was the perfect plan, philosophically, religiously, to end on: merge with the beloved thing, become inseparable from it. But at every juncture of her life, there had been a surprise, and there was one more, one last one, she suspected. It was not enough to meld with this garden. Death resisted that neatness. She experienced a gnawing, the sense of a thing still to be done, a task waiting for her. It unsettled her, in this, the time she most longed for, that she did not yet know what that last unspoken task was. She was waiting. This was her life now. She was waiting for a sign.

2

After her graduation from UMass in 1983, Christina moved to Boston with her boyfriend, a fellow graduate named Charles Binney. Her career goals were only then beginning to coalesce; she found a job at the desk of an emergency mental health services center and supplemented it with a second job behind the counter of a coffee bar on Newbury Street. She thought she wanted to work with adolescents, but was not quite ready for graduate school. The year in Boston was to be a time of respite and exploration.

Charles Binney's career goals were more clearly defined. He was interested in the theater, in acting and directing, and he wanted to audition at some of the theaters in Boston, get some professional experience under his belt before making an eventual move to New York. They lived together in an apartment near Kenmore Square. Their dates were to Fenway Park or to the American Repertory Theater in Cambridge; in summer they found a spot in front of the Esplanade for the Pops Fourth of July concert. Charles Binney was short, compact, athletic (he'd had to drop lacrosse at UMass in order to concentrate on theater), with a head of bushy red hair and a fringy beard. He'd played Horatio at UMass, and the tutor in *A Month in the Country*. In almost all ways, Christina considered him as being ahead of her: ahead of her sexually (more eager, though also more needy), ahead of her in ambition and career goals, ahead of her in his willingness to take on life. He was extremely kind, nurturing, physically gentle with her, and he loved to bring her things in bed—coffee, undercooked muffins he was learning to bake, the sports section of the *Globe*—but during their whole year together Christina could not lose the sense of being a secondary figure, a supporting player. It was not that she felt in danger of Charles Binney leaving her. It was only the belief she'd held since adolescence, that the true drama of her life was still waiting, she had yet to find it.

After the disappointment of Jack Palumbo the summer after high school, sex had been relatively easy for her. There had been decent boys at UMass, willing boys. She'd been afraid once of assault, of going to a party school and finding only savages, so it was a bit of a surprise to find boys who whimpered and could barely manage the act, boys who had to get drunk and then to be encouraged. The world turned out to be shier than she'd ever expected, and this gave her confidence. Her beauty did not isolate her from people at college as it had at Norumbega Regional; she allowed herself to fall into a style that was not the most flattering for her. She knew that, but it helped, socially, to affect anonymity. The visit Jack Palumbo had made to her toward the end of freshman year had been a blot, but then everything involving Jack Palumbo had been a kind of blot: the way weirdness had overtaken him during their summer together, the cocaine he'd wanted her to try on that one visit. The only indelible thing he'd left her with was the way he made her feel during their episode of sex. She tried to deny that, too, because it made no sense; it was too mixed up with shame to mean anything. Charles Binney did not make her feel quite

177

that way, but his neediness felt more real, more normal, more what you could expect from a man. She had always believed—it might have come to her through her mother's milk—that relations between the sexes ought to be tinged with a little disappointment.

The great, difficult surprise of her first year in Boston was that her father insisted on visiting her. Norbert was then in his late sixties. His hair, gone primarily white, he wore longer. He'd come to resemble a founding father—patrician, distinguished, a member of the Kennedys' inner circle or an emeritus from Harvard—in clothes he'd bought twenty and even thirty years before, faded blazers, white shirts made from good cloth that looked as if it might fray if you touched it. He arrived in his sporty green convertible, parked illegally. "Oh, they wouldn't give me a ticket," he said in his entitled manner and then threw the tickets away when they showed up under his wipers. He slept on their couch, and sometimes, on a weekend morning, Christina woke to find her father and Charles Binney seated at the small table at which they ate, arguing over a word in the *Globe* crossword puzzle. They bonded, her boyfriend and her father. ("He'll do," Norbert announced whenever Charles Binney said something of which he approved.) But when she came out of the bedroom to pour herself a cup of coffee, they both looked up at her with an expectation so enormous she could barely face it.

"I've stayed away too long," her father announced; they were sitting in the Public Garden, near the place where the swan boats made their turns. "I've been chasing *women*." She was afraid of the part of him that held back nothing. He touched her arm, her knee. How did you tell a father it was perfectly fine that he stay out of your life? "He just wants to connect," Charles Binney explained. "Let him."

Christina suspected it was otherwise: there was nowhere else for Norbert to go. For years he had lived in Norumbega, in a room in his sister's large house. Now the sister, widowed, wanted to downscale. Norbert's financial arrangements over the years had always been sketchy. "Expect nothing from him," her mother had always said. He'd sold his share in the pizza parlor, but where had the money gone? On the bench in the Public Garden, Christina studied his stained clothes, wondered how much longer they might last. Occasionally they saw, walking on one of the paths, a man who seemed to be the actual living model of which Norbert Oakes was the simulacrum—a distinguished man, an old professor or a minor statesman. Boston was riddled with them. Her father would sit up and endure the way the set of passing eyes took in at a glance Norbert's posture, clothes, shoes, coloring, everything about a man that told a stranger whether or not he was to be taken seriously. Somehow they always knew. In recognition of how he'd been taken in and dismissed, her father had an annoying but dependable way of clearing his throat.

At the end of that year, having been cast in only one play, Charles Binney decided he had to try New York. Christina had applied to and been accepted into a master's program for social work at Simmons. "Put it off a year." Charles Binney tried to convince her. "Come with me." It was not a matter of success or failure, of belief or unbelief. She'd always suspected that Charles Binney would do well in life; he was too uncomplicated for failure. It was that she did not want to tag along, to put off goals. They agreed to try to maintain a long-distance relationship, to ride the train between Boston and New York. She was loath to give up the comfort of Charles Binney's muscular, easily encouraged body, the rise and fall of his smooth back beside her in sleep. But she knew—had always known—that this was not enough. "Oh, it's a shame," her father said to her in the Public Garden, when she told him it was unlikely that she and Charles Binney would endure. "He's—*solid*," Norbert said, and punched the air.

Graduate school required that she share a smaller apartment, nearer the Fens. It was also a period of loneliness. Too many of the other girls in her program were dating seriously or else interested in women. There was sometimes Thai food on Friday nights with an intense, bookish group. She slipped away early. Saturday nights often found her alone at a foreign movie. She dated one boy, a Jewish boy, and cut it off when she realized that he was controlling in the extreme; if she gave him half a chance, he'd have eaten her alive.

She was visiting Norumbega—her mother—one weekend near the end of her first year in graduate school when she decided to walk to the pizza parlor to say hello to Richie. It had been years. She thought about Richie sometimes, their odd relationship, his old kindness. Jack was at a table, sitting with his father, the store becalmed on a Saturday afternoon. She had not expected to find him there, and grew self-conscious. She'd worn jeans and a T-shirt that had shrunk and hugged her breasts too tightly. She had not thought carefully enough about her appearance, or had done so only subconsciously (a part of her, she could not fully admit, had enjoyed Richie's obvious desire, and this was in the midst of her lonely period). She could not put her finger on the change in Jack. More flesh on his face? Longer hair? They both stood, father and son, gawky boys in her presence, ready to lay down coats across puddles to ease her passage. She and Jack had not seen each other since the one bad, memorable night.

He had been home, it turned out, for several months, washed up on the shore of Norumbega for what she suspected were complicated reasons. His face said it, his smile, the deep crevice that had appeared in the middle of his brow. But he was not ashamed. He used casual words to explain himself, as though they'd attained an intimacy that prevented bullshit. She liked this. In a sense, he had grown up. That was her intuition, though she did not want to push it. She waited in the weeks after: Would a letter arrive? She also understood—*feared*—that this was only a desire to relieve her own loneliness. His complexity was not to be trusted. Neither was her memory of the sex.

At Christmas he was still there. Her mother told her. Working at the pizza parlor. "The handsome ones, the high school stars, always end up working the ferries," her mother said, an allusion to the trips they made to the summer home on Isle au Haut. She thought of calling him, did not, drove by the pizza parlor one night, perhaps saw his profile inside behind the counter. It was a raw thing, this feeling for him, not to be taken seriously.

Over the winter break when she was again visiting, she found him at one of the long central tables in the library. He had books open in front of him and did not see her. She might have avoided him, instead approached. He was wearing a bulky gray sweater that needed attention. This is the way disaster begins, she remembered thinking. By being drawn, in bleak midwinter, to an old sweater. He looked up, closed the book he was reading. *The Avenue Bearing the Initial of Christ into the New World*, a title she didn't know. When he looked up at her, she understood in the first instant that they were each acknowledging something, like two old acquaintances realizing, late in life, what their full importance to each other has been.

"Here's how it happened," Jack was saying. He was sitting up in her bed while she lay beside him, his face turned away from her. The light from streetlamps penetrated Christina's room on Peterborough Street. They could hear her roommate puttering around in the kitchen even late on a Saturday night, annoyed that Christina had a man staying over yet again.

"Can she hear us?" Jack asked.

"I don't think so. The walls are thick."

"Then how come we can hear her?"

"Tell me how it happened," she said, and touched his back. They'd been together two months. Still, to do this felt enormous, dangerous, to touch a man's back who might answer not just with need but with a larger claiming. Always, since the day in the library, she felt she'd been out on a limb.

"I was sick one night, burning with fever," Jack said. She could see only the back of his head now, black hair falling to the bottom of his neck. "I'd been living with these two guys, the ones Elspeth set me up with, I don't know, a few months. It was always weird, but they never complained that I was there. I mean, I guess they liked it that I was there, in some strange way. And I was trying to get back with Elspeth, just because she was what I knew. I mean, it wasn't good, I knew that, but I thought at least she could help me stay connected to her father."

Christina nodded, though he couldn't see her, and kept her hand on his back.

"And there was one of them who was distinctly nicer to me than the other. John was his name. He owned the store. The other one, this guy Michael, he was always cooler to me. You know how gay guys can be, wearing a little smile, like they think they have your number. Well that was him, with that little smile.

"And this one night, it was the two of us, alone. I'm burning with fever."

"You said that."

"Did I? You know how you get when you're really young? You get these intense, wild—*fevers*. They just come up. The next day they're gone, but while they're on you, you feel like you're going to die. And I'm sweating like crazy. Michael is the only one home, so he looks in."

Jack took a moment to look out the dimly lit, light-charged window.

"And we've never, like, been all that friendly. But I can see he cares. That I'm sick. He looks at me. He doesn't even ask. He goes and wets down a towel. A hand towel. And he comes back and starts swabbing down my body. Cold water. Not really cold."

Again he stopped. From behind she could see him rubbing his nose.

181

"Just nice. Kind. But erotic, too. I mean, I knew that. A gay guy is swabbing down my body to bring down the fever. But you also can't pretend it's not erotic. I mean, the guy is loving me. And so I, you know, respond."

He turned his head slightly, as if checking on whether she was following, whether she understood. Maybe he sensed the change in her coming through her hand, still on his back but now stalled there.

"And I guess that's like an invitation. So he does—you know—he does what a gay guy would do."

It was the confessional part of him that was so strange, the way everything had to be told, every unflattering, true thing. And perhaps there was this innocence to him, too, that he always believed he'd be forgiven, come out at the end of it cleansed. He did not know the part of her that was stopped, like her hand, by these stories.

"I mean, you know what I'm talking about, don't you?"

"I think I do."

"That he blew me."

"Yes. I got that. You don't have to say it."

He moved right past her objection, like he didn't hear it.

"And there I am, dying of fever maybe. But this is kind of great. And afterward John comes home. His lover. And it's like, 'Jack's sick. I swabbed him down.' And they joke about that. I can hear them in the kitchen, eating Chinese food and joking about swabbing me down."

He lay back. He could tell only so much of this story before exhausting himself, covering his eyes with his hands, then turning to her—not to *her*, but to some part of her body, breasts or shoulders or the area just under the breasts where the rib cage meets the belly, nuzzling there, escaping into her. That intensity of his, like he still couldn't believe it, that he was in bed with Christina Thayer at last.

He had been marked, she knew that, by the deaths he'd endured—the doctor, Elspeth's father, and then this man Michael. But the exhaustion of his life was reenacted in his way of burrowing into her, in the middle of these stories, with just that one part of his body. Except it never felt that way, that it was only one part. With other men, yes, the boys at UMass, they made love with their penises like boys directing a toy remote control car from a position several feet away. But with Jack you felt the whole of him was going into you. It was different. That was as much as she could say.

182

And then, after making love, it was like he had refreshed himself. He asked her to stay awake.

"Jack, I'm tired."

"No. Let me tell more. Just a little more.

"He kept—I mean, it went on a few months. He'd come in when John was away. It became this weird, polite thing. He'd just have this smile. This weird little negotiation—like, *may I?*"

"Didn't you have anywhere to go?"

"Christ, I was lost. Just—lost."

It was a place she didn't want to go, this passage, this inevitable next passage.

"I mean, he was being kind. He was making me feel good about myself. I guess I needed somebody to do that. After the doctor died. After that whole thing. And John never knew. At least I thought John never knew. So that when he got sick—Michael—and I wanted to help, John looked at me, like, why aren't you running away from this?"

There was an abruptness—a wild, physical charge—to the way he got out of bed, went into the bathroom adjoining her room, poured himself a glass of water, stood over her, watching her without watching her. Are you with me? Are you still accepting me? Just barely, might have been the answer. But he needed to take it to that edge.

"He had AIDS," Christina said.

Jack sat down beside her.

"HIV, yes. It was before anybody knew much about it. HIV. Then AIDS."

"And you wanted to take care of him."

"Yes, I did. I wanted to be part of it. I thought I owed somebody something. I wanted to help keep somebody alive. But it was like their—love. Their love affair. It was the last thing they had to do together. They had to get him to die. They didn't really want *me*."

The way he lay beside her then was like a collapse.

"We can finish it some other time, Jack. You don't have to tell me the whole story tonight."

"No. I do. There's so much. I can't go around with all of this in me and, what are we supposed to do, go have a coffee somewhere? Go have a *date?*"

"Okay."

"So I go out and get a girlfriend. A job and a girlfriend. Just so I can

183

feel normal. But it's nothing. It's not anything that means anything to me. What means something is this guy dying."

"Jack?"

"Yes?"

"You had relations with him. And he had AIDS."

He grew very quiet beside her, his hand over his eyes.

"I'm fine. I've been tested. Like a million times."

"Yes, but doesn't it take time, sometimes, I mean, for it to show up?"

He didn't answer, because of course he didn't know. Loving him was like accepting a death sentence. She thought that sometimes when she was away from him, in class, at her field placement in the center for adolescents in Brighton, or even walking around Boston, just getting from place to place. The rest of life had an unreality to it. Jack was more real than the trolleys or the coffee bars or the bearded, thin men or the long-skirted women with bold, excitable faces who taught her classes. She was aware, even jealous, of the part of the world that was free from the consumption of loving Jack Palumbo. Other people could go out for pizza and laugh. They could watch television. It was like being sick and becoming aware of how thoughtlessly the healthy assume the normalcy of their state. Don't you people realize how lucky you are!

"I don't have AIDS," he said.

It hardly matters, she thought. You'll kill me anyway.

"Finally"—on the bed, resuming the story—"John let me help. Just do stuff. Cook for him. Michael wasn't eating much. I did their laundry. I did stuff. I felt useful. I stopped having a girlfriend, you know. I just wanted this pure time. I wondered if this was what Dr. Wooten meant. That this was what I was supposed to do. Find this good part of myself. Like the time when I was just in love with you. The beginning. When I was like a monk. When I first went to the city."

"You weren't in love with me."

She knew he wouldn't hear that. He had convinced himself of what was true.

"I wanted, just, like something pure. To do his death. To be useful. And then that happened."

"Okay."

"And I knew afterward that John knew. He knew everything."

She listened to him swallow.

"That was the crazy time. After. New York seemed crazy to me.

184

All these guys dying. Their friends, the ones who had helped out with Michael. What was I supposed to do? That's when I came home. I thought I wanted to go into a monastery. Like Joan. Just—escape. I wrote to her and she wrote me back. Just one word: *No*."

He laughed, not wholeheartedly. Christina tried to fall asleep then. If she fell asleep, she wouldn't hear anything more. Was this love? she wondered sometimes—this urge, in the middle of the day, to just *get* to him, to get to his body and to *him*, with all his difficulty, to cover herself in him? She thought it must be. Love. It was like nothing she'd ever felt before. Beside this, her time with Charles Binney was like child's play. But the difficulty of saying *yes, absolutely, love* was nearly always with her.

"Hey. You listening?"

"I'm tired."

"You want me to shut up?"

She turned back to him. He was so large a being she was afraid to touch him sometimes, as though to touch him was to ask for more than she could handle. But she did. Touched his nose, his chin, his eyes to close them. She wanted some kind of power in her powerlessness, if only to make him sleep. Could she do that? Could she have power enough over Jack Palumbo just to get him to sleep? She touched him below, too. He was as easy to rouse as Charles Binney had been. Then she climbed on top, thinking this would do it, one more time, their third that night, and he would sleep. But he kept his eyes open. He kept looking at her as she rode up and down, like: What are you doing? Not literally—he knew that much. But what are you *doing*? He was the first man she'd ever known who made you explore every impulse you had—not so much in words, there were no words to sex with Jack Palumbo—but in the way he stayed with you, made you go a little farther than you even thought you wanted to go. And she knew this would not get him to sleep. He was too alive in his exploration of her desire for him. He couldn't know enough about it.

When she finally collapsed on top of him, he turned her over and entered her from behind. The way he touched her ass before doing that was the most thrilling feeling she'd ever experienced, proprietary and tender and even, in its own inexplicable way, *fatherly*. But he hadn't been doing it very long before he stopped.

"Jesus, I'm tired," he said. "You don't really want me to be doing this anymore, do you?"

185

"No, it's fine."

"No. It's like you've had enough. I can feel that. It's all right. I don't need to come again."

But he lay there looking at her, clearing her hair away from her eyes. Her hair had grown damp.

"Christina."

"I would love to sleep."

"Am I hurting your sleep?"

"Yes."

"Go ahead. Sleep."

He put half his body on top of hers, as if to protect her from wolves.

"Go ahead," he said, and touched her face, covered it with his big hand. "Go ahead."

She tried hard. She went into thoughts of Norumbega, the strangeness of once having passed this man in the corridors of the high school and never seeing him, knowing him only by what others said about him, seeing him as large and cartoonish, like an oaf in a comic book. So much of life had been like that then. She had been climbing a long time into some semblance of a life, some skin that felt *vital*. This felt the closest she had ever come. But was it love? The question was tormenting because she knew something would come of this, of being with him.

And as on many other nights, the energy expended in his self-presentation finally knocked him out—he fell asleep first, and she watched him, his eyes closed, the passage of air through his nostrils, the movement of his lips. He will kill me, she thought. This man will kill me. Even that did not seem a good enough argument to leave.

They were married in late summer 1988. Twice she tried to escape, once very close to the wedding. He wanted it more than she did, as if something legal would cement things, make their union irrevocable. Neither of her parents approved. Norbert shook his head in a kind of mock despair. "After that other one, that very *good* one." Norbert's sister had by then moved out of the big house into a smaller one, taken her brother in again as boarder for what was meant to be a limited time. These were the days when Norbert began his long, surprising, and ultimately successful courtship of Christina's mother.

As for the mother, her only advice to Christina was, "Make sure you have something for yourself."

After two years working in the home for adolescents in Brighton, Christina completed her degree, was given a permanent job there, a large raise. This might have been the phase of her life where she branched out, explored Boston city life, ate in good restaurants, dated another kind of man, thought ambitiously. That imagined life—orderly, desirable— existed alongside the one she was living, with Jack working in restaurants, a waiter, bringing home sometimes two or three hundred dollars a night, money that dwarfed what she was earning. But a waiter. Before the marriage they rented half of a two-family house in Belmont. Jack planned their life for them in a way she tried to convince herself was not oppressive. The housing market was at its peak, but he thought it would drop soon, it would be a good time to buy. It was her reasonable mother speaking through her when the words rose inside: I do not want you to be losing your hair and still be driving into Boston in a pair of black pants and a white shirt to stand in front of tables and say, I'm Jack. I'll be your server. To be subsisting on tips. I do not want the threat of cocaine to hover over us both. It was the late eighties. The Boston restaurant scene, she knew very well, was a killing field of coked-up chefs and bartenders. She was alone until two in the morning on Friday and Saturday nights. Around the two-family house in their more modest section of Belmont, she spied on her neighbors, ambitious Bostonians, couples with babies and minivans, young lawyers, women who worked in finance. On Saturday nights she saw the lights in their windows, the cars arriving, the babysitters being ushered home.

When Norbert discovered her Friday and Saturday night solitude, he started visiting again, bringing Thai and Vietnamese food from restaurants in Cambridge, and videos he wanted to watch on their VCR. "Do you know, I've never seen *Gandhi*?" he said, as though this should explain his long visits. Gandhi was still cavorting with Margaret Bourke-White when Norbert fell asleep in the chair. Christina made up the couch for him. "Don't mind me," she heard her father say when Jack came home, and she tried to pretend she was asleep when he came into the bedroom and undressed. He smelled variously of Asiago cheese, coriander, and petite sirah. He also had a sixth sense as to her wakefulness, and she had to work hard to keep herself from making the low, groaning sounds she knew her father would hear. If Norbert expected a resumption of the Three Bears existence he'd shared with Christina and Charles Binney, he found Jack far less solicitous of him, and far more rude.

Still, Norbert came, on Saturday nights, with *Gandhi*, with *Terms of Endearment* ("Oh, this is wonderful," he said, "so tender," and then fell asleep before Debra Winger even died), with *Midnight Express* ("One thing I'm happy to say I've escaped in my life is homosexual rape!").

Christina's life was squeezed between the needs of adolescents she saw between eight and four, a father she saw for long stretches on Saturday nights, and a man who seemed to be ramming her into marriage the way he might have rammed a door open with a log. The image, she thought, was not inappropriate: he kept trying to rip her open sexually in a way she was growing tired of. She did not need so much, she had no wish to be explored so deeply. A few months before the wedding she told him she'd changed her mind.

"What, is it because I'm still a waiter?"

No, it wasn't, at least not entirely. But that became a convenient enough excuse. She moved in with her mother, into the big house in Norumbega, bought her own car. Her mother approved without saying so. Jack called incessantly, willing to make any compromise but threatening nothing. She noticed that. That he never said, I'll kill myself. Never said, You know how easy it is to score cocaine? Instead, through restaurant connections, he got a job as a drug rep, working for one of the large companies. "It's just like the restaurant business," he told her one night on the phone. "It's all about being sexy, and feeding people." He described the large spreads he and his partner brought in to medical practices on days when they were pitching a new product. He also described the receptionists, the nurses, how he knew he could sleep with any of them, but for only the second time in his life didn't want to. "I've taken a cut in pay in order to do this," he said, as though this, too, were an argument in his behalf.

What she convinced herself finally in deciding to marry Jack was that there was perhaps no permanence involved. Marriage might be a phase, something you went through in order to get to something else. That might be the way to deal with Jack. Her mother had never even bothered with the legality, had simply had her baby and proceeded. It might be like that. She needed, in any event, to keep alive the possibility of escape.

She was pregnant a year after the wedding, before she strictly wanted to be. They bought the house in Watertown. Jack took to being a drug rep, he was open about saying, not because he loved the work, but because it made marriage possible. If there was for her something tentative about the state, for him it was entirely consuming. He spent weekends painting their rooms. It was he who bought the pregnancy books, read them carefully, knew every step in the gestation process. "Fingernails this week!" It was he who wanted to take Christina on Saturday mornings to the paint store to look at samples. He was ready to dive into a world that seemed ready-made for them, the welter of early-nineties baby stores in suburban Boston, featuring Snuglis and jogging strollers, paraphernalia to baby-proof your house, car seats, and sun filters. All of it vaguely nauseated her, the bright commercial apparatus that was the opposite of the dream state she wanted increasingly to go into as the pregnancy dragged on.

Their neighborhood in Watertown had once been heavily Italian. From the window of her bedroom, as she sat, hands on her ripening mound, she could gaze out into the backyard gardens where Italian grandmothers in black dresses and dark hose staked tomatoes and dug into the caked soil with their bare hands. Women like that had never had to endure the vacuous language of the pregnancy books, the row after row of hanging mobiles in the Kids "R" Us Jack loved to visit. Sometimes when they passed a jogger, a guy pushing his baby in one of the jogger-friendly strollers, Jack lit up, said, "That's gonna be me!"

"You don't jog," Christina said, but he hardly heard her, awash as he was in a prefab image of himself.

She searched sometimes for the old, erratic side of him—the wildness, the huge, questing animal in him, the unstaunched need to reveal. Was it all eaten up now by the wish to be suburban? She did not know how to explore her resistance to this part of him—it was too new and thus still too confusing. She only knew it seemed to erase him for her.

Late in the pregnancy, there was a thing he liked to do. He'd purchased special oil at the Body Shop in Cambridge, and he rubbed her expanded belly with it. "This is to strengthen it. So the skin doesn't get tired. When you're pushing, I mean." The concentric circles he made loosened the juices in her vagina. She wanted him, and let him know. But he would go inside her this late only with his tongue. More worshipful than desirous, as if he were physically cowed by late pregnancy, made priestly by it. She missed something. "You can come inside," she said. "No, she doesn't want company," he would say, having already named the sex of the child. "She wants the Visitor," Christina said, emboldened, using one of the pet names she had once been so shy about using. The Lodger. The Man Who Came to Dinner (after an old movie they'd watched together on TV). The names became, for her, signposts to a lost wilderness, memories of a long trip they had once taken into a rank, green country she'd been frightened by but now wanted to revisit. Jack didn't appear to hear. It was as if he had closed a door on something, grown respectable. His hair was short, and he wore Ray-Bans as he got into the car every morning to go to the medical practices and announce, "Hey, we've got quesadillas today! Quesadillas and Prozac!" Secretly she wondered if he were himself taking the drug and not telling her.

When the baby was born, she took it out sometimes, in August, into the backyard, hoping to draw the attention of the Italian women. They regarded her from under a grape trellis that provided shade. To them, she was only one of the newcomers, the bland professionals who had come and moved into houses once occupied by garage mechanics and factory workers and had driven prices up and changed the neighborhood's character. The Italian women wore small, suspicious smiles. She would have liked to cross their gardens and offer to help them put up the tomatoes for the winter. Instead, she sat on her own backyard bench and exposed one of her breasts, placed her finger inside her baby's mouth, and encouraged her to open her lips and suck. The primitive action was the most pleasurable part of her day, but the Italian women, watching her, turned to one another and shook their heads, speaking disapprovingly in an island language that didn't carry.

A girl. "OmiGod," Jack had said in the delivery room, in blue scrubs. "Do you believe this? Do you see this?" Elisabetta, they called her, for no real reason. They liked the sound. Blond, like Christina. "She's you," Jack kept saying. "She's this incredible miniature you." The boy was like her, too, though less blond. Born two years later. Joe, they called him. Because every family, Jack insisted, should have a Joe. This began the blurred time of their lives. She could not recall what happened in October 1993, to pick a random date, if her life depended on it. Two babies in quick succession, work, Jack working on the house, breastfeeding, childhood illnesses, toilet training: she and Jack saw each other as figures passing. Their fights were wild, intense, she thought they might kill each other, then just as quickly over, the names they had called each other floating over the ceiling of their bedroom like the reflections of passing headlights while you wait for sleep. This was marriage with small children, she supposed, too many things packed into a closet, you opened the door and they came tumbling out, so you pressed your shoulder against the door to keep it closed, until the soreness was with you always.

Yet you endured. For two weeks in the summer she took the babies to stay with her mother on Isle au Haut. Jack joined them for one. The week without him always left her feeling confined. Her mother's gardening and rigid schedule and long morning swims, the old bathing caps—this all felt like the stranglehold of her childhood and youth, the excessive formality, the presence of a romantic mistake that had taken the form of Norbert Oakes. (Who visited, too, his clothes sometimes found lying around the summerhouse in strange places, though he never came when Jack was there.) When Jack arrived, she felt ravenous for him and quickly sated. After splurging on his body following the long wait, things felt flattened out; she quickly lost interest in him. She thought of herself as cold, crippled by an inability to accept life on the terms that everyone else seemed to accept: that it should be dull, that it should be routine. Did the fault lie in their language, the way Jack could not quite communicate his experience as a drug rep—the driving he did, the meetings at the home office, his encounters with doctors and clinicians—without making it all sound mundane? On the beach, he read thrillers. Once, she asked him about the book he'd been reading the day she'd approached him in the Norumbega library. *The Avenue Bearing the Initial of Christ into the New World.* What was it? "Poetry," he said. He was roughhousing with Joe, the naked little boy brown all over. Jack looked shy when he said the word, as if Christina were asking him to relive one of his old affairs, one of the dark ones, where he'd been asked to do things he was embarrassed to have done. "This guy Galway Kinnell. The poem's about living on Avenue C in New York." It was as if he were trying to iron out his old mystery, to divorce himself from the trials he'd endured, the ones that had drawn her to him when they met up again. It was then that she fully realized how much she wanted that part of him back.

The third baby was the mistake. Their sex came in storms, unexpected, occasionally unprepared for, and this third baby, another girl, was at last Jack's child. Dark, resembling him. He seemed to know it, held her to him in a way that was subtly different even from the loving ways he'd held the other two. He might have been saying *mine*. He

191

might have been saying, no matter what else you do to me, no matter what else happens in life, I have this.

Still, even after three, when she suggested the vasectomy, he looked at her in surprise. So, were they to have six, seven? Was that his plan? To become one of those huge families you occasionally saw in inexpensive restaurants, identical faces lined up on either side of the long tables, the children being urged to order low on the menu. Her mother once casually called her a "baby machine," and that had been a wound. It was perhaps for her mother, she thought sometimes, ashamed, that she did not take the customary time off from work after Zoe's birth, so that she might demonstrate a commitment to career—to a certain kind of life—that would win her approval. You could still be respectable with three small children, though just barely. But never (not, anyway, unless you were rich) with four.

Then, too, she had taken the new job before she'd known she was pregnant with Zoe. Working for a large practice in Newton, seeing adolescent boys and girls (eating disorders, sexual confusion) in a large brick building located between the new, upscale Highlands and Newton Center. She'd often felt helpless in the youth center in Brighton, the problems of her charges beyond the care of talk. In Newton she had an office with a framed Alice Neel print, walls painted beige and tangerine, a soft couch, and leather swivel chairs. She saw upscale adolescents who went to Newton South, to Buckingham Browne & Nichols. When the fetus inside her started to make its movements and bumping shifts, she felt exposed in front of her charges, the life she'd inadvertently put on display less orderly than theirs. Why should this have been important? Yet it was. The boys and girls who came into her office were headed to Harvard and Brown. Meanwhile, there was this small matter of the depression they'd come to her to talk about.

The boy, Adam Goldstein, came to her when Zoe was not yet one, when her breasts were still inappropriately leaking during her sessions, when she sometimes had to excuse herself and go into the bathroom and pump. Some noticed, but Adam Goldstein appeared not to. He came to her in a dark blue blazer, gray pants, a creased white shirt, green tie. His top button was always unbuttoned, and his shirt looked as if it had lived an active life at the Leeds School. She'd barely heard of the place—it appeared hidden, like Jane Eyre's first school, Lowood, somewhere in the thick woods of Waban. "They make us wear uniforms," Adam explained, gesturing to his formal dress, lifting up his tie and waving it, the first charming, self-deprecatory thing he did.

Adam's mother had made the initial call. Marcia Goldstein. She spoke as if Christina would understand everything, they could talk in code. "Hard to describe the problem, but he needs to talk to someone." Adam's mother's voice was modestly seductive; she worked in publishing. In subsequent calls to Marcia, having come to know Adam, Christina could picture the house, one of the mansions of Newton, four or five bedrooms, not all of them filled (Adam had only one brother). The father was a doctor. Ivy clung to the brick outer walls, the lawns manicured and still. A Dominican woman made a snack for Adam and his brother when they got home from the Leeds School. It was a dwelling calmed by assurances. The boys moved toward futures that had been settled long ago, like young princes in a country undergoing a long period of peace. Yet there was affection, too. It was a life, this imagined life, the Jewish life of Newton, Christina had come to revere. If she could not have back the consuming passion of her early years with Jack, there might at least have been this, this image of primal order.

Yet Adam had come to her with a problem and was at first hesitant to speak it.

"My mother talked to you?" he asked, lifting his chin, a motion only slightly defensive.

"Yes, she did."

"But she didn't, umm, I mean, tell you?"

He was sixteen. He had that hormonal charge that made one hand suddenly go up, his elbows splay out for no evident cause. Skinny, and sinewy with young muscle. No one could ever have called him handsome, which didn't rule out beauty. His hair was slightly darker than her son Joe's; it cascaded over his forehead in ringlets that clung to his forehead with sweat. She noticed his skin, its occasional eruptions, its purity. The slight crookedness of his nose.

"Why don't you tell me?"

He stared at her rug a long time, as if his first words would be hugely determinant.

"I run track—" he began.

He followed that utterance by doing something mildly violent to the rug with his foot.

"So there are girls." He looked up. "On the girls' team. We practice together. You know, we talk."

He looked at her, *into* her, as if to seek her understanding before he really said anything at all. Such moments, even for a veteran like Christina, were always affecting.

"We talk."

"Yes."

"And like, you know, they're *feminists*."

She could not avoid a small smile. The word had come to feel quaint.

"What?"

"Nothing. Go on."

"I mean, they *talk* like feminists. It's about, you know, like there's not supposed to be so much even, difference, between us. So you think. Umm—"

He appeared now to be hopping in the chair.

"Take your time."

"Okay."

With each look at her, the intensity with which he'd first regarded her was repeated. It was like someone might look at you if you were keeping them alive—like you might look at a stranger who had found you in a place of limited oxygen and created a pocket of air.

"They're big talkers."

"The feminists."

"Yeah. It's like they make you feel safe to say things."

"Did you say something to them, Adam, that you didn't want to?"

"What? *No*."

"Okay."

"Just. I mean, they make it seem they would *like* you."

He wanted to stop, she could see that. It was excruciating. In a way, the opposite of young Jack. Exposing each small thing made him want to cover the next layer.

"All right," she said.

He'd grown quiet, concentrated on something between them, biting his lower lip.

"Adam?"

"Yeah?"

"Sometimes, in sessions like these, a story comes out over time. It's not really essential that it come out all at once."

His face took on a confused slant.

"You have to learn—part of this process is learning to trust your therapist."

"Why wouldn't I trust you?" he asked.

The question was unnerving in its simplicity. As though the world to Adam Goldstein was a long, unbroken field—mother, father, brother, this new therapist—with only the troubling presence of feminist track-and-field stars marring the view.

"No. They act like they should like you. Because *I* try to be a feminist."

"How do you do that?"

"Well, I try and listen. And like, be *fair*." He swallowed, which seemed a kind of effort. "And you know, you don't— Like, be an asshole."

He glanced up. Was it okay to speak this way in this quiet, sleek office?

"You can say anything, Adam."

"Okay. So you know what I mean."

"I do. I think."

"The guys who just want to score with them. *Score*. That's a stupid word. But you know, you try not to be like them."

"Yes."

"I *try*."

"Well, that's a good thing."

"Is it? *No*. See, that's what's fucked-up. Because they're feminists, but then they *go* with those guys."

There was quiet in the room now because he'd said it, he'd said the thing, revealed the damning truth, but even having spoken it, it retained a residual motion, and he had to stand guard over it, make sure it remained quiescent and didn't try to escape.

She went along with this, quiet herself, and quietly entranced.

"Is that the problem, Adam?"

"Kind of." Or more or less, at least in Adam's view, the whole problem. And not an unusual one. Adam Goldstein had come to discuss the difficulty he had with schoolwork, with concentration, because of the feminist track stars who slept with crude and oafish boys while kind and thoughtful boys like Adam were left to pine in their rooms, wondering what was wrong with them. Yet there was something else, too, something it was not hard to dig for: Adam's wish to explore femaleness, the core of women, the mystery of female desire.

195

"Why do they want . . . I mean, why do they want—" he would ask, before shying away from the hugeness of the question.

Was she expected to explain? The question compelled her as well: how little sense any of women's choices made, including her own. There was no answer; it opened into a vast field, and her job was to calm him down, to convince him that if he waited and learned somehow to lessen his torment, all good things would come. Yet for her it was the question that was important, and that drew her toward him, that he should want so desperately to *know*.

She could watch, from her office after their sessions, Adam walking to the corner to wait for the light, to cross the street to wait for the bus that took him home. She could see the way he lifted his collar in the back, his gaze steady and internalized, his crooked-nosed profile, his greasy, beautiful hair, his gangliness. Something was evoked by him, she didn't at first understand. *Ask more*, she wanted to entice him in those sessions, even while assuring him that the female track stars were only going through a phase. Adam, you must endure. Once, she came upon him and a friend in the CVS across the street from her office. The client following Adam's appointment had had to cancel, so she had run over in her free hour to buy supplies. She heard and then saw him and a friend at the magazine rack, their ties severely loosened, their physical connection to each other, the way they couldn't help but push each other, the naturalness of young male contact. This was what he did when he was not presenting her with his torment. Pushed his friend. Opened magazines to look at pictures of girl celebrities. It seemed at once an offense—he was being untrue to his own pain (she'd convinced herself by then that he was truest, most real, when he was with her)—and an opening into splendor. Such lives these boys had. The waiting parents, the houses, the private schools that engulfed them, the certainties of places ready for them in the larger world. Would he one day simply stop looking, settle for accepting the female, as every other man—as Jack—seemed to do?

It was fall, part of the problem. Newton seemed to her russet, sleek in its autumnal tones, a carefully organized, cadenced city of deep meaning. She was in the long, boring stretch when Zoe was one, Joe four, Elisabetta six. Her life a tangled mass of appointments and pickups— Elisabetta in first grade, Joe in preschool, Zoe in day care. After-school activities for the older two. Swimming. Soccer. Then dinner. Baths. Bedtime. Nothing more existed between her and Jack. This was their careful period, when the unspoken directive each of them understood was to not get pregnant again. An hour of television, bed, his largeness that seemed too large, his back she did not want to touch as she lay beside him. The obsessiveness of their early days she had convinced herself had been not love, but erotic madness. A man like Jack could do that to you, fuck you into willing oblivion, but once you got used to that, what was it, really? There was a place, a further place, they had never managed to get to. This was her present conviction.

She was thirty-five years old. In the mirror, particularly in mid-afternoon, she saw herself becoming her mother. The way time was drawing her face down. Her hair less alive, her chin weakening, her once-perfect ass beginning to widen and elongate. Too late, she realized what a beauty she had been. She looked at old pictures. She had run from it, it had been terrifying to live inside a perfection she saw reflected in the eyes of others. Now it was going before she'd ever figured out a way to do anything with it. The high school years, when she'd sleepwalked, terrified; the college years, when she'd learned how to mask it in order to fit in; the Jack years, when she'd passively accepted worship, believing that to do so was a kind of life. Only here, listening to Adam, did she feel something else. Feel, intensely, what had *not* happened for her. How silly, to be feeling this in the presence of a sixteen-year-old boy.

His story, even his questions, were not, as it turned out, so tormenting as to justify a long treatment, yet he wanted to come to her, she knew that, he needed the fifty-minute talk even when it descended into chat. Occasionally they touched on sex. His masturbatory practices he would not reveal, but he let out an expression once. "MILF," he said, "she's a MILF." Then he blushed. What was a MILF? He smiled shyly. "Umm. Mothers I'd Like to Fuck." She laughed, relieving him of the burden of embarrassment. At the same time, she wondered if, for him, she fell into that category.

"How old are your kids?" he asked her once.

She had been taught to keep her private life unspoken. It was often too confusing for young clients, but there was something thrilling in watching Adam's face as he took in and tried to imagine her life. A small smile altered his features. Still, limits were observed. She would do nothing to disturb the still pool of his life, rippled at its edges by the tormenting currents. But had she failed him in some way, in not engaging him in the deeper questions?

197

The difficult day, the day she thought she would not be able to bear, came in the spring. She had been seeing him then for seven or eight months. Summer was going to form a natural break. Adam was going off to a math camp at Cornell; then the Goldstein family was heading west for a month. Already this presented difficulties for her, but today his face looked different, darker, vaguely chagrined.

"Is everything okay?"

"Sure."

He was not quite looking at her.

"Adam."

It took half a session to come out. One of the feminists, Kristy, not the one he liked the most, but one who would do nicely, had made an overture. At a party they had made out. Now there was the promise of more. Adam did not know what to do. Was not sure he was ready. Sex in his world was not the beery, near-anonymous late-night activity it had been for Christina Thayer at UMass, but a long-discussed, carefully planned thing. Of course. Why should his world in any way resemble hers?

"Do you think this is something you're ready for, Adam?"

"I've got to find out sometime."

It was as though he had come in prepared to make her an enemy.

"Adam."

"I think I should just do it."

He stood up ten minutes before the session was over, his face young, resistant, secretive, as if he must get away, Christina would hold him back. The sensitive part of him invested in her had become a foothold of concrete from which he wanted to break. It did not matter what these girls wanted; he would take what was given. She did not watch him go.

What appeared to her next—in his absence—shocked her. She had not been fully aware of the crater she'd been skirting in indulging this silly feeling for him, but now it opened before her. She stepped to the chair where Adam had sat, still warm, touched the place, the warm place, on her knees. This is madness, she thought. Then, Of course. Of course it's madness. But the thought that she might never see him again was unbearable. She imagined him sleeping with the girl. It was of course the right thing to do. Adam would become accommodated to the commonplaces of sex. But she could not sit here and hear about it. Nor would she be asked to. In the fall he would suggest to his mother that therapy was no longer really necessary. Christina went into the bathroom, sat in the dark. She had twenty minutes until her next client. But it was all she could do, when the time had passed, to emerge.

Everything changed after that. That was the phrase in her mind, though very little actually changed. But she considered it the turning point, the way she had moved to the still-warm chair, the force she had to use to hold herself back from burying her face in the fabric. She did not recognize the woman who had done that, and at the same time she recognized, within herself, no other woman. If at any moment Adam had stood, had approached, come to her, kissed her, she would have been defenseless.

Deep in the night, in the time afterward, listening to Jack's sleep sounds, she thought sometimes of the night he had approached her at the senior prom seventeen years before, the way he looked that night, the danger in him, and the arrogance. The strangeness of feeling that she'd been chosen above others, and then his question: "Why did you choose UMass? You could have gone anywhere." No one until then had ever peered in that far. She'd been thrilled by it; she'd had no idea yet of the depths that lay beyond that layer into which he intruded. And her answer, the only one she could have then given him? She'd been a girl, all those years ago, in search of the common, in revolt against her own physical specialness, which had announced itself in an unwanted beauty. Something had always frightened her. She thought then it must have something to do with sex, and when finally she'd overcome that, and more than overcome it in the feverish time with Jack, she thought she might at last become free of that unnamed, frightening thing in herself.

Jack breathed beside her now, these nights, and she tried to comprehend, as much as she could, her own story. There was no truly comprehending it, of course, she knew that much. No fully understanding why a life should take such a turn, why meaning should so suddenly and fully bleed out of things. Why, in the months after their last session, with Adam away at math camp, Adam in Glacier National Park with his parents and brother, Adam in the arms of the horrible feminist Kristy, his penis thrusting, his little gasps (she wanted to touch his back while that was happening, to soothe him), the explosive young man's orgasm he would have, why in those months the feeling that had started up in his immediate absence—the feeling of despising her own life—should not have abated, but grown. She fed her children.

Their silken hair in her hands while she brushed it felt like an unexpected, unnecessary inheritance, a surplus she did not know quite what to do with. She and Jack made love, and she wanted to cry because of the distance she felt even in the middle of it, even in the midst of her own arousal. She needed this but did not want to know him anymore. Jack still wanted to talk after sex. "This summer, when we go to Isle au Haut, I want to get a kayak. A family one, big enough, I mean—I can take Elisabetta out. Or you and me." She saw it, the sun-dappled water off the island, the water so dark as to look purple in the morning. She saw the way she would protect the children, strap them into life preservers, her carefulness, her good-motherness. You could do all this while feeling nothing. You could go through the motions faultlessly.

What she had feared all along, she thought now, was someone getting to her, making her feel what she felt now, this desolation. Jack had never done that, had perhaps, for all his vaunted prowess, never really been able to. He had taken her to a certain place and then stopped, brought down from some high former purpose, stunned into enchantment by a flat suburban life, placing her within it, pinning her there. Adam would do the same thing one day, once he got to know sex, would accept its domestication. Mystery would bleed out, as would depth, as would the desperate getting to know a woman.

Jack had been that once, that desperate, questing boy. He had wanted to consume her, though, without taking her any farther on the journey he had started that night at the prom. And yet what haunted her in the aftermath of Adam was her sighting of the place that quest might lead to: how far she might have been willing to go if Adam had made the first move. The memory terrified her. She might have set fire to everything—life, children, everything—out of an allegiance to an untapped source.

She did what she had to do. She covered it over. Nothing else to do. Smother it. And in the process, smother Jack as well. Cease to see him. Go through the motions. You teased it, didn't you? You teased the unfaced demon at the heart of your life; then it rose up and looked at you, so that you cowered. Who knew it was so ugly, so demanding? Go away. Go away.

That became her life in the months afterward, that going away. And in the meantime trying to understand how such a demon could have been brought to life by such an unlikely source, such an innocent. A sixteen-year-old boy, a Newton boy, a boy in a school uniform, a green tie.

3

Stella had decided to make the visit alone in late November. Close to Thanksgiving. Richie was worried about her driving to Lancaster by herself.

"What if you get sick while you're driving?"

I won't, she wanted to say; she instead touched him. Their intimacy had deepened over the course of this second onset. She was glad of that. The way she could touch him and say nothing, look into his eyes and nod. Our long journey is nearly over, my boy. We barely understood each other, but perhaps we understand each other now. Her marriage, she had come to believe, was like a long, convoluted Victorian novel full of setups and red herrings that fell into a still pool of meaning toward the end. Like *Our Mutual Friend*, she thought. But she could never say that; he wouldn't understand the reference.

She did not get sick on the drive, but then she'd known she wouldn't. Some part of her, she had come to feel, was able to track her own cancer. The feeling was certainly illusory, but at a certain level she trusted it. She had even come to suspect that at Kingman-Deaconess they were giving her not chemo, but a placebo, something to convince her they believed in the efficacy of treatment. Which they didn't. At her last session, Rhitu had sat across from her in the consulting room and said, "Dr. Kincaid won't be here today. He had a meeting at Brigham and Women's. We're conducting some joint tests." Of course he wasn't there. No need to be. She was to be one of the obvious casualties. In Rhitu's eyes kindness and mild boredom. "And how are you feeling, Mrs. Palumbo?"

She was shown to her cell in the guesthouse by the effete monk who made no small talk. In the stripped-down cell she knelt at the prie-dieu and attempted to pray. For what? She was still haunted by the sense of an unaccomplished task—the thing she knew she had to do before she died—and it occurred to her that on this visit it might have something to do with Joan, a way she might be able to help her daughter.

201

But did Joan need help? A cross with the hanging Christ was mounted above her bed. On the desk was a copy of Saint Benedict's Rule and a single stiff sheet with some words from Saint Romuald: "Sit in your cell as in paradise. Put the whole world behind you and forget it. Watch your thoughts like a good fisherman watching for fish." Outside her window, the gorgeous stripped trees, a late, smudgy sun. She would see Joan at the dinner hour, after the Vespers service.

Prayer would not come. She stared at the cross, hoping for illumination. So odd, an image that had been with her a lifetime, that naked man, the crown of thorns, the sinewy limbs, the head bowed to the left. You were born to it, but what was there to think about in confronting it? "You died, too," she said, just loud enough to hear herself but not loud enough for Brother Philip, somewhere outside the room, to hear. But why should she be embarrassed? "You died, too," she said louder, though now it sounded false.

She stood and approached the cross, touched the little statuette: brassy, like the baseball trophies Jack used to bring home from Little League. She felt the muscles in Christ's legs.

Joan came to her after the Vespers service. Stella had been too tired to attend.

"I'm with you until Compline," Joan said.

Stella was lying down.

"Oh, you're exhausted. I'll cook something."

"I hardly get hungry anymore," Stella said, and took her daughter's hand. "Though sometimes, you know what I get hungry for? The big, meaty sandwiches we used to eat in the Highlands. The meat my mother used to buy in the North End. Mortadella. Capricola. Do you remember that food?"

"No." Joan sat, pulled up the chair.

"Bulkie rolls. The kind they used to sell in the Italian markets."

"I remember those. We have nothing like that. I could make macaroni and cheese. That's my specialty."

"You've gotten prettier."

Joan seemed to blush. "I was an ugly child."

"Not ugly. Plain. You *made* yourself plain."

"Thank you for being honest."

"Well, you're pretty now. Something agrees with you."

Joan turned away for the first time, toward the darkness of the window. There was only a single lamp on, but it was enough for Stella to detect the presence of a secret her daughter was keeping from her.

"You have to eat, though, one way or the other," Joan said.

"So they tell me. What is it, dear?"

"What is what?"

Stella did not feel she had to force it. It would come on its own.

Joan reached forward and stroked her mother's brow.

During Compline, Stella's thoughts were distracted. The church was dark, her daughter indistinct, one of the black-suited nuns (which one?), their high voices lifted in chants that sounded monotonous, the monks on the other side of the church, chanting, baritone-deep, in reply. Joan had willingly gone into this world of rigor and anonymity, of dry religious repetition. Stella could never quite accept it, all these years later, the reality of Joan's decision. At dinner they'd talked of small things: Stella's treatments, the personalities of the other nuns, the sad story of one who had left, one who had been Joan's special friend. Whatever her own intention in coming here, Stella had to wonder at the numbness of feeling she always encountered.

At morning Mass, the abbot's homily began, "I read of a nun once who, when she entered the convent, looked around at the other nuns and remarked to herself, 'These are the chosen? I thought God would have better taste.'"

The nuns, listening, did not quite laugh. The most that could be said was that smiles emerged on their faces. Stella observed them rocking slightly forward.

"The notion that God has 'taste,'" the abbot said, and paused.

Stella had been here enough times to become familiar with this man's style, the mock disgust on his face, the exaggerated Scottishness, his habit of picking his nose while sitting on the altar during moments of abstraction.

"Imagine *strangers*," he said, suddenly louder, as if to force their attention. "Every day we meet strangers. And we ignore them, mostly. In daily life. They are not to our 'taste.' We don't know them. So we go about hoping we can spend our days with those we know, those we like, those who seem like us, who are up to our standards."

He paused again.

"But imagine for an instant the moment of our death. My own mother used to believe it happened in twos. We die in twos. I think

203

she may have been right. We travel to heaven in twos, and this person, this other person with whom we share the most profound *passage*, is a person we may well have ignored in life, passed by, not to our taste. Think of it. We meet such a person in heaven, and our eyes are opened. But here they are veiled. Why doesn't God have better taste? we ask."

The abbot stood there a moment, followed by a quiet stirring. The end of his brief homily. (What Bible passage was it a gloss on? The Good Samaritan? The woman at the well? Stella had been distracted, not paying careful enough attention.) It had great meaning for all the religious ringing the altar, but it left out the sparse congregation. Three women, including Stella, and a man, Hispanic, in workman's clothes.

After Mass, the Hispanic man waited outside the chapel with Stella. Who was he waiting for? Perhaps he'd come to do some repairs. A red truck was parked in the monastery drive.

Joan came to them. She and the man knew each other; each nodded to the other in coded silence. Stella noted his heavy thighs in dungarees, the way he shifted from one leg to the other.

"Angel, I'd like you to meet my mother."

The man turned to Stella, offering a hand that felt meaty and wounded, as if he'd caught it in a machine once and was still recovering. His eyelids lowered.

"Angel has been coming to Mass here," Joan said.

Stella did not know what to make of this. The man seemed embarrassed to have been singled out. There were other nuns passing out of the church, and there were indecipherable looks.

"On Sundays he brings his children."

Her daughter might as well have been revealing a course of study in hot-air ballooning, a hidden, utterly surprising hobby that had taken the shape of a man. Angel seemed relieved to step into his truck and incite its large noises.

In the silence afterward, Joan seemed to be taking in, in a delayed manner, the way the other nuns had looked at her.

"This is not approved of," Joan said.

"What isn't?"

"My evangelizing him. It's been going on for a while."

"He has children."

Joan again seemed to blush. Stella tried to look beyond this hint of trouble.

"He is married," Joan said, affecting cheer. "Two little boys."

They did not talk about it again until late afternoon. Their time together was limited, the lunch they shared the communal dinner of the nuns, all of them seated facing one another at a long table, the prioress at the head, the formality of her calling them to order by ringing a little bell.

In the late November afternoon Stella took a walk. She could not go far. To the main road and back, which was maybe a quarter of a mile. On her return she was overcome, unable to take another step. She sat under a large, leafless oak waiting for the resumption of breath. "Oh dear," she heard herself say aloud, surprised by an assault she was not prepared for. She would have to call Richie, he would have to come and get her. Clouds the color of old, unburnished silver coins filled the sky. There were the white open beaks of emptied milkweed, bittersweet. She waited for breath. It was the point at which it might happen at any time, she knew. Or it could take months. She felt as far from the insulated world of Kingman-Deaconess as she had ever felt, those rooms where the attached tubes, the drugs moving into human systems, the warm female chatter created the illusion that within such a space death stood not a chance. Here was the opposite. Milkweed and bittersweet and dark branches lifting leafless into the sky. *Strangers.* She remembered the priest half shouting. *"We die in twos."* Where, then, was her Other?

She was able finally to get up. On her way back to the guesthouse she encountered Joan, black-hooded, recognizable only by her step, come looking for her. She had to suppress the urge to tell Joan to take off that awful costume, forget the Gertrude business, be *Joan*. At the same time, she had been affected by sitting under the tree, the momentary separation from the living.

"I couldn't find you. I worried," Joan said.

"I tried to take a walk. I wasn't up to it."

She took Joan's hand, then her arm. She wanted something more than they had so far achieved. In the cell, Stella seated, Joan said she would make tea.

"No. Sit down," Stella said. "I want you to tell me about that man."

This time Joan did not blush, stared instead into her mother's eyes. Was this the undeterred, practical look one took on from staring into the face of God all day?

"I told you. His name is Angel. I met him years ago, before I was professed."

Was this a revelation? Had her virginal daughter known a man? Stella could not suppress a thrill at the thought.

"*No,*" Joan said, reading her thoughts, and smiled.

"No, what?"

"Not what you think." The smile lingered. "He was having an affair with a woman who lived in the house bordering our property."

Stella had to say nothing, merely wait.

"I was cheating on my obedience. Walking into the woods. He discovered me. We became friends by accident."

Still, Stella waited.

"You look so shocked."

"Because I am. I didn't know you were allowed men friends."

Joan leaned forward and took her mother's hand. "*Everything* is allowed."

"Surely not."

"If it's love. If it can be justified as an act of God's love."

Stella wanted to lie down now. Not from shock, simply fatigue.

"I'll make that tea."

"I don't want tea. I want to hear about this love life of yours."

"*Don't.* He went off and got married. Do you know there's a whole community of Latinos near here? In *this* part of Massachusetts? And they came here because of drugs?"

"Now I need to lie down."

"Oh, you're shocked. You think we know nothing of these things."

"I thought I'd sent my daughter to a convent. Now I find you're part of some police procedural."

"There were *gangs.* In Springfield. And so the ones who were in danger from the gangs had to move out here, do their drug selling here. They call it turf."

"Sister Al Capone." Stella was on the bed now.

"*Stop.*" Joan was laughing, the color in her face assuring Stella of something, though she couldn't be sure what.

"He told me all this. He wasn't part of the drug-selling crowd. But it was his family. His brother. His *sister.* They all moved out here."

"All right."

"Well, he tried to be the straight one, that's all. He got a job painting houses. But he became involved with this woman." Joan hesitated for the first time. She turned away, regarded Stella's window. This part of the story was difficult, apparently.

Allowing Joan her silence, Stella looked, too. The falling of light—the precise manner in which light fell here, like butter waxing between the trees—she had never seen replicated anywhere else.

"I don't get over this," Joan said more quietly.

"What?" Stella asked. She knew that what Joan was referring to was the light.

"There are many things wrong with this place. But God is here." She turned to her mother. "I'm sorry. That probably sounds very nun-like. Do you feel it?"

Stella glanced up at the tarnished statue of Christ over her bed.

"But it's not *him*, is it?" she said.

Joan looked, too. "Of course it is."

"Tell me more about this man."

"Where was I? He was having an affair with this woman. And I detected—I *saw* something when I met him. A struggle. He knew it was wrong."

The fading light was such that Stella could not quite make out her daughter's features.

"I asked him to come to church."

"And did he?" Stella touched the area around her hip and grimaced.

"Are you all right?"

"No, I'm not."

"What can I do?"

"Nothing."

They sat in silence.

"Can I lie beside you?"

"Yes. If I don't have to move."

Stella felt the heavy, starchy fabric of the habit against her. The silence felt complete.

"He didn't start coming until he had the children. He remembered that I'd invited him once. He brought them."

Stella could not hook up this statement with the earlier parts of the story. Something about drugs. Gangs. She was slipping. The light outside had turned grayer and more urgent.

"Take down that statue, would you, dear?" Stella asked.

"Why?"

"Please. Just do."

Joan did, and placed it on the desk.

"It's as though he won't let us enjoy this. Why the cross? If he's a god of love, why does he insist that we see him on the cross?"

Joan turned to her, a look of surprise.

"Now look, I'll tell you something because I *can*," Stella said. "I think it's that cross that kept me from really enjoying sex with your father."

Joan's look of surprise, turning now to delight, did not go away.

"Since you're a woman of the world, with drugs and married men on your register, I can say this."

"Of course you can." Joan touched her mother's face. "Did you not enjoy sex with Daddy?" she asked.

"I did. Very much. But not as much as I could have. And not without guilt, I'll say that. And maybe it's not all God's fault. I know that much."

Joan considered a moment. "Either way, it's not exactly a tragedy, is it?"

"No, it's not. But I still don't think I want to end this life staring at that particular image."

Stella felt herself drifting. She knew she'd been very articulate, without being certain where the energy for it had come from. It felt impossible now.

"The struggle," Joan was saying, though Stella could not be certain she'd heard this speech from its beginning, "is to see love in that image. Not denial."

Stella thought she just heard that, but she had to work to seize its meaning.

"To see love in it and to feel empowered by that love. That someone loved us that much. If he would give up his son for us, what wouldn't he do?"

A question came up for Stella, but she could not phrase it. It had something to do with Joan and the man. What was his name? Something Hispanic. The terrible thing was, you were in the middle of a conversation and you started to slip into a much deeper place of memory. The heaps of mortadella and capricola her mother had brought back from the North End. The still-warm bags of dough for pizza brought from Mazzola's bakery. And then a night when her sister Lucy had run home from a date, the man had been too forward, Lucy had used the word *rape*, but that had been too harsh, they all knew, it was just Lucy's dramatic way. Why was Stella going there, to the memory of food, of her sisters' early love lives, when her daughter was teaching her how to look at the crucifixion? That was it, that was the subject, and she smiled and wanted to say, it felt *urgent* to say, The crucifix doesn't matter. Something else matters.

"You look like you want to sleep. And I'm lecturing you."

"It's all right."

Joan stood. As Stella drifted, she thought she saw Joan holding up the crucified Christ, staring at it in a way that intrigued her, but Stella could not concentrate on it, because fatigue had grown too strong. The worst would be to step into a sleep from which you did not emerge. She wanted the chance to understand a little better. She reached out her arm to touch her daughter but saw that Joan was no longer there; she had placed the crucifix back on the desk so that Stella could see it in profile, the small, gold tortured body turned toward her. Frank, she suddenly remembered. The name of the man who had tried to force himself on her sister.

On the day Stella planned to leave, she'd packed early, though she decided to stay through lunch. She had put the crucifix back, her late resistance feeling silly. She could not look at it without thinking she had missed an opportunity for understanding. Joan had hinted at something profound, and she, Stella, had lapsed into trivialities.

The room, though. The room and the light, particularly late in the afternoon. It would almost be worthwhile to stay longer than she knew was wise simply in order to experience it again. All the prayer that went on here did something, filled up the air the way the history of cooking fills up a well-used kitchen. Stella received more from that residue of prayer than she got from the services, which seemed a form of spiritual masturbation. She was not afraid of thinking that. Why be afraid? To cower in unworthiness here, to shrink in the face of complexities that had no meaning for her seemed stupid, a repetition of the way she had lived so much of her life. The great mistake, she felt now, was to believe in authority, that others knew what they only pretended to know. If they only told you that when you were a child, you might be able to get on with it. To enjoy sex and mothering, and when a wind hit you that contained in it the essence of the spiritual—of God—you would know what that was and say *thank you* and then move on. That was all she could make out, but was there some way to convey it? To sit in a chair and look carefully at trees was worth a thousand Hail Marys. Then she had to laugh at herself. The wisdom of Stella Palumbo. No one would buy that book.

After Mass, Joan came to her, wanting to know why she hadn't been there.

"I don't like that Scottish priest. I think I've heard enough from him for one lifetime."

"All right." Joan sat.

"Do *you* like him?"

"Not much. No. That's the trial here. To not really like people and yet have your life bound up with them."

Joan's voice had an intriguing briskness, as if something had just happened to her.

"Was he there?"

"Who?"

"You know very well who. Your drug dealer boyfriend."

It had become their joke, containing no meanness.

"You know very well he's not a drug dealer."

"A fornicator, then."

"That he has been."

They were silent, and the silence seemed to contain some new possibility.

"I've never understood a bit why you came here," Stella said.

Joan's smiling face shifted just enough to allow that she'd heard the question without feeling compelled to answer.

"You could have had boyfriends at home."

"I don't have a boyfriend."

There was a bit of hardness there, Stella noticed, but went on. "You're thirty-two now. I could be dandling grandchildren on my knee."

"You've got Jack's. To dandle."

"Yes, I do. But not yours."

Something uncomfortable now lay between them.

"You know she's stopped loving him," Stella said.

Jack had stopped sending letters. Joan assumed he'd gone off into placid waters. She kept photos of his children on her desk. "He doesn't write to me anymore. I used to know everything about him."

Stella wanted to pursue a line of questioning, but she had reached a point in the illness where she had to make decisions. She never knew how much energy there really was; she could drift off at any moment. She had not come here to talk about Jack. "You didn't answer me," she said.

"What?"

"Why did you come here?"

"I had to come here. There was no life for me otherwise."

"But *here?*"

"It's not a decision you make yourself."

"Oh, stop."

"What?"

"Of course it is. There's something you're not telling me."

Staring at her mother, Joan could not go on. She thought of Julian, who had left. Cruelly scapegoated by the mother prioress, a victim of some depression that had left her unreachable. The ones who at first seemed strongest turned out not to be. Julian, who had been cowed by nothing. Joan's boon companion. But it was not that thought that stopped her from speaking. It was the memory of what had sent her here.

"You feel," she said, trying to put it as simply as possible, "the world as it is . . . something opens underneath it, and you *see* that. It's hard to put into words."

"Try, please."

"All right. You become aware of evil." The room could not help but become dark for a moment. Joan wished to be elsewhere, out of the conversation. Something in this conversation felt scouring. "Evil opens."

"I see."

"No. You probably don't."

"Evil opens. Yes, I can't say I understand that at all."

"Unless it happens to you, I think it's impossible to understand. But what comes into you, if you become open to it, is the opposite. Is— love."

Stella detected some strain now in Joan's face and voice.

"This—possibility—that if you just, stay out of life, devote yourself entirely to the pursuit of God, that you can love. And that seems, when the moment comes, when your call comes, something you're being invited by God—being *asked* by God to do."

"Stay out of life? How do you do that?"

Stella could feel it now, the onset of the large tiredness. "I have to lie down again. *Damn*," she said.

"It's all right."

"No, it isn't. We were talking. I want to know more about this."

On Joan's face was a look of disappointment mixed with relief.

"We'll talk more."

But though Stella was able to stay through lunch, she had determined, when Joan approached her afterward to continue the conversation, to conserve her strength.

"I think I need to leave now," she said. "I'm sorry."

"Of course. It's all right."

"Before I become too tired to make it home."

"I've been meaning to tell you. Mother Prioress has given me permission."

"For what?" Worried about fatigue, Stella had become snappish.

Joan retreated.

"To come and take care of you. When the time comes."

"I don't want that."

Again, Joan was forced to uncomfortably retreat.

"I don't want everyone's life disrupted. I don't. Here. Carry my suitcase out to the car for me. I want to be like a dog, go off and die somewhere. Quietly. In the bushes."

"Why?"

"Because it's embarrassing."

"No!"

"Oh, Joan, have you ever *seen* death? The angels do not come and lift you to heaven. It takes forever and it's disgusting."

Joan put the suitcase down. They were nearly at the car.

"I imagine my birth was disgusting," she said.

"I don't remember your birth. In those days they didn't want you to remember."

Stella had grown matter-of-fact. The walls were closing in a little. She had put off her leave-taking as much as possible and would need now the utmost concentration. Only in a remote corner of her mind was she aware that she would regret parting this way.

Joan placed the suitcase in the trunk. "You packed for a month."

"I'm sorry it's so heavy."

"I'll talk to Daddy. I can see you're not up to this. But I'm coming. When the time—"

Stella cut her off. "Fine."

In saying goodbye, Stella reached under the wimple and felt Joan's hair, black and thick. She held on. Can I have this back? The intimacy of your body? She saw something new. The essence of mothering lay in skin and hair and bodily fluids, in inseparability, the necessity of an intimacy that went so deep it could not be called by that name. I have seen your life from the very beginning. I have seen you when you first drew breath. After that, what needed to be said?

Ten miles into her journey home, she had to pull over at the side of the road. She retched into a stand of ragweed blowing in the November wind. She was sitting in the car, waiting for help, when a policeman stopped. It was midafternoon. She asked the policeman if he would please call her husband.

4

The bar was in Fieldston, a surprising place for such a run-down establishment. "Fieldston" had always suggested to Richie what "Norumbega" had once represented: a place of soft wool and suede arm patches, large, purebred dogs, and pipe smoke, where bankers walked on Sundays and rested on lichen-covered stone walls. But the downtown had a bowling alley, a closed theater, a doughnut shop, and this down-at-heels tavern where Ray Desmarais insisted they meet.

They had both retired from ComVac the same year, Richie's retirement long planned, that of the slightly younger Desmarais more sudden, even rushed. Over the years of their working together, their roles had shifted, if only slightly. Desmarais the conqueror, Richie the guy who had to live with a lesser share of the spoils and a plateaued career— had given way to a working relationship where Desmarais had come to respect Richie, even to rely on him.

"Now we're a couple of old farts in retirement," Desmarais had once memorably put it, "and let's face it, golf sucks."

They had a standing biweekly appointment to meet in this bar.

"How is she?" Desmarais always asked at the beginning of every session.

"She's okay. Doesn't complain."

Ray Desmarais's wife, Dee, was, on the other hand, gloriously alive, a great shopper and spender, deeply engaged with her daughters and grandchildren. "The parade" was how Desmarais described the mall-centered life he was excluded from.

These were the afternoons, then, that needed to be filled. Richie understood that Stella didn't always want him around. Though he occasionally tried to duck out on these meetings (they often left him depressed), today he had actually looked forward to this as a respite from loneliness. Stella had been away for two nights at the monastery.

"You ever notice," Ray was saying, "what's written in the bathrooms of these places?"

"I don't notice too much."

"Disgusting. The level of what's disgusting just keeps getting ratcheted up. You realize that?"

"I don't think about it."

"Well, think about it."

With certain men, you let them take the lead. The big talkers, the ones who needed you more than you needed them. You sat with them in a kind of willed absence.

"The tits get bigger, and the dicks . . . my God!"

"How's that?"

Ray Desmarais chuckled. "Go look."

"No thanks. I'd rather not."

"Let me ask you something. In the old days, when you were head of the department, you ever shack up with Dottie?"

Richie, made nervous by the question, moved his beer glass in a circle. Out of the corner of his eye he saw the big, insinuating smile on Desmarais's face.

"'Cause that was the rumor."

"Never."

"Never? No? Shit. 'Cause that was the rumor."

"We were close."

"Close." Desmarais laughed gently. "Close." He tapped his teeth together a couple of times. "Oh my God, I am heartily sorry," he said.

"For what?"

"For all the shit I ever pulled."

Richie paused a moment, trying to make a connection.

"You and . . . Connie Furlo?" He felt uncomfortable bringing up the sexual question. He'd never been that sort of man, an insinuator.

"Nah. That was the rumor?"

"I never heard a rumor."

"So why'd you bring it up?"

Richie shrugged. Let this be over. He was no master of bar conversations, of intimacies between men. Stella would be in his bed tonight. He would sleep. Sometimes he was capable of a sustained illusion: she would live forever, the cancer diagnosis was, if not quite a lie, something they were taking far too seriously.

"I tell you, I was always faithful to Dee," Ray Desmarais said. "Though offers came my way. As they always do. In the course of a life."

It was part of what Ray Desmarais wanted at these meetings, Richie supposed: to expound to a charitable, unthreatening listener, this late-life toting up of the score.

"And then there's that god-awful thing that happens when they don't want it anymore." Desmarais's gaze drifted off to a spot somewhere between their table and the bar. "That happen to Stella?"

No, it had not, Richie might have said, if he weren't embarrassed by the admission. He understood that Ray Desmarais was offering him that rare chance to compare sex lives, but he was afraid of what he might discover. He'd always been afraid that Stella was a little unusual in her ardor.

"You're not saying, so it must have happened. And then life becomes begging." Desmarais laughed, Richie thought, cruelly. "And no response, you know. *That's* no fun. You might as well be jerking off." Desmarais rubbed his hands over the empty table. "Which I don't mind admitting I resort to from time to time. Sixty-five. Is this some joke? Jerking off at sixty-five. And Jesus, it used to go all over the place, coming out of me. Now, hell, now . . ."

After his two hits of Scotch, Desmarais characteristically became quiet, almost melancholy, and it was at this potentially dangerous juncture that Richie usually sought his release. "Time to go," he would say. And Desmarais would come back with, "What's your hurry? Where we going? Empty house, that's all."

To consider how unwanted Ray Desmarais was in his own house only made Richie want to hasten his departure, because he did not feel that way about his own life. If he sensed, correctly, that Stella needed

215

time alone, he was still very much needed, to cook for her, to see to things, to be sure she didn't exhaust herself.

"Will you marry again, Rich?"

Something opened then—ripped open—that he did not want opened.

"I mean, you'll have to excuse me, if the worst happens."

It was said only to be polite. He knew what Ray Desmarais thought. The world—men like Ray Desmarais—had already buried her. It was odd the way he found himself detaching from such moments, receding, going into other moments, sometimes ones from the deep past. He was remembering coming home from Korea with gifts from Japan—pearls, kimonos, dishes—things that had become lost over time. He'd gone to Stella's house in the Highlands, that hothouse of fleshy Italian females. Her sisters had parted to reveal the small one, the one he loved. He'd opened the bag he brought to her. "From Japan," he said. She didn't know what to make of his gifts. He'd understood then that the great weight of his last two years, his time in the wet, foul-smelling country of Korea would have to recede, would have no bearing on the next thing he wanted to happen, which had all to do with her and her uncompre-hending beauty. Such moments felt more real than the moment he found himself in now, this meaningless moment in a bar in Fieldston.

"I never think about it."

He knew Desmarais was looking at him.

"Hell, Rich, you don't want to be alone."

"I'm not alone," Richie said, adamant but quiet. Then he looked at his watch.

"I should . . ."

"Oh sure, leave an old, lonely retiree to drink in solitude."

"No. Stella's been away. She might be getting back."

"What's wrong with you," Desmarais said flatly, as if to an object between them. "You don't see your opportunities."

Richie knew that the man was getting drunk, and wisdom would be to just get up and leave.

"You never think—some forty-eight-year-old? Fifty? Divorcée? Somebody who's old enough so, God forbid, you don't have to start a whole new family. But somebody"—Desmarais licked his lower lip, something that might have appeared a nakedly carnal demonstration of his intent but was in fact just another of the man's unwholesome tics—"who *wants* it once in a while?"

Desmarais smiled, having said it. "Oh Jesus, listen to me. Pathetic." He chuckled. "But let me tell you, from my point of view, that wouldn't be so bad. Fact is, I envy you."

"You envy me."

"Chance to start again."

Richie was about to get up, but Desmarais grabbed his arm.

"Aww, come on, don't. Don't call me an asshole. Don't think I'm just being an asshole. Rich. If we can't talk about this, what can we talk about?"

The man's face seemed empty of malice. They were quiet.

"Go ahead. Get the hell out of here. Jesus, no wonder we were able to bounce you out."

"What are you talking about?"

Desmarais looked as if he'd been waiting for this juncture, but maybe waiting so long that it no longer gave him any pleasure to bring it up.

"All those years ago. In seventy-one." He turned away, maybe slightly embarrassed.

"I know. Seventy-one. But what do you mean, bounced me out?"

Desmarais stared at the table, deciding.

"You think what me and Cedrone did was legit? All these years, you go on thinking that? We used to bowl, the two of us."

"Who?"

"Me and Cedrone."

"You bowled."

"Hatched a little plan. I convinced him you were weak."

Desmarais shook his head, turned his glass around on the table.

Richie supposed this would hurt later, when he let it, when he had time.

"Our plan," Desmarais went on. "To streamline production. You were the logical guy to take over. But we were bowling buddies." The man chuckled. "Fred and Barney." He looked up.

Richie saw something there. Some small plea for forgiveness. This was what had motivated the calls, the meetings in the bar.

"You told Cedrone I was weak."

"Convinced him. Yeah." Desmarais blinked, his old warrior's eyes stopped in hesitation.

"Okay, Ray. You fleeced me. Old news." But it wasn't. "I've got to get going."

Desmarais seemed unsatisfied when they stepped outside. The thick-necked former lineman blinked in the late-afternoon sun. His shirt seemed tight against his neck. He was looking at Richie, still waiting, asking silently, That's all you're going to say?

"If that movie theater was open, I'd go in and take in an afternoon movie," Ray said. "How bad is that?"

The marquee was blank; there was a sign for a weekend flea market hanging under it.

"You could go out to the mall, Ray. They've got afternoon movies there."

"Yeah, but it sucks. Driving there. Sitting with a bunch of women. You know how it is. And what are they showing? Mr. Magoo movies. Flubber movies."

Ray Desmarais looked at him, asking one more time for some unspoken thing. It had been a mistake to take on this man's life.

Still, that last image of Ray Desmarais on the sidewalk was with him on the ride home, haunting him as he tried to move past it, to distance himself from the revelation of how his old, beloved position at ComVac—cigarettes with Dottie, control of production—had been taken from him by sleight of hand. He'd always known, but at the same time hadn't known, and what it left him with now was a desire to get as far away from Fieldston, from the bar, the sidewalk, and to get to Stella. Her presence would make the emptiness go away. Let her be there.

But she was not there. The initial feeling of loneliness—a vivid warning of his future life—hit him as he stepped inside. Would it always be like this someday? The message light on the phone was blinking, and when he pressed it, he heard Stella's voice, her attempt to assert calm, giving him instructions as to exactly where on Route 2 he would find her. She was waiting with what she insisted was "a very nice policeman."

He had no way of contacting her, so he drove in a blind panic. It was twenty miles. How long ago had the message been left? Would she still be waiting now, in the near dark?

He saw the police car's lights flashing at the spot where she said she would be. When he made a U-turn and pulled up behind the police car, he thought he saw the back of Stella's head in the rear window.

The policeman, a husky young redhead, stepped out of the car. "Mr. Palumbo, I offered to take her to the station house. Where it would at least have been warm."

"I'm all right," he heard Stella say, her face small inside the policeman's car.

"Stella, why didn't you—"

She stepped out, which silenced him.

"My suitcase is in the trunk."

"Where's the car? Did you get into an accident?"

"Mr. Palumbo, I found your wife when I was driving by. She was sick. We had your car towed to the Texaco station in Fitchburg. Figured that would be the smart thing."

"She was sick?"

Stella stood beside him, head bowed. "I'm fine."

"She just couldn't drive anymore. And like I say, I wanted to take her in, but she asked if she could stay here. Fortunately, it's been a quiet afternoon."

It could break your heart, Richie thought, the generosity of young men like this who have as yet seen nothing, who do not venture from the places where they've grown up.

"Here." The policeman handed Richie a receipt with the name and phone number of the garage. "You can take your time picking it up. I've explained. There'll be no charge."

"Thank you."

It was cold, and cars passed occasionally. Stella's afternoon was inconceivable to him. The longer they stood here, the more embarrassed he felt in front of the policeman, for his abandoning Stella, for allowing her to be found in this vulnerable state.

In the car, Stella said, "We had a very nice talk. His wife just had a baby. A girl. He described the terrible birth. My God, the child nearly died. To think that still happens."

Her voice seemed to be tamping down on the chaos she'd just been through. Otherwise, they were quiet. The early November night still, the headlights on the other side of the road welcome.

"Tell me what happened."

"I misjudged."

"How?"

"Sometimes I think I'm a little more capable than I apparently am."

She held to a reasonableness that touched and annoyed him. He also resented the design of his Volvo, a car he had bought and paid too much for solely because it was the most popular car in Norumbega. The car had the same design most new cars did, separating the driver from the passenger. Once upon a time, in the old Chevys, he would have been able to reach over and draw her to him.

"How was Joan, Stella?"

"In love, I think."

"*What?*"

"I'll tell you later."

When they reached home, she went up to bed.

"You don't want to eat?"

She didn't answer. There was nothing for him to do downstairs. He was hungry, but he did not want to prepare anything just for himself, and to be separated from her now felt wrong. Her simple presence in the house satisfied some basic desire, but he did not want to be away from her, so he went upstairs.

He found her folding back the covers on the bed. He had caught her naked. She had her nightgown laid out on the bed but had not yet put it on. She glanced up at him. He eyed the manufactured breast, the one without a nipple. Her skin had provided the flesh for it, but it had always seemed false to him, not entirely hers. She saw him looking.

"Come lie with me," she said.

He did, fully clothed. There was light from a single lamp. He tensed up without knowing why as she snuggled against him.

"Tell me about your afternoon," he said.

"I don't want to," she said in a very low voice.

He wondered if she was still frightened. It had to be frightening. Her nose abutted his chin, grazed there. In all their married life, regardless of whatever emotion he had been feeling, certain intimacies had never failed to have a physiological effect. He stiffened mildly, nothing urgent, and was determined to ignore it.

"I had a very nice visit with Joan. But you should know she's in love with a Hispanic man out there."

"What?"

"Don't. I'm telling you things, but I don't want you to get upset."

Her hand touched his chest, rested there. Again he felt physically tense, though of course he hardened a little more.

"You tell me something like that and I'm not supposed to wonder?"

"We'll talk about it sometime. Though that's all it is. I think her days as a nun are numbered."

He swallowed. The news was not unwelcome, though the word *Hispanic* bothered him. Nearly thirty years in Norumbega, and his position still felt tentative enough that dragging in a "Hispanic" would mark him even more than opening a pizza parlor had.

"Richie?"

"What is it?"

"I miss her. I never realized how much I miss her."

There was a silence in which he allowed her time to simply feel what she was feeling. He could do nothing to make it better. He himself could not, would not, allow that lost paternal ache in himself to take over.

She looked up at him, her face simply there, wide open, a thing to be met, perhaps asking for a kiss. He kissed her and, finding her lips dry, reached over to the bedside table for the lip balm he knew she kept there. He applied it to her lips. The caretaking side of him gave him great comfort. She was still naked.

"Aren't you cold?"

"I am. Come under the covers with me."

It made sense to undress, though only down to his underclothes. She got under first, and watched him. He was half hard, pushing out against the cloth of his shorts, and she smiled in her private way, noticing it.

In spite of that, he was surprised, even a little startled, when she reached for it under the covers. That did the trick. He went all the way hard, though he still couldn't fully imagine they'd make love now, not after this afternoon of hers. He retained the belief that she was holding it appreciatively, for reassurance or comfort. She snuggled up and lifted her face. No, it was real. What she wanted was distinct.

He touched her hair, the sparseness of it that still struck him with a kind of wonder, that this could happen to a woman, she could lose the feminine privilege so easily. His hand lifted off her hair and sought her breast, but he decided not to go there. The false breast was the one that was readily available to him, and it brought up things he did not like to think about, and so his hand lowered, found a buttock. He wished for more flesh there. With mild panic he realized that each place he sought—hair, breast, ass—when it was reached, did something to soften him. His hardness, having peaked at her touch, was in retreat, and soon, he understood—it had happened once or twice lately, he'd had to excuse himself—it would evaporate altogether. But that must not happen today, not after the day she'd had, so he closed his eyes, and it was terrible, but as if he were dredging something usable from the muck of his own afternoon, he drew up an image of Dottie, himself

fucking Dottie, as he had done not in life but in the rumors Ray Desmarais had told him about, and though Dottie's body had never strongly
appealed to him, in his imagination now, here, it did. In his imagination
was another Richie Palumbo, not the one he'd stumbled into becoming,
but a harder and more ruthless version of himself, not "weak," but
strong, fucking Dottie over a desk. While rumors swirled. Then, when
that was finished (it was enough to allow him to penetrate Stella), a
worse fantasy, an old one, an ancient one, young Christina behind the
counter. Never could he allow himself to imagine doing it to his own
daughter-in-law, though he could not resist the memory of an afternoon
after Christina's second baby was born, visiting her in the hospital. It
was just the two of them, and he'd come in when Joe was suckling at
her breast. After the initial embarrassment she had decided it was all
right to show him, to display this. She must have been happy that day. A
baby boy at her breast. She'd wanted to show him, and the image (not
really erotic, but wonderful nonetheless) had lived with him forever.

Stella was moaning now, and that always helped. But he needed to
keep up with her, and in order to do that, he knew he needed to move
on from the Christina fantasy. The fantasy that came in its place, the
one that worked (though he hated that it worked), that took him all the
way to the end, involved him not at all. It was the image of Ray Desmarais fucking Connie Furlo. This never happened, Ray had insisted.
No matter. To think of it was to bring back everything he had despised
about the afternoon, but it was also brutal and savage and exciting
enough to work here in his mind, and what was going on in his mind
had a direct connection to his degree of hardness, and this physical
result was all Stella knew or need know. So it went on. Connie Furlo's
brassy blond hair, those late-sixties women whose glamour was really
a layover from the fifties, a cheapness in its last summer flowering before it turned entirely unattractive. Enough to see her bottle-blond hair
falling over the edge of a couch in the office, a pin falling out, a holding
barrette, her mouth opening in mingled panic and pleasure (as Stella's
was now), and Desmarais on top of her. The man was probably huge—
you never fully thought these things out, but in some corner of your
mind the imaginary assessment of other men always went on—and it
was a strange pleasure to become the younger Ray Desmarais fucking
the younger Connie Furlo in some long-ago unspooling, Richie becoming, in this moment, as strong as this imagined man, not capable of being
"fleeced" by a couple of bowling buddies, but tough and huge—yes,

that—and full of a quantity of juice that would go—how had Desmarais described it?—"all over the place." And this took him to the end, through Stella's orgasm to his own now customarily weak one (about this diminishment, Ray Desmarais had been unfortunately right). Weak, but enough. They didn't matter, his orgasms, not anymore; they were like an old file of things that must be saved but rarely consulted.

Stella said "Oh," and he touched her face, relieved to be back in the world of the real. He kissed her forehead. She need not know what it had taken to achieve this. She did not have to know what was projected on the screen of his mind, and he did not have to think about it either. It was boxed away, as so much had to be, and if you unpacked it all, there would be no living. Instead, pull the covers tighter around her, let her sleep, and when she awoke in an hour or so, have something warm waiting for her to eat, downstairs.

5

In midwinter Jack asked his mother if he could accompany her to Kingman-Deaconess some Monday for one of her treatments. Didn't he have to work? Jack allowed that he could easily take a day off, that he felt he had been remiss in his duty toward her, and that beyond all that, he wanted to. Just the two of them, without Richie.

She instructed him where to park and waited for him in the lobby. They passed the children's ward, where a little girl in purple pressed her hands up to the glass. There was no knowing anything. It could be her brother or sister who was afflicted, though Stella retained a memory (perhaps an imagined one), as the elevator doors closed, of sparse, knobby hair.

"Those are the children," she said to Jack.

The lighting was dim inside the elevator.

"I got that."

It was not a surprise to find that people looked at him—the receptionist, the nurses. She was glad they did, proud to show him off, her big son in good clothes. Richie had told her that Jack had once revealed that he was making more than a hundred thousand dollars a year. He'd worn an expensive-looking purple shirt and a leather jacket. But these were not the clothes she'd have chosen for him, if the truth be told. They were perhaps too slick.

"Is this your son, Mrs. Palumbo?" Jeannine, the pregnant nurse who'd taken over her chemo treatments, asked. "Your mother's one of our favorites."

"Oh." Stella shook her head, disparaging specialness.

"When are you due?" Jack asked.

"April. This is my second."

Jack was smiling widely, the social side of him easy and prominent. Stella sat, the needle went in, Jeannine told Jack about her older child—it had all become like a tea party, a gathering where everyone knew one another, but which was of no particular importance. That the chair would be empty someday, her body replaced by another, hardly mattered. The nurse would have her baby and barely remember Stella Palumbo (or if she did, she would remember her only as being "nice").

Stella looked hard at the flesh on Jack's face as he watched the news of the president and Monica Lewinsky on the TV. He'd become a professional smiler, and it had created certain ridges where there didn't used to be any. She tried to re-create the more youthful face, the intense seriousness he'd had as a boy.

They were alone, Jeannine having gone off to attend to someone else. Perhaps Jack had anticipated something more dramatic than the two of them sitting in chairs, Stella's hookup, the cheerful medical staff, the TV.

"Does this hurt?" he asked, leaning forward.

"Not really," Stella answered.

Once every three weeks she met with Dr. Kincaid directly after the chemo. The doctor was a merry sort, young and curly-headed. She could picture him playing with his children after work in whatever enormous house he lived in, in whatever upscale town.

Jack seemed to pick up on Dr. Kincaid's bland comments, Rhitu's affected concern.

"I've been reading," Jack said, injecting himself into the conversation. "Listen, I'm in the drug business, so I know all about the bullshit. But shark cartilage—I've been reading about shark cartilage. As an inhibitor."

Dr. Kincaid's eyes receded, as if he were a bright student who'd just been accused of cheating by a teacher he didn't particularly respect. "There's a lot of experimentation going on," he said.

"Well, that's what I'm talking about." Jack was smiling in a way that, Stella supposed, got him what he wanted in a lot of other venues. "Because it's clear this isn't working, isn't it?"

What was it he knew? Kincaid looked at Stella as if to excuse what had just been said. Rhitu looked at the floor.

"We're very hopeful," Kincaid said, glancing back at Jack.

"Well, that's good. I'm glad you're hopeful. But in the meantime, there are experiments going on, and . . . I don't know if you've read about the treatment Bob Guccione's wife is undergoing."

"Who?"

"He's the publisher of *Penthouse*."

Dr. Kincaid blinked. It was as if someone had breached the splendid fortress of his house out in—where? Winchester? Acton?—broken down the door, and assaulted him while he read to his little boys.

"I know. *Penthouse*," Jack said. "Come on. It doesn't matter. It doesn't matter if she's like a convicted killer. It's a treatment that's working. I read about it. You should, too."

Jack was speaking with an urgency that embarrassed Stella a little. He was making her more important than she was. It seemed in bad taste to be doing what he was doing, in this neat room where she always met with Dr. Kincaid and Rhitu, where they made their little jokes and indulged in their petty assurances. She was surprised to find she did not want that delicacy ruffled. In his leather jacket and his slightly garish shirt Jack seemed not of their world: cheaper, somehow, not to be as deeply trusted.

That was her first thought.

Her second was that she loved him for what he was doing. He had brought his briefcase, and she thought perhaps he had brought work with him, but instead he took out photocopies.

"I'd like you to look at these," he said, handing them over.

Dr. Kincaid took them and pretended to peruse them. Rhitu looked over Kincaid's shoulder, her eyes intense.

"We will," Kincaid said. It was false. He gave Jack his reassuring smile.

When Rhitu and the doctor had left the room, Jack said, "What bullshit."

"Oh," Stella said. It seemed to be a word she was using all the time now, a full-service syllable.

"They'll never take a look. They don't want to save you. It's too much work."

"Don't say that."

He looked at her. "Why not? You know you have to fight the medical establishment, don't you? I mean, you know that."

"I don't know any such thing."

"Well, I'm telling you."

"You're a good boy."

"Don't tell me that. This is not about me being a good boy."

She felt now, in a more urgent way, their out-of-placeness in the vacant room, among the medical books and the plastic spiral notebooks on the desk. They were out of their depths here.

Jack hit his fist lightly against the arm of his chair.

"They should be trying everything."

"Somebody else is going to need to come in here."

"You worried about that? About taking up too much space in the world, Mother?"

"Lots of people get cancer."

"But there's only one I care about."

In the elevator, she took his arm. She wanted an intimate moment. She felt the smooth leather of his jacket.

"Sometimes, before we go home, your father takes me out for a cup of tea."

He hesitated. "You want that?"

The smell of leather, the way he leaned toward her, the faint scent of whatever he'd put on his face after shaving, she thought this was what it would be like to be a woman with him. To sink under the weight of his calm authority.

"There's a Starbucks—" she suggested.

He drove into the heart of Boston, parked in a garage, then walked her into a hotel lobby. The restaurant was raised above the lobby floor. He told the hostess, "My mother wants tea," and the woman nodded. A waitress brought a selection of teas, a china cup, a sliver of lemon. They sat at a small table.

"Starbucks," he muttered, and shook his head.

"Nothing for you?"

"Nothing."

She sipped her tea. Piano music was piped in. This was a world she didn't know. Hotels. The staff all looked as if they were waiting for the rush that would come at any moment.

"Let me ask you something," Jack said. "Do you want to be a good patient, or do you want to live?"

She put the cup down. Her vision was suddenly blurry. She wiped at her eyes.

"You okay?"

"I'm fine. This happens sometimes."

"Do you want me to get you something?"

"No."

After a moment he said, "Do you not like that question I asked you?"

"Not very much. No."

"Why?"

"It's a difficult one."

"You and Dad." He shifted in his chair. "There's a kind of person. Don't let me offend you. I'm in this business, okay? There's a kind of person, they become a patient, it's like becoming a lamb being led to the slaughter."

"I don't think that's the case."

"This guy Kincaid. I researched him. He's not the best."

"Oh, he's very nice."

"I'm sure he is."

She looked up at her son. It was a performance she was giving. She wondered if he knew. Did he think of her as simple? Was willed passivity the same as simplicity?

"I'm upsetting you."

"Not at all. You want me to see the best doctor. You want me to *fight*."

"Of course I do."

The waitress came and poured more tea. A cheap girl in faux-elegant waitress's clothing. She and Jack shared a look. Stella wondered what it meant, then decided it meant nothing.

She would have liked to find some way to talk to him about Christina, rather than this difficult subject. The waitress brought a fresh lemon. The staff here had too little to do.

"Now listen," Stella said, forcing herself, but also feeling brave. "I think there are people who *should* fight. Young people. People with young children. I don't expect you to understand this. If I spent all my time fighting this, I think there's something I'd miss."

"What's that?"

227

"I wish I knew. But I feel there's something else I should be doing."

He smiled at her in a very gentle way—*almost* as though he understood—and she closed her eyes against her own difficult response to that smile: her intense regret, almost a stabbing feeling inside, over the years when she hadn't loved him enough. Was the whole end period of life a constant reexperiencing of the things one had done badly? She wanted to tell him she was sorry. More, to do it over. Yet she suspected that if she went back, it would be just as hard. He had had those years of hairiness and blank-eyed surliness, where he'd been either in his room or wanting to escape, and perhaps taking drugs. She had thought he'd never be handsome. The T-shirts he wore had been soiled monuments to antisocial behavior. It had come as almost too big a shock when he suddenly started to look handsome to her, his skin smooth, hair grown soft, the molting that had taken place his senior year. Then had come the night she found him naked with the girl. She'd never told him. It remained her secret.

"How is Christina?" she asked, and studied his face for the first response.

He seemed calm, unruffled by the question.

"I think she's tired. I think it's a lot. Three." He reached for her tea and took a quick sip. "Having a two-year-old. Hard."

She did not say anything, but went on staring at him.

"What?" he asked.

Then she wondered if he even knew, if any of what she perceived was known to him.

"Something you want to tell me, Mother?"

"No."

"Oh, come on." He smiled widely.

The separation between them felt both opaque and huge. He wanted to convince her to fight for her life, and she wanted to convince him to—what? Certainly not to leave Christina, but to recognize something.

"Come on," he said, still leaning forward, tapping his knee against the bottom of the table playfully.

How could Christina be so thick, so stupid, not to see what she had before her—to see that she had *Jack*. And what more could any woman want? Was it possible that even Jack could become boring, that the sight of him, night after night, the predictability of him could wear a woman down? Even Stella wanted to reach out and change things about

228

him—the shirt, the slight thickness of his skin, the incipient coarseness of his face. The sight of his body all those years ago on the couch, open like a young biblical warrior resting after his battle, returned to her. He'd had a kind of heroism then, and an innocence. She traced his thighs in her memory, the casing of his balls, the splendor in her own mind of thinking, He is beautiful. My son is beautiful. She had no shame anymore about those feelings. What a ridiculous feeling was shame.

Jack shook his head, still smiling. "Okay, listen," he said. "I've got to use the men's room. You okay?"

"I'm fine."

The waitress watched him after he'd asked directions. He'd taken off his coat; Stella saw his body moving across the lobby. A salesman. Her son was a salesman, with that young middle-aged pep they all had, that incipient surliness, too, that she always associated with sports bars. Did young men, in order to survive, always have to become rougher? Jack swam in the world, he was conversant with hotels. She should have been glad. He did not have to be, forever, what he once was.

But she was alone now, and it was awkward. The waitress glanced at her and didn't smile. Only with Jack here, with that aura of sex and gold credit cards, was social kindness drawn out of such people. Otherwise Stella was a woman asking for too much attention.

But alone—he was taking a long time—his question came back to her. That will not to live, to accept this, to accept what seemed now the blatant lies of Dr. Kincaid and Rhitu. In her accustomed place, in her house, in her garden, at Kingman-Deaconess, even at the monastery, it made sense, her reaction. A kind of passivity felt called for, as though her life were caught in a groove and wouldn't move on. Illumination would come of passivity and waiting; she might be dying for a very long time. Here in the hotel it came to her not as a thought, but in the form of panic. There was no thought to have, no illumination, no grand final task, no *other* she must seek out, the double who would accompany her to heaven, as the priest had promised. Instead, death would just *happen*. A set of elevator doors would open, and there would be blackness, and a small, still voice inside her would say, Go ahead. Step inside. And she would, just as she'd done everything difficult in her life, by simply doing it. Her hand went out, uncontrolled. Why had she done that?

"Are you all right?"

Jack was above her. She wanted to reach out for him and ask him to save her.

"I'm sorry."

"Jesus, don't apologize." He was looking at her in such a way that she knew she must look crumpled and old.

"Oh, this is terrible."

"What is?" He sat across from her and clasped her hand.

"I wanted to be *good*." It was not what she meant to say, though she knew inside what she meant. Something about getting through without letting on how difficult this was. She became fussy. She finished the last of her tea.

"We can pick up Zoe early today. We finished early," Stella said, wondering what edges and shavings of panic might be showing up in a voice she was trying to control.

"She needs her nap," Jack said, looking at his watch, then at her, still concerned. "You want to tell me what just happened to you?"

If it were spring, she might have suggested that they step outside, even take a walk in the Public Garden. These last few weeks had been a welcome period of strength. Rarely did she find herself tiring helplessly. But it was late January. The world closing in on her, her son closing in with his body. They'd never quite been in the right place. It had been so brief, his senior year, the late-night tea, the two of them in the kitchen, the silence that had felt so comfortable. His gift to her had been the return, years later, when he came home from New York, wrecked somehow, to live in his room, to work with his father in the pizza parlor, to haunt the library and bring home stacks of books, like a young divinity student, God-besotted, tortured. Christina's insertion of herself into his life had ended all that.

She shook her head. Her hand was in his hand.

"Okay, here's what's going to happen," he was saying. "I'm going to get hold of all your reports and send them to somebody else. Don't say anything. You're going to meet with this other guy. You're going to hear what he has to say. Okay?"

There was no explaining why the image in her head was one of the two of them driving in a very fast car. In the front seat. Her hair waving. In what county, what landscape? She saw it for an instant. She saw them.

Jack put his head down, resting it on her outstretched hand.

"You've got to forgive me. I've been aloof. I haven't taken this in hand enough."

"Oh." That word again.

"I've let Dad handle it. He's hopeless."

"Don't say that."

"Dad is a dreamer."

She never would have imagined those words coming from his mouth. Were they true?

"And my life . . ." he said.

She caught her breath. She wondered what he understood of his own "life."

"What?" she asked.

He lifted his head, shook it, waking himself up. He raised one hand for the waitress.

"What about your life?"

"Just the tea for the two of you today?" the waitress asked, there too quickly.

"Big spenders," Jack said, smiling. He slipped her a credit card. The tip would be large. What about his life?

He never answered. She could not bring it up again. Something in his face forbade it.

They drove to the day-care center in Watertown. It was before Zoe's nap, and she looked as if she needed one. The way she reached out her arms to her father was a greeting Stella and Richie never received. Jack held Zoe and flicked her little widow's peak, which was wild.

"What are they doing with your hair?" he said. "What do they do to your hair here?"

The workers at the day-care center laughed. They liked Jack, as all women liked him.

"She won't let us comb it."

"No. Just me, right?" Jack said.

Zoe lifted her hand up to her widow's peak. She kept her eyes on her father, as if she wanted to offer it to him. She was his belonging; she gave herself to him entirely.

"Shall we go home and comb it?" Jack said.

"Yes," the child answered.

He drove Stella home first. On the way, Zoe fell asleep in the backseat.

"My day is fucked now," Jack said. Then, "Sorry."

"Oh, you think I've never heard such words?"

"I think you've probably heard a lot of words."

He smiled, like he was flirting with her.

231

"We might as well drive now, let her sleep. You mind?"

"I don't mind at all."

Outside, the snow had taken on a thin crust of ice. It shimmered. Jack was driving beyond Norumbega, into the network of hidden towns beyond it, towns that were not really towns. Woods. Lakes. The roads were slick, but he negotiated the icy curves well. They were not speaking. She closed her eyes, but not to sleep. It took her several moments to realize that this was how she had seen them in her vision in the hotel restaurant, though in the vision it had not been winter. Their hair had been flying in the wind, but here they were in a warm car, listening to classical music. She'd assumed her vision had had something to do with the afterlife, a moment in some other-earthly sphere where they might someday be together. But here it was, in the middle of an ordinary day.

"Who do you like in the Super Bowl, Mother?"

She waited a moment. "I don't know. Who's playing?"

They both enjoyed the little joke; the tone achieved between them felt liberating. Jack smiled and tapped his fingers on the steering wheel, in tune with a swift passage in the music. She hoped that they could drive like this forever. There were words they might say—a conversation she might press him on—but here there seemed some larger possibility contained in the silence between them. She was back in her room, waking in the middle of the night, tiptoeing downstairs, finding him. In her own life, she had never quite achieved the desired thing, the tipping into a desired sensuality that had so tortured her. But she had had that moment.

"Oh" was the simple word that escaped her now, and he looked at her curiously, as if to ask what she meant.

6

When, in the spring, she found herself still alive, she had to determine whether it was worth planting things. If she were to die in summer, would Richie notice when the dahlias had grown tall enough that they needed to be tied to stakes? Would tomatoes fall, bruised, split open, a haven for bugs, before he remembered to pick them? She thought she might leave him a note, but it had always been an article of faith with her that when the end came, it would come so swiftly that she would have no time to tidy up these loose ends, and a note given to him in May, when the tomatoes were only potted six-inch stalks, would not be remembered in August.

She did plant some things. The doctor Jack insisted she go to had far less time than Dr. Kincaid had, but he was, in his cold way, more encouraging. The new regimen was harsher and made her more sick. He was older than Dr. Kincaid, a foreign doctor with a wit like Henry Kissinger's, where there was a delay before you realized he'd made a joke.

"I have terrible news for you," he said. "I see some shrinkage in these tumors."

"Why is this terrible news?"

"Your son tells me you've already made out your will."

There was no Rhitu, no gorgeous deep eyes to stare into to offset the facts of her illness. Her chemo treatments shifted to another hospital; she was acutely aware of the differences, small and large. The children's oncology ward was not to be found. Sleek elevators lifted her up to the place where an older, brisker staff waited. She kept looking for a warmth that arrived only in patches.

When she complained of this to Jack, he said, "Listen, Mother, you have to measure the seriousness of your care by how miserable the staff is. It just means they're taking the cancer seriously."

Then he couldn't resist adding, "The other place, it was like walking into Mister Rogers' Neighborhood. That was the instruction they all got from that clown Kincaid. 'Ease her passage.' They were going to put you on a little choo-choo toward heaven."

It changed things; it did. She was under orders from Jack to will herself into a new seriousness. But she'd preferred the dreamier treatment; it asked less of her. She missed Kincaid's cackling boy's laugh, which made her feel like his intimate.

One night in May she woke beside Richie and knew instantly she'd been tossed out of sleep into a wakefulness that would not go away. Such moments—increasingly regular now—she did not mind. When death was so near (as she still believed it was) who needed sleep? This gave her a little more time, and she seized it. She went to the window, fighting pain in her hip, lifted the window as much as she could. The moon was sufficient that the outlines of her pea vines were visible. Good that she'd planted them.

In some part of her mind she had a vision: herself walking naked in her garden on a moonlit night like this. She thought that was the sort of thing a dying woman should do. But because it was lodged so exclusively in her mind, she rejected it. It came too much from the world of books or else was something she'd seen in a movie. She put on a robe and sneakers. She felt her tense, skinny legs appreciatively. They had never gotten old and lumpy and thick. At least she had that.

At the back doorway, she tightened her robe. May nights were always colder than you'd expect. Almost certainly, she'd frightened an animal, stepping outside. She sat on the old painted aluminum chair she'd dragged over, near the garden, to have a place to fall into when fatigue came during gardening. It was damp; the damp would come through the robe. She'd get a chill. No matter.

At night the pea vines had a wonderful, abnormal stillness that she knew was deceptive. They were looking for something to ascend to. It made her tired to think that she might live the whole summer, might have to go through the whole succession of things growing. Here, this was enough. May. The inception of lilacs, everything about to pop. She had said goodbye to her children, though she would go on seeing them. Jack would bring the grandchildren to the house; they would look at her wide-eyed, having been told by their father that Grandma was "sick." She offered cookies and a cheerfulness that felt exhausting. What else were you going to do? Joan kept threatening to come, though she seemed to be waiting for the peak moment, the moment of peak helplessness, so she could bring her crucifix and her strange God into the house. At the last minute Joan would say, Do you understand now? holding up the crucifix and asking Stella to embrace it. I'm afraid not, my dear, she would say. I am as far from it as ever.

How long could she sit here before doing her body damage? Already she felt creaky and uncomfortable. But she hungered for such moments. Her sisters called incessantly, wanting to take her places— shopping, lunch. Richie hovered. You wanted to prepare, but the world wanted to distract you, as if the thought of your own death was one you shouldn't be allowed to have. "Some are shrinking," the new doctor had said, "but maybe some new ones are growing." She reached out to touch one of the runners of peas, its tendrils nosing upward like a newborn's fist, searching for something to grasp.

The animal she had scared was perhaps coming back. She waited, hearing the small shuffling noise. Rabbit. Skunk. Raccoon. Possibly a small deer. These were the encounters you wanted. In children's books, the ones she loved to read to her grandchildren, an animal was always leading a child into the world beyond doors, beyond gardens, lifting its head and looking back to be sure it was being followed. They were stories about trust, stories suggesting that the world contained some hidden, interior meaning you'd been blind to all your life. The Catholic Church in its stupidity had tried to squeeze all that meaning into a crucified body. No, that was not anything you could follow. She would tell Joan that when she came. They would continue their always truncated, frustrating discussion.

Or maybe not. Maybe tonight the deer would come and lead her through a door. She smiled to think it, and then, as though watching her own mind, thought, This is how we comfort ourselves, with such stories. Close to death, we wait for the full illumination. But of course there was no such thing. The crucifix came to her again, and she touched her knee. She didn't want to believe that it was not about some moon-drenched illumination, but about suffering and the wild, conceptual love of that long-haired man on the cross. To feel that we are loved and then slaughtered, is that all it comes down to? She stood up, felt exquisite pain in her hip, went down onto one knee. Oh God, would she have to wake Richie? Was this what she got for this desire, unquenched nearly all her married life, to steal time away, to be alone?

She did manage to get up. She had scared the animal away again. For a single, panicky moment she thought it had been her last chance to die beautifully, to escape into a story like a child heroine, pigtailed, blond. Her hip throbbed. Was this where all the unshrunken tumors had migrated? It would all be quite real, she understood. Suffering. Pain. A fight for breath at the end? She saw herself clawing the air in some soiled hospital bed (Let me be alone there, please!), and the face of one of the nurses who had been so kind at Kingman-Deaconess, only now with her nurse's lips turned down in disgust. I was my mother's small, undemanding last child, she heard herself saying, by way of excuse, to the young, pregnant nurse. Forgive me. But perhaps there was nothing about the human, nothing *in* the human, that could completely forgive in the face of stench, of suppurating sores, of groaning and demand. Perhaps this was the moment when you fell into the hands of the heavenly father and *got* the crucifix. You will not come to rest until you come to rest in me. Still, some stubbornness rose. She did not want to give in, as everyone seemed to, to that final promise of someone waiting to catch you on the other side.

She grasped the chair with one arm. How would she explain to this God, waiting to catch her, her own life? Its complications. How would she excuse her resistance to her post-Korea husband, when the sight of his body had repulsed her at the beginning and she had thought, I will marry him, but I don't love him. And then her children, too, the extreme aversion—Jack as a boy, Joan as a frightened teenage girl. All your life you wanted to run, didn't you, from what restrained you. She felt a head nodding in response, said aloud, "Who are you?" heard no answer. Fear had gripped her now, she wanted to be held, and the pressure she felt was to allow someone to hold her who wasn't there, whom she knew not to be there. She was angry at him, the unseen God of the cross, for perhaps being right about everything. We get things endlessly wrong, and then we die. *Yes, that is it, that is it exactly. Now come to me.*

If there were something in her life she could remember as being its center, something good she had fought for, something she could take honest pride in, she might have been able to battle this unseen God. But there was nothing. She felt—no, she *experienced* her own humility, the way the parts inside, after the long, biding time that was active life, were claiming her. We are what you are now. Not memory. Not history. Just this ache, this pain. In her cell at the monastery she had said "You died, too"; now the words echoed back to her. *Yes I did,* the man-Christ was saying. *I did indeed. I felt everything you felt. I begged for it not to happen.*

Her hand went to her face. She knew it was over. She'd gone as far as she could go. She could meet this God no more than she'd already done; it was his to do next. She felt the internal closing of a door. Everything from this point on would be imagined, willed. God had escaped like the animal she'd frightened. She'd have liked to call him back, but she was frightened of him, too.

When she turned back to the house, she saw that a light had come on in the bedroom. Her absence had awakened Richie. Something she'd come to understand about marriage: you could rail against it, but it inhabited you physically. Like a drug. It was true. There were these withdrawal moments, the body craving its induced easements. Richie had woken because his unconscious body knew she was not beside him.

"Richie?" She had not said it loud enough for him to hear. But she could see lights coming on. When she saw the kitchen light, she knew he was close.

"Richie," she said again, not much louder.

He appeared in the doorway in his blue pajamas, his hair mussed, looking sleep-dazed and confused. He did not say anything, and she wondered if this meant he didn't see her.

"I'm afraid you're going to have to help me," she said, no louder than before, but the small motion of his head told her he'd heard.

"What happened?" he asked.

She had to search for an answer.

When he started toward her, she lifted her hand.

"No," she said. "Put on slippers. The ground is colder than it looks."

His head rose toward her, as though she'd said something deeper, more intimate. His face took on the look of a boy receiving instructions from his first girlfriend: this is how to love me.

Then he disappeared, went inside. She waited. A small panic: What if death came now, while she was waiting? She grew anxious for him to come back, it seemed to take forever. He was wearing a bathrobe, old, cracked slippers, the first he had found. Not those, she wanted to say, knowing he had better, warmer ones. But when he was there, she collapsed into him.

He held her and touched her hair.

"What the hell are you doing out here?" he asked, unable to keep the mild annoyance out of his voice.

"I'm a crazy woman," she said. "Remember?"

She hardly knew herself what she meant.

"Stella." It was as though she were already in some alternative space he had to call her out of; this was what she feared. Speaking eloquently, loudly, and then understanding that no one heard a word she said.

"You loved me once," were the insane words she spoke.

"What are you talking about?"

She shook her head. It didn't matter what she said.

"Let's go in," he said.

She leaned into him. Then, after a moment, he lifted her up. It astonished her. This was not something he should do, she wanted to caution him. But then she realized. He was not straining. She had grown tiny, weightless. *Cancer*, she thought, this is *cancer*, the word itself at a distance. He carried her into the house.

"Not the stairs," she said.

"Stella, I can do it."

"No." She insisted. He put her down. Grasping the banister, she lifted herself up the stairs, not without difficulty.

"We should have moved," he said when she was at the top. "Gotten a place that was all one floor."

She looked at him then, as if to allow him to measure in her eyes the absurdity of what he'd just said. Leave the house? The great, defining, life-changing house? She found her way into bed. He followed her, his body attentive to her, as if she might need one more thing. Sex? She smiled at that. Was he ever hopeful for that, even at this late moment when there was hardly anything left of her?

"Richie?"

"What is it?"

"How small am I now?"

"What are you talking about?"

"How—"

She could live with the absurdity of the question, though he could not. She went into it, felt down her body, collapsed stomach, thin legs. She was all still there, but even a being in miniature considers itself complete. She needed some proof. She took his hands and forced them to feel her. Stomach. Legs. Arms. She felt his erection against her and smiled. Hope. God. Undying hope. Not tonight, my love. Just feel me. *Feel* me.

Two weeks later, in the morning, she told Richie she had arranged to meet her sisters at a restaurant in Boston.

"In Boston? Why are they taking you out in Boston?"

"I asked them to. I wanted to go back to the North End."

She asked that he drive her to Waverly Square, where she could catch the bus into Harvard and from there maneuver herself to the North End.

Which to him sounded crazy. "*No,*" he kept insisting. Why weren't her sisters picking her up?

"I *asked* to do it this way. Of course they wanted to drive me. But how many more times do I get to take a bus? Or a trolley? I want to do this. Really. I feel strong enough."

"I'll go with you."

But she insisted. So, unhappily, he left her at the bus stop, waited in the parking lot across the street until the bus came. She knew how she must look, small, helpless, caved in, an old woman at a bus stop. Her little prayer was that he would not have to wait, watching her, too long.

The bus came. Her second prayer: Let me have strength enough to go through with this. It had all been a bluff, of course, her avowal of strength. She was praying increasingly these days, though this did not mean anything, really. Her little encounter with God in the night garden had evaporated, but left something in its wake. A dialogue had opened. She grasped the metal support of the bus while she sat. She enjoyed seeing the houses of Belmont, Watertown, the stores that were still there from time immemorial, the ones that had changed.

In the cave of the subway stop at Harvard, she walked, longer than she'd have liked and getting lost once, to the train line she needed. So far, so good. No huge fatigue, though she stopped once or twice, rested on benches to be sure. The fact was she was not certain of the stop, only of the general vicinity she needed to get to, and she hoped that if she did get off at the wrong stop, there wouldn't be too long a walk.

Which of course there was. Unresearched plans like this always went awry. It was a trolley she had taken, and when the neighborhood looked enough like the one she wanted, she got off. But when she realized her mistake and asked a pedestrian for directions, she was told she'd have to walk about a mile. She sat on a bench and despaired until it occurred to her she could just get on the next trolley and continue until she got closer.

This time it worked. She could see the neighborhood was right. Kingman-Deaconess was over there in the burrow of hospitals, one seeming to rise directly out of the next. There was even the Starbucks she and Richie used to go to. After she'd done what she needed to do today, she might go in. For old times' sake.

But as cheerful as she felt at this moment—the sight of the Starbucks, the nearness of Kingman-Deaconess—it came over her anyway, by surprise. Was it excitement that made her have to catch her breath and then feel that she was losing it, so that she staggered a little on the curb and then sat on it, on the curb itself, there was no bench in sight. Pedestrians passed, a blond woman wearing a tight bun and a good brown suit, caught in conversation with a man. The woman's eyes went to her but did not ask if she could help. Good. There was no help to be offered that she could accept. Let them see her as a bag lady. She would sit here until she had strength enough to stagger on. She could not think of what lay beyond the achievement of her goal. Impossible to think that, or of the strength she would need to get home.

Finally she was able to stand. Making her way slowly, walking close to walls, reaching out occasionally to touch them, she reached Kingman-Deaconess. A small wave of nostalgia greeted her in the lobby. This is where I used to wait for Richie, on that seat. Nostalgia for *this*? For chemo? Why not? It had been the ritual of their late marriage, had come to define it in these late stages. Oh, how I have come to love you, she thought, thinking of Richie, and it felt like a small defiance of God. You try to kill us, from birth, and then we love. That is our revenge. At heaven's gate you reach out and say, Here I am, the beloved, and we turn around, waiting for another to join us. How you must hate that.

She shook her head. Stupid thoughts. She made her way to the corridor she sought. The doorway was surprisingly hard to find. A receptionist was there. Two of them, in fact. They did not even ask the obvious question. She formed her own excuse.

"I'm waiting here for my granddaughter."

"Name?" The woman was black. Some of them had a severity, good earrings, style.

Stella pretended not to hear, sat.

Having come all this way, it was a disappointment. No one else was here. But she knew she looked harmless, an old woman, decently dressed; they would leave her alone.

She had expected, in her imagining of this, that she would enter their world. Slides. Blocks. Puzzles. The bright colors she'd noticed each time she came. But those things seemed to exist in some inner sanctum. Here were only copies of *National Geographic* and children's animal magazines.

It took a few minutes before a woman and two children entered, the woman dressed in a maroon jacket that could have been either hideously expensive leather or a cheap imitation. Jewish, she could tell, with short hair, a mannish haircut, and a quick, deliberate manner. The two children were a boy and a girl, and the appointment was for "Sean," or perhaps "Shawn," which could have been either, couldn't it?

"You two wait," the mother said, and spoke to the woman behind the desk.

The children were hesitant to leave their mother's side, the boy slightly braver, he wandered a bit. Stella sat in such a way that she might provide an invitation. But how did you do that? She unsnapped and snapped her bag. Both children looked at her with mild suspicion. Neither approached.

But we will go to heaven together, she said silently to one or both of them. She was remembering what the priest had said: "We die in twos." But now that she was here in this room, her plan—the plan that had finally occurred to her as the last act of her conscious life, to find among these children her accompaniment to the next world—felt absurd. She had intended to make some connection with one of these children, to perform one final act of tenderness. Conceiving it one sleepless night, she had thought it had seemed perfect, brilliant, the answer to the question that had haunted her all along: What was the thing she must do in order to fully prepare? Now she understood that the children would be ushered into the play area, which was of course off-limits to her, and she would be here alone, and soon enough one of the two women behind the long desk would ask, Who again was that grandchild of yours?

The two children, she could see now, were extraordinarily beautiful. That young Semitic look, dark hair (both of them full-headed, so the cancer could not have gone deep yet, or else the treatment had only just started), and large eyes. Was it a disappointment to find a child *not* close to death for this encounter? She shook her head.

"Do you want to take them into the play area?" the receptionist asked. "She's running a little late."

"Sure, in a minute," the mother replied. "I need to make a call. May I use one of your phones? It's local."

You could tell—watch carefully and you could always tell—the relationship of the staff and the patient, which of them did annoying things all the time, like ask to use the phone, and which were beloved because they asked so little. Stella, in all her time as a patient, had tried to join the latter club. The mother dialed and the children looked at Stella.

Oh, she should just go. She'd expected it would be so different. This last, beautiful encounter. This penetration of their world, which had so intrigued her. She wanted pathos—bald heads, little knitted caps. What she got were two healthy-looking, gorgeous Jewish children. One of them might well be dying, like her, but how was she to know?

A mild argument had started between the two children while their mother spoke on the phone, a tense call if her tone was any tip-off. Some people had no shame about exposing their battles in public. The little girl came and sat next to Stella.

After a moment Stella said, "Hello," but the little girl seemed not to hear her, intensely focused as she was on her brother.

"Are you Shawn?" Stella asked.

"What?" the little girl asked, looking up.

The child touched her nose, as if to pick it. Her hair was so thick. Like Joan's as a girl. Stella hadn't recognized the connection, not at first, and as she did, she turned away. Blinded for a moment.

"What?" the little girl asked again.

She was leaving them. She was leaving the little girl Joan had been. How was it you pushed all this away in your concentration on yourself, your neat, beautiful death that would be so unruffled if only you could work it, arrange it that way. You forgot this other thing, the past that receded, all the days of their childhood when you simply endured, day after day, lunch and dinner, taking them to school, the playtimes, the endless afternoons, the silences, and the sudden tears they always shocked you with. You were leaving all that behind. The epic of dailiness.

"Don't pick your nose, Shawn," the mother said, turning to the girl. She was still involved with the phone call, and the little boy, the brother, the one who would survive, scratched at his mother's jacket.

Stella tried to see beyond the blindness that had afflicted her, the wet eyes. Finally she was able to regard the little girl, who sat still and seemed to hold the suspect finger, the nose-picking finger, in her other hand, as if to hold it down. Stella blew her nose and turned and regarded the child, who looked up at her.

"So you're Shawn."

The little girl didn't answer, looked at Stella. Had she ever seen such big eyes? All right, then. You. In all the world. You. By this accident. You, or someone enough like you as not to matter. We will ascend together. *Stranger,* the priest had said.

The little girl took her hand, the one that had been picking her nose, and ran it along the cloth of Stella's light jacket. To feel the fabric or to clean the finger? Did it matter? This was allowed. She offered her jacket and more. The little girl smiled, brazen and apologetic at the same time, accepting, Stella could not help but believe, the offer of company she had come here, to this place, this unlikely place, to make.

FIVE

THE BOOK OF JOAN

Early Summer 2007

1

There was no understanding, and ultimately no controlling, the sounds an old house made. Still, they all came to Richie as urgent warnings. Gutter drips, furnace belches, heating ducts that seemed to have trouble breathing, the scratching sound that could be the sign of animals inhabiting the interior walls. He found himself, all the time, on the alert, so much so that when his attention was called for, as it was now, he had to rouse himself out of a distracted state.

Above him he could hear the unpacking, and that, too, was a distraction.

Meanwhile, the boy waited.

"I just want you to tell me about Korea," the boy said.

"What do you want to know?"

The boy had the book of photographs open before him. A film of impacted dust blurred some of them. They were all from Korea, old Kodaks with white, mottled edges.

"Who's the cat?" was the boy's first question. He smiled as he asked it, clever, hiding something? A way of making fun of him? Richie could not tell.

The small black cat was being held by a soldier whose name Richie should have remembered, but couldn't.

"We named that cat Vidoki," Richie said, pleased that he remembered.

"What's that mean? That Korean?"

"It's Korean." Was it? He couldn't remember. He had not been asked these questions before. His children had not wanted to know about Korea. Nor had his first set of grandchildren, Jack's children. The Korea photographs had gone into a box at the back of a closet. Then one night at dinner Joan had mentioned to this boy that Richie had served in Korea, and the boy's face was lit with interest. "Why'd we have a war there?" the boy had wanted to know. He talked fast. There was in his speech patterns a quality Richie called "jive," without really knowing what the word meant. "When was this, the fifties? Was everybody crazy in the fifties?"

Then out had come the box, the scrapbook Richie had assembled years before. But Richie was wary of this boy, with his dark skin, his long lashes, his air of absolute ease and happiness in a new world that, by rights, ought to have intimidated him.

VD. That was the derivation of the cat's name, Vidoki, the soldiers' little joke. Which of course could not be revealed to this boy. As if to move past the subject, Richie turned the page, and there she was, a face he didn't at first recognize, then did.

"Wait wait wait," the boy said when Richie started to turn the page, and he placed his dark hand over Richie's. "Who's she?"

The Japanese girl had been captured looking upward, the sun creating a glare that obscured the left side of her face. Her pose was nearly formal, pathetic. She was a part of the past that Richie had always hated, the inescapable part. He closed his eyes and listened to Joan shifting a piece of furniture on the floor above him and wondered if she was scratching, doing damage to the floor. He ought to rise, he ought to go up and tell her: be careful.

"Who is she?" the boy asked again, and now Richie disliked him for his relentless prodding. He wanted to go up and announce to Joan that it was too much to impose on an old man, the insertion into Richie's home not only of this boy but his older brother as well. But if he went upstairs, he would have to confront the even harder thing.

"Sightseeing," Richie said. "A sightseeing guide, that's all."

The boy looked directly into his eyes. Always a shock, this unapologetic peering in. The other grandchildren, Jack's three, had always treated him as a given, an object of little interest. Whereas this one, this Felix, had taken to him immediately, for reasons obscure. But was he making *fun*?

"She a geisha?"

"I told you what she was."

246

"Come on. She was a geisha."

The boy smiled, as if understanding perfectly Richie's subterfuge. As if saying *you can tell me* and then wanting to laugh about it. But Richie had no intention of being seduced. Neither was he lying. The girl had been introduced, among a group of others, as a sightseeing guide. Tokyo, 1953. All the young soldiers had been ushered into a room. No one remembered how the rumor had started, who told them to go to this particular room where a man would be waiting. Where there would be girls. They will show you around the bombed-out city. He had never told Stella.

He flashed out now in anger. "She was no geisha. Jesus, where do you get your ideas?"

"You shoot anybody over there, Popi?"

Was the boy actually willing to move on or just trying to calm him down? Worse, was this another one of his clever subterfuges?

"No. Nobody."

"Ever fire your weapon?"

"No."

"You carry an M1?"

"M15. Why do you want to know all this?"

"I like the history of the world. I like knowing what happened to people before."

Felix tilted his head coyly. Richie could never be sure whether any information he gave this boy wouldn't be used later, in private. He heard Felix and his brother laughing sometimes in the room they were allowed to stay in, Jack's old room.

They had not yet fully moved in. There was hope there, that Joan had not yet completely made up her mind.

"If you turn the page, I can show you where we patrolled."

Felix leaned forward, continued to peruse the photographs of the girl. If Richie had meant to hide the fact of her from Stella, why, in making this scrapbook, was the display so bold? Had he been trying to say something to Stella in those early years that had been gradually rubbed away, to be replaced by the official self, the less raw self? He had a moment of trying to scratch back. He had a moment of believing Stella was still alive and he ought to be embarrassed.

Again, there was a sound from upstairs. This time Richie stood, called up,

"What are you doing?"

"Nothing," Joan called down to him. "It's the suitcase you hear. I'm just trying to back it into a corner without lifting it."

"Be careful."

"I will."

Remorse was the feeling most common to him now in his dealings with Joan. Remorse and confusion. Who was the man named Angel, and why were Angel's two sons suddenly present in Richie's life? He could not answer. It had all happened too fast, without adequate preparation. Joan's asking if they could come here had been careful, couched in the language of concern. It would be good to have help now, wouldn't it? But who said he needed help?

Then there were moments like this. Her small voice, abject. "I will." Wasn't he meant to rejoice that she'd at last taken on life?

The boy still waited. But they could hear her now, her heavy step on the stairs. She was coming down. When she appeared before them, he had to confront her belly, and it always had the same effect. She was undoing what he had made. The young girl who had to be coaxed out of her room had finally been fully coaxed, but rather than a tender romance with life, she had had a sordid affair with it. Her belly, just beginning to push out against her cheap frock, was the evidence.

Joan smiled at him. "Ready for lunch?"

"We're looking at geishas," Felix said.

Joan's face hovered between questioning and amusement. "Really?"

"Look." Felix lifted the book, brought it to her. She looked at the photos of the girl, then at her father. "Your daddy knew her."

"Daddy?"

"He's been having fun with me, that's all. A bunch of boys in Korea. Let me have it."

They did; then Joan and Felix seemed to share the joke with each other. Joan, sensing Richie's hurt, came forward.

"Would you like to feel the baby, Daddy? I think I feel movement today."

"No, that's all right."

She was too old for this—too old to be having a baby—though he could not remember her age. Was he supposed to touch her belly? Were they to make the leap toward an intimacy they hadn't shared since she was a child? Who said? Who made these new rules?

He moved away, went into the kitchen, stared out into the yard, which had been Stella's preserve. The many-paned windows framed it. In early summer, things she'd planted years ago still shot up through the soil. He couldn't concentrate fully—too much memory intruded—and when he felt Joan behind him and saw the boy outside, he wondered how much time must have passed. How long had he been standing there? There were these lapses, he knew that much. The unaccounted for.

Joan placed both hands on his sides, drew herself closer so that the small baby mound pressed against him, rested her head sideways against his back. She wanted this now: full access to him.

The boy was in Stella's garden—the shock of black curly hair, the long legs that were ahead of the rest of his growth. Coltish. He kicked at the winter detritus, as if to allow the green shoots easier access to the sun. Then he bent down and studied what was coming up.

"He doesn't mean to tease you," Joan said. "Look at him. He's interested in everything. He's interested in *you*. He's never had a grandfather."

The boy, having perused the garden, turned on his heels and headed toward the front of the house. Richie suspected he would head to the town center, perhaps toward the library, perhaps elsewhere, making an innocent display of himself. Look who's moving into the Palumbos'! Could Richie stop him? He seemed to have the strange idea that he was *welcome* in this town.

"Who was she, Daddy?" Joan asked. He had to stop a moment, to try to remember. Who was Joan referring to? Above him, a creaking in the house disturbed him, and he looked up.

2

Perhaps, Joan thought sometimes—long after the drama that led to her leaving the nuns—the whole difficulty had been that she'd chosen to return to the monastery in winter, in the month of January, after her time spent at home following her mother's death. Stella had died in August 1998, and Joan had come home to take care of Richie. To cook for him, to see that he was all right. The mother prioress had encouraged her to do this.

But being back in the house in Norumbega in those sweet autumn months had only made her want to stay. The comforts of childhood were there. Richie, it turned out, had not needed much attention, not then, not at the beginning. He'd already eaten breakfast most mornings before she came downstairs; it was more often he who cooked for her.

In the afternoons, both she and Richie had ritually lain down for naps. Life—the active part of life—need not go on. The enormous light of September entered the room where she lay. Stella's absence had seemed vast. Also, comforting. In those days, Stella seemed to be hovering over the house, holding them both in her grasp.

It ought to have been God's. That was the difficult argument she had with herself as she walked, post-nap, in the afternoons. She ought to have felt God's grip, His presence, more than she did, been more secure in the belief that her mother had gone to Him, was being received in His embrace. Instead, there was evidence of Stella's continuing presence. Tiny moments in the house. Once, her father had asked her to carry some of Stella's sewing things up to the unused room on the third floor. On the last step, always a tricky one, she felt herself falling backward. An invisible hand had been there to steady her. She could explain it no other way. According to all logic, she should have fallen.

During that time, she found herself looking forward to the comics in the *Sunday Globe* with an eagerness that surprised her. They were a treat she hadn't allowed herself in her girlhood, when she'd been preparing for the monastery. But they formed now, in this time of grieving, a reintroduction to life. The adventures of Adam, a paunchy man with several children, whose main impulse seemed to be to survive the daily chaos of family life simply in order to settle, at the end of the day, on a lumpy couch. The family of "For Better or for Worse," enduring the trials of marriage, children, teenage dating, all of it driving the chinless mother into a state of mild, just-bearable shock. In only one comic, "The Family Circus," was there a spiritual element. A family whose round, simple faces seemed all cut from the same cloth had their lives watched over by a deceased grandfather standing on a cloud. In his afterlife the grandfather wore the golfing clothes he'd worn in life. To Joan it made sense. It was the way she thought about her mother now, this cartoon version of eternity. Only inches away from the living, she watched. At any moment Joan expected to hear her voice: *Do this.*

In the midst of her time caring for her father, she'd received a note, forwarded to her by the mother prioress.

Dear Sister Gertrude,

It took some prying for me to get the story out of the nuns. Some of them wouldn't talk to me. They told me your mother had died and you went away. They wouldn't tell me where. I am sorry for you and I will pray for your mother. I don't want you to think my prayers are such a big deal, or that I'm holy or anything. You know I'm not that. But I will do it.

What they wouldn't tell me is whether you are coming back. All they said was if I wrote, they would send it to you. I still bring Hector and Felix on Sundays. Felix has an easier time with the Mass than Hector does. He's a quieter kid, more patient. Hector is getting a little mean, if you really want to know.

I'm sorry. I'm just going on here about my kids and you're in mourning for your mother. I know she must have been a good woman. I remember I even met her once. I hope you had a good relationship with her and that this time is not too hard for you.

Write and tell me when you will be coming back and how you're doing.

Yours,

Angel Lopez

She'd folded it, put it away, had always meant to write him back. "Angel Lopez," as if she wouldn't remember him otherwise. It was a sweet memory, his arriving with the first of the little boys at Mass one day two years before her mother's death. "From the ice, remember?" he'd said, and then asked if he could talk to her.

He'd never known how much his subsequent visits and their conversations had isolated her from the other nuns and subjected her to their criticism. She felt far away from all that now, in the very different environment of home. How silly it had been, though, to be forbidden to talk to a man. The mother prioress had spoken to Joan about it only once.

"Word has come to me. A young man comes to Mass and delays you afterward."

"Surely you've noticed him, Mother."

Anselm allowed that to pass without responding. "It's the delay that concerns me."

"He wants to talk sometimes."

"Perhaps he should speak to Father Alfred."

"No, it's me he wants to talk to."

Something had made her brazen in the ten years since arriving here. It had been noted.

"Why you? I wonder. I wonder, too, whether you did well in ignoring that advice I gave you when you first came here as a girl."

When Joan, deeply embarrassed, said nothing, Anselm added, "To date, I mean."

"I know what you meant, Mother."

"We're not evangelizers, Sister Gertrude."

She had allowed that to sit. Joan determined only that she would endure this conversation.

"His children are beautiful," she said.

"As are all God's creatures."

Perhaps her continuing attention to him had arisen out of spite. Julian had left the monastery by then. Her friend, her confidante. (That, too, had always been disapproved of, their "special relationship.") Julian had been the victim of a depression that would not go away; it kept her, for a long while, from eating. The nuns had not known what to do with this; it made them shun Julian, cruelly. Julian had been a "cynic," some said, her depression seen as a comeuppance. All the nuns save Joan had followed Mother Anselm in this scapegoating.

Joan had gone to see Anselm once to complain about this, a risk, she knew. It would flag their "special relationship" in a way that might not be of help to Julian.

"I don't know anything about depression. That's a clinical term, isn't it?" Anselm had answered quite simply. "Sister Julian needs to attend to her bodily needs. Without that, there's no service to God."

In the silence and the space created between them afterward, Joan perceived the organization of the religious life in its inhuman aspect. No one was to hold up the private wound and cry *Me!* They made no provision for it. Though in the end they did bend. Julian was asked if she wanted to see a psychiatrist, but the offer, coming so late, seemed ungenerous, a sop, and Julian elected to leave.

Why then, Joan had to wonder afterward, should she turn away a friend like Angel, when the community of nuns rendered love so conditional? This had led to a great confusion, broken, if only briefly, by her mother's death. But she was never sorry she had not turned Angel away.

At home after Stella's death, she thought increasingly of the possibility of a permanent return to the world, of a life of service not so strictly controlled as the life of the monastery.

The most attractive possibility would be to live at home, attend to her father's simple needs, pray the hours she'd become accustomed to, but alone, in the back of a nearby church. Yet as the days at home went by, she became aware of another force, one she would have called acedia—the will to do nothing—if it hadn't felt so strangely alive. Like a living pulse running through her stomach in the area of the liver, long suppressed, now announcing its own beat. What was it? A *desire*? Was that what it was? A simple desire for something in the world?

Whatever it was, it had not gone away when the time came for her to return to Lancaster. After months away she could find no more excuses. Sister Anselm would not accept a plea for more time involving the fact that she would miss delivery of the *Sunday Globe*, would miss "Adam" and "For Better or for Worse" and "The Family Circus." It was a rainy January when she returned, the grounds of the monastery slick with ice, the postholiday diffusion and emptiness present. Sister Monica slipped on her way to the car for a grocery run and broke a bone in her arm.

Joan's time at the priory had ended, and she knew it had ended, though that was a sentence she would not allow to appear fully formed in her mind. The nuns all asked after her mother; there was politeness, kindness, occasionally genuine concern. But each time she took a walk and came to the place where she'd found her mother returning from her own walk on that last visit, she felt something like a clamp descend over her heart.

Her mother's messages were not yet clear ones. Joan felt at times that they could come from anywhere; some Sunday the grandfather in "The Family Circus" might act as a conduit for Stella's messages. On his cloud above the little family, inside the bubbles within which comic strip figures spoke, he might become sibilant and profound; the vast Boston readership would be dumbfounded and move on to the next comic, but Joan, its intended recipient, would have missed it.

She sometimes thought of her mother as she'd appeared during that last visit, returning from her walk, close to death yet buoyant. Stella

253

had been insistent with Joan, wanting to know all about Angel (there was nothing to tell, not yet, all of that was still far away), even annoyed, as if she'd known she had limited time to get to the nub of some truth the two of them had never quite reached together. What was that truth? Stella had seemed thrilled by the simple fact of Angel, a man in Joan's life. They'd come close to a conversation they never before had the courage to have.

If Joan could have, she might have told her mother now about the moment that had begun this life for her, the moment she separated from all of them. Her deciding day. She wanted to probe it now, to probe everything, the hidden beginnings of her life.

She had been seven or eight years old. They'd all been in the car, near Christmas, in the midst of a town. "Stop here," Stella had said. Certain things were of course vague. Perhaps it was Waltham or Watertown, in the days of the still-thriving downtowns, late sixties or early seventies, large, open movie palaces, stores that were not chains, women's dresses in the windows, the white mannequins posed. Stella had gone into one of these stores, and they all waited, the car idling, the heat a solid texture among them. Jack's stillness, his young male alertness—she remembered that, too—his intense need for his mother stored in his body. You remembered certain scenes from your childhood as if an X-ray of the senses lay before you. The way they all waited. Tiny flakes of snow, the windshield wipers turned off. Then Stella returned, carrying a package.

It had been near Christmas, so there was reason to believe that the package might be for her, Joan. But she'd felt none of that potential excitement. Instead, an absence intruded, something so strong it nearly had a face. There was her mother, a woman coming out of a store, and Joan waited for a feeling that ought to arrive at any moment. Love. Safety. Assurance. She felt, instead, the onset of terror. Her mother was only a being like any other being, one of millions in the world, who went into stores, who told their husbands to wait, who anticipated the bright wrapping performed by a cheery salesgirl and then stepped out into the light snow. Her mother's simple woolen coat seemed a harbinger of some elemental lack of defense against a threat that lay in wait. There is no safety, no safety at all. How did a seven- or eight-year-old perceive this? Yet she had.

Later, in the literature of nuns, she read that others had moments like this, a moment of cruel detachment from the world, of receiving a separate call. One wrote about waving goodbye to her father from a train, another about being at a big family party. The details were always different, but the result the same: a calling that began as a separation.

Then her mother had entered the car. A very simple scene. Stella turned to Richie, he to the package in her arms. A silent message passed between them, perhaps his disapproval, her defiance. Very small, a scene that might take place between any couple, hundreds, thousands of times in a marriage. Nothing, really.

And yet, everything. Sometimes, as a small girl, troubled by the beginnings of insomnia, Joan had had a vision of things being stacked, large slate stones, one on top of another. Here was something like that in the car, a sense of large, crushing units falling one on top of the next. Though it was only her father's look, her mother's response, those things seemed to contain a terrible weight. A chasm lay between these two people. How had she described this moment to her mother once? "Evil opens." Not exact, but words as good as any. An awareness of the vast emptiness at the heart of the world—a man and a woman and the nothingness that might exist between them. She remembered turning away. *They cannot save or even protect me.*

In the lives of the saints, this is how it goes: at such moments the child turns away, and there, on a street corner, in a field, by a fountain, the Virgin appears. Sometimes draped in flowing robes, other times more simply dressed. Her hand out, or not. On her face, the peace that passeth understanding. An open road carved into sheer rock.

For years Joan tried to pretend she had seen the Virgin at that moment. It would have made things so certain, so simple and elegant and complete. But she had not seen anything at all but snow falling, the shops, women coming out of them, the lit marquee of the movie theater. Nothing but that. All of it alive, blazing, full of an alternative reaching out to her. *Go that way*, she had heard, or not heard. *You are denied the other.* For years she tried to piece together the components of that moment, to determine why it had been so strong. And failed.

But now she listened—as if at the very edge of this story—for Stella's whispering commentary on that long-ago day. Had it been not God, but fear? She listened, as if words might come from anywhere, from a tree, from the wind. The hand that had held her up at the top of the stairway was also, she could not help but feel, pushing her forward.

3

Jack's daughter Zoe was twelve now, an awkward age, thick glasses, dark hair cut short, almost to the scalp. She carried a book at every available opportunity. Today, on the day they were going to help Joan and Angel move into the house in Norumbega, it was *Show Boat* by Edna Ferber. The library copy was old, with yellow tape peeling off the old slipcover and a picture on the cover of a black man heaving a big purple bale. She read in the car, so deep into the book she probably didn't remember he was beside her. When he had the chance, Jack looked at her, at the muscles in her neck. At a stoplight he couldn't resist reaching over and kissing her neck, biting it gently.

"Stop." She swatted him away.

"I'm giving you a hickey."

"What's a hickey?" She still had not looked up from her book.

"It's something—in the old days, in the ancient days of courtship—boys would give girls. Big red blotches on their neck. It was a sign of—something." He glanced down to make sure she was listening. "Possession, maybe? The girls would wear makeup to cover them when they showed up the next day at school. But it was selective makeup. They wanted to pretend to modesty. But they also wanted to show their classmates that they'd gotten one."

Zoe looked up, stared ahead for a moment, taking it in before going back to her reading.

She had become, at twelve, his receptacle. He'd always had one, first Joan, then Christina, now this little girl who endured it all, as he supposed the others had: the epic of Jack. At forty-six, he was becoming aware that it was not such an epic as he'd once believed, that his story had grown a little depressing. He was a man separated from his wife, on a bewilderingly long track for divorce, who had lived an early life of sexual splendor but now didn't. At low moments he went so far as to consider himself, and especially his latest sexual accommodations—the ones he had made in the wake of the separation—pathetic.

His youngest child was the only one of his three who would have sat still for his stories. The two older ones were Christina's children, had always been. Some difference lay in this one. He'd known it from the beginning; something kept her apart and made her more like him. He had a vague awareness that this was not going to be entirely to her benefit.

It was a Saturday, late June. School had recently ended. His and Zoe's connection to each other was manifest in the way he'd known she would come with him today, without his asking, to help with the move. Though she'd brought the book, and though in every visible way she pretended to be absent. Sometimes he would incur a slight wound on his body. Fixing things, or playing racquetball after work. He would mention it to her, weeks would go by, and then, out of nowhere: "How's that cut?" Or a small thing at work, a problem he was trying to work out, something he had spoken about once, briefly. She retained that, too. She would look up from her book only for a second or two to ask after his difficulties, but the fact that she remembered at all, that he lived in her in some way, left him moved beyond words. Also unsettled. It felt wrong for a daughter to so willingly bear a father's burdens this way.

The others had long ago gone off into their lives. Christina, after the separation, had found a place in Newton so that Elisabetta could go to Newton South, where she was a varsity forward in soccer, starred in *Le Bourgeois Gentilhomme* and *Camelot*, and, about to become a senior in the fall, planned to apply for early admission to Brown. She would of course get in; no one doubted it. Watching Elisabetta on the stage, Jack had the uncomfortable sense of watching a killer at work. No one was safe, least of all the boys playing opposite her, who looked cowed, prepubescent, helpless. She'd acquired a finish before anyone else had; she had Christina's looks, with some confidence-inducing additive composed of horseback-riding lessons, creative writing for middle schoolers taught by a published novelist in Cambridge, and the coup of having been chosen to play Clara in a local ballet company's production of *The Nutcracker* at age twelve.

Joe was following in his sister's footsteps, though in a different school. Christina had insisted, for reasons Jack could never understand, that Joe attend a private school in Waban, the Leeds School. The idea was insane, the tuition astronomical, but Christina could not be talked out of it. A vague and finally unprovable argument about "learning disabilities" had been placed before Jack; Joe would do better there, Christina quietly maintained. When Jack dropped the boy off or picked him up at the Leeds School, he had the sense of entering not an institution of learning, but a Rolling Stones training camp. All the boys seemed to be working hard to affect the louche attitude, the "Under My Thumb" air of sexual entitledness, the thatchy, unkempt hair of a young Mick

257

Jagger. The school's one insistence that it *was* a school lay in the fact that the students were required to wear vaguely Etonesque school uniforms.

Within this world, Joe's single rebellion seemed to be his look: he wore his straight blond hair so that it fell in long bangs across his face and hung just over his neck in the back. Jack caught him smoking once, while he was waiting to be picked up. "What was that?" he asked once Joe was in the car. After a long moment, a low breath out, a checking of the text messages he might have received in the time since putting out his cigarette and entering the car, Joe turned to him. "What?" "The cigarette you were smoking." "It was a cigarette," Joe said. Then he put in his earplugs to listen to his iPod. Jack pulled over, ripped the earplugs out, causing the boy to reach up and touch his offended ears. "Don't. Do not fucking smoke, all right?"

The look Joe sent back to him was one Jack had come to hate: you cannot get to me. Jack's rage at him was always a bit more than was strictly warranted. His own son had become a boy of a type Jack had never fully approved of: drenched in class privilege and entirely unapologetic as to the fact.

His children were with him on alternating weekends, but even on those, the two older ones found excuses to be elsewhere. This in spite of the fact that at the onset of the separation, Christina had insisted he keep the house in Watertown "for stability." She seemed to have everything worked out rationally in her endgame, down to the mediator she selected. It was not entirely a shock to him when she told him she wanted to move out. Christina's withdrawal had been gradual. A man less in love with her would have noted the signs earlier than Jack had, but even he had finally come to see them as unmistakable. Still, three years into their separation, a part of him could not accept that this might be permanent.

With too little to occupy his thoughts, he went over the marriage constantly: Were there things he could have done to halt Christina's slide away from him? Were there things he might still do? What he always remembered, when all else failed, was a poem of Rilke's.

He'd come upon it in his poetry years, the wild years of Elspeth and Dr. Wooten, of John and Michael and gay, dying early-eighties New York. In the poem, Orpheus had gone down into the underworld to bargain with the King of Hades to save Eurydice. The classic deal had been struck: you can lead her out if you don't look back until she's in the light. And at the last moment, the heartbreaking moment, of course, Orpheus looks back, thinking she's out, but she's not, not quite. Rilke's addition, his brilliant gloss on the legend, was that at the last moment, realizing that Orpheus has screwed up, that she's got to return to the underworld, Eurydice smiles.

That seemed now to Jack, as he looked back over his marriage, as true as anything else he might come up with in explanation. Look at the evidence. Christina was tending now to her father, the still living, crustaceous, seriously ancient Norbert Oakes. In the big house, with her mother, whose long gray hair had been pulled into a tight bun as if to confirm a family policy of sensual austerity, a mother who wore long, bulky skirts to hide the bulge of her WASPy belly. Christina seemed to have gone back willingly to the confinement she claimed she'd always felt with these two. She'd even begun referring to the deadbeat who'd sired her as "Daddy," a term of affection she never used when they'd been married. The recent past was nothing, really. Their time together, nothing, just something she'd needed to do in order to get her three children, and then to get them into good schools and make the first two, anyway, into an unapproachable prince and princess. There were all kinds of narratives to explain failure, but this was the one he'd currently settled on. Christina had needed this particular descent, for reasons he could never fully understand. But that did not make it permanent.

He glanced down at Zoe. The place where he'd kissed her (not really giving her a hickey, he would never go that far) had left a very small red blotch, his mark. Christina would ask about it, no doubt: You're giving her *hickeys*? Something more to tote up in the negotiations that always went on even after everything seemed settled. Christina taking an eraser to the past, history getting rewritten: I was never that. Or *that*.

But of course she had been. That was the one thing he could hold to in these difficult years, while he waited.

The sexual accommodation Jack was ashamed of, and spoke to no one about, had started three years before, a few months after Christina moved out, when he made the decision to attend his twenty-fifth high school reunion.

Because there was no place large enough to fit them all in Norumbega, the class of '79 committee rented a ballroom in a Boston hotel, which, as it turned out, was a little too small for the gathering. The old classmates rubbed up against one another, flashing pictures of gawky children. Not many remembered—very few of the men he spoke to, at least—Christina Thayer, who of course wouldn't have dreamed of coming to this event. When he tried to describe her, to jog people's memories, he found himself becoming a little defensively rhapsodic, which grew embarrassing. "Oh *yeah*," some of the men said. "She was blond. Quiet. *Her?*"

It was late in the evening before he ran into Ellen Foley. Perhaps he'd passed her and not quite taken her in. She was now the sort to blend in easily with a crowd: the large glasses, the simple dress making no display of its expensiveness, a slightly exaggerated thinness. "Oh my God," she said. "The man who broke my heart."

"Ellen. Jesus."

She maintained a dryness and an ironic tone—a habit of not quite meeting his eyes—as they related life histories. She was a lawyer specializing in family law, traveling often to assist at long-distance adoptions. Married. Two daughters. She pointed out her husband, a man nearly as thin as she was, dapper, with a neat mustache. (He resembled Dickie, the less interesting of the Smothers Brothers.) Also a lawyer.

"I'm separated at the moment," he had to admit. "From—"

"From Christina Thayer. Of course you're separated, Jack. I'm surprised it lasted this long."

He was halted for a second or two.

"Have you been following my life, Ellen?"

She smiled but would not answer. It seemed more important to redirect the conversation, to let him know in her subtle way how well she had herself done: the house in Sherborn, a summer place in Maine. It might have ended there, except that toward the end of their little chat he noticed, in one of her nostrils, a small, perfect round of snot protruding, and he knew she would want a friend—an intimate—to point it out.

"Listen, Ellen," he said, "this is embarrassing. Do you have a tissue?"

She opened her purse—small, gold—and he spied a pack of cigarettes inside. She handed him the tissue.

"No. Don't be embarrassed. It's for you."

It had been a small intimacy, they were briefly a married couple, it made them both laugh a little, though he could tell she was a bit upset about the flaw in her self-presentation.

"Listen, I saw your dirty little secret," he said.

She looked, for a moment, like she'd been exposed.

"You want to go out and have a smoke?"

When they were outside lighting up, leaning against one of the pillars that held up the hotel's overly elaborate portico, they both became aware of a potential opening—something like a private joke remembered only by the two of them. It excited Jack, this little break into his more glorious past, but he sensed a hesitation on Ellen's part. She might have felt the same as him, but it would be up to him to go forward.

"You probably don't remember," Jack began. "Something you said to me a long time ago when we were—dating."

"Did we *date*?"

"Yeah, I think that's what it was."

She smiled, but not fully. What it felt like was that she was holding back full approval of him. They were miles from who and what they had been, yet he felt, in her eyes, that he was still what he had been: having not ascended into the aristocracy of Boston law or finance, he was still Jack Palumbo, boy. When he described his job to her, he could see her vision of him, hot-rodding around with a car full of drugs.

"You said when I was older, when I was a father, you wanted me to call you up."

She looked blank.

"I said that? I wonder why."

Though he had no right to, he'd expected something more, that this earlier request had come from a deep stratum within her. "Well, I guess—I mean, I guessed then. That it meant something. You were a deep one, Ellen."

"A deep one? Jack, I was the most depressed teenager on the face of the planet. Even you must have guessed that."

They were interrupted by the appearance of a couple looking for their car, the valet dashing up to collect the ticket stub, so they went off to the side, sat on a low wall bordered by hedges.

"What do you mean, 'even me'?"

"You were so happy-go-lucky. Why were you even fucking somebody like me?"

He hated it that the word came out of her mouth so coarsely. Was everything about the past to be dismissed this cavalierly?

"I thought you were kind of cool," he said. "A challenge."

"Like you could make me happy."

"I thought that. I guess. So here I am. I'm a father now."

As she gazed at him, was some need or vulnerability in him showing? Her gaze lasted a long time, finally giving way to one of her tiny, maddeningly evasive smiles.

"Psychotropic drugs were the things that got me out of my misery, Jack. Not some happy-go-lucky high school boy."

Her answer hadn't given him what he wanted, but he played along. "Aren't they wonderful? I sell them."

"Did you become interesting, Jack?" She pressed the lit end of her cigarette against her heel, putting it out.

"Jesus, what kind of a question is that?" He waited a moment, still trying to read her. "I had a complicated marriage. *Have* one. Does that make somebody interesting? I've got to say, you're looking at me like you're disappointed."

"No, it's not that. I just wonder why you haven't asked me a single question about myself."

"Okay. How's your marriage?"

"You're obsessed with that subject, aren't you?"

"I guess that's how uninteresting I've become."

"It's adequate. My marriage."

"Okay."

"Which sounds like it's leagues ahead of yours."

"Mine had its moments."

"I bet."

"Listen, it's been really good seeing you again, Ellen, but maybe we should go back inside."

She touched his knee, a gesture he was not ready to interpret except in the most basic way: to stop him from going.

"Jack. I'm sorry."

"I feel like you want to rake me over the coals. For marrying her."

She didn't comment, instead turned slightly away from him. In the silence, he felt the possibility of the conversation they were not having, the one they could not quite figure out how to have. The one she, in her eighteen-year-old's wisdom, had known a quarter century ago that they ought someday to have. *When you are older, when you are a father, I want to know you.*

"Are you seeing anyone, Jack?"

262

Though she'd asked it directly, he still hesitated from inferring anything. Still, his interest couldn't help being piqued.

"Jesus, I'm barely separated. Give me a little time. I'm just getting used to it. Mostly my life these days is cutting the mold off the bread on Saturday mornings. You know what I'm talking about?"

"No."

"Bachelor life. I have a daughter I adore."

"You said three kids."

"Sure I did."

Her eyes narrowed a little, another small, enigmatic but less detached smile.

"Was it worth it?"

"God, you're still a little bit pissed at me, aren't you? For marrying her."

"Of course I'm not."

"For dumping you at the prom. That's what this is about, isn't it?"

She shook her head, smiling in reaction to his teasing manner.

"This all happened a hundred and six years ago, and you're still pissed."

"I'm not . . . pissed."

"Okay, listen. I'm going to try to explain something. Maybe I owe you this. That night, at the prom. That night I was very cruel to you. Don't ask me how I know this, but when I looked at Christina that night, I felt like everything important I had to learn about myself was in her. Do not ask me how I knew that. Moments like that make a young man cruel. The urgency of them. This is going to sound really stupid."

"What is?"

"The phrase in my mind right now? Really stupid. I had to get to her. She held my capacity."

Her eyes widened again, and he felt a little embarrassed by that overblown phrase.

"Does that make any kind of sense?"

"Help me out," she said.

"Look, when you're young, you think you have all this potential for—"

"For what?" She was smiling. She thought she knew exactly what he meant.

"I don't think I can go on without sounding like an idiot."

263

"Oh, *try*." She was still smiling, clearly teasing him. "Tell me, Jack, about your capacity."

"All right, I'm sorry I said that. And I'm not going to offer up another thing until you do." She looked at him again. If there had been some intimacy achieved, she seemed to be turning away from it, as though she'd remembered an appointment. She asked him if he wanted another cigarette, which felt like a kind of sop.

"I yell at my son for smoking," he said. "No thanks. One's enough."

"Then I won't either. And I think, if I don't go back inside now, I'll be missed."

She stood, dusted off the seat of her dress. He followed her inside, and for the rest of the night he watched her. He could not quite believe he'd said such foolish-sounding things, and as a result, he drank too much. Still, he watched her as she stuck close to her husband, anxious for some sign from her. The husband placed his hand on her back a lot. Jack thought of the word *couple*, and it was as if he were watching a living definition of that word. But something seemed not quite right.

Two weeks after the reunion he received a note.

"I think I want to know you again," it said. "As little of your capacity as I seem to hold."

He considered not responding. Was there something dismissive in her tone? They e-mailed for several weeks, and in the end he gave in. He convinced himself this was something he was doing only to allay his loneliness, the sort of affair that could never hurt him with Christina. It would be his secret; she need never know.

Right away, as soon as he and Zoe had arrived at the house, he could see that his father was upset, cranky and shuffling from room to room. The old man had nothing to do during the move—Joan and Angel wouldn't allow him to lift anything—but he kept imposing himself, following things as they came in, boxes mostly, and the boys' furniture, objecting to certain placements, grumbling when corners were knocked into.

His father was failing. At least that was Joan's view of it. An old man who was beginning to forget important things, who could not be trusted to live alone. She was bringing her new family to live in the house, and though Richie hated this change (he'd told Jack as much, lucidly, Jack thought), it was happening. Joan would have her baby here—still an astonishing sentence for Jack to form. Joan having a *baby*.

That there were complications for Jack involved in this move, he only half admitted. The change effectively forced him out; he would not be the one to save his father, if such a thing needed to be done. Not him, but Angel, who would be here, who would repair things. Not Jack's children, but Angel's running through the house.

In the end, these were inadmissable thoughts. He was going to be supportive of Joan. He did not need to be master. He was here to help, and when Joan took him aside and said, "Please distract him," he instantly agreed.

"Dad, let's go out, let's take a walk," Jack suggested, but Richie only looked at him as if he were crazy. So, after a couple of other failed attempts, Jack gravitated toward his old room on the second floor, where the older of Angel's two sons, Hector, was moving in.

Of all of Joan's new family, Hector was the one who most intrigued Jack. Tall and at fifteen not particularly handsome, he wore his hat in the newish affectation of black and Hispanic kids, squatted atop their heads and pointed off to the side. When Jack was growing up, anyone who wore his hat that way would have been singled out to be made fun of, but it had become somehow the essence of young male hipness. That this particular style had to be made room for in his father's house seemed to Jack amazing.

Standing in the doorway, watching the boy survey his new space, Jack thought he'd never seen anyone look so out of place. Hector moved around the room less like he was preparing to live in it, than like he was casing it, seeking out exits, looking for the weak spots in the walls. Jack wanted to tell him to relax, but felt he hadn't yet earned the right.

All he said was, "When you get to the high school, look for a guy named Shelton. History teacher." Jack did not know, in truth, if Mr. Shelton was still there. "Tell him you're my—whatever you are. What are you, my nephew?"

"I guess."

"He'll watch out for you."

Did Hector seem offended by that suggestion, like he *needed* looking out for?

"And when you see him, tell him he was right. Tell him I screwed up."

Hector couldn't focus on what Jack was telling him. The boy, trying to look tough and indifferent, looked exhausted by change.

"There's a good view out here," Jack said. He took Hector to the window, where they both stared out at his mother's ruined garden. He wanted to touch Hector in a friendly way, assert some *uncleness* to show affection and support, but the touching part felt too weird and might be misconstrued.

When he looked out at the long field behind, something came over him, a sense memory of what it had felt like to be seventeen, eighteen, the thing you lost with the onset of age, that stream of infinite potential. He wanted to find some way to convey this to Hector, a sense of what was waiting to happen. He turned to the boy, but all he could see was Hector's confused sense that nothing, nothing all that good was waiting, that all that lay behind the house was a field, not a symbol of potential, but one of emptiness.

"You gotta see my room."

Hector's younger brother, Felix, was in the doorway. Felix, anyone could tell you, was going to be the blessed one in this family, the one who would have an easy time. Taller and thinner than his brother, he had an elastic-looking body. He reminded Jack of Gumby.

"Yeah? You like it up there?" Jack asked. "I always wanted to live up there. My father would never let me. He wanted to have us all within sight."

"Yeah, that's the way he is."

Behind Felix, he could see Richie climbing the stairs up to the third floor.

"Dad, where you going?"

"I've got to show them."

"Show them what?"

They followed the heavily breathing Richie upstairs into the room that had never been used before. Richie didn't like the way Felix's bed had been positioned, the headboard just under the slanted eaves.

"What's wrong with it?" Jack asked.

"He'll wake up, he'll bang his head. They should sleep together, I think."

"Come on, let me have my own room, Popi. Besides, I don't wake up that way anyway. I don't wake up and sit up straight. Popi, what do you think, life is like the Three Stooges?"

To demonstrate, Felix lay down on the bed and then popped up straight, faking banging his head.

"That is what *Curly* does, Popi. What do you think, I'm Curly?"

Richie shook his head, unamused. Their relationship was a mystery to Jack, this boy's freedom to dig into the most absurd aspects of Richie's character.

"What if we—" Jack began. "It's a beautiful day. What if we take the kids out on the lake for a canoe ride."

Richie looked at Jack as if the whole issue of the lake—of the other things he might give this boy, in addition to the comfort of this large house—were something he had not yet considered: You mean they get *that*, too?

"Come on, we can steal Norbert's canoe."

Richie seemed not to understand.

"I use it all the time. I'm sure everybody does. Kids steal it and take it out on the lake."

"What's the lake?" The boy lay on the bed, smiling, anticipatory.

"Nobody ever told you about the magical lake in this town?"

"Nobody. Ever."

"Well, some of the most important things in your high school career are going to happen to you on that lake."

"Like what?"

Had no one really told him? To Jack it seemed inconceivable.

"Don't talk to him like that," Richie said, turning away.

Jack had to follow his father into the hallway.

"You make it too easy," Richie said, shaking his head.

Angel was coming up the stairs, so Jack didn't have a chance to pursue the meaning of Richie's words. Angel's shoulders slumped deferentially in Richie's presence. He was not a big man—Jack was taller by several inches—but he had density to him, and it seemed that he was always trying to make himself physically less imposing in his father-in-law's presence.

Angel motioned Jack into the stairwell so that they could be out of Richie's hearing.

"Listen, Joan wants to make him lunch, calm the old man down, have the two of them be alone together a little while. Maybe you and me could drive out to Hinckley. I got one more dresser out there I couldn't fit in the last load."

There was a kind of false closeness in the gesture Angel made—his hand resting on Jack's shoulder, like they were becoming partners in the enterprise of managing Richie. Jack did not quite trust it, but he went along. When Joan had written Jack about the man she was going to marry (the shock of Jack's life, that letter), she suggested that he go to the book of Samuel, Chapter 16, and read about the summoning from the fields of the boy David. "Then you'll understand my new husband," she'd written. Jack had had to go in search of a Bible, but after he found the passage (*"ruddy, and withal of a beautiful countenance, and goodly to look upon"*), he thought this was a typical Joan move, to sanctify it somehow. She was marrying not a Puerto Rican construction guy, but the boy-God. Angel had turned out, in Jack's view, to be much more ordinary than that.

Still, Jack thought, as they sat together in the cab of Angel's truck, there was the sex to consider. Or *not* to consider. His virginal sister and this man. How had it happened? He would have liked to know, but he had a suspicion that any foray he might make into this area would inevitably lead to the sex games he and Joan had played together as children. Even that term—*sex games*—seemed too extreme, though when he'd told Christina about them, she hadn't shied from using the term *abuse.* "No," he'd answered. *"No." Abuse* conjured for him an image of sulfurous brothers thrusting their penises into defenseless girls. He would never have done that. He had only wanted to show her his body. Needed to. It had been their intimacy.

Sometimes—now, for instance, in this truck with the silent, unsuspecting Angel—it occurred to Jack that his way of getting close, his notion of intimacy not simply with Joan, but with all women, had been misguided. He was coming, almost certainly too late, to the understanding that there were parts of him—wonderful parts, erotic parts, deeply private parts—that he had enjoyed immensely but had, in the end, depended far too much on. In New York with Elspeth, he had seen an Italian film about a man so frustrated by his erotic failures that he took an electric carving knife to his penis. The movie ended with an image of the man holding it up after slicing it off, a big red hunk of meat. It had lately become a symbolic image for Jack, himself laying down his own lopped-off organ on Christina's doorstep. Severance from the mistakes of the past. Okay, I'm other things, too. I am other things.

These were his thoughts while he drove with Angel, waiting for

268

what he assumed must come, some intimacy, some effort toward closeness. Even an accusation would be welcome—You messed with her, didn't you?—if only to give Jack a chance to defend himself. But Angel simply drove, wearing a half scowl, until at a certain point he stopped at the side of the road and let the truck idle.

Was there a point to stopping here, beside a long, fenced field that might have pastured horses?

"Umm," Jack said, to prod the scowling man beside him, which made Angel chuckle.

"You wondering why I stopped here?"

"I am."

"Wait'll you see this bureau. Piece of shit. No reason we had to come back here for it."

Jack folded his hands, settled back. Tell all, my friend.

"Tell you the truth, I just had to get out of the house. He makes me nervous."

"My father."

"Sure. No good reason. This is going to be—a challenge."

Jack nodded. If Angel had just needed to get away, why had he brought Jack?

"This is where I found her."

"Found who?"

"Your sister. When she was living with some monks up here. Not the original place, the place she left. She moved in with some other monks. You know all about that, right?"

"I know some of it. Not all. It's kind of confusing."

"These woods are full of monks, you know? She left the nuns, but she didn't know where to go. Not home yet. Some monks up here—their order doesn't even have a name, or if they do, it's just a crazy name, Brothers of the Heavenly Something. They've got a house, with a little guesthouse. Like a kind of monk motel. They took her in."

Angel sniffed, looked down the road. Was that a cocaine sniff? Jack had to wonder. Interesting. It would be a shock to learn that about this man.

"They operate a little thrift shop. They put her to work there. She didn't know how to use a cash register." Angel smiled. "Joannie. She was trying to be an ex-nun. Not as easy as it sounds, I guess. You leave God that way, that's a big deal. This is where I found her. Walking on this road. Looking *little*, you know?"

269

Jack nodded, begging for more. But Angel only looked away, and then there was the disappointment of his putting the truck into gear.

They passed through the town of Hinckley, its Dollar Store, its nail salon, and then the procession of abandoned buildings that spoke a little to the myth of Angel's appearing here in this country of horse farms, monks, and ancient stone walls. The small, old manufacturing base had left behind not only the cement of its old factories but houses in varying shades of decay, shelter for those who had to run away, as Angel's family once apparently had to. Another story Jack only half knew.

The two-family house was on a rise, graceless and brown-shingled, with a stairway leading to the second floor latched to the outside wall. They climbed those outer stairs. Within the house Angel seemed even more internalized, as if not willing to allow Jack to see his true feelings about having taken Joan here, raising his sons here in this shabby place. The rooms had the lifeless blankness of rentals between tenants. Jack had never been here, never been invited, but what struck him, after trying to wrap his mind around the thought of Joan living here, was the shock it must be for the boys to be going from this house to the house in Norumbega. In what must have been one of the boy's rooms, a Lil Wayne poster had been left up, half hanging. An abandoned enthusiasm, or something they had been told not to bring? To ask Richie to confront the world of Lil Wayne apparently above the imaginations of Joan, Angel, or perhaps the boys themselves. Jack took it down, rolled it up.

"What are you doing?" Angel asked.

"They left this. They'll want it."

Angel scowled again, drew Jack into the room where the old bureau was. It was an unimpressive piece of furniture, with a couple of the drawer handles missing.

"All the way out here for this," Angel said. He put his hand on it and regarded Jack, couldn't miss the way Jack was studying these surroundings, though he was trying to do it surreptitiously.

"You're probably thinking, this is where this guy took my little sister?"

"I'm not thinking anything."

Angel stared into Jack's eyes for a moment, making the decision not to be defensive. "It's what I'd be thinking. You know how it is—you been divorced."

"I'm not divorced yet."

"Right. But you know what happens. All your money disappears. Don't ask me why. I was the one taking care of the kids. Mostly."

He sniffed—that cocaine suggestion again; Jack was almost sure it was his own history he was picking up on, not Angel's.

"You don't have to apologize."

"I'm not. I do okay. We're not going to be any kind of a burden on your father."

"I never thought you would be."

Angel continued to look at him, as if waiting something out.

"Joannie thinks it's important we be around for when he fails."

"How's he failing?"

Angel was smiling a little, like the answer would be obvious to anyone less thick.

"No. I don't get it. How's he failing?"

"I don't see so much, but Joannie tells me."

"I don't see that."

Angel gestured that they should lift the dresser. It mildly annoyed Jack that this man should have the power to open and close subjects, revealing only so much before pulling back.

"Maybe we should just take it to the dump," Angel said when they'd maneuvered the dresser down the stairs. "Doesn't go with that place."

"You can make that place anything you want."

Angel's look warned Jack against any kind of condescension.

"No, I don't think so. I think we honor the old man. Honor the house. It's a beautiful house."

"Okay. Your call."

"Maybe you never thought so."

"Thought what?"

"The house. Never thought it was beautiful. It was yours, you grew up in it. Maybe you took it for granted." They took the dresser to the dump and unloaded it. Jack had put the Lil Wayne poster aside and kept it in the cab of the truck.

When they got back to the house, everyone was finishing lunch, and Jack made the suggestion again. The lake, a break from the day's activities. He managed to coerce Hector into coming. Felix and Zoe were already on board, and Richie had to be convinced. With Richie beside him in the front seat of the car, Jack looked into the rearview mirror and saw the faces of the three children. This new, strange mixed family. Richie should have been proud.

"Hey, I saved your poster," he announced to the boys.

Neither of them seemed to know what he was talking about, though later he heard them talking together and thought he heard the words "Lil Wayne" spoken in a disparaging manner.

Norbert no longer bothered to lock his canoe. It was there for anyone. Felix helped Jack slip it into the water. Jack was surprised when Richie wanted to come. There were three of them in the canoe, Felix in the middle. Jack called to Hector and Zoe on shore. "You're next!"

Hector had not bothered to come down to the shore. He sat on a bench near the line of trees, near the sign listing the rules for the town beach. He sat there like he did not believe this world was his now. He would have to be convinced.

They were nearly in the middle of the lake when Jack began to perceive the strangeness in Richie. His father was rowing, but he was staring off at a distinct spot in the middle of the lake.

"You know how to swim, right?" Jack asked Felix.

The boy was wearing one of the old, moldy life vests that had been stored for years under Norbert's canoe.

"Somebody'll have to save me. Help!" Felix said. "Tell me the magic."

"What? Of this lake?"

The boy nodded.

"You're going to have to find that out. You okay, Dad?"

Richie appeared not to hear. He was rowing listlessly, still staring at the same spot.

"Dad?"

"I'm ready to go back now."

"Go back where?"

"Go back home. I don't know what they're doing."

"They're okay."

"No." Richie dipped his oar in hard to turn the boat around.

"He gets nervous," Felix said to Jack, apologizing for Richie.

"You maybe want to take a rest on the shore, Dad?"

"No. I want to go home."

"We promised these kids."

"It's all right," Felix said. "It's okay." The boy seemed to have more understanding of Richie than Jack did. It had become a strange urgency for Jack to show the lake to this boy, and then to Hector.

They rowed back to shore. Richie stepped out of the boat and began to walk to where the car was parked, not stopping to acknowledge the two children who had been waiting.

"I guess this is it," Jack said. The kids did not seem to mind as much as he did. The water of the lake and his own past were so intermingled that to leave it physically was to deplete himself and to give these children less than he wanted to give them. For young people to be so willing to forgo their own pleasures in order to indulge the old seemed a small crime against nature. But no one complained as they marched back to the car, where Richie was settled into the passenger seat, staring straight ahead.

"What'd you see out there, Dad?" Jack asked, but it seemed Richie had already moved well beyond him. It was then that he heard the boys in the backseat joking about Lil Wayne.

4

In the sixth month of Joan's pregnancy, she was up a lot at night, and because of the configuration of their bedrooms, her being up woke Richie. He slept lightly and had trouble getting back to sleep once he had woken. Because it was late August, he could take himself outside, which was what he liked to do, sit in Stella's garden in a bathrobe. He did not fully understand, or remember, that this was the very thing she had done near the end. There were things troubling him, things he could not let go of, though he couldn't quite hold them either, or link them up in a way that felt cohesive.

He thought it might be the house doing this to him, the manner in which the house had changed, the way he was woken sometimes not just by the sound of Joan getting up but by the sound, deep into the night, of the two of them in the next bedroom. He would rise, thinking the sound was coming from Jack's room, that he was back in the late seventies, Jack's high school years, and that Jack had taken Christina into his bedroom, that the sound was coming from Jack and Christina and he must stop it. Before he reached Jack's room, he was always stopped because the sounds were coming not from there, but from his daughter. Here was the new world. Stella was no longer with him; Joan was home with a man. He would get back into bed, but then, on nights like this one, he could not sleep and he got up again.

It would not hold still, the world. That was the thought he brought to the night garden. It galloped. Perhaps Stella's being alive had held it together. After her death, things had fallen apart quickly. Joan's leaving the nuns had been the first of the great changes.

He'd visited Joan in the guesthouse of the monks, where she'd moved after leaving her monastery. He'd gone there often, though the visits were difficult, especially his having to witness her shabby new surroundings, a great fall from the simple grandeur of the old abbey. Her life had seemed to him even more constricted than it was among the nuns: a plain room, hours working in a thrift shop selling old clothes that brought back to him the scents carried by the men he'd hired in the early days of the pizza parlor. She'd been alone there, and though he wanted to ask her what her plans were, she always cautioned him in ways both verbal and nonverbal not to demand an accounting of herself. She was doing what she was doing. She felt its rightness, its necessity.

Did she ever think of returning to the nuns?

No, that was impossible.

As to why, what had happened, she shook her head against that question and smiled enigmatically.

So was it to be this, forever?

No. She was certain of that. Rest assured, it would not be this forever.

What he could not tell her then, just two years after Stella's death, was that he himself had fallen into an affair with a woman in Norumbega. Evelyn Petterino, only the second Italian in the town. She and her husband had come there long after Richie had blazed the trail; now she was a widow. They'd met in a book club set up in the library. He never read the books; he'd gone there just to relieve loneliness, which was the same reason he started with Evelyn. But sex had finally developed with Evelyn, and with sex had come a shame when he visited Joan, as if he carried within himself something inadmissible.

During one of his visits, which happened to be late in the spring, he and Joan sat together in the garden behind the monks' house. There was a small enclosed garden, a statue of the Virgin, a bench. They had reached the place where speech was not much of an assist to them. In the garden that day, Richie had thought of where he was going after

274

his visit with Joan, to the home of Evelyn Petterino, and for the dozenth time, being with Joan made him think he should end it. Seek purity. At least seek solitude and whatever honor existed in keeping himself decent and alone. This sense of a secret—of a kind of inner corruption that he had to keep from Joan—stymied his efforts to help her. But just as he was thinking this, Joan did something astonishing. She was wearing a cheap pink cable-knit sweater that did not quite match the purple shirt she wore underneath. Suddenly, as if in reaction to the warmth, she took it off. She closed her eyes and, breathing deeply, thrust her chest out. He could not help seeing that she wore no bra. Joan, with no bra. He saw the tops of her white breasts peeking out under the purple cloth of her shirt and wanted to cover them. But Joan had been open to the day, and perhaps to something more. As if to signal that opening, she rested her head on his shoulder.

In this other garden, Stella's garden, some echo of that moment came back to him, though not so clearly or so rationally. It had become harder to move forward, to link up that moment with all the ones that followed. But he came always to the essential thing, that Joan had continued her movement toward the flesh and he toward the ascetic—or toward emptiness, really. He'd gone ahead and broken it off with Evelyn Petterino because he'd come to believe that only in solitude could he find something of the primal order he'd always hunted out in this town, in this house, the vision of beauty seen in the November night thirty-eight years before, the still center of the world that had unexpectedly beckoned him when he found himself lost here. What such thoughts always brought him back to was a sense of failure: his effort had not been enough; he had not seized enough, or maybe he had never been able to impress upon his children sufficiently the power and beauty of his vision. He could not avoid the fact that some flaw in himself was at the heart of his failure.

Because such thoughts were difficult, he reacted physically. He stood, shaking a little, and tried to calm himself down. It could drive you crazy, this endless rehashing of things. He moved out of the garden.

In doing so, he passed through the side yard, where so many of Stella's flowers soldiered on all these years after her death, with next to no care coming from him. He ought to do something about this, stake them, something. When he reached the road in front of the house, he became aware that he was dressed only in a bathrobe.

Before he could do anything about that—and what was there, really, to do? he didn't want to go back inside—something in the road before him provided a distraction. There was just enough moon to see by, and the sight of the road opening at its western end into wilderness had always done something restorative to him, providing a reminder of what he was connected to by living here. The statue in the town center commemorating a certain moment, the night when the call had gone out, the spring of 1775; it had been the first thing to draw him here, hadn't it? The shadow of that statue falling on the town green, the potential connection to a purity that might allow them to transcend all that was potentially petty and small about the Palumbo family, their Italianness. It might all be bathed and made pure in this town, free from chaos, like the man in the muffler taking the night air in a city as old as history. He had himself consistently fallen from that vision. It was not just Evelyn Petterino and not just what had happened with Joan. It was the pizza parlor; it was every choice he had made that had pulled them back into pettiness. That had been the failure. He was thinking all this—lost in such thoughts—when he saw the headlights approaching.

It was unusual to see a car this late at night. Perhaps that was why he felt a strange certainty that he knew the person driving. Still, he stepped aside; they were at least a quarter mile away, but if they came too close, he knew he'd be blinded. It might have seemed a gesture of politeness, a form of gallantry, a man in a bathrobe stepping to the side of the road to let a large car pass. Never mind that it was three in the morning. He would not even consider the absurdity of his being out there at all.

The car seemed to be making its way over ruts, as if what Richie knew to be a smooth, well-paved road had given way to its original self, a path for wagons, sheep, cows, horses, deeply grooved, barely navigable. The car bounced a little, then came closer. An enormous silver grille bracketed by throbbing headlights.

It slowed and then stopped. The headlights did not go off or even dim. Perhaps it was a neighbor, someone being let off after a late night, though the car was parked in the wrong place if that was the case. What Richie saw—the car was silent now, or humming so quietly it was the next thing to silence—was the lit ash end of a cigarette being tossed out the window.

Then the car moved slowly toward him.

It was a Lincoln.

When it was close enough for him to see inside, he did not recognize either of its inhabitants. The man in the driver's seat must be his age or older, with close-cropped gray hair, a large face, formidable nose. Not a tall man, but stocky, with the overburdened eyelids of an old sensualist. He was dressed in a jacket and tie, the tie loosened, the clothes, it was somehow clear, of long duration. Beside him was a woman with an abundance of hair, a glittering tiara holding it in place, in a dress that looked sparkling and perhaps purple, a woman considerably younger than the man, though still not young. She gazed at Richie with a smile, as if she knew him.

"Out for a late stroll?" the man asked.

That was all it was, just a couple out driving who thought he was unusual. But ought he to recognize these people?

"I'm . . . yes . . . I walk," he said, moving his arms in a general westerly direction, wondering if the words connected in the way he intended, and seeing from the man's quizzical expression that they probably didn't.

"I live here," he said more firmly. "This is my house."

"Oh, I know that," the man said.

Richie stood a little straighter, sensing danger.

"How do you know that?"

"Because I sold it to you, remember?" the man asked. Then he turned to the woman, as if the two of them were sharing some joke.

"You're Ronnie," Richie said. "Greeley."

"That's right."

The man nodded, smiled at him, something up his sleeve. Richie, disoriented, thought for a moment that some part of their old agreement had maybe gone unfulfilled: he still owed money, and Ronnie had come to collect it.

"You're out late," Richie said, to say something.

"Are we?" Ronnie turned to the woman. They had no shyness about them. Whatever they'd been doing required no excuse.

"Sure, it must be three, four in the morning."

Ronnie looked straight ahead. Some part of him appeared unchanged from the early seventies, when Richie had first encountered him. He had seen Ronnie from time to time, but only from a distance, and not for years.

"Let's go," the woman said to Ronnie; what Richie caught in her was the essence of the good-time girl, the woman who had aged but

277

still sought the party, something like what Evelyn Petterino had been, but socially more hungry.

"I drive by here sometimes at night," Ronnie said, still looking ahead. "Nostalgic moments for me, believe me."

"Sometime you should come in. I'll show you around. Show you what we've done."

Ronnie looked at him, the historic coldness in his eyes.

"That'd be nice. Sometime," Ronnie said. "Tell me, what have you changed?"

An accusation lay in the question, as if Richie had no real right to have changed anything; it had not been in the contract. Richie stepped back a foot or so. What if Ronnie were to see the house's new black inhabitants? Perhaps he could pretend they didn't really live here.

"Years have gone by."

"Yes."

"It was an old house to begin with."

"My mother died in that nursing home we sent her to. You know that, of course."

Richie said nothing. His hands were in the pockets of his robe.

"I didn't. I assumed."

"You assumed she died?"

"Yes."

Ronnie laughed. "Well, that's good. Because she'd be about a hundred and fifteen now if she hadn't."

Ronnie's smile was large but still not warm. And though the woman beside him started to laugh, it was caught short by something when she looked at Ronnie. It was clear they were not long intimates.

"But still," Ronnie said, his right arm back on the steering wheel, turning it slightly though the car was stationary, "maybe she'd have had a longer life if I'd let her stay. What do you think of that?"

"I don't know," Richie said. "She was starting to get a little unsteady. Wobbly."

"Sure she was," Ronnie said. He looked at Richie. It was the look one man gives another man when they are agreeing to maintain a common lie. But something in Ronnie's eyes wanted to challenge his own posture, move past it.

"Ronnie, let's go," the woman said.

Ronnie ignored her, staring at Richie. It seemed to go on forever, that look, becoming coercive, with something of the quality of a hand reaching out and grasping Richie by the collar.

Then Ronnie turned away. "Yeah," he said, as if he were returning to some old, dark agreement with himself.

The woman leaned over and whispered something in Ronnie's ear.

"Oh Jesus." Ronnie shook his head. "Can't you see I'm talking to my friend here?"

It was terrible to watch. The woman, who had to be sixty, was helpless with some need Richie couldn't guess.

"For God's sake, you've got the whole—you've got Mother Nature here," Ronnie said, and then turned to Richie, raising his eyebrows.

The woman settled back, looking deeply unhappy.

"Go ahead."

"I will." She got out of the car and came around to Richie's side. He saw the dress, clearly a dress for dancing. Where had they been? There was nothing, no place appropriate for such a dress in the western direction, only towns like this, quiet, fast asleep at three in the morning.

She did not ask Richie's permission. She went behind a bush that was at the very edge of his property. In deference to her privacy, Richie turned away, though he could hear her. It was a quiet night. Ronnie had no such respect for her intimate needs. He watched, his eyes amused and disgusted at the same time, yet keenly focused, fully absorbed.

"The twat," he said. "Jesus. Look at it. The bush."

Richie closed his eyes. "Don't," he said.

Ronnie looked up at him, eager for a fight. "Who are you?" he asked.

Richie couldn't leave, though he wanted to. He knew that to do so was to give them permission to deface his property further, which he believed Ronnie was not above doing.

"Who are you?" Ronnie asked again. "Better than me?" He laughed. "The two of us. We did it together. You know that. Forced an old lady out of her house. *Wobbly.* Christ." Ronnie chuckled grimly. "How we deceive ourselves."

The woman came back, her tiara at an awkward angle. She was trying to steel herself against embarrassment, adjusting her dress. She got into the car, disgust caking her features like inexpertly applied makeup.

"Okay? Better?"

The woman, angry now, didn't answer.

Ronnie raised his eyebrows again to Richie, long-suffering but smiling at his own joke. "Okay," he said, and worked the gearshift into drive. "Just remind me, what'd you pay for this?"

Richie shook his head. "I don't remember."

Ronnie smiled. "Sure you do."

There followed a long sigh, and the car began its eerily slow movement away. Richie watched it fishtail a little as it passed his house, and he had a fear—sudden, not quite rational—that Ronnie was going to plow into the house. But the car disappeared.

In its absence, he looked again up the road in the opposite direction. Impossible now to imagine that he'd ever had common cause with the souls of those long-ago riders, or with anything like purity. Very much with him was a sense of Ronnie and the woman, larger than they'd actually been, immense figures of corruption who had somehow managed, from the very beginning, to pull him over to their side. He felt compelled to go to the place where the woman had squatted to pee. He wanted to dig up the shrub there, plant something new. Impossible to think of leaving it defiled.

When he turned back toward his house, he saw the figure of Mrs. Greeley standing there waiting for him. I can walk straight, she said. You see? He'd known it all along. There'd been nothing wrong. He had consigned her to death.

"Daddy?" Mrs. Greeley said, and he could see then that it was Joan, waiting for him in a bathrobe, the bulk of her body under it having deceived him. She'd been there awhile, watching him. He knew that.

"Are you all right?"

He wanted to tell her to go in. He could not face her, feeling the humiliation Ronnie had imposed on him, the weight of the old woman's death he had at least partly caused.

"Go inside."

"No," Joan said. She shook her head.

"Go inside."

She waited, unbudgeable.

This was the hardest, had always been the hardest, the way love was offered when you felt you least deserved it, despised yourself the most, how you had to rise to it. Love, that egomaniacal force, insisted on its rights. He wanted to push her away.

Instead, he moved toward her, head down, prolonging the short journey.

"Did you see that car?" he asked.

She didn't answer. He stared at her, waiting for her to say something. He pointed.

"The car that was just here."

He knew she had been there long enough to see it. Time was not that deceptive. Was it?

She reached out and took his hand.

"I'm sorry I keep you up," she said.

He shook his head.

"I know this is hard for you, Daddy."

He reached for some part of her, blindly, clasped the sleeve of her robe, wondering what his eyes revealed.

"The car," he said again, begging for her to corroborate what he'd seen. I've sinned, he wanted to say. I've sinned. The image of Ronnie Greeley, the man's dead mother, even that long-ago Japanese girl, all of them gathered at the periphery. Life was a list of such things. They waited, those you have used, those you have not done right by, for this point of maximum vulnerability, to point a finger.

Because such weakness was too much to bear alone, he turned on Joan.

"You never should have," he said. "You never should have."

He was not quite pointing at her belly.

Joan waited, with her nun's patience. Then, holding him tight, she led him back into the house.

5

At the beginning of her time as a guest at the monks' house in Claxonburg, the time just after she'd left the nuns, Joan renewed her old ritual of taking walks in the morning. Claxonburg was not far from Lancaster, where her old priory had been, and there was always the danger of being seen by a nun driving by on a shopping run or one of the brothers on his way to the dentist. Even in this time of freedom she could not help feeling she was doing something wrong, was about to be found out, that she would have to confess to the prioress.

Each day, though, she pushed herself forward. She was up at dawn, so she had time. Every day to go a little farther, past the farmhouse that sold wood, past the green painted house that had thirty-six windows, past the dip in the road and the long field where there was nothing, and then a house set far back. Each day she had to say to herself, No one is waiting to punish you for this. The large figure of Mother Anselm had to be steadily shrunk until it diminished.

I am brave, Joan remembered saying to herself, a small self-encouragement. To have left the safe life of the nuns, which she had come to see contained love but not the kind of love that had slowly become a necessity. Which was not the bodily, she was sure of that, not the carnal. But neither was it the love of the nuns, which was for God and only conceptually—and sometimes grudgingly—for one another. One day she would write to Julian, but not yet. It was too sad to imagine the two of them meeting, in simple, unstylish dresses, in a coffee shop. Too much with them would be the presence of the bridegroom they'd been unworthy of.

The true shock of those days, the thing she finally had to gather to herself, was to understand that beneath the years-long effort to live without a self, the retarded, squashed-down, mangled, half-choked but ever-patient and still breathing self had managed to stay alive. Its reappearance made her laugh—the simple revealed truth that this is how life works. We try to kill ourselves, but we don't die. This, more than anything she'd been asked to believe in at the monastery, was the message of God. *Go and live, difficult as that will be.* Or was it not God, but her mother offering that directive? She wondered sometimes. Even Anselm, when Joan had come to her with her decision, seemed to understand, and only nodded. No fight for her soul. The soul had fled elsewhere.

So the walk felt brave, as did the discipline of her day—returning, breakfast, Mass, the hours in the thrift shop, the dinners she made herself, sometimes in the presence of what few other guests came to this house. She was looked upon by them as strange, but that was all right. Brother Didymus, who had befriended her on those social occasions when all the religious in the area met, had taken her under his wing. He came when he could, sat with her, understood. The rules were less rigid here, an openness was possible. His way of consoling her was to tell her stories of his own past: his post-high-school, pre-monastery career as a carnival barker and a drunk. He made her laugh. Brave, all of it, to live this life.

It was eight months after she'd left the priory, eight months at Claxonburg working in the thrift shop, eight months of pushing herself farther on her morning walks, when one morning the truck stopped ahead of her. One of its brake lights was out, she noticed. It stopped next to the stone wall bordering the empty field.

A man stepped out of the truck and stood in the open door watching her approach. She was afraid at first. His stance was what made him recognizable. His hair had been cut shorter, and there was something newly coarse or untended-looking about him. It had been two years.

When she came close, he said, "I never thought I'd see you again."

"Hello, Angel."

He squinted at her. The next question he asked, he asked with his hand, gesturing to the road down which she'd come.

"They told me you left."

"I did."

He reached up and rubbed his eye, which still had sleep in it.

"How are the boys?"

Again he narrowed his eyes, as if her every utterance required careful interpretation. "They're good."

She could see that they were not. She could see, further, that trouble had come into Angel's domestic life.

"What happened?" she asked.

"That's what I want to ask you."

She smiled. "I couldn't tell you in a million years."

He looked offended. Astonishing to believe that someone like him could be hurt by her having cut him off.

"I'm sorry," she said.

"What are you sorry for?"

She simply nodded, as if he would know. "Things haven't gone well, have they?"

He had an abrupt reaction.

"Where are you headed?" she asked.

"I got a bathroom to finish. House in Petersham. I almost never take this road."

"Are you still bringing the boys to Mass?"

He worked the door handle of the truck, as if testing it.

"Weekends have gotten weird."

She waited a moment before speaking.

"You're divorced."

"You got to know everything, don't you?"

"I do."

"Okay. Separated."

Then he looked down, as if only in speaking the words did he begin to feel embarrassment.

"I'm sorry."

"Yeah. I'm not."

"Why not, Angel?"

He stared at her as she remembered he'd once done in the woods, when he was trying to reveal without words that he'd been coming from the bed of a woman who was not his wife. What was it he'd said then? "I'm a sinner, Sister."

"Listen, where you living?" he asked now.

"Right up the road here. In the monks' house on the curve. I'm in the guesthouse beside it. I have a room."

He took that in with some solemnity.

She pushed forward, not exactly knowing why.

"I could make you dinner some night," she said. "It's not forbidden anymore. It's different there."

The solemnity did not leave his face; the sense of taboo felt stronger now than at any moment previously. Leading her on the ice, or delaying her after Mass with his babies in his arms, there had been the unspoken barrier that had made him smile and want to push past it. With no barrier, he looked cowed and disbelieving, as though he wanted her to be closed off, barred from him—and from whatever chaos he represented to himself—by the religion he respected.

"I'm not a very good cook. You should know that."

She wondered if he even heard that.

"I'm walking," she said, as if holding to her ritual was the important thing now, even after the gesture she'd just made, which, she knew very well, had invited in the element of danger all her new rituals were meant to keep out.

He did not come for weeks. Then there was the night she returned from the thrift shop and found him sitting in the main room of the guesthouse, a pair of work gloves resting in his lap. He was slouching in his chair. Seeing her, he sat up.

"This all right?" he asked.

His clothes were soiled, his face.

"This is fine." She stood over him. "The best thing I make is macaroni and cheese, but if you need something more quickly, I can make vegetables and rice."

"Macaroni and cheese is all right."

He seemed nervous, cast his eyes from side to side. "Nobody else here?"

"We hardly ever have guests. It doesn't matter."

Some understanding lay between them from the beginning: this was to be balm in his life. The rest had grown wild. The two angelic boys no longer entirely his, and at risk. He glanced around the guesthouse, as spare as a prison, but a prison full of crucifixes.

After dinner she walked him out to his truck. In early autumn, there was still just enough light to see by.

"Why'd you leave?" he asked.

"Impossible," she said, just the one word.

"Got to get you some better clothes," he said.

It pierced her: not insult, but intimacy. Like he'd touched her.

"I don't have to call you Sister Gertrude anymore."

"No. I am Joan Palumbo."

He repeated her name. It may have been the first time she saw him smile fully.

"What size you take? What size dress?"

She shook her head.

"No. Let me."

"I've never in my life thought about such things. There's no need to think about them now."

He studied her so long and completely that she had to turn away. She understood it was a look that was possible only when a man has looked at a lot of things, has judged things previously believed worthy to be not so, has learned to look carefully. She blushed under the force of this look, and he smiled at this power he had.

"No," he said finally. "You should."

Before he got into his truck and drove away, he said, "I can come back?" and she nodded.

She walked down the road, not yet ready to return to the confinement of her room. She had performed the priestly service. It was as if she could remember the feel of his tongue as she'd placed the host upon it. (She was ignoring the moment that had made her blush.) This was what he needed, and she was free now—she felt this—to do for others, to not feel locked in by the limitations and the order of the nuns.

On her way back she saw Didymus in front of the guesthouse. He was smiling slyly. When he wanted to joke with her, he affected an Irish brogue.

"Milady has had a guest."

She gestured dismissal at his insinuation and passed by him.

One day she came back and found a box on the table. A piece of paper with the words "Joan Palumbo" written on it. She recognized his hand-writing from the letter he'd sent after her mother's death.

Inside was a simple black dress. It had a belt. She put it on. Slightly large on her, it made her breasts disappear. She looked at herself in the mirror. In her own view, she looked mousy. She pulled up her hair. No, this would not do. Even the presence of her mother's encouraging voice could not convince her she was ready for this next step. But she wore it the next day to work, and Didymus commented.

"Very fetching."

That day, she returned to her room, put it back in the box, put the box away, and went back to wearing the haphazardly matched clothes Didymus and she had bought together on their trip to the Goodwill store in Leominster, having not found anything suitable in the monks' own store.

Angel's arrivals were unpredictable, unannounced, and sometimes weeks went by without a visit. Then she would arrive home from the thrift shop to find him in the chair.

You could not always eat macaroni and cheese, so she kept a supply of other things; she learned to make shepherd's pie (Didymus, as he became aware of Angel's continued visits, bought her a cookbook), chicken cacciatore, ravioli with sage butter. Angel expressed little surprise at whatever was offered, ate what she presented. Sometimes in the midst of dinner he wore a distracted look, like a hand of darkness had been laid over his features. Then he would look up, as if she had caught him in the depths of a private moment, asking for privacy while still not pushing her away.

"What happened to the dress?" he asked once.

"Oh, it was too big."

"So I'll return it."

"No."

She hoped he would know what she meant. All would be lost if he tried to turn her into something other than what she was. He must not even look for the other thing.

Sometimes he helped her with the dishes afterward, and they walked a little before he got back into his truck. The great humiliation he was undergoing was happening elsewhere. He did not speak of it.

"How come you never wrote me back?"

"When?"

"When you were gone. After your mother died. And then you came back. You never wrote to me and asked me to come back to church."

"I assumed you would."

He did not comment.

"It had to be for you," she said. "Not to see me. Coming to church had to be for you."

"You're talking like a nun."

"Am I?"

"Your religion. Nothing can be personal. Nothing can be just what you *want*."

She turned and headed back. He'd grown annoyed. These were the difficult moments, full of presumption. She did not know how he defined things between them. He gave himself the right to chastise her, to *dress* her, and that was troubling.

Otherwise, their relationship proceeded without explanations, without signposts, naturally. She preferred this. Somehow she knew when he passed from separation to divorce, without having to be told. The weeks when he did not visit took on the feeling of a retreat. For her, it was all God sometimes, all prayer, still. The difference was that she no longer needed the imposed discipline of the religious life, the coldness, eyes averted at the sight of another's need. She still missed the communal singing of the psalms, the time in church, the physical comfort of being part of a flock.

When spring came, she stopped wearing a bra. No decision preceded this. She enjoyed the feeling. Her breasts were not large and problematic. It seemed a response to the change of weather, a request on the part of her skin.

Angel noticed. He smiled one evening at supper, looking. He held a piece of bread and gestured with it.

"Good," he said.

She knew what he meant, blushed.

"Now the hair. That's the last thing."

She reached up to touch it. "It's impossible. It'll stay like this forever."

"All you need is a hairdresser." He was practically laughing, so delighted was he with his suggestion. "In town. I could make an appointment."

"You'll do no such thing."

They ate in silence awhile.

"Are you dating again?" she asked. The strange question—difficult to ask, peremptory—seemed as necessary as placing salt and pepper before him.

He looked at her uneasily, questioning the very question.

But when summer came, he suggested, one night after dinner, that she accompany him to what he referred to as a "swimming hole."

"I don't have a bathing suit," she said, and he smiled.

She got up and started the dishes.

"Joannie." She heard his teasing voice from where he sat at the table. He rose and dried the dishes, standing next to her.

The way he said her name, it was like that was his job, to bring her out. What had to follow such teasing was a silence, her imposition of the required boundary. He was quiet, drying the dishes. She saw the place where he'd cut himself shaving, just under the line of his sideburn, and turned away from it.

He dried and said, "I wouldn't mind swimming, that's all."

"You can go." Then, "How did you cut yourself?"

He reached up to touch it.

They looked at each other, and Joan was frightened for the first time by her own forwardness, and by the look he returned. She searched for the correction, but she could not quite bring herself to say, *Go.*

Then she realized by his manner that he was in his own way as nervous as she was.

"If you want, you can take me there. I won't swim, but I'll watch you."

He turned to her, trying to interpret.

"That doesn't sound like much fun for you."

They drove to the place where he had to park. It was near a stream. He led her down a path, and she could see that he was alert to the potential for other people being there. There was a place where the water pooled, became deep. He seemed cautious.

"I don't have a bathing suit either," he said, as if in apology for some earlier, more sordid thought, the one that had arisen in the kitchen and followed them here. That was the thing in him she liked the most, his capacity to be self-chastened.

"Are you wearing underpants?" she asked.

"I am."

"Then go in in those."

She sat on a soft place on the bank and watched him undress. He turned away from her; he had that much shame, or courtesy. The skin under his T-shirt was a shade lighter than the skin above. He was thirty-six. His was not a boy's body. There were slight rolls above the band of his white underpants and a netting of red marks on his back, a birthmark that had never faded. Above, in the area of his shoulders, were the corded muscles.

He dove in quickly. She thought of John the Baptist and wondered if her mind had been so deeply trained by Scripture as to have lost the capacity to apprehend the world in purely secular terms. But when she forced herself to do that, a coldness crept in. A man named Angel Lopez, a Hispanic man with dark skin (it seemed to affect her for the first time, the color of that skin), thirty-six years old, a divorced man with two sons was swimming three-quarters naked in a stream, having taken her there in his truck to watch him. Was this a truth of love? she found herself asking. The minute you remove yourself from immersion in it, see the brute facts of the other, you grow cold and frightened. Then, immediately, she began to shiver. The word *love* she had not anticipated.

"You sure?" he asked, turning to her in the water.

"I am." She could barely get the words out.

He splashed around, happy.

"Beautiful. My spot. My special spot."

She forced herself to nod so that he would believe she was all right. It was coming over her, overwhelming, in a great wave.

"I hate it when there's somebody else here," he said. "Makes me feel like it's not my own special discovery."

Allow him this, she told herself. She was praying to be taken away. To frame this in terms of John the Baptist had been worse than foolish.

Then Angel came out of the water.

"I should have brought a towel," he said. He was refreshed, happy, no longer ashamed. The hair on his chest, wet, curled downward, pointing that way. Always astonishing, in paintings, in life (those few times, all of them involving Jack), to see the bunching below, its presence so real yet so easily denied, or avoided, in daily life. A thing they carried with them like a second presence. It was coming toward her—she thought "it" while understanding that what made her shiver was not "it" at all, but the way the word *love* had burst out, surprising her.

"Jesus, you're shivering."

She shook her head to deny it. But she felt her skin turn blue.

"Hold on," he said. He put on his pants, ran up to where the truck was parked. He came back with a blanket. He covered her with it. She felt its soiledness, its caked parts. It didn't matter. His arm was over her shoulder.

Was he so far from it? This terrified her perhaps more than anything else, that he could hold her this way and seem so unaffected. He was a friend. That was all he'd ever thought about her.

"Better?"

She nodded. He smiled. Then he stood, a kind, unaffected man. His fear and uncertainty before, in the kitchen and when they'd first arrived here, what had they meant? Some passing thought, that was all, that he could defile her so easily, which he had mastered. She'd been a fool to leave herself so open.

"We should get you home, get you in a shower."

He lifted her so that she was standing. She had never felt so small, so humiliated. This was what love did to you, humiliated you. She would lie on her bed tonight with the lights off. She would think of him and remember every moment.

They drove, and he checked on her. Curious, that was all.

"I'll be all right," she said when they were back at the guesthouse. It was just growing dark. One guest, a woman, sat in the common room reading. The guest looked up at them from out of a space too internalized to contain accusation.

"Place I can wait?" Angel asked.

"No, I'm all right."

"I want to be sure."

She had him sit in an empty room.

When she came out of the shower, dressed again, she found him sitting. Her hair was wet, tied in a towel. It made him smile.

"You see?" he said.

"See what?"

"You're pretty."

It had been said like a brother, an innocent brother, might say to a sister to encourage her. He led her to a mirror in the room, forced her to look at herself. She saw instead his reflection behind her. Whatever had been there before—all the signs of his aging, decay, loss that she'd noticed the day he stopped in his truck on the road before her—all of that was gone, leaving behind only what was beautiful about him.

And in his face, this: he understood nothing. Or else had willed himself not to.

She began to dread the times he came. She made the dinners but tried not to look at him or to offer much. Sensitive, he knew only that something had changed. When she did look up, she caught the hurt, the poverty of understanding in his face. He had wanted a friend, that was all, an ex-nun to care for him. What could be safer or more simple? Yet the times he had moved her physically beyond that—"See? You're pretty," his hands on her cheeks, so that she could still feel them hot against her—had moved her literally beyond the place where she could be what he needed.

And as it went on, he seemed to grow younger in her eyes, the boy in the woods, chastened, seeking a mysterious absolution. That was what he had come to her for, not the messy emotional involvement she was beginning to feel. She knew there were others for him. There was a woman somewhere. She knew it. Joan was for innocent friendship, chosen for torture.

"Well, the fact is, you must tell him," Didymus said one night, quiet, sitting in the chair near her bed, she on the bed, dusk, the light an invitation to some unnameable golden thing, someone else's perfect life descending for us to look at but not to live.

She shook her head.

"No, there is no choice here. You must."

The joking man who had taken her under his wing, who had looked upon her with that sly smile when he'd been a visitor at the Lancaster monastery—*knowing* her somehow, in a moment's glance—could become something else so quickly, this man in the chair, attentive, without ego, harsh in his judgments, her priest.

"Or let me tell you what will happen. He will continue to come and you will suffer. For months or years, who knows? And then one day he will make the announcement that he is marrying again. And your heart will be crushed within your body."

She closed her eyes. "I have endured worse."

"Oh, have you? In *this* area?" He was smiling slightly. He shook his head. "Terra incognita, Joan." He bunched his fist and tapped his heart, the mea culpa.

Then he stood up, looked out the window.

"Terrible that the only experience I had was that one summer at the carnival. I slept with women, Joan. But I didn't love. I knew already what was calling me. Terrible."

There came the night of reckoning. In the end, unavoidable.

Dinner. Something simple. She remembered pouring milk, grating cheese.

"I'm not an idiot, you know," Angel said midway through the dinner, which up to that point had been silent. He put down his fork in the midst of lifting it.

She glanced up, surprised, not comprehending him at first.

Late summer. A year had gone by since the day they'd found each other on the road.

"What?"

"I said I'm not an idiot."

After a moment he looked to the side, considering.

"Did Didymus speak to you?" she asked, literally quivering.

"No, Joannie, Didymus didn't need to speak to me."

He took her hand and led her outside, and they sat on a bench facing the woods. He could have led her anywhere, could have slaughtered her. She had lost the power of resistance and wondered if she were capable of hearing anything he might say.

"I want you to understand what you're getting into. I mean, if . . ."

He patted her hand slowly and deliberately, then kneaded her fingers, each touch affecting her so deeply she felt uncertain of her own consciousness. There followed a confession. She heard some of it. Her vague recollection was that she nodded a great deal, said yes over and over, but none of it was real, or even fully heard.

What was his confession? Bland, she thought, trying not to think like God, to think only like a woman. But perhaps this *was* thinking like a woman, this believing that none of it mattered. Women, mostly, his sins with women. At one point a huge fear rose in her that having said all this, he would go, having declared things impossible. At which point she would melt into the ground.

But then there was a silence.

"I'm scared, too," was what he said, finally. "In case that's any consolation."

Near darkness helped. "Are you sure?" she asked at one point, not even certain that he heard her. A part of her—a large part—could not believe it, to feel the sheer border-crossing wild freedom of exposing her breasts to a man for the first time and having him look at them. And to touch the muscles that lay between his neck and his shoulders. She touched them gently, touching a man for the first time, unsure of the tensility of everything. Was she capable of hurting him? He was nineteen, twenty, a boy in the woods. Why had this not happened years ago? "I always knew" was a thing he said then, or at another time, she could not remember. It hurt immensely, but that did not matter. Neither did the fact that even with her lack of experience, she knew it was not entirely successful. Worth it all to touch his neck afterward, to feel his panting soul and allow her own cry to escape. *"It does not matter it does not matter it does not matter"* were the unexpected and, as it turned out, incorrect words she heard coming out of herself before he covered her mouth with his own.

That had been six years ago. It had taken that long to progress, to marriage, to a pregnancy neither of them thought likely or even advisable. She was forty-three. Angel asked if she was going to take the tests. She answered no, she would accept what came.

There was no cousin across the hills to run to, no gestating synchronous fetuses to leap toward each other in recognition, John the Baptist in his mother's belly leaping toward the just-announced Savior. No one told you that what you got was not the Magnificat, but loneliness and questions. Angel went to work, her father hovered, the boys went off to school, one troubled, the other centered and curious. With her they

293

were deferential: they had never known a woman like her, a woman so shy. Their father's passion for her must have been at least as much a mystery to them as it was to her.

Yet a passion it was, even if a strange one. The poses of married life were ones she had never believed she would encounter. Even after six years they left her only mildly ashamed; more, the feeling was astonishment and gratitude. The sight of the top of a man's head down there between her legs, the sheer, unyielding determination with which Angel went about such business. Had her mother felt the same astonishment? She would like to have known. Her mother had died too soon; she would have been so *useful* now. But then, Joan reflected, if her mother hadn't died, she might still be among the nuns.

So she was alone with all of this change, Joan Palumbo in the realm of ordinariness, praying in the desanctified chapels of her father's house. She was having a child at forty-three, a child who might well be deformed in some way. She could sense Angel's withdrawal and fear sometimes, as though he were already making his peace with something that would alter things between them, not for the good.

But there was more to his potential withdrawal than the threat of an imperfect child. The minute he'd seen her father's house, something in him had grown uncertain. "You're not going to want me in that house," he said to her. She tried to reassure him, but he held to the sense that some late awakening in her, some smoky manifestation of class would ultimately doom him. She could not convince him that she would happily have remained in the house in Hinckley if it weren't for her feeling that she should be here for her father.

No, it wouldn't be class that doomed them. It would be this other thing. No man who knew sex as Angel did would be satisfied with her. To Joan it all seemed temporal, charged; she felt like a woman on a hillside, a wounded soldier had come to her, lost from the war. She'd nursed him, he'd impregnated her, but the time would come when he'd have to go back.

In the fall, the boys at school, Angel at a construction job in Orange, she made her father lunch. Since the night she'd found him outside, insisting on the appearance of a "car," something seemed to be troubling him. But then, all his lapses troubled him. She wanted to ask him about this, but they had no language for it. She wondered how much he even apprehended it. He blamed her, she knew, for her own sexuality, that unexpected, unpleasant intrusion into his life. She could accept this, though with difficulty. She knew by now how much it had been a mistake to impose intimacy on him at the beginning of her stay here, to ask him to touch her belly and the moving child. She sensed keenly his withdrawal from her expanding flesh. She was mortified when sounds came from Angel during sex, sounds her father in the next room might hear. She sometimes wished sex itself might stop, to give her father peace. But not really.

If there was any room for hope that the two of them, father and daughter, might be able to accommodate each other at this stage of life, it came from something that had happened recently. In a corner of the bureau in the room where Richie slept, his marital bedroom, she had found the photograph of the Japanese girl Felix discovered in Richie's scrapbook. He had placed it there. She knew for a fact it had not been there until recently. She would like to ask him about it, but she didn't. Not yet, anyway.

Underneath it she had found a list of Japanese names scrawled in his handwriting, possible names for this woman, as if he were trying to remember her.

It seemed to Joan—though she was not sure how—that it was some kind of message to her. Because the perception was clear, she wanted to leave him a response of her own. Its content rested like a cloud above her head, like the clouds over cartoon characters, she thought. She wanted to offer him comfort, as if the two of them were on some swiftly moving stream and they must hold on, that was all. He needed only to accept the full being he had once been. Then he could accept the change in her.

Find the girl's name, Daddy. Find it or decide on one, but tell me all about it, *tell me*. I will forgive you for whatever you did. Not that there is anything to forgive. *Sex*, Daddy? We do not have to forgive each other for sex. That is the *last* thing we have to forgive ourselves, or each other, for.

The thought was astonishing. Nonetheless, it felt true.

6

The ritual had become a familiar one now that they were this deeply in. Jack always arrived at the hotel first; that was their agreement. The hotel clerk handed him not a key, but a card. Occasionally one of the clerks recognized him and called him "Mr. Palumbo" with some semblance of familiarity, but without warmth. Jack would have liked warmth. Outside their lives as clerks, he knew, these men and women lived in too-small apartments with mothers and brothers and grief, but in their lives as hotel clerks, they assumed a finish that allowed them silently, subtly, to judge him. Ellen, who paid for the room, always had to leave his name.

The room. Ellen had made the request that he be there ahead of her modestly, so it was easy enough to comply. But it always depressed him to wait. It was the noon hour, one, or whatever fit her schedule. The sheer draperies had been drawn, the local menus splayed out, a notebook of recommended Boston nightlife. Studying these, Jack was troubled sometimes by the implied belief that we were all expected to be satisfied by the same things. Everyone would want to eat in restaurants with names like Dolce Vita and Toscano and, afterward, attend shows like *Nunsense* and *Shear Madness*. He felt that—the generic place he had come to inhabit, his life now pretty much the same as anyone else's.

He would have liked to say to someone, *I am Jack*.

The need had never before appeared—the necessity for it, the desire—in a life where "Jackness" had always been self-evident. But it waited for you, didn't it, this moment in a hotel room where, after all the screaming *I am Jack*–ness of your young life, even your early middle life, a river was crossed.

Sometimes when Ellen arrived she was still talking on her cell phone, and she smiled apologetically at him. An adoption involving a Russian baby had gone awry, plane reservations would have to be changed. Sometimes these conversations dug fifteen or even twenty minutes into the hour they had together. He was never sure why he allowed this to go on, except that he had hoped from the beginning, and had never quite given up hope, that these meetings would allow him some connection with who he'd once been, an original self he could still recover and perhaps bring to Christina to undo the turn life had taken that forced them apart.

One afternoon in the early fall of 2007, when Joan's due date was approaching, he got up off the bed while Ellen made the brief call she said she had to make. He stood at the window looking down into the side street, where he could see a woman in a business suit clutching a shopping bag. A wind started up and the woman touched her hair. He thought of his mother without knowing why. The night she'd come downstairs and found him lying with Ellen. He'd known she was there, sensed it, though he kept his eyes closed. For years, his secret. But as she lay dying, when he held her hand, he'd felt each of them acknowledging the moment, their old erotic bond.

He heard the end of Ellen's conversation but did not turn around until she said his name. She seemed to acknowledge the awkwardness of the moment by drawing up the sheet so that it just covered her crotch.

"Will that be all right?" he asked.

"What?"

"The adoption you were talking about."

"Oh. Yes. Fine. I mean, the birth mother was having some last-minute doubts. It happens. I'm sure it'll be fine."

Perhaps she was wondering why he wasn't coming closer, why he just stood there.

She was going away for two weeks. It happened every year at the end of September. Both her daughters were in boarding school at North-field. Her husband and she waited until this time to go up to Maine.

"Will you miss me?" she asked.

"Sure."

He sat and touched her big toe. They had fifteen minutes left, which could be stretched into half an hour if need be. She was waiting to see if he'd be aroused again. Sometimes it happened. But something was bothering him today.

"What—" he started to ask, feeling a brief awkwardness. "What do you two do up in Maine?"

In all the relationships of his life up till now, only a few had involved cuckolding another man. The feeling of moral embarrassment was unfamiliar. Ellen looked at him, curious as to why he should be asking. She reached for a cigarette and lit it.

"We take long walks." She exhaled. She looked at him with the blankness of a good, slightly bored poker player, a part of her perennially closed.

"Do you—"

"Oh, Jack, what a silly question that is."

She was smiling, becoming playful again, though her having covered herself took things into another, more cerebral area of play.

"It's not silly," he said, and meant it.

297

"All right," she said. "Yes. We do."

"Okay."

"Are you shocked by that?"

Once, he thought, he'd known everything about women.

"When you're—"

"Jack."

"No, this is important."

"Jack, I don't really want to talk about it."

"We've got to."

She looked at him, the cigarette in her hand, her chin slightly lifted, and he saw in her eyes that she understood he was on the verge of leaving her, of saying *no more*, that the conversation was crucial that way, her answering these questions in a way that satisfied him was crucial. He also saw—and this was the surprise—the place in Ellen that had developed over time, that allowed her to survive her childhood and her depressions, the part that would be fine—or if not entirely fine, at least *okay*—if he left her now. He was not that important.

"Why do we have to, Jack?"

She put out her cigarette, scrunched herself forward on the bed, reached out, and touched the back of his neck. He bent forward. Her gesture felt comradely, but it opened a space in him he was afraid to have opened. Because what he wanted—what such moments always made him want—was an immersion so entire that he would cease to be himself. He wanted to escape into someone—into Christina—in a way that was no longer available to him. But even as the possibility had fled, the yearning, the simple desire stayed behind. He felt himself a weight too heavy to carry. A woman was *for* that. To unload into. Yet all the silly, cheesy metaphors for sex—the *weight*, the *unloading*—didn't get it right, because the thing you wanted to unload wasn't really sexual at all and wasn't contained in any part of your body. It was the internal burden of yourself. Here. Take this. For a bit, anyway.

She was kissing him now. It had taken him a few moments to realize, to catch up with his own physical self, because he still wanted to have the conversation they'd only started, the one where she explained to him what they were doing together, and what she and her husband did, and what was the secret of life, its essential, maddening truth. That was where he was internally, though externally something else was happening. He'd become aroused, and she was fondling him. She had an elegant way of caressing his penis, her long fingers feeling for parts of it she was now deeply, historically familiar with.

"No," he said, because he didn't want to indulge in the act of sex while feeling emotionally absent.

She appeared not to hear him or else ignored what she heard. After kissing him more deeply for several seconds, she climbed on top of him. As she did, he noted it all: her clipped pubic hair, all the neat, efficient parts of her, this being who was what had become of "Ellen Foley," along with her money, her career, her hard-edged belief in what she did. The only thing missing, apparently, had been a man like Jack Palumbo to fuck her.

So he became what he became weekly, ritually—the only thing she really wanted him to be—Jack Palumbo fucking her.

It took no time at all for her to get where she needed to get, and when he heard her response close to his ear and felt the subsequent appreciative kissing of his ear, her taking the lobe fully into her mouth in erotic gratitude, his emotional distance didn't matter anymore. He was a creature of habit. You just did it, that was all; on some unspoken level it didn't matter who was under or on top of you, except of course it did, and the awareness would not quite leave him that he had been spoiled for this, spoiled by love, spoiled by Christina. That fact could not be changed, not by two or even by three times when Ellen cried out appreciatively and reached down and cupped his balls in that gesture that seemed so generous, so mature. Even as he enjoyed this, he knew how he would feel when it was over, and he tried as hard as he could to put that moment off. But when the moment came, he looked at Ellen and put off for another week the breaking-off words he'd rehearsed, not yet willing to admit that these meetings had become more important to him than to her.

An hour later he was parked outside Christina's mother's house, thinking how it had never changed for him, not since the time he had first come here and Christina showed him her room, when they stood in white clothes, bone hard, panting, in that exquisite state of denial he had felt it was so essential to maintain. There are houses that preserve things, they are like museums of adolescence, they archive your early lust. That was how he always felt entering the house. But today

299

his feelings seemed like the residue of the hour he'd just spent with Ellen.

Waiting outside, he found himself remembering when his daughter Elisabetta had been cast as Guinevere in the Newton South production of *Camelot* three years before. It was one of her early triumphs—to be cast in the lead as a freshman. This beautiful girl with young skin like Christina's had been, skin like a palimpsest, its colors giving way to deeper colors waiting to emerge. Elisabetta had not yet known how beautiful she was, and it had marred her performance. Not at the beginning—she was terrific at the beginning, when all she had to play was King Arthur's child bride, blushing and astonished by everything in the new kingdom. But later, when she had to fall in love with Lancelot and then play the betraying wife, you could no longer believe her; she'd been too young to understand power and choice. There had been a moment toward the end when the big, bearded, husky senior playing Arthur was alone on the stage, his world fallen apart, his perfect kingdom sundered and at war with itself, when he called to the little boy he'd chosen as a messenger. The words he had to speak expressed Arthur's late-life understanding that we are all simply drops of water in a rushing sea. "'But some of them sparkle!'" the senior had cried out with surprising force. "'They do sparkle!'" Hearing those words, Jack had undergone an embarrassing moment where tears had come to his eyes. Arthur was talking about *him*, one of the sparkling ones! God. Such moments. *Stop.* In the car, outside Christina's mother's house, he covered his face, pushing the thought away. Then he got out of the car, composed himself further, and prepared to go inside, where his children and his ex-wife (he had to think of her that way) and her parents were waiting for him. It was Norbert's ninetieth birthday. Jack was surprised to have been invited and had taken the rest of the afternoon off—the post-Ellen part of the afternoon—in order to attend.

The front door was open. He could hear them in the back. The dimmed afternoon light in the front parlor made him stop. The old furniture. The beautiful oak tables and the lamps. Christina's mother's books from the fifties and early sixties. *By Love Possessed*, *The Wapshot Scandal*, the dustcovers faded. It was a world, this room. Coming into it as a young man had been like entering the heady air of privilege itself.

It was faded now, of course. Still, Jack took his time. There was a lot to remember, to take in here in this room where he was rarely invited. Those early days when he and Christina had become lovers and would drive in from her apartment to spend a weekend, and he would sit and revel in the fact that Christina looked so *released*, a new easefulness manifested in her body as she moved through these rooms that had once so burdened her. Her gratitude to him had still been mixed with moments where she felt she had to be cautious, could not quite trust him, could not quite trust herself *with* him. In her bed, watching her look down at him, he could see the way her face dealt with ambivalence, that sense that there was something sordid about him, about what they were doing, something not entirely worthy of the internal being she'd always protected in herself. What he had taught her, what he had tried to teach her, was that if you didn't embrace the sordid in life, you never *got* to life. That seemed, even now, true.

Elisabetta was in the hallway talking on her cell phone, pacing. As she moved to within sight of him, she glanced up, but her eyes did not register him, not significantly; they were absorbed in the call.

"What?" she said into the phone in a tone that could have implied anything at all: love, annoyance, sexual enrapturement, a missed deadline.

Elisabetta was not tall: that was part of the trick of her. She had a wonderful round behind you could not miss; she always wore tight jeans. Today, this being early fall, she wore a pale green sleeveless turtleneck sweater sculpted to her breasts. Her features were so exquisite you did not miss the want of height. Her blondish hair, worn long, hung in ringlets, and she curled one around a finger near her ear as she listened to the person on the other end and looked up at, but did not acknowledge, her father.

He stood there waiting for something.

It was not quite surliness he noted on her face. Not quite annoyance either. It was incomprehension.

"But then we'll have to be late," she said into the phone.

The importance of their high school lives, the earthshaking consequentiality of everything! He felt it. He wanted to be generous to her. He willed himself not to matter.

"Noooo," she said into the phone, seriously annoyed with whomever she was talking to.

Whatever the very good, very mature, very responsible urge to absent himself, to allow her her phone conversation, to simply move past her, he found he could not quite sustain it.

"Elisabetta," he said.

She looked up. They had not seen each other in a week. She seemed to be looking at his lips, trying to place him.

See me. Look at me.

He would like to have slapped her. He didn't. But he would have liked to, just to get her to acknowledge him. Here I am. I matter.

I am your father. I am Jack.

Zoe arrived to save him.

"I thought that was you." Her face in the doorway confirmed that for her at least, he still took up space.

"Come on in." She took his hand. But there was something forced in her tone, like she was trying to sound happier than she was. Was it a warning?

At the round table in the large kitchen, lit by windows on three sides, the windows small-paned and hung with herbs, Norbert bent forward over a crossword puzzle. Joe was very close to his grandfather, their heads nearly touching.

"Don't tell me, I'll get it," the old man said.

"Grandpa, you don't know pop culture stuff, you need help," Joe said. In spite of the boy's annoyed tone, he seemed secretly delighted by the old man's deep stubbornness.

"I *know* pop culture. I knew pop culture when you were in diapers, young man."

Norbert's hair, entirely white, crested backward inadvertantly into what had once been called a duck's ass. He'd attained, at ninety, an unearned air of distinction. He had survived, that was all. Jack knew the man had done nothing, achieved nothing in his life, been faithful only to himself.

"How are you going to answer 'texting diminutive,' huh?" Joe was asking, half laughing. "Two letters. First one *R*. Tell me."

Norbert turned to Jack, not because Jack had made any noise upon entering, and not because he'd been anticipated, but only in order to deflect Joe's goading of him. The old man's face, in age, had grown enormous. He was wearing half-glasses. He'd gotten heavier, stout, his pants held up by suspenders, a large change from the dapper man he'd once been. What had never died was the air of competitiveness he'd always had concerning his daughter, so that even now he could not resist casting a mildly disgusted victor's gaze toward Jack. Christina was standing at the counter with her mother, opening the box that contained Norbert's birthday cake.

"Perhaps you know," he said to Jack. "Two letters, texting diminutive."

"Try *R U*," Jack said.

Norbert took a moment before smiling, a slow-growing crease beginning to divide the lower half of his face. "*R U*," he repeated, and tapped Joe on the head a little roughly. "And this young scofflaw thought I couldn't get it."

"Strictly speaking, you didn't," Joe said.

Norbert wrote the letters in with enormous lip-smacking satisfaction, pronouncing them aloud as he wrote.

"Daddy's here," Zoe said.

The others had not looked at him yet. Christina and her mother were folding down the flaps of the cake box and trying not to get frosting on their fingers.

The two women, both glancing up at the same time, shared a coloring. They both seemed to be getting *whiter* with age. Though Christina's mother was much the heavier of the two, Jack could see in Christina's hips the evidence of an incipient spread she did not seem to be fighting much. Perhaps having just come from Ellen—the weight-obsessed, gym-haunting Ellen—made him more keenly aware of that, though it was possible, too, that finding imperfections in Christina had become a study of his.

"Good, you came," Christina's mother said. "You can take this out from under us, but don't throw it away. Fold it and we'll take it to recycling."

She was one of those women, deeply concerned with her carbon footprint, who drove a Prius and made her own trips to the town recycling center.

Norbert looked up from over his glasses, watching Jack fold the cake box. "Throw it in the trash," he stage-whispered.

Joe laughed.

"I heard that," Christina's mother said.

"Of course you did," Norbert said, studying the crossword. "Having despoiled, we now feel that virtue can save us."

"Which it can," Christina's mother said, opening a box of candles and placing them like battle markers over the terrain of the cake face.

"I'm ninety, I'll remind you," Norbert said, eyeing the candles.

"No one's forgetting that," Christina's mother answered.

"I expect to have to blow out ninety candles."

"We're opting for symbolism today, Norbert."

"Oh, fuck symbolism," Norbert said, and winked at Joe, who followed the conversation as if his grandparents were magisterial in their eccentricities, a privilege to be related to. "Besides, it would be good exercise for my lungs."

"We don't want to test them."

"*Ninety* candles, or I won't blow out a single one." Norbert smacked the table.

Christina's mother turned to Jack with her characteristic talent of regarding him without feeling there was anything particular to *see*. He was a collection of molecules with a name and not much of a heritage, who had been somehow responsible for bringing her grandchildren to life.

"The recycling, Jack, is on the porch. Be good, would you?"

He did as he was told, took the box out to where there was a pile waiting and the regulation blue container for recyclable bottles. After he'd folded the box neatly and placed it on the pile, he turned around and saw that Zoe had followed him. She stood in the doorway in a pair of shorts and a top that hugged her still unformed breasts. She looked a little pale. He was touched that she had followed, though uncertain why. Why did your children love you? Why? Elisabetta's and Joe's relative indifference to him made more sense than his youngest's attachment. It was a helplessness—a form of depression—he perceived in her now. She was looking at the floor, not at him.

"They driving you crazy?" he asked.

They heard Norbert's loud voice coming from inside. "'Language of literature Nobelist Shmuel Yosef Agnon,'" he was shouting. "Six letters! Anyone know it? Anyone?"

"You want some cake, don't you?" Jack asked Zoe. He wanted to lighten the moment, whatever it was. He also wanted to get back inside. He knew he should be taking the time to bring whatever it was out of her, but he was too excited to get back to Christina.

"Come on, Zoe. It's okay."

By the time he guided Zoe inside, Christina's mother had finished her preparations with the candles.

"Norbert, I'm going to light these and bring them to the table, so you'd better put away the crossword."

"She doesn't like me doing this," Norbert announced to Joe. "Sharp-

ening my *mind* this way. She'd rather it became soft. You know what
Norman Mailer said women want, don't you?"

"No," Joe said.

"Babies with dicks."

"Norbert, that will do. Put the crossword away."

"Well-hung infants." Norbert winked again at Joe, who loved this.
"Now tell me. Agnon, his language."

"I would think *Shmuel* might be a hint," Joe said.

Lifting one eye exaggeratedly, Norbert said "*He*brew" and began
to write it down just as Christina's mother finished lighting the candles
and brought the cake forward, singing "Happy Birthday" in a high,
colorless soprano. Christina, to Jack's mild surprise, joined her mother.
Having barely acknowledged him, she was now smiling as if this mild
travesty of a birthday party (had Norbert just said the words "well-hung
infants" and not even been *chastised*?) were something truly special.
Regarding them, mother and daughter, they seemed to Jack like elec-
trical appliances plugged into nothing; the juice they worked off of was
an emanation of this room, their sustenance here something he had
never understood.

"Wait," Elisabetta said just as the cake was placed in front of Norbert, who looked at it unhappily. "Don't blow them out without me."
She sat at the table, holding her phone, checking once more for texts.

"You've arranged all your various arrangements, I assume," Norbert
said. "So you can join us. We peons. We vassals."

"Hannah is going to have to be late picking me up." Elisabetta
turned to her mother. "So it would be good if I could take the car and
drive myself."

"Your grandfather is going to blow out the candles," Christina said.

"All right, but . . ."

"I'm doing no such thing," Norbert announced.

"Norbert."

"*Nine?* What am I, an *infant*? He can do it."

Norbert had turned, surprisingly, to Jack.

"Don't be silly, Norbert."

"Well, someone has to, and it's not going to be me."

Christina's mother, in her mild domestic frustration, turned to
Jack. She didn't like the idea at all.

"What if Joe does it? If you insist on being silly and stubborn."

"No." Norbert covered the lit candles with one hand. "Jack, or no one. Jack, or they blaze down into this lovely frosting."

It was, Jack supposed, a trap of some kind. Norbert was smiling slyly, an under-the-breath smile he barely tried to hide. Perhaps it was done simply to annoy Christina's mother. When she turned in his direction, her eyelids were lowered, like she were giving away the keys to some old, secret chest containing family heirlooms.

"I suppose someone has to do it," she said. "Though this seems silly."

There was something irresistible in the moment. A way, even, of getting back at Christina's mother. But though he knew it was the wrong thing to do, Jack leaned forward and blew out the nine candles. He saw immediately afterward that a small glob of his spittle had landed near one of the candles. No one would at first admit it, though he could see Norbert's smile widen in reaction. After a couple of seconds' silence, Christina's mother picked up a napkin and removed it, a gesture whose subtlety called more attention to it than a loud announcement of its existence would have.

There was a quiet then, a sense of them all paying a bit too much attention to Christina's mother throwing the napkin away. In Zoe's face, Jack saw a continuation of the look she'd given him when he'd first come in, like she was warning him against something. It was like he was visiting a family he barely knew. He had tried to adopt their private language and failed, and Zoe kept witnessing his failure, feeling it in a way he could not.

"Did you make a wish, Norbert?" Christina's mother asked.

"I did," Norbert said.

"What was it?" Joe asked.

"World peace."

"No, really."

"Conversion of the heathens."

"He'll never tell," Christina's mother said. She was cutting and then dishing out cake onto napkins to save on having to wash plates. "But one thing I can assure you is that it had nothing to do with any of us."

"Damn straight," Norbert said, and bit into his cake.

"He's the most selfish man alive." Christina's mother, making a heavy joke, seemed not to have gotten beyond her annoyance at the way Norbert had outmaneuvered her on the candle blowing.

"And *ninety*," Norbert crowed. "*Ninety*. Let this be a lesson to you."

"What's the lesson?" Joe asked.

Rather than answering, Norbert looked up suddenly at Christina, as though she'd done something to draw his attention. She hadn't. She was simply accepting a piece of cake from her mother. But her vacancy in the room—the fact that she alone had said little up to this point—was what Norbert was suddenly noticing, and addressing. She took a small bite of the cake, and when Jack looked at Norbert watching her, he sensed that they were both feeling the same thing: this remote woman held both of them hostage by never quite giving enough.

"Wish me something," Norbert said directly to her. There was a tenderness, a plea in the way he spoke, a tone Jack had rarely heard from him. "My darling."

Christina seemed surprised to be singled out this way. The slightest blush appeared on her face. Her mother looked at her, expectant.

"Wish you what?"

"A birthday wish."

She went on chewing. She said nothing at first, and Norbert waited.

"Let me think."

"Shouldn't have to think. Should be brimming with good wishes for the pater."

The great surprise, the great, continuing surprise was that Norbert seemed so willing to display an unvarnished need for something from her.

The second surprise came when she turned at this moment to look at him, at Jack. He had no idea why he'd been invited here today, had suspected it was Zoe's idea. But he thought he detected in her look—and hoped it wasn't just something he was putting there—the notion that it was she who had insisted on his presence. It gladdened his heart. She might still come back. It was stupid to indulge such a thought, but every hint that it might still happen made him forget that.

Just as quickly as she'd gifted him a moment's recognition, it seemed to go away. Or else she erased it.

"I'll wish you ten more years, Daddy."

Norbert seemed for a moment to be chewing on her words, testing them for bitterness, or poison.

"Only *ten*?" he asked in exaggerated disappointment.

What she had given him was not enough. That was what he had decided. The moment turned sour.

As Jack looked around the room now, he noticed that Zoe had

307

retreated into a corner, as if trying to effect a removal from the scene. She hadn't taken a piece of cake. No one had offered.

"Doesn't Zoe—want?" Jack asked, and it came out—he was not certain why—like another of his faux pas, the things he could not manage to say correctly in this room.

"Zoe, don't you—"

She shook her head with some urgency, as if he mustn't call attention to her, some damage would be done.

"She doesn't—*like* me," Norbert said. "*That* one."

The same sourness, and readiness to do harm, that Christina had elicited was in his face as he pointed to Zoe.

"I just don't want cake," Zoe said.

Norbert placed his elbows on his knees and leaned forward, as if to beckon her to him. "No, you don't like me."

Jack moved toward her, to stand beside her. The essential thing seemed to be to not allow this man to reduce her to tears. He felt, as he did this, a sense of their separateness, their joined darkness in this sea of blondness. He gently squeezed Zoe's shoulder and felt that she was better defended against them than he was.

Norbert regarded the two of them. Some film appeared over his eyes, veiling them, giving him the appearance of someone farseeing. Then he said something Jack didn't immediately hear.

Christina's mother and Christina herself looked at Jack expectantly.

"What's that?" Jack asked. "I didn't hear."

"He said, 'How's your father?'" Christina's mother said.

"Good," Jack answered. Rote, protective.

"You know," Norbert said, and, at least at the beginning, nothing more. Some inward impulse had overtaken him, because he looked out the window, away from everyone, and seemed to have dropped whatever thread of a thought he'd started out with.

"I allowed your father to stay here," he said finally.

"How's that?" Jack asked.

"I sold him my store at a great disadvantage to myself. A *great* disadvantage."

Norbert was still addressing something unseen by any of them, something outside the window. Jack looked at Christina for a reaction. There didn't seem to be one, though she wouldn't look at him now.

"I would think that's ancient history now, Norbert," Christina's mother said.

"Very advantageous terms," Norbert said. "Otherwise, you know, you'd still be in the hinterlands. The Italian ghetto." He lifted a last forkful of cake to his mouth, spilled it on his lap. "Damn. I can't . . . even . . ."

"It's all right." Christina's mother stepped forward. The white frosting had spilled and stuck to Norbert's generously tailored crotch, and Christina's mother took a napkin to it, working away at the crotch in what seemed an unconscious series of gestures until Norbert's face took on its own quite conscious look of bliss, his face like a boy's upon discovering, for the first time, the ecstasy of orgasm. This woman, tending to his mess, working at his crotch, was accidentally pleasuring him. Norbert turned to Joe, who seemed embarrassed and unsure of his own reaction, but because it was his grandfather giving him permission to do so, he smiled collusively.

Finally Christina's mother looked up, caught the looks on both their faces, took the napkin in her hand and threw it away, and washed her hands. She looked uncomfortable, only vaguely humiliated. Norbert, the conqueror with soiled pants, regarded her from his seat, the smile intact on his face.

"My love," he said, as if in triumph, "did we embarrass you?"

"It's time for us to go," Jack said.

"Us?" Christina's mother asked.

"Yes. Me and Zoe."

"Jack, I don't think you understand. We have some festivities planned."

"Pin the Tail on the Donkey," Norbert shouted. "And such."

"I promised my father I would bring Zoe by."

Christina's mother did not believe him. In her eyes was the old disapproval, unmasked. A question hung fire.

"Is that so? You made another plan, after we invited you to Norbert's ninetieth?"

The immense compliment conferred was meant to be understood.

"I did. Yes," Jack said, and looked at Zoe.

"This spoils things, then, doesn't it?" Christina's mother said.

"I don't know," Jack said.

The two older children seemed indifferent to his leaving.

309

"Zoe?"

She nodded and left, said she had things upstairs, her schoolwork. Jack, regarding these others, put down his napkin full of cake. Christina's mother looked at it as if his not having touched the cake was not the least of his sins.

He left them without saying anything else.

In the living room, he caught his breath. It could still hold him, this room. He realized that you could have a liberating moment—his abruptly leaving them like that, spiriting Zoe away—and then in the next instant be caught. He would always be a boy here, thrilled to have been invited.

"Jack?"

He heard Christina's voice behind him, turned. She was frozen in late-afternoon interior light, which captured half her face and left the other half in shadow. She could have been her mother thirty years before, except for something he recognized even now, even in the withdrawn Christina, this woman half in shadow, endlessly retreating. A will to be other. The truest thing he knew about her, which she had spent this latter part of her life denying.

"That was rude," she said.

"I guess."

Was that to be it, then, this small chastisement? Why had she even bothered? Why not just let him leave? What he held out hope for—always, and stupidly, in spite of himself—was some admission that what she had chosen in place of him was *less* than him. But he also knew—or thought he knew—that it had not been for her a matter of holding two different values next to each other and choosing one over the other. He saw it in more emotional terms. She had grown afraid of something in him. That was his conclusion. He was waiting for her to become brave again.

He took a step toward her, inadvertently, old instinct.

She did not move.

"So," he said.

She only went on looking at him.

"You doing all right?"

"Yes."

"In Newton."

She looked at him, as if to register how odd it was that he needed to mention the town where they both knew she lived.

"We going to have a talk sometime about Elisabetta's tuition next year?" he said.

"Let's have her get into Brown first."

"She'll get in."

Her face did something he thought he understood, and didn't like: What did he, Jack, know about such things, he who had never even gone to college? Did that count against him, too, in the long array of Reasons to Have Left Jack Palumbo?

"We'll see, won't we?"

"Yes," he said, "but I don't have any doubt. And that'll make next year an expensive year. With Joe going to that stupid school."

"It's not a stupid school."

The truth was, he had no idea why they were talking about this. He had had no intention of bringing up tuition. It was, instead, as though he still looked for ways to thrust, unconscious ways to get inside Christina.

"It *is* a stupid school. You ever pick him up there?"

"Of course I do. Jack."

Her face had changed very suddenly and in some indecipherable way.

"What?"

She shook her head, shooing away the internal thought. There were vaguenesses always now between the two of them, moments when he felt she wanted to tell him some truth that would, he was sure, have helped him in the end but from which she held back, not wanting to hurt him in the present. Maybe she was trying to make some excuse for this afternoon. He sensed it was something larger she was trying to tell him. If he were objective, he could have looked at her and thought, She really is nowhere near as beautiful as I make her out to be. She is a woman, like any other woman, growing old. But he knew he would have thrown himself into a fire for her—not for *her*, not for this woman before him, but for the one who, he believed, still inhabited her, the one for whom he'd once made it possible to skip through this room, freed of its constraints, in his heroic years.

"This is what you want, then?"

"This?"

"Your father. The kids in beautiful schools?"

He had asked that before, many times. Still, he supposed he would go on asking it out of the endlessly renewable disbelief with which he regarded the end of his marriage.

What he wanted most of all, though, right now, was to touch her. For a second. To return to the old belief that his body could make things happen. That it no longer could, that it wasn't being allowed to—some large part of him still could not accept that. So he lifted one hand and held it away from her face, waiting for her to retreat. She did not. She went on looking at him, not in repulsion, but not in invitation either. She was only confirming what had to be reconfirmed: his pastness, his uselessness and lack of power in the present. Then he discovered something clinging to the hair just under her ear.

She did flinch a tiny bit as his finger approached.

"Frosting," he said. "In your hair."

Her eyes, still not quite trusting him, allowed the invasion of her private space. He held the strands of her hair a second too long as he rubbed the frosting out. Then, on his hand's withdrawal, he allowed it to linger and graze her cheek. She colored a little. Finally, he brought his finger to his own lips.

Her eyes closed a second, in embarrassment, he was sure. Something tender came out of him, something fighting with desire. Whatever it was that composed her limitation with regard to him, he understood that it was as much a part of her as anything else had ever been. We do have these brief moments where we rise above ourselves. We do. But they are brief. *Some of them sparkle. They do sparkle.* It had always been his job to encourage that sleeping part of her.

"Come back," he said. She pretended not to have heard.

Zoe was in the doorway now. Her book bag. Her short hair and her seriousness and her heartbreakingly skinny legs.

It took him a moment, but then he said, "Okay?"

Zoe nodded her head.

"You want to wait outside just a minute, Zoe?"

It was a mistake. To force the issue here, he knew right away it was a mistake. But Zoe did as she was told, and he and Christina were alone together.

"You heard what I said."

"I'm not coming back, Jack."

"Because."

"Yes. Because." She hesitated. "Stop waiting."

He grasped her arm. Everything was a mistake, everything was the wrong thing.

"Do you see her pain?" He knew he was using Zoe now; it was not his noblest moment.

Christina removed his arm. "Whose?"

"Your daughter's."

She looked at him as if fortifying herself. He knew her defense: her older daughter was thriving. Their son, too. She had never wanted the third. The third, the one who loved him, was the mistake.

"It's fine, those other two, Christina, but this one needs us to be together. You see that, don't you?"

"I have to go back."

"Christina."

"Don't grab my arm again."

"What are you doing for sex, Christina?"

She looked offended. They might as well have been back at the table at the senior prom, Barney Hunt between them. Except that this time she would allow him no opening.

"Because that was important to you once."

She didn't respond, didn't give him the satisfaction.

"And now you're fading. You're fading away."

"Am I?"

"Yes."

"Well, okay then. I'm fading."

It seemed astonishing to him, the conversation, his desperation, everything. He did not want to go back to the Parker Meridien, to the blanched life of his affair. He wanted the old intensity, to tell her stories, to tell her everything. There were things he had left out. There were still possibilities.

"Don't keep waiting, Jack. Don't. All right?"

"Why not? I saved you from these people. They're *awful*."

It was too much, it was over the top, it was exactly what he could not make her believe. He took her by the arms again, and it was her resistance, her half-disgusted face that made him not let go, made him feel that if he only held her long enough, he might have her one more time, in this room, Zoe waiting patiently outside, the dissolute party continuing in the next room. There might be a restoration on these dusty chairs. Never mind that he'd already had sex twice on this day. He was Jack Palumbo. Twice was nothing.

She was angry at him, though

"*Stop!*"

He put his face close to hers.

"Stop," she said more gently. "Don't make me pity you."

"Why not?"

"Jack. Understand this." She waited a moment, deciding something. "I never loved you the way you thought."

He stopped. It sounded too harsh, though gently, even hesitantly spoken. It made him embarrassed for her. He even smiled a little, to excuse her.

"I never did."

"What are you talking about?"

"Your whole sense of things, Jack. It's wrong."

He went on looking at her. It was like seeing the first signs of dementia or physical failing in someone you love. You wanted to be reassured that you had not seen what you just saw.

"You suffocated me, Jack," she said quietly.

Still he waited.

"What are you talking about?"

"I've got to go back inside."

She turned away from him and tried to return to the kitchen. Once more, he grabbed her arm.

"Stop. Please."

"I don't know what you're saying."

They were silent in the way only couples can be silent. He was reassured by that, that they were still a couple in this regard. They retained joint ownership of a small territory.

"I really do have to go back," she said.

"Why? You can't tell me something like that, and then, what, it's over?"

She looked at him as if to say of course she could. He saw pity in her eyes, too.

"Explain suffocation. Okay? At least do that for me."

Perhaps she tried. There was a moment, a silent one. She shook her head. Too much to try to tell him about the day Adam Goldstein had left, how she'd understood then the impossibility of going back to her marriage and finding it anything more than a farce. Then had come the gradual diminishment of memory. She could no longer recall the chaos of feeling of the early days, her bed on Peterborough Street, the charge she had felt on the way home to him. He had been a body, that was all. Had he been more than a body, something, she was sure, would have endured. It was impossible to go beyond that. Again she shook her head. She refused to hurt him that deeply. Let him have an illusion.

Jack saw all this as a shadow passing over her features.

Zoe had come back inside. She did not have to say anything. She simply looked at both of them. They must have seemed strange to her, her parents, who retained no sense of once having been together, of having come together in the early exhaustion of their love to make her. Except that, Jack kept thinking, Christina was insisting that there had been no love to be exhausted. She'd never loved him. Or that he'd suffocated her. It was mixed up in his mind.

He looked from Zoe to Christina. There was a choice, a very simple one. One of these women loved him, one did not. That is, if you wanted to face the facts as they were presented to you. Which he didn't want to do. He wanted to take the world and make it something other than what it was. Something larger, sweeter. Take a beautiful girl from her little table at a prom and transform her by means of love and sex, dick and mouth and *will*, and make of her a receptacle huge enough to take in Jack Palumbo in all his colors and his size, his passion and his energy and his will to love. Was that suffocation? How else did you love if not with your whole suffocating self?

"You loved me," he said. "Do what you want. Just don't fucking pretend you didn't love me."

He turned then. He actually made the choice. Surprised by himself, he took Zoe with him, and when they were in the car, he put his head against the steering wheel, expecting tears to come, surprised when they didn't. He supposed it was out of respect for Zoe, out of a desire to protect her, that he held back. Zoe waited patiently, as though she knew everything. But of course that was foolish. She couldn't know everything. She was just a girl waiting for her father, a girl doing the work of separating herself, for her own survival, from her parents' unaccommodating passion.

"Sorry," he said.

"It's okay."

That was the only discussion they needed to have. But he didn't let it go there.

"You understand much of this?"

It was too complicated a question to ask a twelve-year-old. She bit her lip in internal reaction against what she was being asked to understand.

He started the car, and they drove in a long silence in which he was mostly embarrassed by himself, by what he had said, by the scene he had forced. Beside them, the beautiful town, the water of the lake opening. The young, wild, resistant part of him still wanted to embrace it all, to take himself and Zoe into some exultant moment. Instead, he stayed with the weight of his own solitude, honoring the limitations of her understanding, going over what Christina had said.

When they got to the house, they came upon a strange scene. His father was digging up a bush in the side yard. Felix was standing with him, next to a wheelbarrow holding another plant. What Richie was doing looked like a strain, too much for him. "Dad, why don't you let Felix do it?" Jack asked.

Richie looked up from his work, like the question had no bearing on anything, was merely confusing.

"I've got to get rid of this bush" was all Richie said.

"I keep telling him to let me help him," Felix said. "But look, he let me pick out this plant."

Felix looked proud of his choice. The new bush had small pink bulbs, and Felix touched them. "We're going to put it in."

Jack took the shovel from his father and finished the work. He had to dig deep, the root ball was deep. He worked up a sweat, but it felt gratifying. His father stood just over him until he'd gotten to the base of the root, and then he asked Felix to help him pull it out. Some of the roots clung so deep they had to be clipped. Only when it was fully out did Jack ask, "Why'd you want to do this? What's wrong with this plant? It's healthy."

Richie shook his head, and they loaded in the new plant. Richie had the peat moss ready, and Jack shoveled in enough dirt so that the new roots were covered. Felix touched the buds, and Jack said, "We should have watered the roots."

"It's pretty, though, isn't it?" Felix said.

Jack's shirt was dripping with sweat. He watched his father walk to the back porch, where Joan, huge now, was watching from the steps. Hector was there, too. Richie went to Joan and stood in front of her, and they seemed to be exchanging something that Jack was cut off from. Richie reached out and touched Joan's belly delicately, grazing the circumference. The act looked difficult for him, something he was forcing himself to do.

Zoe watched from near the house. Jack wanted to offer this scene to her as another exhibit of his aloneness. He'd always been separate, creating a private sphere for himself, a place big enough to act out his vision of himself. "Suffocated," she'd said. He felt unconnected to anything.

"Who wants—" he said, not sure what the next words might be. "Who wants to go to the lake?" It was the only idea he could think of. Pathetic. His lake, he was always going there.

They all looked at him. It might have been a non sequitur he'd spoken.

Hector was the only one who finally responded. "That old tin can canoe?" he asked.

"Yes. Sure."

"It's gonna sink."

"Not if it hasn't by now."

There was a stillness. Richie sat on the stoop, below Joan. Joan touched his hair.

"Sure, I'll come," Hector said.

"Felix?" Jack asked.

"I'm gonna watch my plant."

"You think that'll help it grow?"

"No. I think I'm in love with it."

Hector stood.

"All right," Jack said.

The two of them started toward the car.

"Wait," Zoe said.

"You want to come?"

She came close to him. She didn't have to say anything. He wanted to tell her she didn't have to save him, or even help him now. She could take care of herself, she could start doing that, the time had come. But he allowed it.

The tears didn't come until he was driving. He turned up the radio to distract them both, but he suspected that neither of them was fooled. He was emptied of the tears by the time he was out of the car, loosening the canoe.

"We can all fit?" Hector asked when Jack was floating the canoe. Jack was wondering if the boy was being kind to him now, if he had noticed the tears.

They rowed to the inner lake. Zoe seemed to understand her father's mission and sat quietly at the helm, staring ahead. Hector, sitting on the crossbar in the middle, leaned over and ran his hand along the water.

"Don't tip us," Jack said.

"It's me who can't swim good," Hector said. "Me who'll drown. You'll be fine." Then he said, "Where we going, by the way?"

"You'll see."

They portaged to the inner lake. It was something he wanted to show Hector.

"That's the most beautiful thing you'll ever see," Jack said when they were there.

"That? No, it isn't. That's a *lake*."

"All right."

"That's just a *lake*. I've seen lakes."

"Yeah, but this one's yours."

Hector stared out at the water a moment, then turned back, smiling. "No, it isn't."

Jack smiled back. Okay, he thought. That's what they would do. Take their time to make things their own, in their own way. That was healthy. Maybe that was the best legacy he could pass on: Don't have my crazy romanticism. Don't.

"Take it out."

"What?"

"The canoe. Take it out."

"By myself?"

"Sure."

"You'll save me if I drown?"

"I will. Yes."

Jack and Zoe sat and watched Hector as he got into the canoe and hugged the shore.

"Go out farther," Jack called to him. "You won't drown."

"No. No. I'm not going to risk it."

It was crazy. This kid, this virtual stranger to him, this boy with dark skin, out on this lake, Jack's sacred place. Taking over. But that was what Jack wanted without knowing it was what he wanted, this boy to take over. Then he understood something. It had never really been his. He had believed that. It had been given to him for a while, that was all.

Still, he could not quite lose the sense of wanting to tell Zoe, of wanting to tell Hector, what had happened here, what he had been once. The more he thought this, though, the more it started to shrink, all of it, the lake, his past. What had really happened here? He had seen a girl swimming, and that moment had had a force of transformation for him. You had to blink them away, the moments of light. They were at the same time nothing and everything. You had to blink them away, and you had to hold on to them.

He was surprised then to find himself remembering Dr. Wooten. Something Elspeth had written him after it was all over, after the doctor was dead. Something that man had believed about Jack. That he was capable of grace, if he could figure out a way to be. Had he done that? Had he found a way to make beautiful things happen? Where was grace? It was impossible to know.

He remembered the time afterward, the time after the doctor's death, after Michael's death, after the time of AIDS in New York, his coming home, his haunting the Norumbega library, his search. That had been him at his best, he thought now, that crazy search, not his long enthronement of Christina. His lostness. That had been the closest he had ever come to grace.

He turned to Zoe. She was far away from him. Good, that was where she belonged. They would live the unromantic life, Zoe, Hector. They would not make his grand mistake, to turn a simple girl into something more than she had any wish to be. He had suffocated her. Still, he had had his moment. He had not shied from grasping the most important thing that had ever been offered to him. He waded into the water. Just past where Hector was rowing, little bursts of joy sneaking over the boy's face, he saw again the beautiful girl who'd once swum here in a tight black bathing suit. She was looking at him curiously, invitingly, wondering why he didn't come farther in. Why it couldn't have been simpler. He watched her swim away until she disappeared. Then he was sitting at the long table in the Norumbega library. Christina came in and saw him and turned away, did not approach. Would that have been better? He went back to the little girl on the shore and took her hand.

He shouted to Hector, "Don't go out too far. Don't go out to where I can't save you."

Hector, newly brave, smiled at him and went out farther.

"You don't need to save me," he said. "I can save myself."

319

7

Joan's baby—a girl—arrived in the middle of December. A horrendous delivery, twelve hours of labor before they panicked and performed a C-section.

The child was consuming, as she'd been promised a baby would be. She could not imagine a world beyond this one, these days of being so entirely needed. Things that appeared on the edge—her lost, sinking father, her husband, the boys whose first semester at Norumbega Regional had been, predictably, easy for Felix and less so for Hector. All a fog. Winter light. When something from the world outside of her daughter's needs intruded, she became aware of the wealth of extra-natal concerns that would someday demand her attention. At moments she thought of the impossibility of what she had taken on. He would leave. Angel would leave. This man beside her, who had had in his life so many women, how was it possible that he should remain with her? Was the urge that had drawn him toward her, the link they had formed in their sequence of strange conversations, strong enough to withstand what must be going on in his body? You could think such a thought only so long. Before long, the baby always woke her. She sat in a rocking chair in a corner of the room, looking out at the frost that laced the window, at the field behind the house, then at her husband lying in bed, half awake, a hand half raised. Would it ever cease being strange, the presence of this man?

One day in February, when the ice had frozen solid on the lake, Angel, rooting around in the basement, found an old pair of skates and told Joan he wanted to take her skating. She laughed.

"Two months postpartum," Joan said. "You want me to skate."

"You've wanted to skate all your life," Angel said.

Sometimes, when he said things like that, she became aware of another thing he might be saying. His aggressiveness at such moments masked what she thought of as shyness, a plea that she not forget something.

"Who'll watch Julian?"

"Your dad can watch her."

She resisted, he insisted, and finally they roused Richie, who was sitting by the fire in the downstairs sitting room, dozing.

"You watch the baby while we skate?" Angel asked.

"No," Joan said. She knew enough to know how scared that would make Richie, alone here with an infant. She would never do it. It was not safe. He would forget the baby, go and do something else. Angel did not understand, not fully. "He'll come."

She thought they would only look at the frozen lake, take the baby for an outing. She thought Richie might enjoy that. It was a winter afternoon. The boys were in school.

Richie was hesitant to leave the fire.

"House won't burn up," Angel said. "I promise. We just cleaned the flues."

Richie looked at him as if for direction.

"The flues. They're all right. Come," Angel said, and put his hand on Richie's shoulder and guided him to the car.

The clarity—or what amount of clarity had come to light in Richie's increasingly clouded existence—was that he had to give it over. Everything he'd earned, claimed, taken. It had to be given over to these dark-skinned people. That was what he thought, at his worst. I was given this house—*took* it, really, caused an old woman's death in order to get it—so that I can give it to a family of dark strangers. That was a hard thing for him to accept, and he fought it until in the end all that seemed possible was a truce. And a sense that this was what had to be. Otherwise the Ronnie Greeleys of the world got to keep it, and that was an even more unacceptable thing. So he held his dark-skinned granddaughter and followed them through the snow to the edge of the lake until this brief glimpse of clarity was eclipsed. Angel strapped the old skates on a resistant Joan and laughed at her and goaded her. Richie held the baby, who stared at him with dark, clear eyes. He smiled at her. She looked at him as if she did not quite accept the smile.

"They're rusty," Joan said about the skates.

Angel bunched up some snow and ran the blades through it. It made no difference.

"You been wanting to do this stupid thing all your life," Angel was saying, and he led her out onto the ice.

She looked back once at her father. "Are you sure you're okay?"

Richie nodded.

The ice was lumpy, not smooth, and she was frightened of falling. Her body, which had astonished her by its ability to hold and give life, was still healing. So she would go easy on herself, not allow Angel to force her into anything she wasn't ready for. He held her hand and slid alongside her. It was just possible to skate over the bumpy terrain.

She kept an eye on her father. It was conceivable, with his memory loss, his new absentmindedness, that he might drop Julian or place her down and wander off. She had this double responsibility—an old man and an infant. So she kept close.

"Okay, I think that's enough," she said.

"Joannie." Angel held her face in his hands. "Skate."

There it was, that plea. He did not want her to forget how it had started, with him freeing her that other day on the ice. It was as though he did not want to move too far from that moment. And she would go along for a while. At the same time, she fully understood it could not stop there. They could not live a myth: his freeing her, her gratitude. She did not know how she understood that, but she did. It had maybe been what had led Jack to say to her one day, "It's crazy. You're the only one of us who's going to be free. You, the scared one."

She allowed Angel to increase her slide—she let out a little scream—and then she watched him take off, sliding just ahead of her.

Here it was, what she had perceived once as a little girl: the horror and emptiness of two people clinging to each other. Impossible. Run from it. Except here it was. You entered it. She finally understood why.

And Angel was looking at her, too: Don't be so afraid of this. Don't doom us with worry. Look at us. We're skating.

She had to go along with that, the cold, the risk. Had to. She smiled at him.

Richie watched them both. It was almost as he had once imagined it, this claiming of something that had initially not been his. It had belonged to the Indians once, then the settlers, then the revolutionaries and farmers, and finally to the men in tweeds, men who worked in banks, men in mufflers who had never really earned it. But if he closed his eyes halfway, he could imagine it was his now. His daughter was the little girl the boys would line up for, the dark-skinned man out there his handsome, accomplished son. All the pain could have been avoided, all the missteps. This, this scene—this vision altered only by the half closing of the aperture of his eye—was what he had come here for, fought for, believed in. They would come here, and all would be wonderful, wonderful, wonderful.

The little girl in his arms suddenly let out a wail.

Who was she? Briefly, he did not remember. She did not fit the scene he had just conjured. But he held on to her anyway, rocked her as if she were Stella. Stella, in the last days of her pain, asking him to hold her and rock her, and please be with me in this, please.

ACKNOWLEDGMENTS

My gratitude to my uncles Anthony and Tom Ferlazzo; to Dr. Steve Eipper, Jake Zucker, Rick Kaufman, Adin Thayer, Alice and Dan Melnik, Debbie Forman, Henry Dreher, Mary Jane McGovern, Marla Akin, and Laurie Binney; to my readers Joann Kobin, Eileen Giardina, and Jim Crace for their guidance; to Jim Magnuson for keeping me gainfully employed when I needed to be. To Sloan Harris, for his stringent realism and honesty, always tempered by his extraordinary humanity, and to Kristin Keene for her help at ICM.

To Jonathan Galassi for his continuing support and insight, and to Jesse Coleman for the thoughtful, smart, sensitive editing we're all told no longer exists. Also to Maxine Bartow for her meticulous copyediting and to Chris Peterson, this book's excellent production editor.

To my children, Nicola, Henry, and now José, for allowing me entrance to worlds that would otherwise be closed to me. To Eileen, for her always wonderful questions, which are always the right ones.

I am indebted as well to Jeremy Harding for the phrase "the place that other people call the world," and to Mark Edmundson for "the heart's desire to break," in his introduction to Freud's *Beyond the Pleasure Principle and Other Writings*. For help in my research into the lives of nuns, I relied on the first-person testimonies collected in *Contemplative Nuns Speak* (Helicon Press, 1964). Finally, I would be remiss in not acknowledging those individuals who provided me with details of monastic life, but who have asked, for reasons of privacy, not to be named. It would be ungracious not to thank them here.